MYSTERIOUS MYSTERIES OF THE ARO VALLEY

MYSTERIOUS MYSTERIES
OF THE ARO VALLEY

DANYL McLAUCHLAN

VICTORIA UNIVERSITY PRESS

VICTORIA UNIVERSITY PRESS
Victoria University of Wellington
PO Box 600 Wellington
vup.victoria.ac.nz

National Library of New Zealand Cataloguing-in-Publication Data

McLauchlan, Danyl, 1974–
Mysterious mysteries of the Aro Valley / Danyl McLauchlan.
ISBN 978-1-77656-047-9
I. Title
NZ823.3—dc 23

Printed by Ligare, Auckland

To Sadie, who told me to put a monster in it

Mathematics may explore the fourth dimension, and the world of what is possible, but the Czar can be overthrown only in the third dimension.

—V.I. Lenin, *Materialism and Empirio-Criticism* (1909)

PART I

I

A hero's return

Danyl stepped off the bus then stepped away as it pulled out from the kerb, splashing up sheets of spray. Its tail lights mixed with the lights reflected in the wet black streets. The hiss of its tyres mixed with the rain.

And the rain was cold. So cold. He took shelter under a leaky shop awning and watched the bus continue to the end of Aro Street then turn left and vanish. It was just past midnight. Midwinter. He'd been away for six long months, but now he was back.

Back in the worst place in the world.

The shop windows were dark. There was no one around; no other vehicles on the road. He took a minute to get his bearings, surveying the terrain through the curtains of rain. He stood in the rough centre of things, halfway along Aro Street which extended from one end of the valley to the other, with streets and alleyways running down to it like streams feeding a thirsty river. The valley itself ran from west to east. It was surrounded by hills on three sides, with the eastern end open and adjoined to the Capital, which Te Aro was geographically in, but culturally and economically and spiritually and sociologically and politically not of. Lower and mid-Aro Street was lined with shops and apartment buildings, barely visible through the darkness and the downpour. The rain pooled on the road, turning it into a muddy sea. The wind swept ominous patterns on the water.

Danyl's reflection gazed back at him from the window of a badly parked van. He was a once-attractive man reduced by hard times to mere handsomeness. His light brown hair was long and wet, swept back from his face like an otter's fur.

His glasses were blurry with raindrops. His fine aristocratic features were hidden behind a scraggly beard tinged with premature grey, and he'd gained a lot of weight in the months he'd been away: a side effect of his medication. His clothes were simple but elegant: navy woollen trousers and a rust-coloured tweed jacket, both stolen that morning in a daring raid on a thrift store mannequin. He wore a leather satchel slung over his shoulder. His eyes were clear and bright: twin blue flames gleaming from between a wet brow and pudgy rain-streaked cheeks. Their gaze swept the road and the houses and hills then settled on Devon Street, a narrow road connecting with Aro Street.

The eyes narrowed; the fire in them flared. He stepped out into the rain.

A short, damp minute later he stood before his old house, studying it from the opposite side of the road.

It was a two-storey wooden building with paint peeling from the walls and a front garden crowded with weeds. There was a mail slot in the front door and this was stuffed with letters and pamphlets and community newspapers. They spilled out onto a mound on the path. The windows were dark. The curtains were open. There was no sign of habitation.

The gate creaked and stuck. Danyl forced it: it groaned open. He kicked his way through the sodden mire of junk mail and weeds to the front door, cleared the debris clogging the mail slot, then took a tiny but powerful torch from his satchel. He knelt and shone it through the slot.

The hallway beyond was empty, a region of shadows and spiderwebs and dust. The house was deserted; it had been for months.

And that was a mystery. The house was owned by Danyl's former girlfriend, Verity: she threw him out when she ended their relationship. He still didn't know what went wrong between them: his deteriorating mental condition and financial dependence on her may have played a role; he wasn't sure. He'd never had the chance to find out: a misunderstanding with the criminal justice system had forced Danyl to leave Te Aro, and events had conspired to prevent his return. Until now.

He'd expected to come back and find Verity back in her old house. Comfortable perhaps, but lonely. Remorseful for the way she'd treated certain people in her past. Repentant.

Instead she was gone. Where was she? And why didn't someone else move in and occupy the abandoned home? Property rights in Te Aro were porous. Empty buildings did not remain empty for long. There were always vagrants looking for shelter and experimental dance groups looking for performance space. They occupied bankrupt shops and the houses of the intestate dead. Where were they?

He closed the lid of the mail slot and stood up, and the beam of his torch lit up a series of deep scratches in the wood of the door at head height. A message. He stepped back to inspect it.

Death to the Agents of the Real City

Danyl frowned. People in Te Aro scrawled death threats on each other's doors all the time. None of it meant much—but something about this particular threat troubled him. He ran his finger along the wooden stubble, tracing the letters, trying to fathom their meaning, but no answers came.

His stomach growled, reminding Danyl that he was not only cold and homeless but also very hungry. His original plan was to have Verity welcome him into her house and her arms and then cook him something delicious and nutritious, and feed it to him while sobbing and begging his forgiveness for throwing him out. But this no longer seemed viable. He needed to adapt his plan. Improvise. And his top priority now was to eat before he collapsed of hunger.

There might be something edible in Verity's kitchen.

Nothing fresh, obviously. But maybe muesli? Noodles? Maybe salted nuts, if the fates smiled on him. He fumbled around in his satchel and found his old house key. He wasn't sure it would still fit, but it did. He turned the lock and then hesitated.

Because he wasn't technically allowed to be there. Just before Danyl left the valley Verity took out a trespass order against him, barring him from the property: a final, baffling gesture of malice. He was legally forbidden to enter his own home.

But he was cold and really hungry. Shouldn't the law make an exception for that? Besides, Verity wasn't even there. He wasn't trespassing so much as entering her home while she was away and ransacking it in the dead of night. Surely there was no law against that?

He unlocked the door, forced a semicircle in the pile of junk mail, and stepped over it.

2

How to eat in Aro Valley for free after midnight

Danyl walked through the dark, silent house, remembering the life he'd once lived in it. His relationship with Verity had lasted for about eighteen months. They lived together for less than a year between these very walls, beneath this now leaky roof. He'd been blissfully happy during that time, except for the money problems, and their fights, and his undiagnosed clinical depression, and he thought that Verity was happy too.

But she wasn't. He knew that now. Partly that was Danyl's fault. He was mature enough to admit that. But Verity had problems of her own. Shadows from her past; things she didn't like to talk about or, if she did, wanted to talk about when Danyl was trying to sleep and didn't feel like listening. These things had reached into their sunlit life together and contaminated it. Now, walking around her abandoned home with its cryptic threat scratched into the front door, he suspected that those same shadows had reached out and taken her, pulled her back into the darkness she'd climbed out of. And—he was just speculating—maybe those very same shadows had also reached into Verity's pantry and taken all the non-perishable food.

Because something had. The doors to the kitchen pantry were open and all of the Tupperware containers were missing. The glass jars for rice and pasta were empty. So were the nuts. The crackers. The noodles. Almost everything was gone: a few sad bottles of vinegar and sesame oil were all that remained.

Who took Verity's food? It wasn't a common thief. Everything else in the house was exactly as Danyl remembered it. The TV and stereo were in the lounge. Verity's photographs were still on the walls. Constellations of dust spun about in the beam of the torch.

He climbed the stairs and checked the bedroom. The bed was unmade. The closet was full of Verity's clothes. No clues. And no food. Nothing for him here but memories and hunger and weakness and silence.

Wait. There was something else, something missing. Danyl crossed the room to the waist-high bookshelf by the window. This was where Verity kept her scrapbooks and photograph albums. There was a large gap in the centre of the bottom shelf. Some of the books had been removed.

He found them in the bathroom. The toilet was filled with spiderwebs but the bath was filled with ashes. The pages from Verity's notebooks had all been torn out, tossed into the bath and burned.

Their discarded cardboard covers lay in a pile by the washbasin. Danyl knelt down and sorted through them.

Journals. Someone had burned Verity's old journals. These dated back to her childhood; they were filled with drawings and teenage secrets, dreams and poems and longings; Danyl had sometimes flipped through them to laugh at them when he was bored. Why would anyone destroy them?

One of the discarded covers was marked *Verity. Age Fifteen. Private.* It was splattered with mud and warped by water, long dried. Danyl picked it up. The pages were gone. Ripped out. The inside cover was blank but, looking closer, he saw indentations. The mark of a pen pressing hard against a page that was subsequently torn and burned.

He took a scrap of paper and a pencil from his satchel and, holding his torch between his teeth, laid the paper flat upon the inside cover and traced over the indentations with the pencil, watching the invisible marks beneath appear as gaps in the field of graphite.

A complex network of curves pooled across the empty page. It looked like a prehistoric pattern drawing, or an elaborate mathematical abstraction in the shape of a spiral. When Danyl looked at it from the corner of his eye the spiral seemed to pulsate, then when he looked at it directly it froze back into place; impossible shapes asserted themselves from the complexity then dissolved back into chaos.

Danyl had seen this spiral before. Oh yes. But what was it? What did it mean to Verity? He looked at the front cover again. *Age Fifteen. Private.*

Verity grew up in a quiet seaside town, near an old abandoned farm. She once told Danyl that this farm was raided by the police. They were looking for a fugitive hiding out there, but the fugitive escaped. Not long after that Verity ran away from home and never returned. All of this happened when she was fifteen.

Why did she leave? Danyl didn't know, but he would ask her when he found her. Because, he now vowed, he would find her. She was in trouble, he was sure of it, and he would help her, and in her gratitude she'd forgive him and take him back and everything would go back to normal. In a way this was better than his original plan to simply show up on Verity's doorstep and have her waive the trespass order and beg his forgiveness, a plan that was, in hindsight, unrealistic. But if Verity was in some kind of terrible danger from a dark horror in her past, and Danyl rescued her from it . . . Forgiveness, right there.

He grinned, folded up his spiral drawing and slipped it into his satchel.

The house trembled as another gust of wind shook it. Rain drummed against the roof. Danyl stood by the front door and considered his next move.

Before he could look for Verity he needed to eat and sleep. But where? He was broke: the bus ticket back to Te Aro had wiped out all of his savings. The only allies he had in the valley were Verity, who was missing, and Steve, who was once Danyl's closest friend.

But that friendship hit a rough patch six months ago when Steve was called upon to testify at Danyl's trial, to vouch for his sanity and good character. But when he took the stand he told the court that character and sanity were illusions, systems of control, and perhaps it was the judge and the legal system that were mad, while Danyl was the sane one. Most of the threats Danyl had screamed as he was dragged from the court after his sentencing were directed at Steve. But a few months later—after Danyl's court-appointed physician found the right dosages and his mood stabilised—he forgave his friend and sent him a few letters, apologising and describing his new, medicated life. But Steve never replied.

So Steve's house was an unknown. Steve might not even live there anymore, and it was in a gully on the far side of Devon Street, accessible only via a steep hill which Danyl would have to walk up in the rain. And even if he still lived there, Steve was not the type to keep food in his house.

Then Danyl's hungry gaze fell upon a leaflet lying on the hallway floor: junk mail from the mail slot. It advertised the Autumn Equinox Aro Valley Council Election. Beneath this was a map leading to Aro Community Hall and the slogan: 'Say Goodbye to Yesterday and Hello to a Brighter Future Tomorrow. Tonight!' The date on the poster was two months ago. The map sparked a memory in his starved and failing brain.

The Community Hall was just around the corner from Verity's home. It was a mostly sheltered walk with no hills. There were doorways and alcoves for Danyl to sleep in and, more importantly, there was a crèche where the preschool children of the valley played on their non-competitive playground and tended their vegetable garden.

Five minutes later Danyl squatted in the crèche garden groping for the base of a carrot. When he had a firm grip he tugged it free of the earth and held it up to the rain, rinsing off the dirt.

He sank his teeth into the vegetable's damp flesh and groaned with delight, then grabbed at another carrot with one hand and a clutch of spinach with the other. He shovelled both into his mouth, snapping his head back to swallow the raw leaves. Eventually his feeding frenzy subsided and he stopped to look around.

The vegetable garden was in a square raised bed. Two scarecrows stood on either side of him, swaying, their painted smiley faces grinning into the sleet. There were sticks in the dirt around the sides of the garden, each bearing the name and photograph of a rabbit, goat or hamster living somewhere in the valley for whom the vegetables were intended.

A few more minutes of gorging and Danyl was satisfied. He sat back on his haunches, belched and spat out a small stone. Then he yawned. It was time to sleep.

The crèche was one of four buildings that made up the civil and administrative centre of Te Aro. Next to it was the Community Hall. Behind the hall was a nest of offices where the council staff worked and plotted against one another, and the separate chamber of the valley's lone elected Councillor. All of these buildings faced a concrete games court. Beyond the court sat a squat, windowless building: Te Aro Archive.

Danyl headed for the archive. The doorway was set deep into the side of the building: sheltered and private and dry. And it faced the sun. The light from the dawn would wake Danyl long before the savage preschool children of Te Aro arrived and saw what he'd done to their garden. He made himself comfortable on the concrete steps, took a bundle of rolled up clothes from his satchel and rested his weary head upon it.

Voices woke him.

It was still night. The rain had stopped and the wind had died. The voices came from across the courtyard: loud but garbled, like a radio stuck between stations.

Danyl sat up. He looked around. Nobody. Darkness. And still the voices came: a confusion of echoes, impossible to make out. They came from the far end of the courtyard. But there was nothing there, just two bare walls intersecting.

Wait: there was something. A flutter of light. Danyl crept closer. It came from the gutter running around the edge of the courtyard, and it cast a faint spectral glow upon the base of the wall. Kneeling, he found a small drain set into the ground. It was half concealed by leaves and rubbish. The voices and flickering lights came from below, accompanied by what sounded like music. A flute or recorder playing an old, discordant tune, familiar but impossible to place. Then the music faded. The voices stopped. The lights died away.

They were probably just maintenance workers down there, Danyl decided. Making sure the underground stormwater drains didn't overflow because of all the rain. In the middle of the night. To haunting music.

He yawned and went back to bed, nestling up against the metal reinforcing around the door. He'd heard something about tunnels beneath the valley. People called them the catacombs, and of course there were stories about them. Urban legends. Tales of disappearances. Rumours of an ancient evil. These thoughts circled Danyl's mind once, twice; then they spun away as he fell asleep.

3

The treasurer

'Hey!'

Danyl grunted awake. He was spreadeagled in the entrance to Te Aro Archive. The sky was dark but the horizon was flushed with light. Someone leaned over him: a hand fumbled against his face. A woman said, 'Hello? Hello?'

Danyl slapped the hand away. If you slept outside you often woke to find people interfering with you. He'd learned to be firm with them. 'Leave me alone,' he warned the woman. 'Or I'll scream.'

She stepped back, admitting a little pre-dawn light into the alcove, and said, 'You can't sleep here. This is council property. You're polluting our alcove.' She prodded him with something hard. He whimpered and sat up. 'You are stealing value from the ratepayers of Te Aro,' she told him, prodding him again. 'You are—wait. Are you Danyl?'

'Yeah. Well, maybe. Who wants to know?'

She drew closer but not too close. 'Danyl! It is you!'

This woman was tall with medium-length black hair parted on one side. Her hair fell over the other half of her face in a dark wave. She wore a black shirt, a long wool dress and a black raincoat. She held an aluminium golf club in one hand and a white leather purse in the other. Once, Danyl would have been struck by her beauty. He would have scrambled to his feet, smoothed his hair, tried to ingratiate himself with this woman by making her laugh, trying to win her approval, apologising for polluting her alcove. But that was the old Danyl. Six months of powerful antidepressants had cured him of this cowardice before beauty by ridding him of any sexual impulses, and even though he'd been off his drugs for a week

21

the effect still lingered. It gave him perspective. Wisdom. He didn't have to debase himself before someone just because she had pretty eyes and a nice figure. Not anymore. He sat up, drew his head back and said in a cold voice, 'Do I know you?'

'We've never met,' the woman replied. 'But it's very fortunate that I've found you.' She extended her hand for Danyl to shake. Then her eyes flicked to his forehead and she drew it back. 'There are insects in your hair.'

Danyl tipped his head forward and brushed his scalp with his fingertips. 'Those are just spiders,' he explained as they dropped to the ground and scuttled away. 'You get them when you sleep outdoors. They're attracted to the warmth.'

'That's horrible. You shouldn't have to live like this.' The woman's face was a mixture of arachnophobia and genuine sorrow. Danyl glared at her. All he wanted was to sink back down on the concrete step and close his eyes. 'Did you want something?' He didn't try to hide his hostility. 'You seem to know who I am, but I've never seen you before, and if you don't mind'—he gestured at the spiders scurrying across his pillow—'we're trying to sleep.'

'But you can't sleep here. This building isn't zoned for dormancy. And it's not safe.' She glanced about, then whispered, 'This valley is a troubled place.'

'Troubled?'

'Very troubled.' She leaned closer. 'Like I said, this is a fortunate meeting. For both of us.'

'Who are you? What do you want?'

'I'm Ann. I'm the new Te Aro Council treasurer. I have an offer to make you. A transaction between equals. My office is just over there.' She pointed at the small warren of prefabricated offices tucked behind the hall. 'Come. Hear what I have to say.'

'I don't—'

A knowing smile played across her face. 'I'll give you a muffin.'

Danyl's eyes narrowed. 'What kind of muffin?'

'Poppyseed.'

He flicked another spider from his earlobe. 'Help me up.'

Ann unlocked the door leading to the council offices and led Danyl into a large, dark, low-roofed room. They waited while the fluorescent lights buzzed and flickered, died, then burst into sickly life to reveal six wooden desks separated by waist-high metal partitions. The desks were covered with piles of paper and folders stacked beside dark computer screens. Each desk was messier than the last except for the one in the far corner of the room, which was bare. Danyl smelled disinfectant; this smell became stronger as Ann led him to the clean desk.

'Have a seat. Sit anywhere. Not there, that's my seat. Don't touch it. Here.' She gestured towards a swivel chair. 'Tea or coffee?'

'Tea, please.'

'Dandelion or fennel?'

'Coffee, please.'

The kitchen was a narrow bench in the corner of the room. Ann filled a kettle and washed cups while Danyl looked around.

The room was a square with a door in each wall. One door led outside; the next through to the town hall, and the next to the toilet. The last door had a handsome brass doorknob and a brass plaque reading 'Chamber of the Councillor', and this led into a separate building. A window in one wall looked out over the quad; the window on the opposite wall gave a view of a small private courtyard.

Ann spoke from the kitchenette. 'I've been in Te Aro for six months. I took this job just after you went to trial. I read about you in the newspaper.'

'The media blew all of that out of proportion.'

'I realise that now. At the time I thought you were crazy, that they were right to commit you. But now I understand that the things you screamed at your press conference were true. There is something strange about this valley. Something malevolent, but hidden. Is that why you're back here? To destroy it?'

'Actually I'm just here to find my girlfriend,' Danyl said. 'Technically, ex-girlfriend.'

'Verity? The photographer?'

'Yes!' Danyl found his heart fluttering, beating out a complex and secret code. 'Do you know her? Do you know where she is?'

'No.' Ann set a crested community council mug on the desk beside Danyl then took a seat opposite him at the spotless desk. 'She disappeared shortly after your trial. No one's seen her in months. And she isn't the only person who's missing.' She lowered her voice to a conspiratorial hush. 'There are others. No one knows how many. People go out late at night and don't come back.'

'Like who?'

'All sorts.' She waved her hand at the empty room. 'Some of my colleagues on the council staff are gone.'

'How many?'

'Aside from me? All of them.'

Danyl sat back in his chair and sipped his coffee. Too hot. He looked at the empty desks. They were coated in a thin layer of dust: unused for weeks. He said, 'Where did they go?'

'Nobody knows. That's where you can help me.'

Danyl nodded. He saw where this was going. He said, 'You want me to find out where everyone has gone. Bring them all back.'

A vertical line appeared in Ann's brow. 'Well, not everyone. The disappearance of the council staff has been quite good for local government. The savings on salaries alone! We're hitting all of our budget benchmarks and the residents of Te Aro are happier than ever.'

'How do you know they're happy?'

'The volume of complaints to our website has dropped to

almost nothing.'

'Because so many of them have vanished?'

'Possibly. But I'm just the treasurer. I have no legal responsibility for residents who disappear. I do, however, have responsibility for the council's scholarship student.' Ann opened one of the drawers in her desk and took out a folder. 'This is who I want you to find.'

She took a photo from the folder and slid it across her desk. Danyl leaned forward to inspect it. It showed a hideous teenage boy with short spiky hair, dirty glasses, eyes that looked like raisins set into mounds of dough and a weak mouth above a cascading set of flabby chins. He stood in Te Aro Hall holding a certificate and smiling horribly at the camera.

'The Te Aro Fellowship is awarded to one exceptional student every year,' Ann explained. 'The winner receives a tiny amount of money, a year's residency at Te Aro Scholar's Cottage, and a fern. The winners are usually arts students but this year I convinced the council to grant the award to Sophus.' She indicated the repellent boy in this photo. 'He's a mathematician.'

'Really.'

Ann nodded. 'A gifted and brilliant number theorist. I studied maths myself before I came to Te Aro, so I had a particular interest in his work. I thought I could guide him. Steer him towards the breakthrough I know he's capable of. But now he's vanished.'

'Maybe he met a girl?' Danyl looked at the photo again. 'Or not.'

'No, there's no girl. He hasn't fallen in love with a person. He's fallen in love with mysticism. Everything he said before he vanished points to him being ensnared in a cult.'

Danyl frowned. 'Why would a brilliant mathematician be attracted to a mystical cult? Isn't maths all about pure reason?'

'It's supposed to be.' There was a bitter edge to Ann's voice. 'But sometimes mathematicians think . . . impure thoughts.

They ask the wrong questions. Dangerous questions.'

'Like what?'

Ann looked around the office and pointed to a stack of paperback books on a desk. 'Consider those books,' she said. 'They're real objects. All of our senses interact with them. There are words printed inside them and those words describe things that we encounter in the real world. But the words themselves don't exist. They're just symbols. So the word *book* describes a book, which is real, but the word *book* has no physical reality. Do you follow me?'

'Yes. Partly. Not really.'

'Some mathematicians wonder whether mathematical objects are real, like the books, or symbols like the words inside the books. At first they seem like symbols. The number two is just a description of two objects, right? It's not real. You can't reach out and touch the number two. But!' She held up a cautioning finger. Danyl tipped his head sideways and squinted. 'If we look closer, it seems as if numbers really are real. Consider the pile of books again. There are four books in it. If you wanted to you could pick them up and reorder them. How many different ways could you arrange them?'

Danyl set his jaw. He was not a naturally gifted mathematician and this upset him because he liked to think of himself as smart, and the fact that he could barely count undermined this notion. He blamed his lack of mathematical aptitude on an early childhood illness: he was off school with measles for a week and while he was away the rest of his class learned subtraction and Danyl never caught up. Now his mind went blank. He tried to think. How many ways could you order four books? Was it the square root of four? The log? What was 'log', anyway? No, wait—wasn't it just simple multiplication? Four books, four different positions . . .

'Sixteen,' he said.

Ann said, 'Twenty-four.'

'Twenty-four. Yes.'

'Four possible positions for the first book times three for the second, times two for the third one for the fourth equals twenty-four.'

'I get it, yes. I meant to say twenty-four. What does this have to do with your missing student, or Verity?'

'I'm getting to that. If there were five books there are 120 ways to organise them. Six books, 720 ways, and so on. If you divide each of these numbers by one and add the series together it tends towards a number called the infinite sum. The first few digits of the infinite sum are 2.71828 but it goes on forever, never repeating. It's what we call an irrational transcendental number. It's closely related to pi and the square root of negative one, which are also important irrational, transcendental numbers. And it appears in physical systems. The infinite sum controls the rate of radioactive decay in atoms. People spend their entire lives studying this one number. They go mad thinking about it.'

'Is that what happened to your student?' said Danyl. 'He went mad thinking about a number?'

'He didn't go mad. He asked himself the question that mathematicians aren't supposed to ask. He thought about the thing they're not supposed to think about.'

'What's that?'

'If numbers have no physical reality—if they're just symbols created by humans—then how could we find a number like the infinite sum embedded in the deep structure of the universe? Any other intelligent species studying radioactive decay will encounter this same irrational number. Therefore it must be real. But if this number is real, then surely all numbers are real? And if they are, where are they? How does the universe interact with them? How do our brains comprehend them?'

Danyl thought about this for a few seconds then asked, 'What's the answer?'

'No one knows,' Ann replied. 'But that's not the point. Maths is supposed to be about logic. Reason. Reality and incompleteness are outside the parameters of mathematical enquiry. That's why some mathematicians turn to mysticism. They seek unorthodox paths to the truth.'

'And you're afraid your student took one of those paths?'

'I'm sure he did. There are things he told me just before he disappeared. And you know this valley. There are sects, cults, tribes of nudists living in yurts. Worse. Sophus and I fought the night he vanished. He claimed he'd stumbled upon something here in the valley. A path leading to a breakthrough. He mentioned someone or something called Gorgon. Tell me,' Ann whispered, 'does that name mean anything to you?'

Gorgon? It sounded familiar. Then Danyl remembered the children's rhyme. Back when he lived with Verity, he was often woken by the sounds of children playing in his neighbour's yard. Yelling. Screaming. Singing. He wanted to complain to the council: get some local ordinance passed preventing the noise of children's games exceeding a quiet murmur, but Verity wouldn't let him. Danyl remembered well the words to all their songs, one of which went:

> *Be me*
> *Seem me*
> *Or Gorgon will see me*
> *Hide me*
> *Blind me*
> *Or Gorgon will find me*

He recited this for Ann and her eyes gleamed. 'Yes,' she said, 'yes. Sophus's disappearance and the rhyme must be connected. What do you think it means?'

'I'm not sure,' Danyl admitted.

'But you can find out. You can look for Sophus where I can't. I've contacted some of the local sects. None of their cult leaders will talk to me because of my position at the community council. I represent authority. Bureaucracy. But you were arrested in a bizarre scandal, taken into custody by the police and diagnosed with an acute mental illness. That makes you a hero to these people. They'll talk to you. And while you're searching for Sophus, you can stay in the Scholar's Cottage. Sleep in a warm dry bed instead of a damp concrete stairway. And I'll feed you.' She opened her satchel, took out a muffin and handed it to Danyl while fixing him with her gaze. 'Say yes.'

Danyl took the muffin. He sat back in his chair and considered Ann's offer. It sounded appealing. A roof. A bed. More muffins. He drummed his fingers on the table, thinking.

His doctors had stressed the importance of stability and relaxation in managing his illness. A regular routine. Regular meals. Regular sleep, ideally indoors on a bed and not in a concrete entranceway. If they were here they'd advise him to take the deal.

But his doctors were not infallible. After all, they had warned Danyl that if he stopped taking his antidepressants the consequences could be dire. Yet a week after discontinuing his medication there had been no consequences; on the contrary, he felt fantastic. Alive! So his doctors didn't know everything.

Danyl took a bite of muffin and smiled, and Ann smiled back. But there was something hidden behind her eyes. Something calculating. Remember where you are, a voice in Danyl's head cautioned him. Te Aro, where nothing was as it seemed. Beneath the valley's superficial quirky charm lurked depths of madness. Danyl had forgotten this in his time away, but he remembered it now. His goal was to find Verity. Help her. Maybe she would take him back, and if so he would stay. Otherwise he should leave the valley again.

And what about the treasurer and her missing student? Should he get involved? Maybe Verity's disappearance was related to this mathematician's and in seeking one he would find both? But probably not. People vanished mysteriously all the time around here. And he didn't trust this attractive and generous treasurer. She was trying to draw him into something sinister.

Danyl swallowed the last of the muffin and decided he would not be drawn. 'I'm sorry,' he said to Ann. 'I can't accept. I don't need a place to stay. I'm going to find my girlfriend today. I hope you find your . . .' He gestured at the horrible teenager in the photograph. 'Thing. And thanks for breakfast.' He brushed the muffin crumbs from his beard and stood and walked to the door. He was almost there when the treasurer spoke.

'Danyl?' Her voice was low. Ominous. He turned. Ann steepled her fingers. 'You'll never find Verity by yourself. But I know where you can start looking.' She nodded at the photo. 'Find Sophus. Then I'll tell you. Otherwise you could look forever and ever and find . . . nothing.'

4

The Free Market

Danyl had thought about Verity a lot in the days since he had released himself from the hospital. What happened? Where did it all go wrong?

One afternoon stood out in his memory. About a month after Danyl moved into her house, Verity came home early from work and suggested they go to the market together. 'It's in Aro Park,' she explained, pulling open the curtains while Danyl sat up in bed blinking in the flood of late-afternoon sunlight. 'It's called the Free Market. It's subsidised by the council. They wanted to give the residents of the valley an alternative to global capitalism so they set up stalls where people can barter for goods and services as equals in a trusting, loving environment.'

'Do they sell food?'

'Yes, but you don't want to eat anything from there. And stay away from the organic beetroot juice. I've heard stories.'

Danyl sat up and swung his legs over the side of the bed, watching Verity as she moved around the room. She was in her late twenties, average height but small-framed so she seemed shorter than she was. She was pretty but not as pretty as she could be, Danyl felt, if she grew her hair longer and dyed it blond, and wore makeup and short skirts and tight tops instead of jeans and T-shirts. Her shoulder-length black hair fell over her face, which was pale even in summer. Her eyes were green. Or maybe brown; it was hard to tell in the bright sunlight. He reminded himself to look at Verity's eyes more.

'Get up,' she ordered, moving to the window overlooking the street. 'I want to get photos of the fair before everyone goes home.' She pulled up the blind and then hissed and stepped backwards.

'What's wrong?' Danyl sensed danger; he started to climb back beneath the bedclothes. Verity stared, a shocked expression on her face. Her eyes flashed—they were actually kind of grey —and she scanned the road, her hands on her hips.

Danyl asked, 'Did you see something?'

'I don't know. There was someone standing on the corner of Aro Street looking at our house.' She shook her head. 'They're gone now.' She smiled at him. 'Probably just a ghost.'

There were dozens of stalls. Hundreds of people browsed them, or danced in the middle of the park to the band who played 'Three Little Birds' over and over again. The smells of cinnamon and cannabis and burnt halloumi hung heavily in the air.

Verity and Danyl walked through the crowd. Danyl looked for a book stall. Verity took photos. She had another exhibition coming up but she didn't know what it would be about. Her last photography exhibition consisted of gloomy monochromatic photos of the Aro Valley, and it won an award for Most Troubled Young Artist. 'I don't know what to shoot,' she complained. 'It can't just be Te Aro again.'

They passed a stall selling handicrafts: children's toys, drug paraphernalia, woollen hats. Then a stall selling organic beetroot juice. A sign above it read: *The Rumours are TRUE!* A long queue of silent, expectant men stood waiting. Verity put her hand around Danyl's arm and hurried him on.

The next stall sold more toys, bongs and woollen hats. So did the stall after that. But at the end of the row was a drab canvas tent with a blackboard in front of it reading: *Fortunes Told! Secrets Unveiled! Beware! Dr Zuzanna's Cards Predict a 20% Chance of Rain!*

'A fortune teller!' Verity turned to Danyl. 'Do you want to go first?'

'I'm not going in there. Don't tell me you believe in this nonsense?' Danyl and Verity hadn't been a couple for very long and they were still learning things about each other, not all of which were pleasant. Verity was unhappy to learn that Danyl couldn't cook or clean while Danyl was appalled to discover that Jane Austen was Verity's favourite author. And now this. She believed in psychics and he didn't.

She said, 'It'll be fun.'

'Fun? These people are frauds. Is it fun to give your money away to someone who tells you lies?'

'Yes,' Verity replied. 'It's fun. It's a fantasy. And how do you know they're frauds? I've seen some strange things in my life. Things that defy rational explanation.'

'Ha! So you do believe in them! You're like a child, Verity. What if—' He held up a cautioning finger. 'What if the fortune teller tells you something that you'll do in the future and you decide to do the opposite? Boom. Paradox.'

Verity did not acknowledge the metaphysical consequences of this question. Instead she said, 'I'm going in. Here's your spending money.' She took five dollars from her wallet and handed it to him; Danyl accepted it with dignity. 'I'll meet you by the feminist cake stall in twenty minutes.' Then she disappeared inside the tent. Danyl glimpsed a candle-lit interior and a framed degree from the Royal Oxford University of Astrology in Lagos hanging on a coat stand. The flap closed.

The second-hand book stall was at the far end of the market. It consisted of a dozen tables with books laid out in packed rows. More books spilled out of cardboard boxes nested beneath the tables. A sad, tired-looking man with white hair sat under an umbrella at the back of the stall. A handwritten sign beside him read *Books $5*. The only other customers were a man and a woman huddled together by the self-help section. They wore wrinkled clothes and looked pale and unhealthy. Danyl turned his back to them and inspected the fiction shelves.

Danyl had once worked in a second-hand bookshop; he'd

found it very calming to browse around stacks of old, forgotten books—flipping through manuals for obsolete technology, the vanity-published memoirs of businessmen and the forgotten bestsellers of the 1950s. He did so now, and a clever idea came to him: Verity was getting her fortune told by a psychic. Well, Danyl would tell her fortune too, via bibliomancy. He would buy a book at random and whenever Verity cited her fortune teller, claiming that some random event in her life was foretold by the cards, Danyl would flourish his randomly chosen book, read a passage from it and improvise an equally plausible forecast. He cackled to himself. His five dollars would buy him hours of joy.

He stood between two tables, closed his eyes and, smiling, spun about in a circle then reached out, groping for a book. His fingers danced along the spines, waiting for an impulse to pick one. In his mind he was already anticipating the way in which he'd torment Verity if the book was a dictionary. Or a poetry collection. Or, best of all, a romance novel. He grinned, blindly extended his fingers and reached out.

A hand gripped his wrist. Danyl gasped and opened his eyes. The unhealthy couple now stood on the opposite side of the table glaring at him. The woman held Danyl's hand; she shook it and croaked in a flat, oddly accented voice, 'These books are not for sale.'

He snatched his hand free and puffed up his chest. 'Of course they are,' he replied. 'Ask the shopkeeper.' He pointed at the sad, white-haired man, but he was gone. Vanished, along with his chair and his umbrella. In his place were three more pale, wrinkly clothed figures. They were moving books from the tables into cardboard boxes then loading the boxes on a trailer.

'These books are not for sale,' the woman said again. 'These books are ours now.'

'Who are you? What's going on here?'

'We are the Cart—' the man began, but the woman raised her finger to his lips, silencing him. 'We are nobody,' she intoned. 'Just some friends out for a walk who decided to purchase this entire stock of used books. Is that so suspicious?'

'I guess not.' Danyl smiled at the woman. 'I just need one book,' he explained. 'To play a joke on my girlfriend. Any book. I'll pay.' He flourished his five-dollar note.

'We don't want your worthless money,' the man replied. He had a triangular face, four very large front teeth and a truncated nose. He looked like a goat, and now he reached across the table and shoved Danyl's shoulder. 'Spend it on something else,' he sneered. 'While you still can.'

All his life Danyl had been a coward. And, like all cowards, he could sense greater cowardice in others. The goat-faced man was afraid, putting on a show of bravado to impress the woman he was with. So Danyl stepped back to the table, picked up a book and jutted out his chin.

'I'll go. And I'll take this with me,' he said. 'Unless you think you can stop me.'

'Careful,' the woman said, laying a hand on the Goatman's shoulder. 'We can't cause any trouble. It's not time.' She looked Danyl up and down, bathing him with her hatred. 'Yet.'

'That's right. It's not time.' He smirked at the Goatman then glanced down at the cover of his new book. It was a guide to beautiful French Kampuchea.

Then someone poked him in the back and he dropped it. He turned, ready to fight or run, probably run, but the person behind him was Verity. She looked serious. She said, 'We have to go.'

'I'm just arguing with these cave fish,' Danyl replied. He gestured at the Goatman and his associate, who stood watching him, hostile and silent. 'They won't let me buy this obsolete guidebook, but I say—'

Verity cut him off, poking him in the belly this time, making him squeal.

'We need to go home. Now. There's someone waiting for me there.'

'How do you know? Did the fortune teller tell you?'

'Yes.'

'Oho! Well, I have a fortune for you!' Danyl fumbled for his book but the Goatman snatched it away. Danyl lunged for it. The Goatman stepped out of reach, then Verity grabbed Danyl's arm and dragged him away from the stall. She pulled him into the crowd; the last thing he saw was the Goatman grinning in triumph, his huge square teeth gleaming in the sunlight.

'The fortune teller said that an old friend was looking for me.'

'So?' Danyl and Verity walked along the old road leading to their backyard, shading their eyes from the glare of the sunlight. Verity hurried; Danyl trotted behind her putting on little bursts of speed to keep up. 'I thought you said it was just a bit of fun?'

'You remember earlier when I looked out the window? I thought I saw an old friend. Someone I thought I'd lost forever. That can't be coincidence.'

'Who is this friend?'

Verity didn't reply. She stepped through the hole in the fence leading to their backyard, and stopped.

The yard was a field of midday summer sunlight. The shrubs and trees glowed. The back of their house was a white plane with the sun reflecting in the windows. At the base of the plane was a black rectangle: the door leading into their kitchen. It was open.

'Didn't we lock that door?'

Verity didn't answer. Instead, she said, 'She's here,' and moved towards the open doorway as if in a trance.

'She?' Danyl followed, nervous but curious.

'Someone I grew up with,' Verity replied. 'We were close when we were teenagers.'

'Very close?'

'Not like that, idiot. We ran away from home together. We were looking for something, but we fought about the best way to find it. When she left I thought she'd gone forever.'

They were close to the kitchen now. The darkness unknit itself: through the door they saw a suitcase, the dim outline of the table, a chair facing the doorway and a pair of bare, tanned legs extending from the shadows into the light.

'What were you looking for?' Danyl said.

'We were looking for a great man,' said a voice that came from the shadows about the chair. It was confident and amused, but at the same time hostile and cold: like a receptionist in a doctor's office. The legs uncrossed. Danyl noticed tattoos around each of the ankles. Complex spiral patterns.

'We were looking for a great man,' the voice repeated. 'One of the greatest who ever lived. And you found him, Verity. You found him, then you abandoned him for the sad little creature beside you.'

5

Eleanor

The rain had stopped. The wind blew sprays of icy mist up from the puddles and down from the trees, aiming it directly at Danyl. He stood on the street outside Aro Park, remembering the Free Market and the terrible events that came after it.

He sighed. He knew where to go next. The one person in the valley likely to know Verity's whereabouts. But he hesitated. Surely there was another way. Someone else? Anyone?

He looked around for inspiration. The sun was a vague grey blur just above the horizon. It was about nine in the morning. People should have been stumbling home from parties or making the way up the hill to the university, but there was no one about. Danyl was alone. There was no alternative.

The house was nestled between two apartment buildings. It was an old bungalow, handsomely refurbished with leadlight windows and fresh white paint. A sign on the door read: *The Dolphin Café is closed until further notice.*

The front windows were dark. Danyl pressed his nose against a frosted pane of glass. From deep inside came a faint glow of electric light.

His memory stirred. The Dolphin. How many times had he come here with Verity, laughing as they walked through the door; holding hands at a cosy table, taking their time over a romantic dinner before hurrying home to make love? At least twice. He sighed and tried the handle. It opened.

The hall was dark. There were three doors spaced evenly along the left-hand wall. They led to the dining room, the kitchen and the manager's office. The light came from the office.

Danyl softened his footfalls. He looked into the dining room. It was empty: chairs stacked on wooden tables, dusty wood-panelled walls receding into shadows. A sliding door in the opposite wall led into the service alley behind the restaurant. It was open: a confusion of muddy footprints criss-crossed the floor, leading from the alleyway to the waiter's entrance to the kitchen. He heard a clatter of bins coming from the alley. Three large men passed back and forth carrying sacks of rubbish.

He moved on before any of them glanced his way. He passed the kitchen—the door was ajar; the space beyond looked chaotic. More footprints criss-crossing the floor, several large basins stacked in a mound on the bench.

He reached the end of the hall and gave the office door a nudge. It swung inwards, revealing a cramped room dominated by a cluttered desk. A thin woman with a narrow face and huge black eyes sat at the desk. Instead of her customary white chef's apron she wore a sea-green bathrobe with a matching towel wrapped around her head. She rested her bare legs on the top of the desk. Spiral tattoos snaked around her ankles.

Eleanor.

Oh yes. Eleanor and Verity were old friends. They grew up together. They ran away from home together. Then they parted ways, forever, or so Verity thought, until that sunny afternoon two years ago when Eleanor appeared in their kitchen. Tanned, thin but muscular from her endless hours of yoga, with long straight hair and a face that looked serene and jolly until she looked at Danyl.

She'd been living in a Taoist monastery someplace in Asia, she told them. The Golden Pavilion of Complete Perfection. She ran the kitchen there and spent the rest of her time meditating on the nonexistence of reality, until one day an electrical fuse blew, plunging the Pavilion of Complete Perfection into darkness. Eleanor trudged down the mountainside to buy a replacement fuse at a nearby town. While she was waiting for the electrician to open his shop, she sat in lotus position in the dust beside a noodle stand, flipping through international magazines. She came across a story about Verity's photography award. 'There was a picture of you,' Eleanor explained from the dark interior of the kitchen. 'And there was this.'

She took a piece of paper from her pocket and laid it on the kitchen table. It was a crumpled reproduction of one of Verity's acclaimed Te Aro photos. It showed a hillside dotted with half-ruined buildings. It was taken from the bottom of the hill looking up. A gravel driveway flanked with weeds wound up the slope, terminating at a house at the top of the slope, perched on wooden pilings. Behind the house a bare stone cliff loomed out of the frame. Verity looked at it with a grim expression. Then she turned to Danyl and said, 'Can you give us a minute? Ellie and I need to talk.'

And that was the beginning of the end. Eleanor moved in with them. She slept in their spare room. She ignored Danyl, and he did his best to ignore her. He pretended she wasn't there, pretended she wasn't doing nude yoga in his backyard every morning to greet the sun, and whispering, always whispering to Verity.

The house filled with these whispers. Danyl heard them in the middle of the night when he woke to find Verity's side of the bed empty; Verity in the spare room sitting cross-legged on the end of Eleanor's cot, whispering. They always broke off when he entered the room. He overheard fragments of conversations: words that meant nothing to him at the time: the city, the chemist, the conduit, the spiral.

Then one happy day, Eleanor left! She bought a crumbling old house on Aro Street and converted it into her restaurant, She worked all hours to build a kitchen, convert the dining room and garden, and recruit staff; occasionally she slept on a couch in her office. She was still on the periphery of Danyl's life: a darkness on the horizon, still encouraging Verity to leave him, and trying to make him feel bad about himself because she was building a successful business out of nothing while he spiralled into depression and total financial dependence on Verity. But at least she wasn't living with him anymore. Life went back to normal. For a time.

Now Verity was gone from his life but Eleanor was still here. She sat behind her desk in her stupid little office, with schedules and lists and diagrams covering the walls, frowning at her silly little smartphone as she tapped away at its screen. Eleanor hated Danyl. He knew that; and also that she would never intentionally reveal Verity's whereabouts, or tell him anything helpful. But perhaps she could be tricked? Could her hatred be turned against her? Perhaps—if he took her by surprise. He raised his hand to knock on the door.

'Aren't you supposed to be locked in an asylum?' Eleanor did not look up at him. 'Did you break out?'

Danyl transformed his knocking motion into a casual stroke of his hair and replied, 'It wasn't an asylum. It was a residential treatment facility. And I released myself under my own cognisance.'

Eleanor put down her phone and leaned back in her chair, regarding Danyl with a sour expression. 'And now you've come back to Te Aro.'

'That's right. I think you know why I'm here.'

'To beg for food?'

'I don't need your charity. Someone already fed me breakfast. No. I've come for Verity.'

'Verity threw you out.'

'I want to give her the chance to fix that mistake.' He stepped into the room. 'I've been to her home. Our home. It's been abandoned for months and there's a cryptic threat carved on the door.'

'Oh?'

'It said "Death to the agents of the Real City". What does that mean?'

'I don't know.'

'I think you do.' Danyl took another step towards the desk. 'I think that you think I don't know anything about what you think. But I know more than you think about what I know you think.'

'OK. Time for you to leave, Danyl.' She reached for a brass bell on her desk. 'Allow my kitchen hands to show you the gutter outside the door.'

'I also know about the farm.'

Eleanor's hand froze. Danyl continued. 'You and Verity grew up together. Best friends together in a tiny seaside town.'

Eleanor did not move.

'Verity once told me about an abandoned farm on the outskirts of that town. She liked to go there when she wanted to be alone. Until one day the police raided it. There was a fugitive hiding in the farm buildings. Some kind of scientist. He'd set up a clandestine laboratory deep in the woods. The authorities brought in bulldozers and knocked it down. Any of this sound familiar?'

Eleanor was silent. Danyl opened his satchel and took out the mud-splattered journal cover. 'I found this in Verity's bathroom. Someone burned her old journals but they left this cover, dated the same year the police raided that farm. And the same year that you and Verity ran away from home together, never to return. You know what's inside it?' He flipped the cover. 'Nothing. And the fact that it contains nothing means something.'

Eleanor leaned forward, rested her elbows on her desk and cradled her head in her hands.

'I think you and Verity crept onto the farm,' he went

on, 'after the police raid but before the bulldozers. I think you found the fugitive scientist's hidden laboratory, and you saw something. But what?' He smiled. 'You'll never tell me, of course. You hate me. And there's no way to recover the contents of this notebook.' He cocked his head to one side and his smile widened. 'Or is there?'

Eleanor still did not reply. Danyl reached into his satchel, took out his etching of the spiral shape and laid it face up on Eleanor's desk. 'That's the reason the two of you ran away all those years ago, isn't it? You were seeking the spiral. Verity is still seeking it. It's why she's disappeared. What is it? Where is it? What is the Real City? Where is Verity?' He stood before the desk, looming over Eleanor, his arms folded. 'I'm not leaving here unless you tell me everything.'

There were three kitchen hands, each a head taller than Danyl, all lean and heavily muscled. They held him up by his arms and legs and carried him face down through the hall and out the door. 'Are you going to leave quietly?' one of them asked Danyl, who swallowed and nodded. The kitchen hand said, 'Set him down nice and easy.' They swung him to his feet and steadied him as he found his balance. 'Don't come back,' the same kitchen hand said, in a tone that was both friendly and heavy with implicit violence.

'Danyl.' Eleanor was in the doorway. Her arms were folded; the flaps of her dressing gown whipped in the breeze.

'I really don't know where Verity is,' she said. 'She's disappeared. That's what she does. She left her home, and then me, and now you. I know you don't believe me. You think I'm your enemy, and that everything I do has some sinister motive.' She shrugged. 'It's true that I never liked you. You were bad for Verity. You were a sick guy. When I heard you were getting treatment, taking medication, I was glad for you. You needed help. And now here you are, back in Te Aro raving about farms and spiral patterns and scientists, and looking for Verity. But she's gone. There is no mystery. There is no plot. Forget about Verity, and this valley, and whatever you think is happening here.' She pointed to the beginning of Aro Street, where it connected with the rest of the Capital: he saw lit buildings, cars and pedestrians on the roads. 'Go now,' she urged him. 'Leave this valley. Go back to your doctors. Your treatment. Get out while you can.'

6

The familiar face

Danyl walked up the hill on the north side of the valley, heading for Steve's house. This was a cottage located in a narrow gully accessible only via a near-vertical ascent of Devon Street. It was still raining; still cold. He took many breaks as he walked up the steep and winding way. He huddled in burnt-out garages, or beneath crumbling walls scoured with graffiti and weeds, panting to catch his breath, and he thought over Eleanor's parting words.

When Danyl first went on his medication he worried that the powerful mood-altering drugs would take away his identity, his free will; turn him into a happy, obedient zombie; destroy the real Danyl. Enslave him. But when they started to work and his depression dissolved he realised that the previous Danyl —Unmedicated Danyl—wasn't free. He was sick, horribly sick, and the drugs had cured him. The new Medicated Danyl was the free Danyl. The real Danyl. Once a lowly grub, now transformed into a beautiful, soaring but heavily drugged butterfly.

Unfortunately that feeling didn't last. Medicated Danyl was calm Danyl. Controlled Danyl. Temperate Danyl, who felt no highs or lows. Medicated Danyl never burst into tears when the sensors for the automatic doors at the supermarket failed to detect him, but neither did he roar with laughter when something truly hilarious happened, like seeing a stranger walk face first into the doors at the supermarket after they failed to open for them. The most pleasure Medicated Danyl ever took from life was an amused smile. After a few months of calm and sanity, Danyl realised he missed Unmedicated Danyl. Maybe that was the real Danyl after all?

Now, after a week of being Unmedicated Danyl again, Danyl felt very real. But what if he was deluding himself? What if Eleanor was right and Unmedicated Danyl was psychotic Danyl? And, if that was so, which Danyl was the real Danyl? How could he tell?

These thoughts troubled him as he panted and gasped his way up the hill, gritting his teeth and leaning into the wind. Eventually he reached the great bend in Devon Street. To his left the road curved around and continued up the hill and out of the valley. To the right the slope dropped away, descending to a narrow gully. He looked down on the dismal collection of damp sunless houses below, the most wretched and lichen-encrusted of which was Steve's.

It was mid-morning, about 10.30. But the sunlight did not reach the lower depths of the gully. Ever. It was a region of shadow and mould.

Steve's house was a small single-storey box: an old cottage with peeling paint and curtains covering the windows. It was reached via a long, crooked wooden staircase. The steps were loose concrete bricks: they were slick with slime.

As Danyl descended, making his way deeper into the gloom, he saw the yard. One of the terms of Steve's tenancy was that he keep the garden neat and well-tended and free of weeds, and Steve's response to this burden was to routinely spray the entire property with industrial defoliant. The result was a bland expanse of mud surrounding the entire house, extending to the fences on all sides, broken only by the skeletons of dead trees. A path of churned ooze led from the bottom of the steps to Steve's front door. When Danyl reached it he noted that there were many different footprints embedded in the mire: different shoes, boots, different sizes. They all looked recent. Steve's front door was ajar.

Steve would never leave his front door open. And why were dozens of footprints leading to his house? Would dozens of people visit Steve? No. Never. Danyl stopped halfway to the open door and called out, 'Hello?'

No answer. Maybe Steve was sleeping? He slept for about eighteen hours a day so this wasn't unlikely. Danyl knocked on the door. The house creaked. Water dripped from the gutters overhead. He touched the door with his fingertips. It swung inwards.

Steve had entered Danyl's life one fine summer morning at the German Bakery on Aro Street. It was Verity's birthday, so Danyl took her out for breakfast. They sat by the window and ate apple tarts and drank black coffee. When they finished their pastries, Verity paid at the counter then went to the bathroom. Danyl glanced through the newspaper, and when he looked up a moment later a stranger sat opposite him.

Before he could speak, the stranger reached across the table and grabbed Danyl's hand. 'Don't get up,' he said in a low but cheerful tone. 'Keep smiling. Pretend we're friends having a nice, normal chat.'

He was a man of average height and average build. He was dressed identically to Danyl in old black jeans and a faded grey T-shirt. His head was shaved; the contours of his skull were pleasing to the eye. His smile was warm and open. He had dimples in his cheeks and laugh lines around his eyes. He looked like a crafty, dissolute Buddha trying to scam his way to enlightenment.

Danyl frowned at the fingers grasping his wrist and asked, 'Who are you?'

'We don't have much time,' the stranger replied. 'Let's not play games. I know who you are, you know who I am.'

'I have no idea who you are.'

'I'm the guy who is about to blow your mind'—the stranger released Danyl's hand and briefly mimed his head exploding— 'with the truth. Your name is Clive.'

'My name is Danyl.'

Steve considered this information for a few seconds, then replied. 'Listen, Donald. Do you ever have the feeling that the world is not as it seems? That there's a deeper reality, a hidden reality all around us, but that something or someone is concealing the truth from us?'

'I think everyone feels that,' Danyl replied, having heard these ideas many times since his arrival in Aro Valley. 'But I think that paranoia about the nature of reality is really just a coping mechanism. Reality is what it is, but it's so chaotic and complex our minds struggle to comprehend it. So we invent these conspiracies to tell ourselves that there's a deeper simplicity. It's more comforting than accepting the truth, which is that our world is random and meaningless.'

'Exactly. Well said.' The stranger smiled then leaned across the table. 'The real question is this,' he whispered. 'Who is making us paranoid and why? What are they trying to conceal?'

'That's not—'

'What if I told you I had proof of a conspiracy?' He took a folder filled with papers and photographs from his backpack. 'A massive conspiracy that stretches across space and time? A conspiracy operating right here within Aro Valley. A conspiracy that your girlfriend Verity might be involved with? A plot against reality itself?'

Danyl thought for a second. 'I would be intrigued,' he replied. 'But also completely disbelieving.'

'Disbelieve this.' The stranger flipped to the middle of the folder, then glanced in the direction of the bathroom. 'Tell me, what is you think your girlfriend does after she leaves the house in the morning?'

'She goes to work at an art gallery.'

'Oh? Does she?' He smirked knowingly. 'And was she at work yesterday at 1.15 pm?'

'She was probably on her lunchbreak.'

'Indeed. And do you know where she went for this lunchbreak?'

Danyl nodded cautiously. 'She said she went to the library.'

'She did,' the stranger said. 'But the real question is: what did she do there?'

'Got some books out?'

'Correct. And what books did she get?'

'I don't know,' Danyl said.

'Ha! So she doesn't tell you everything.'

'She told me. I just wasn't paying attention.'

'I have a colleague at the library,' the stranger continued. 'He keeps an eye on things for me. Tells me who is reading the wrong books. Researching the wrong subjects. Finding the wrong answers.'

'Is that legal? What about people's privacy?'

'What about the books' privacy?' the stranger demanded. 'What about the right of knowledge never to be known? Take a look at this printout of all the books your girlfriend borrowed yesterday. Tell me what you see.' He slid the printout across the table.

Danyl read the list. 'These are mostly art history texts.'

'And?'

'Verity is an artist. A photographer.'

'Keep reading.'

'The rest are mostly cookbooks.'

'Indeed,' said the stranger. 'And it gets worse. Look at the last entry on the list.'

'Emanuel Swedenborg's *Journal of Dreams*.' Danyl looked at the stranger. 'So what?'

'Do you know who Swedenborg was?'

'Wasn't he some kind of Swedish mystic?'

'Emanuel Swedenborg,' the stranger replied, 'was the greatest psychic in the western tradition. In 1741, when he was in his mid-fifties, he was a world renowned physicist. He was at the height of his scientific career. Then he began to have visions. He manifested astonishing psychic powers. He documented the first of these visions in his *Journal of Dreams*. On this page'—he produced a photocopied document—'Swedenborg described a luminous pathway spiralling up through the stairs towards heaven with groups of angels ascending and descending it. Now . . .' He smiled reassuringly. 'I bet you're wondering what the visions of a Swedish mystic who lived three hundred years ago have to do with why I follow your girlfriend around on her lunchbreak?'

Danyl nodded.

'Look at the top of the list,' the stranger continued. 'She's also borrowed a book about William Blake.'

'That crazy poet?'

'He was a poet,' the stranger admitted. 'But Blake was also Britain's greatest visual artist.'

'What about William Turner?'

'Any idiot can paint a steamship on fire in the mist, Danyl. No. Blake was the master. He was heavily influenced by Swedenborg, so we shouldn't be surprised by this.' He slid a reproduction of a Blake watercolour across the table. It showed an impossible spiral stairway, rising up through the stars, that was populated by graceful figures, some of them winged, carrying vases or baskets or children. The stairway terminated in a distant, radiant sun. *Jacob's Ladder*, painted by Blake circa 1806. Very different from the path to heaven described in the Book of Genesis, but identical to Swedenborg's vision. The painting is obviously based on it. How do you explain that?'

'I guess Blake read Swedenborg's journal,' Danyl replied. He found himself enjoying the stranger's torrent of nonsense. His life had been very quiet of late: Eleanor had moved out; Verity spent all of her time working on her new photography exhibition: a secret project of which he knew nothing. Danyl himself had been trying to finish writing his novel, but he spent more and more of his days asleep. This stranger's babble was like rain in a drought, and he delivered it with such a confident cheerful air. Danyl should have been alarmed that this deluded man was stalking Verity and recording her movements, but the stranger's merry eyes made it all seem harmless, even fun. 'Blake painted his painting based on the passage in the journal,' Danyl continued. 'But now you'll claim that he didn't.'

'You're right,' the stranger replied. 'In that you were totally wrong.' He stabbed the painting with his finger. 'The journal Swedenborg recorded this vision in was never published during his lifetime. It was lost until a century after his death. A researcher stumbled upon it hidden away in the Royal Library of Stockholm, in 1854. Twenty-seven years after Blake died. According to the memoirs of Blake's friend William Varley, Blake saw this spiral stairway in a vision, just like Swedenborg. Two men, decades and countries apart, both imagined and depicted this same unique image. If we asked either of them to explain this, they'd talk about revelation, about divine inspiration. But we'—Steve waved his hand, encompassing Danyl and himself—'we are men of the world. We don't believe in such superstitions. But then how do we explain this mystery?'

'Coincidence?'

The stranger smiled indulgently, then his expression turned serious. 'There are many of these coincidences throughout human history. Too many to be a coincidence.' He leaned closer. 'These manifold visions have an origin. An author. What is their agenda? All art and all storytelling has the same purpose. To manipulate the audience. But here the audience is all of humanity. Something wants to influence our thoughts. The development of our civilisation. The destiny of our species. But who? And why? I believe that your girlfriend'— He tapped the list of Verity's library books—'is involved in this plot. I don't know if she's an outsider, like myself, or one of the puppet-masters ringleading from behind the curtain. I want you to help me find out.'

'If our thoughts are being manipulated by someone unknown,' Danyl asked, warming to the subject, 'then how do you know you aren't being manipulated right now?'

The stranger clicked his fingers and pointed at Danyl. 'That is a very perceptive question,' he replied. 'How indeed?' He said this again, softly, to himself. He opened his folder, flipped through the remaining papers inside it, then paused and licked his lips. 'After all, my own thoughts . . . I could be part of the plot, and I wouldn't even . . .' He trailed off then, and after a minute of silence he coughed and announced, 'I have to go now.' He took the library list and photocopies and stuffed them into his folder, which he tucked under his arm. Then he stood. 'Don't speak of any of this to Verity. Keep an eye on her. Monitor her for unusual behaviour. Don't tell her anything. I'll be in touch.' He hurried out of the bakery and ran across the road.

Verity returned from the bathroom. She watched the stranger vault the wall to Aro Park, catch his foot on the lip and fall out of sight behind it. She said, 'Was that man sitting in my seat?'

'Yes.' Danyl finished the last of his tea.

'Who is he?' Verity picked up her handbag. 'What's his name?'

'Steve!'

Danyl stood in the unlit hall. It ran all the way through Steve's house. There were five doors leading off it: the back door was open, leading into the backyard. The other four led to the bedroom, lounge, kitchen and bathroom: they were all closed. Danyl paused on the threshold, sniffing the air.

The house smelled of sweat and urine. It felt empty.

The first door opened onto the lounge. It was even darker than the hall. He tried the light switch just inside the doorway, but nothing happened. The window was a vague rectangle to his left, covered by a heavy curtain. Danyl pulled ineffectively at the curtain. It was nailed to the window frame. He grunted and tugged harder until the fabric tore, admitting a ragged ghost of light into the room.

Steve's lounge was never a well-decorated, harmonious space, so whoever pushed all the furniture against the walls and covered the threadbare carpet with a dozen foam mattresses had improved the decor. There were cheap woollen blankets scattered around the place. There was something missing, and it took Danyl a minute to realise what it was.

Steve's decrepit, disgusting couch and chairs were crammed up against the wall where the bookshelves had once stood. The shelves themselves were disassembled and stacked in the corner, but Steve's vast and precious collection of self-help books, neo-phrenology texts and horror novels were all gone.

Danyl returned to the hall and opened the next door. Steve's bedroom. The bed lay on its side, tipped against the wall to make way for more mattresses. He checked the small closet built into the back wall: Steve's clothes were all there—formerly blue jeans and formerly white T-shirts, all equilibrated to a muddy shade of grey by Steve's inability to set the correct water temperature on the washing machines at the local laundry. Pinned to the back of the door was a scrap of paper. On it was written:

Thinking cannot accomplish anything—unless you THINK it can

Danyl smiled at this. Steve was addicted to stupid inspirational aphorisms copied out of his self-help books. They used to be taped up all around his house, dozens of cheerful sentences urging the reader to follow their fears and face their dreams. Now they were gone. His books were gone. Steve was gone.

Danyl returned to the hall and tried the next door. The bathroom was small. It contained a toilet, a wash-basin and a bath with a shower stand at one end. There was nothing else in the room except for another quote taped to the bathroom mirror:

YOU are NOT a butterfly dreaming you are a man
Because butterflies lack the neurological complexity to dream

Steve did not cook, so he'd converted the kitchen into a study. Access to the fridge and oven was blocked by a row of heavy filing cabinets. The kitchen table was empty. The linoleum floor was covered with scuffed, muddy footprints leading a complex dance back and forth then leading to the back door, which was open. Beyond the door lay another tan field of mud.

A gust of wind shook the door. It swung back and forth, creaking and bashing against a yellow rubbish bag which was trapped in the doorway. The bag had split, spilling its contents on the floor. Danyl sorted through them with the tip of his shoe.

Syringes. Latex gloves. A dozen empty bottles of disinfectant. Dozens of adult-sized nappies all swollen and reeking of urine. Some of these were things you'd expect to find in Steve's rubbish. Others were a mystery.

The footprints on the lino headed straight towards the doorway and the rubbish bag. Beyond it they inverted into depressions in the mud leading directly to the shape of a human body imprinted in the ooze, arms outstretched, about two metres from the door. The footprints then reversed direction, weaving an unsteady route back to the house. Danyl stepped over the bag and walked across the mud to the indentation. He knelt beside it.

Whoever fell here had landed face down and made a surprisingly clear imprint. The area above the back porch was sheltered by a corrugated plastic roof, and this had protected the footprints and the impression from the rain. The fall could have happened this morning, or days earlier. Danyl could make out the shape of the buttons on their jacket, their outstretched fingers. Their face.

The circular pattern of footprints around the imprint reminded Danyl of something. He stared at the mud, and then his hand touched the notepaper inside his pocket: the etching of the spiral pattern he found in Verity's notebook. He remembered Eleanor—his confrontation with her that morning. Her parting words as she stood in the door to her restaurant. There is no mystery. There is no plot. Forget about Verity, and this valley, and whatever you think is happening here.

He'd almost believed her; almost abandoned his search for Verity and left the valley. Now he stared down at the finely detailed imprint in the mud and made a low growling sound in the back of his throat; because the face that was so clearly outlined there was Eleanor's.

7

The entrance to the labyrinth

The night rose from the ground like a tide. The shadows brimmed and pooled, flooding the streets, drowning the valley. The lights from the streetlights and houses were tiny remote dots separated by a great sea of darkness.

Danyl stood in the sunken depths of the service alley behind the Dolphin Café. The sliding door leading to the dining room was closed but not locked. He pulled it ajar, admitting a sliver of radiance into the dripping alleyway, then he slipped through and eased it shut behind him. He circled the dining area and hid under a table near the hall. He listened.

Ten hours had passed since he'd discovered Eleanor's face imprinted in the mud outside Steve's cottage, and Danyl had not been idle. First he took a nap on the sofa in Steve's lounge. He woke eight hours later, keen-witted and ready to act. Next he finished the packet of cereal he found in the kitchen and then left the cottage, making his way through the empty valley. It was twilight. Rush hour. Even in the depths of winter there should have been people getting up and going out to teach yoga classes, or to beg for change from commuters in the Capital. But when Danyl turned on to Aro Street he saw no one. There were few lights on in the houses. The windows of the apartment buildings were grids of darkness. Everywhere was deserted. Abandoned.

Everywhere but the Dolphin Café. Now Danyl hid in its dining room. He heard the wind outside. The distant hum of refrigerators in the storeroom. Low voices. He took his shoes off and put them in his satchel, then crept to the hall.

A burly kitchen hand stood in the door to Eleanor's office. Eleanor's voice carried past him. Danyl waited for a second but the kitchen hand seemed stationary, his back to the hall, so Danyl tiptoed in the opposite direction, making for the kitchen. The man did not turn around.

The kitchen was empty. Two stoves were set against the far wall: broad stainless steel ranges with massive extractor units above them venting into the roof. A bench ran between them. Dozens of copper pans hung from hooks on the wall at head height. Danyl checked the hall, then hurried over to the stoves and set to work.

He took down the smallest pot he could find, set it on a stovetop and lit the gas burner. Next he rummaged through the drawers under the bench. They were filled with jars. He took out a jar labelled 'Bay' and dumped all of its brittle leaves into the pan. He repeated this again on the other stovetop with another pan and another jar of dry herbs. The room soon filled with the scents of toasting oregano and warm bay leaf.

The kitchen hand was still in the doorway listening to Eleanor, whose voice came down the hall in low, unpleasant waves. Danyl crept back to the dining room and hid. He waited, and in less than a minute a web of smoke drifted along the hall. It grew thicker. A few tendrils entered the dining room and a voice cried, 'Fire!'

Danyl ducked his head beneath the table. Footsteps pounded. When they reached the kitchen, yells broke out. Danyl waited for a few more seconds in case of a latecomer, then he crawled across the floor and looked down the hall.

There was an awful lot of smoke in the air. Even the door to the kitchen was hazy. He saw two moving blurs beyond it: Eleanor and the kitchen hand. They were yelling at each other, their words interrupted by fits of coughing. Danyl turned away as his eyes stung and, squinting, with his arm over his nose and mouth, he hurried down the hall into Eleanor's office and shut the door behind him.

That was better. Still a bit smoky though. He drew back the curtains and opened the window, partly to clear the air and partly to jump out of it if anyone came through the door. Then he turned his attention to Eleanor's desk.

There was an antiquated laptop which was not switched on. A box of tissues. A paper tray containing utility bills. Scattered multicoloured Post-it notes with names and numbers scrawled on them. Nothing useful.

There were three drawers. Danyl tried the first one. Not locked! That was the genius of his plan. If you set fire to something, people are unlikely to waste time securing their workspace. The drawer contained pens, a stapler, cold medication, packages of tissues, hand cream and a large roll of cash.

He frowned at the money. It was an odd thing for Eleanor to leave lying around, especially in a restaurant that didn't have any customers. His hand hovered above it, then withdrew and shut the drawer. Danyl was many things, but he was not a common thief. He was here for knowledge and revenge, and possibly art and love.

He opened the next drawer. A box of teabags. An accounting ledger. He tossed these on the floor and uncovered . . . Eleanor's cellphone. Jackpot. He picked it up and touched the screen. The display flashed on. No PIN. No password. Danyl slipped it into his pocket, shut the drawer and made his way to the window. He raised one leg over the sill, then withdrew it and walked back to the desk, opened the top drawer and took the roll of cash. He slipped out the window and into the Te Aro night.

He ran across Aro Street, putting distance between himself and the restaurant. He stopped when he reached the park.

Sooner or later Eleanor would figure out she'd been robbed and come looking for him. He needed to get off the streets. He saw a narrow pathway between two large apartment buildings and jogged towards it. A car engine coughed in the distance; he broke into a sprint and reached the safety of the path just as headlights swept the empty road. He flattened himself against a brick wall. The car hissed by.

It was raining again but only a light drizzle. Danyl felt good. Very good. His cheeks flamed; his heart beat with a strong, proud rhythm. His blood sang in his veins. He wondered: if he were still on his medication, would he feel this joy? Would he have the wit and courage to set fire to a restaurant and then rob it? Surely not—the very idea would have seemed insane. And where would sensible old Medicated Danyl be now? Nowhere. Lost and bewildered, certainly not hiding in an alley holding Eleanor's stolen cellphone, his pockets stuffed with her cash.

He touched the screen of the phone. It lit up with a ghostly blue light. He tapped his way through to Eleanor's address book then scrolled down to the end of the alphabet. Verity was the last entry. He tapped it. The phone auto-dialled.

Verity. At last. What should he say to her? Give her his pre-rehearsed speech? Demand answers? Beg her to go out with him again? He didn't know. Danyl had a tendency to overthink things; he knew this about himself. He schemed schemes, formulated elaborate plans and then when things didn't go the way he hoped he was lost, he fell apart. Much better to improvise. Go with the flow. Like he did at Eleanor's restaurant. He'd gone in without any complicated, pre-conceived plans, started a fire and come out smiling. That was the way to get things done.

The phone kept ringing then forwarded him to voicemail, where an electronic voice invited him to leave a message. The phone recorded his silence for a moment. He hung up. He'd try again in five minutes.

While he waited, he explored the alleyway. It was not a cheerful place. Its entrance was lit by light from the street, but that did not extend into its depths. Dark apartment buildings loomed on both sides. Rain dripped from steel stairways and the landings of fire exits high overhead. The walls were plastered with posters advertising the two-month-old community council election.

Danyl was about to try Verity's number again when he heard footsteps. Someone was walking along Aro Street, splashing their way along the footpath. They moved at a slow, hesitant pace. An innocent passerby? Or a burly kitchen hand? Danyl shrank deeper into the shadows, backing down the alley as the footsteps grew nearer. There were several large skip bins here. He ducked behind one and watched as a lone figure appeared on the path. They stopped and turned to face him: a shape outlined by a halo of lamplit rain. Danyl froze. He could see the shadow's breath steaming in the cold, and he held his own breath and waited.

The shadow stepped into the alley.

Danyl's instinct was to run but he stopped himself. He didn't know where the alleyway went. It might have a dead end, and he was well hidden where he was.

The person came closer. They stopped just short of the bin and rummaged through a bag, muttering something. It was a woman's voice, and as she neared he could make out the words. 'One. One three seven. One. One three seven.' She took something from the bag and pointed it. Danyl flinched, blinded, as the alleyway flooded with light.

A torch. She had a torch. Danyl squatted on the ground, exposed, watching helplessly as the woman examined her surroundings. She peered at the graffiti on the walls, which was the usual incomprehensible multicoloured scrawl. She shone the torch down the stairway leading beneath one of the buildings. Finally she shone it at the skip bins, lighting him up like a nude on a spotlit stage. She looked at him for a moment, then said, 'Hello.'

'Hi.' Danyl shaded his eyes.

'Are you looking for the entrance?'

He squinted, confused. 'The entrance?'

'To the labyrinth.'

'The what?'

She dipped the torch. Danyl blinked away the afterglow, and when the blotches of light faded they were replaced by the face of a very, very pretty woman with short spiky hair, and features so sculpted and delicate he checked her ears to make sure they weren't pointed. She wore jeans and a black raincoat, and carried a black leather handbag over one shoulder. 'Wait.' She stepped closer. 'I know you. You go out with that photographer.' She clicked her fingers trying to remember. 'Verity. Am I right?'

'That's right. But we don't—'

'I knew it. What's your name again?'

'I'm Danyl,' said Danyl.

'I'm Joy.' She stepped forward again and extended her hand. Danyl came up on his knees, held out his arm and shook it. She stepped back. 'How is Verity?'

'Well, we broke up. Now she's vanished.'

'That's too bad.' Joy made a sad face. 'You'll meet someone else,' she assured him. She flicked the torch around the alleyway. 'Maybe not here, though. Take a dance class. That's where I met my boyfriend.'

'Thanks. That's good advice.'

'No problem.' Joy shone her torch back into Danyl's face. 'So what are you doing here?'

Danyl wasn't sure how to answer that. He didn't want to get bogged down explaining everything about Verity, and Eleanor, and the fire and all the rest of it. Instead he just said, 'Working.'

'Whaddya do?'

'I'm a writer.'

'Ah.' This seemed to make sense to Joy. She relaxed her posture, turned her back on him and went back to studying the graffiti. She walked the length of the alley. She examined the fire exits and the steel doors leading into the apartment buildings and made disappointed noises when she found they were locked. Then she walked back to Danyl. She said, 'A lot of my clients are writers.'

'Clients? What do you do?'

'I'm a drug dealer. Here—' She tucked her torch under her arm, rummaged around in her purse and fished out a business card. He ventured forth from the shadow of the bin and took it, then squinted at it in the spill from her torchlight.

Joy
BSC Chem Msc Pharmacology
Ask me about my Phenethylamines

He turned it over. On the back was a phone number and an address on Norway Street. 'Nice. Are you here on business?'

'Not exactly,' she replied. She looked around the alleyway again and stepped closer to Danyl. 'Let's stop pretending,' she whispered. 'We both know why we're really here.'

'We do?'

'Of course. We're both looking for the same thing. But I left the blue envelope at home—with my boyfriend—and I don't remember the signs.' She shook her head, rueful. 'I wish I wasn't so high right now.'

'You're on drugs?'

'Just a little pot. And a low-grade hallucinogen. And a few wines to loosen me up. Maybe that's why I can't find the way?' Suddenly her eyes widened. She reached out and grabbed Danyl's arm. 'I know what we'll do. We'll team up.'

'Team up?'

'You're right. The blue envelope said to come alone. Otherwise I would have brought my boyfriend with me. I have a boyfriend. But,' she waved her hand, 'we did come alone. It's not our fault we arrived at the same time. So now we'll find the way together.'

'We will?'

'Sure. With my brains and your'—she flicked her eyes over Danyl—'beard, we'll find the labyrinth in no time. You take that side. C'mon. Get to work.'

This, Danyl thought. This right here was the problem with Te Aro. You couldn't even hide in an alleyway at night without someone stumbling along and babbling at you about labyrinths. But it was too soon to venture out onto the street. Eleanor would still be hunting him. So he tagged along behind Joy as she inspected the alley.

The graffiti did not yield any clues. The doors leading into the apartment buildings did not budge. She shone her torch up a drainpipe. When they reached the back of the apartments, where the alley branched in divergent directions, she said, 'You go that way,' and gestured with her torch, directing him into a region of total darkness. She went the opposite way.

Danyl took Eleanor's stolen cellphone from his pocket and used the screen to light his path. There was nothing in this branch of the alley but piles of plastic bags and leaves wedged against the walls in waist-high drifts, and a tall concrete wall signalling a dead end.

He walked back to the intersection and down the other branch of the alley. Joy must have turned a corner because her torchlight was nowhere in sight. He held up his phone again and halted.

This branch of the alley was identical to the other one. It was narrow, filthy and short, terminating in a high concrete wall. There were no exits. No windows. Nothing to hide behind. And it was empty. Joy was gone.

8

The mysterious deep structure of the universe

Danyl backed down the alleyway. He felt very nervous. If a beautiful woman could disappear here in a matter of seconds then so, logically, could he. He eyed the high walls, the dripping gutters, the bins, and then turned and ran back to Aro Street.

But as soon as he stepped onto it a car rounded the corner. It moved slowly, with no lights on. One of Eleanor's kitchen hands drove it; Eleanor herself sat in the passenger seat scanning the road.

Danyl dropped to the ground beside a mound of twigs and leaves clogging a stormwater drain, ducked his head and tried to look like debris. The car rolled by, tyres whispering on the wet road. When it was a safe distance away he looked up. He watched the car continue past the park and round the curve in the road, out of sight.

But she'd be back. Where could he go? The streets weren't safe, but neither was the alleyway. He needed to get out of sight, inside a building somehow. He needed sanctuary.

The lights were on in the offices behind Aro Community Hall. Danyl hid behind a tree watching the pathway for a few minutes, making sure the way was clear. Then he ran to the office, crouched below the window and peered over the rim. Yes. Ann the treasurer was there. Alone at her desk, her back to the window, papers spread before her.

He tapped on the rain-streaked glass. She looked up, surprised, then smiled at him and held up a finger signalling him to wait. She gathered all the papers on her desk, shuffled them into a stack and locked them in a drawer. Finally she rose to admit him.

He explained everything to her, more or less. He told her about the alleyway and Joy the drug dealer, and that an evil Taoist cook was searching the streets for him. He didn't bother to mention the fire, or Eleanor's cellphone. Ann listened, absorbing everything.

'You said you'd help me find Verity,' he said when he'd finished his story, 'and give me a place to stay.'

'My offer still stands, of course,' Eleanor replied. 'If we are not bound by what we say, we are bound by everything we don't say.'

Danyl thought about this, blinking rapidly, then he said, 'Do you think Joy's disappearance is linked to what happened to your mathematics student? And your colleagues? And Verity?'

Ann stood. She motioned at Danyl. 'Follow me.'

She led him to a window at the back of the office. It looked out on a tiny concrete space walled off by council buildings. She pointed at a door in the opposite wall and said. 'That's the Scholar's Cottage. It's where my student—Sophus—lived until his disappearance.'

'Cottage?' Danyl peered through the gloom. 'It looks more like a small shed.'

'The term "cottage" is aspirational,' Ann explained. 'Also, it comes with a fern. The last time I saw Sophus was three weeks ago. We talked right there.' She pointed at her desk. 'Sophus claimed he was close to a breakthrough in his work. The answer, he said, was here in the Aro Valley. He explained that he'd been studying mathematical patterns hidden in the valley itself.'

Danyl asked, 'What kind of patterns?'

'Secrets embedded in posters for missing animals. Graffiti on the walls. The distribution of shoes tossed over power lines. I told him he was rambling. That he sounded crazy.

He apologised and said he hadn't slept for days. We agreed to talk again the next morning. I went back to my work.' Ann gestured at the cottage. 'About an hour later I glanced out the window and saw him in the courtyard catching rain in a pan. Then he went to go back inside, but stopped when he saw something poking out from under his doormat. A blue envelope. He opened it and looked inside it. Then he went into his cottage. I never saw him again.'

'Joy mentioned a blue envelope. And something about a labyrinth.'

'Yes.' Ann frowned, thinking, then turned to Danyl. 'You said she was muttering something when she entered the alley. Can you remember what?'

'I think it was a number,' Danyl replied. He concentrated, remembering. 'One three seven,' he said. 'I think it was one three seven. Could that be an address? Does it mean anything to you?'

'It means something,' Ann said, her voice grave. 'Oh yes. It confirms all of my worst fears. We're dealing with mystics.'

'Is one three seven a mystical number?'

'In a way. One divided by 137 is the approximate value of the fine structure constant of the universe.'

'The what?'

'The electromagnetic coupling constant.' Ann saw the blank incomprehension on Danyl's face. 'Let me explain.' She pointed to the light in the courtyard, glowing softly through the drizzle, illuminating the door to the Scholar's Cottage. 'You see that light?' she said. 'You know how it works?'

'Not exactly. Electricity, somehow? Actually, not at all.'

'It's very simple. Electrons in a high-energy state travel through the wires. When they reach the filament in the light bulb, they drop into a low-energy state and when they do that they release a photon. Trillions of photons stream out of those bulbs every second. They bounce around the room changing slightly as they come into objects with different colours and properties until they bounce into our eyes and bind to a new electron in a photoreceptor that sends a signal to our brain.'

Danyl looked at the light. He said, 'Huh.' He felt a little ashamed. All his life he'd been seeing things, yet he had no idea how seeing worked.

'At the beginning of the twentieth century, physicists wondered about the strength of the interaction between electrons and photons. It's not difficult to calculate.' She wrote an equation on the condensation of the window with her fingertip. 'It's the charge of the proton divided by the quantum of action multiplied by the speed of light in a vacuum. When we solve this equation we get this number, which physicists call the fine structure constant, which is about 1/137. Now, normally when you carry out equations in physics, you end up with a number and a unit. The speed of light gives you a distance that you can travel over time, and you can measure that in miles, or kilometres, or whatever you want. The photon charge gives you the strength of the charge, and physicists like to measure that using a unit called coulombs. But when you calculate the strength of the electromagnetic interaction, something interesting happens. You get this number'—she pointed to 1/137—'but no unit. No matter how you measure the other variables in the equation, it will always return this specific number. It's a dimensionless constant hidden away in the deep structure of the universe. Now, here's where it gets strange.'

Danyl nodded and said, 'Huh' again.

'Where did this number come from?' Ann spread her fingers. 'No one knows. Einstein wondered if God had any choice in the way He designed the universe. Could He have built it differently, or is this universe in which we exist the only viable option? Of course, there is no God. That's a false metaphysical premise. But it turns out that if the fine structure constant was slightly larger than it is, there would be no carbon in our universe and probably no intelligent life. If it was smaller, you wouldn't get star formation and the universe would be a cold, dead, lifeless place. So this number'—she pointed again—'must have this exact value, because if it didn't we wouldn't be able to observe it. Philosophers call this "the fine-tuning problem": why does the universe seem like it's been designed to allow the existence of intelligent life?'

Danyl asked, 'What's the answer?'

'No one knows. That's what Sophus was working on before he got distracted studying scraps of paper he found in the gutters of Te Aro. He wanted to solve the tuning problem by enumerating the fine structure constant. If he could relate it to the number of dimensions in the universe, or to some significant mathematical value like pi or the infinite sum, then he could say: "There's no fine-tuning problem because the electromagnetic interaction must have this value. It's all part of a logical framework and not an arbitrary number that just happens to allow the existence of complex life." Sadly, there are plenty of lunatics out there who try to link the fine structure constant to codes in the Bible, or the secrets of the Illuminati. That must be how whoever is behind these disappearances snared Sophus.'

'What do we do next?'

'We search that alleyway,' Ann replied. 'First thing tomorrow, after we've slept. And if we don't find anything, we need to track down one of these blue envelopes and see what's inside it.'

'Do you think that's safe?' Danyl asked. 'Joy and Sophus saw inside their envelopes and they disappeared.'

'They were weak,' Ann assured him. 'Sophus was young and confused. Your drug dealer was on drugs. But you and I . . . our minds are robust. Powerful. Don't shake your head.' She reached out and took his arm. She smiled at him, and some long dormant region of Danyl's brain fluttered. 'Don't underestimate yourself. You've only been back in the valley for one day and you've pinpointed the location of the disappearances and revealed the nature of our enemy. You're better and stronger than you think. Perhaps all those others vanished because, on some level, they wanted to. But not us.' She met his gaze. Her eyes were clear and black and deep. 'You and I will not disappear.'

9

The giant

The next morning, Ann was gone.

She'd ordered Danyl to meet her at her office at 8 am, but he slept in a little so it was 11.30 before he emerged from the Scholar's Cottage, where he'd spent the night.

The cottage was a tiny space containing a single bed, a desk and a dead fern. Posters of mathematicians covered the walls. At least, Danyl assumed they were mathematicians. They were black-and-white portrait photos of elderly bearded men with bulging eyes. Danyl was too tired to undress when he went to bed; he just collapsed, face down under their bulbous gaze.

When he woke he burrowed under the blankets for a while, warm and drowsy and happy and safe; not quite remembering where he was but content to be there. Then the events of the previous day came back to him unbidden: Steve's empty house, the alleyway, the fire. He realised he was not safe. He was in Te Aro. People were disappearing and he needed to find Verity and get out of the valley before whatever took them claimed him too.

And he remembered stealing Eleanor's phone. He'd switched it off before he went to bed out of a paranoid notion that Eleanor might be able to track it, somehow, and hunt him down while he slept. He turned it on now and dialled Verity again. Still no answer, and the clock on the display informed him that he was late to meet Ann.

The door to her office was locked. The entire council building was dark and empty. Danyl stood outside it, shivering and hungry, wondering what to do next. Return to the Scholar's Cottage, climb back into bed and wait for Verity to ring or Ann to show up? That seemed like the smart move.

But he was hungry and there wasn't any food in the cottage. Also, what if Verity didn't call, and Ann didn't return?

He pressed his nose against the office window. Maybe Ann had left behind some sort of sign, or clue? And that's when he saw it: on her desk, a blue envelope with the top torn open and the contents removed.

He returned to the Scholar's Cottage and climbed back into bed. That wasn't a long-term solution though. He needed to find Verity. Ann had claimed to know where she was, but Ann was gone. She'd opened a blue envelope, taken whatever she'd found inside it, and vanished. She wasn't coming back.

Then Danyl had an idea. His mind flashed back to Joy the drug dealer standing in the alleyway, stoned and bewildered, staring at the graffiti. *I left the blue envelope at home.* He fished through his pockets and found her business card. Yes. Her address was there, and on Norway Street, not far from the Community Hall. So there might be an envelope at Joy's house with the mysterious contents still inside it. Find the envelope. Find Ann. Find Verity.

Danyl bounced up and down on his feet, delighted with his brain's performance. Medicated Danyl never had clever ideas like that. His mind just drifted along, responding to stimuli but never pulling its weight. Now it was back in the game. Danyl felt invigorated. With his brain on his side he felt he could accomplish almost anything. He washed his face in a nearby puddle then headed towards Joy's house, a spring in his step.

The address on the card led him to a flat sunlit section. A concrete path ran across a lawn; steps led onto a wooden porch running along the front of the house, which was a nondescript cream-coloured wooden building with frosted windows and a peaked red roof punctuated by skylights.

Danyl knocked at the door. His stomach rumbled. No one answered, which made sense. Joy had disappeared, after all.

71

She had repeatedly mentioned her boyfriend, though, and Danyl thought this boyfriend might let him in and feed him breakfast then hand over the blue envelope, but apparently not. Perhaps the boyfriend didn't even exist? It was probably just a clumsy way for Joy to signal that she wasn't romantically available to Danyl. But she didn't know about his medically induced impotence, so the joke was on her.

He tried the door. It opened.

That was odd. You'd think a drug dealer would have better home security. Then he pictured Joy drifting out her front door late last night, her eyes glazed over, letting the door swing shut behind her then trailing down the hill towards the alleyway. Still, he hesitated. This wasn't like breaking into Verity's parents' house or Steve's house, or setting fire to Eleanor's kitchen. This was a stranger's home. He knocked again and called out, 'Hello?'

Still no reply. He stepped into the darkened interior of the drug dealer's house.

It consisted of one very long room separated into different spaces by the arrangement of the furniture. Just inside the front door was the kitchen area with a white tiled floor, segmented off by a dining table atop polished wooden floorboards, then black leather couches facing a large flat-screen television. A Japanese-style divider stretched between a tall wardrobe and a chest of drawers. A door-sized gap in the divider led to an unlit space that had to be the bedroom. Grey light filtered in from evenly spaced skylights.

Danyl began his search in the kitchen. He looked in cupboards, drawers and the refrigerator. When he was finished, he made a breakfast bowl with organic muesli and frozen blueberries. He topped this up with goat's milk, took a spoon from the cutlery drawer and groaned with pleasure when he tasted the first spoonful. Then, chewing and swallowing, he walked to the dining table at the far end of the kitchen.

The kitchen was covered with papers. Danyl walked around

it, craning his head to read them all. There were photographs of graffiti, copies of the Te Aro Community Volunteer Newsletter with some sentences underlined, others blacked out. Words scrawled in the margins. Beside the newsletters were graph pages covered with complex algebraic equations. The number 1/137 was at the bottom of one of the pages, underlined and circled with red ink. Also on the table: a large ashtray filled with ash. The reek of cannabis hung heavy in the air.

He rummaged through the mess, but there was no blue envelope. Just beyond the table, though, lay a pile of clothes. Danyl knelt down to inspect them.

Black leather boots. Black jeans. A black T-shirt. That's what Joy was wearing last night in the alleyway. Danyl frowned, thinking. Most people in Te Aro owned multiple black T-shirts and pairs of black jeans. So the pile of clothes on the floor might not mean anything. But it might mean that Joy had reappeared, somehow, and then returned home and taken off her clothes.

His frown deepened. If Joy was here, naked, then it might not be appropriate for Danyl to be in her house, creeping towards her while eating her blueberries.

He called, 'Hello? Joy? It's me, Danyl. The guy from the alleyway.'

No reply. Danyl ate another spoonful of food and moved deeper into the house.

He passed the couches and TV. The TV sat atop a long, polished wooden shelf filled with books and records. A stereo occupied the far end of the shelves, which were flanked by rectangular speakers. More clothes were scattered on the floor here. Black female undergarments, along with some sort of weird, oversized, bifurcated blanket made of blue denim.

Beyond the lounge stood the dresser and room divider. Danyl walked between them and entered the bedroom. The bed was huge, with a massive, flesh-coloured duvet piled in the centre. He circled it to verify that the bed did not contain a pretty naked girl. There was a narrow door on the side wall near the bed. This led to a bathroom—the only separate room in the house—and he glanced inside it. Danyl had had nasty surprises from bathrooms in the past. But this one was empty.

He turned around, and after a moment he drew in his breath. Lying on the floor just beside the bed was a bright blue envelope. He cried out, 'Aha!' and stepped towards it. And then the gigantic man sleeping on the bed snorted and stirred.

Danyl froze. *The bed wasn't empty.* The bed wasn't empty! When he checked earlier he'd been looking for a naked girl, so he'd failed to notice that the flesh-coloured, oddly stained duvet was actually a huge, naked, muscular man with a shaved head and tattoos. The huge man coughed and rolled over. The bed groaned under his weight.

Danyl was paralysed with fear. He knew this sensation well. It happened to him a lot, and right now he was roughly in the middle of the fear–paralysis spectrum: he could blink and twitch his fingers, and he did both of these things while the huge man climbed out of bed and stood before him, yawning and scratching his belly, which was covered with tattoos of skulls and roses and eagles and knives. He shouted out, 'Joy!' Then he walked past Danyl and around the bed, heading for the bathroom, his uncircumcised penis slapping audibly against his leg. He disappeared into the bathroom. Seconds later came the sound of a torrent of urine coursing into the toilet.

Thoughts flapped around Danyl's mind like a plastic bag in the wind. This must be Joy's boyfriend. Why didn't he see Danyl? Why did he walk straight past him? How loud his urination was. His urethra must be huge! And why didn't Danyl see him earlier? A gigantic, dangerous man lying on the bed in plain sight!

Then he understood. When he looked at the bed he'd expected to see a naked girl, not a terrible giant. His brain had filtered the giant out. And the same thing had happened to the giant! He didn't expect to wake up and see Danyl in his bedroom so he walked right by him. Also, the light was bad, and Danyl's jacket blended in with the plaster walls and the murky grey light from the skylight. That was lucky. But his luck wouldn't hold. The giant would eventually stop urinating and walk back into his bedroom. He'd see Danyl and then he'd hurt him. That's what Danyl would do if he found a strange man in his bedroom. If he was capable of hurting anyone, which he wasn't, and if he had his own bedroom, which he didn't.

The blue envelope lay at Danyl's feet. At least he'd found what he came for. All he had to do was grab it then run for the door. He was going to make it.

He knelt down to pick up the envelope but, as he reached for it, he felt an odd little jolt inside his brain. It wasn't painful; it felt like the static charge you get when you touch a hot car or an escalator handle, only it was inside his brain. He shook his head and reached for the envelope again, but his brain jolted once more. What was happening to him?

Danyl's mind flashed back six months to his doctor's office, when he was first prescribed his medication. 'You may need to take it for the rest of your life,' the doctor warned, waving the little bottle of pills before Danyl's eyes like a hypnotist. 'If you ever discontinue it, the process must be carefully managed. Otherwise there could be dire consequences. Mood swings. Cognitive disturbances. Irrational behaviour. Maybe even *brain zaps*—sudden shock-like discharges inside your brain.'

Danyl hadn't experienced any mood swings or irrational behaviour, although he reminded himself to look out for them in the future. But this was definitely a brain zap. He gritted his teeth and lunged for the envelope one last time, only to snatch his hand back as his brain jolted him a third time. He hissed in frustration.

Then the roar of the giant's urination stopped. The toilet flushed. Footsteps shook the floor. Danyl scuttled to the bed and dived under it, rolling out of sight just as the tree-trunk-sized legs of the giant came into view.

The giant moved back and forth across the bedroom. He stepped into a pair of fluffy brown slippers. He yelled out 'Joy!' again.

There was dust under the bed. There was always dust in these situations: Danyl knew not to breathe through his nose but to open his mouth as wide as possible and inhale and exhale, slow and deep. That way he wouldn't sneeze. He could see the blue envelope out of the corner of his eye but he also knew not to reach for it, or even turn his head to look at it. Beds were fine places to hide in theory, but they were often cluttered with forgotten bric-a-brac, and the slightest motion could spring open a suitcase or send an empty wine bottle rolling across the hardwood floors.

He did not move. He waited. He took slow, steady breaths. Things would be OK. The giant would take a shower, eventually, or go outside to look for his girlfriend, and Danyl could make his escape. All he needed to do was keep calm and not make any silly mistakes.

He closed his eyes, turned his head and rested his cheek against the cool floor.

Eleanor's cellphone rang.

10

Surprise Symphony

Danyl didn't have a phone of his own and in his terror of the giant he'd forgotten about stealing Eleanor's, so when Haydn's Surprise Symphony started playing, he thought he'd nudged an old alarm clock, or something. Then he realised the sound was coming from his jacket pocket. He pulled out the stolen phone. The ringtone grew louder. The caller ID flashed a name on the glowing screen.

Verity.

Danyl stared at the phone in perfect comprehension. Of course it was Verity. He'd called her half-a-dozen times from Eleanor's phone; now she'd seen those missed calls and responded, and this chain of events would lead to Danyl being beaten by a huge, hairy naked man. He pressed the button to terminate the call but it was too late. Far too late. The house shook as the giant approached. 'Joy?' He knelt down.

Danyl shifted backwards, wriggling to the other side of the bed as soundlessly as possible, getting ready to break cover and run. The giant was on his knees trying to see under the mattress, but he was too large. Instead he fumbled beneath the bed with a massive dinner-plate-sized hand. Danyl cowered just out of its reach. Then the hand withdrew.

'Joy?' The giant sounded angry. 'Joy?'

Danyl needed a plan. He needed tools. He glanced around and saw a power cable connected to a bedside lamp, some empty condom wrappers, a giant woollen sock and a ballpoint pen. And there was something else: a small steel box near the head of the bed. He tried to pull it towards him but it was fixed to the floor. The lid was open. Danyl wriggled closer and looked inside. The box was filled with vials of pills.

He remembered Joy standing in the alleyway saying, 'I'm a drug dealer', and passing Danyl her card. *Ask me about my Phenethylamines*. This was Joy's hidden stash. Danyl's mind raced. Maybe he could combine the drugs with the power cable and the condom wrappers and fashion them into some sort of weapon? He tried to think, to concentrate. But then he twitched as his brain jolted him yet again. His doctor's voice came back to him. 'The discontinuation syndromes will be aggravated by stress.'

Yes, Danyl thought at his brain: I know you're under stress. I'm under stress too, and I need you to find a way to get us out of this situation, not make it worse. His brain replied with a second sullen zap, then his eyes—still casting about wildly—focused on a distant object on the kitchen table, halfway across the room, visible through the gap in the room divider. An old-fashioned corded telephone with a keypad.

Danyl had Joy's business card in his pocket. Did it have her home number on it? Would phoning it distract the giant? Possibly not, but it was still better than trying to build a weapon from a sock and some pills in less than five seconds. He took out Joy's card and punched the number into Eleanor's phone, his damp, trembling finger slipping on the keypad. He keyed in the last digit just as the giant's massive hands wrapped around the bedframe and began to lift it into the air.

Danyl rose with it. He'd grabbed the underside of the mattress and braced his feet against the base. This wouldn't hide him for long, though. Maybe another second—and then the giant was tipping the bed onto its side and kneeling down, first his torso then his massive face coming into view as the bed tipped sideways. The phone's display flashed: *Connecting . . .*

The giant's eyes were the size and intensity of candescent light bulbs. They swept the area below the bed. A mere flicker of its mighty ocular muscles and it would look directly at Danyl.

The display on the phone changed to *Ringing*, and the telephone on the other side of the house rang out. Danyl clung to the mattress, his teeth clenched, his breath trapped in his lungs. He hung there like this for a very long time—between two and four seconds—while the giant looked over its shoulder in the direction of the phone. Then it stood, letting the bed drop back down. Danyl lost his grip and fell to the floor, but his whimper of pain was drowned out by the thunder of the giant's passage.

The phone stopped ringing just as the giant reached it. It snatched it up and, when it heard nothing but a dial tone, spun about and returned to the bedroom. It lifted the bed again and looked underneath. It looked behind the dresser and glanced into the bathroom. It called out 'Joy?' Then it stomped back to the kitchen, muttering to itself.

Danyl was in the bathroom, lying in the bath below the rim, trembling with fear, holding Eleanor's stolen phone in one hand and something clenched in his fist in the other.

He uncurled his fingers to reveal a mass of blue paper screwed into ball.

Ha! The blue envelope! Danyl had picked it up on the way to the bathroom and he'd done so without thinking about it so that his brain couldn't stop him. Brilliant.

There was something drawn on the outside of the envelope, visible between his white knuckles. He breathed out, very slowly, and further unclenched his fingers.

The envelope opened like a flower. Inside its torn petals was a picture of a spiral.

11

The plot against reality

Verity's second photography exhibition opened on a warm evening in mid-summer. The party was held in the showroom of Te Aro Art Gallery. This was a large, bare room with white walls and polished wooden floors.

Danyl arrived late. He'd overslept. He'd been sleeping a lot, recently, and even when he was awake he never had any energy. He'd barely written a word of his book. He'd even forgotten that Verity's exhibition was today until he woke to find a Post-it note stuck to his bare belly, reading:

Darling. I know things haven't been right between us, but my opening is at five and I'd love you to be there.

Verity

The gallery was crowded and loud. Danyl squeezed through a group of nudists clustered around the doorway and peered through the throng, looking for Verity. He found her on the far side of the room talking to a circle of artists and critics. Eleanor stood beside her, nodding as Verity explained her work.

Verity pointed at something on the wall, and at first it looked like a black photograph with no frame, but as Danyl moved closer he saw it wasn't a photo at all but a black plastic box approximately the size of a thick, hardback book. He took another look around the room. There were about twenty of the black boxes on display. No actual photographs could be seen.

What was going on? Danyl wound his way through the crowd to one of the boxes and examined it. There were no distinguishing features. It was just a black box. A card on the wall beside it read: *Title*: *Dimensions III. Please do not attempt to look at the art.*

He noticed a man and a woman standing before the adjacent box. They were inserting their hands into a hole in the bottom of the case and making little cooing sounds. Danyl did the same. At first the case seemed empty, but after a few seconds of grasping, his fingertips encountered a slick glassy surface. It was a photograph.

Then a voice whispered in Danyl's ear, 'I warbed you about thib.'

Danyl snatched his hand out of the case and turned around. The hideous whisper had come from Steve, who had a mouthful of hors d'oeuvies. He grinned at Danyl, revealing a row of parsley-coated teeth, and gestured at the box on the wall. 'This ib part of it. Part ob the plob against reality.'

Danyl had seen quite a bit of Steve since their first encounter in the café. He lived in the Devon Street gully and most afternoons he dropped by Danyl's house unannounced. Steve was a psychologist, he'd explained on his first visit when he strolled into the lounge without knocking, kicked off his shoes and put his feet up on the coffee table. He was eight years into his PhD, which was something to do with the history of the Aro Valley, although he admitted he was still nailing it down. 'My supervisor retired and died,' he explained. 'And none of the other lecturers knows about me. So that gives me a lot of academic freedom. I mostly follow my intuition, intellectually.' He unbuttoned his pants and reached for the TV remote.

Steve borrowed a lot of Danyl's detective novels for research and this seemed to relate to his thesis, somehow. When Danyl brought up Steve's allegations about Verity, Steve just winked and said, 'I'm handling it,' and went back to watching a talk show about reincarnation romance. But now he swallowed his mouthful of hors d'oeuvres, pointed at the black cases on the wall, and said, 'This is what I warned you about. Art.'

Danyl looked at the plastic rectangle fixed to the wall. 'Art?'

'Art is one of the ways in which our perceptions of reality are manipulated,' Steve replied. 'Consider sunsets. We think they're beautiful, but only because artists have programmed us to think so. What if sunsets are actually quite ugly?' He tapped the side of his head. 'Think about it. Have you talked to Verity about this exhibition?'

'I've been pretty busy—'

'Come.' Steve took his arm. 'Listen.' He manoeuvred Danyl through the crowd, stopping only to sweep a passing platter of mini-pizzas into his mouth. They circled the room and came up behind Verity, who was explaining her work to a frowning, nodding, grey-haired pot-bellied nudist couple.

'You've come here to see a photo exhibition,' she said. 'But you can't see the photos.'

'It's very clever,' the nudist man assured her, but the nudist woman shook her head. 'Why can't we see the photos?' she demanded. Her partner huffed loudly and rounded on her. 'You're missing the point. Imbecile!'

'No. She's right,' Verity said. 'Anyone can take a photo and display it for people to see. I want people to think about my photographs as objects they *can't* see. Consider this box.' She took the black plastic box off the wall and flourished it. 'We perceive it through our five senses. We can see it, touch it, smell it, taste it and listen to it.' She knocked on it. 'But our five senses are limited. They don't provide a complete picture of reality. We don't see all of the box.'

'What don't we see?'

Verity replied. 'Almost everything. This box feels real, right?' She waited while the nudist couple touched the box to satisfy themselves that it did, in fact, exist. 'But it—and everything else we see, including ourselves—is mostly empty space. A vacuum occupied by fluctuating mathematical objects called probability waves. The waves can't co-exist in the same location as one another—no one knows why—so the box can't collapse in on itself, or fall through my hands and then through the floor and down through the earth. That's why it seems solid. But really, it, both of us, all of this'—she gestured at the crowded gallery—'is nothing.'

The nudists seemed immensely pleased by this notion. 'What was your inspiration for all of this?' the man asked.

'My friend Eleanor.' Eleanor nodded dourly at the couple as Verity continued. 'Ellie's a Taoist. Taoists know all about contemporary physics. They've known it all for millennia. We'd be fools to think our current scientific understanding of reality is definitive. Who knows what remains to be discovered?' She turned the box on an angle. 'Perhaps the photograph inside this box extends off into other dimensions that we can't yet see? It seems to be smaller than the box but perhaps the real photograph dwarfs us all in both scale and intricacy? It might be part of some vast machine or even a living creature that only intersects with our perception of reality in tiny, insignificant ways. We could be inside the body of some vast and apprehending beast, but the only way it projects itself into the sliver of space-time that we experience is through the photograph inside this box.'

'You see?' Steve tugged Danyl away from Verity to the corner of the gallery. 'Didn't I warn you about your girlfriend?'

'You did.' Danyl frowned, confused. Verity's photographs were usually of buildings, or landscapes or female nudes that were a critique of the objectification of women, somehow. All this talk of reality was very unlike her. There was something strange going on. But Danyl doubted it had anything to do with extra-dimensions. No, the evil was far more proximate. He glared at Eleanor, then turned as Steve gripped his arm and said, 'We have to see what's inside these cases.'

'Why?'

'Weren't you listening to your girlfriend? She's talking about reality. Openly. Flagrantly. She's part of the plot against reality!'

Danyl said, 'I never really understood the plot.'

Steve pointed a cheese puff at Danyl. 'If you change the way people think about reality then you change reality itself. And, as I explained when we met, someone or something is manipulating our civilisation—our species—into perceiving reality a certain way. Your girlfriend and this exhibition are part of that.' He gestured at the plastic box nearest to them. 'We need to break one of these open. We'll have to come in at night. Disable the alarms. Does this gallery have a dog? You know, like they do at junkyards? We'll need to drug it, or win its trust. And the boxes themselves may be alarmed. It will be incredibly dangerous. Are you free later this evening?'

Danyl squinted at the box on the wall. He glanced around to make sure he wasn't observed, then took the box off its hook, squeezed it between his hands and cracked it open.

He picked apart the plastic shards, revealing a photo of a drawing. A complex rendition of a large, interlinking spiral.

Danyl lay in the giant's bath staring at that same spiral image on the outside of the blue envelope.

The top of the envelope had been slit open; he could see blue paper inside, folded over, lines crossing over the crease. Writing? Drawing? Danyl didn't know, and he wasn't sure that the bathtub of an angry giant was the best place to find out. Not with the giant still lumbering about outside the doorway, grunting and muttering. So he slipped the envelope into one pocket, and the still-blinking but now muted phone into another, and willed himself to focus on his escape plan.

There was a window above the toilet but a latch prevented it from opening fully, and Danyl would never fit through the gap. He could smash the glass and then climb through, but the giant would hear the sound. No, the only way out of the house was through the front entrance.

Danyl waited and listened. When the giant's footsteps moved away, heading towards the far end of the house, he climbed out of the bathtub and peered around the door.

The beast was in the kitchen, lumbering between the fridge and the bench, preparing itself a drink in a glass the size of a vase. The path out of the bedroom area was through the room divider, but this path was in full view of the kitchen. The giant would see Danyl instantly. He had to find another route.

He slithered over to the bed and then to the bookshelf. This was stocked with texts on pharmacology, small-business management and sadomasochistic erotic art. The top shelf was at waist height: it held an old-fashioned record player and a stack of records. A wooden set of drawers separated this area off from the kitchen.

He made his way over to the shelves on his hands and knees and examined the record player. They were a dead technology everywhere else in the world, but the subculture of Te Aro had formed a deep emotional attachment to these devices and they were standard issue in most houses. This one was attached to two speakers, one of which lay just beyond the set of drawers. Between them was a gap large enough for Danyl to crawl through, by which he could access the other half of the house without being seen by the giant.

A plan took form in his mind.

He crawled back to the bed, stripped the sheets and made his arrangements. He wriggled beneath the bed and disconnected the extension cord connecting the bedside lamp to a distant power plug. He took a handful of pills from the box and scattered them on the floor. Next, he wound the cord around the headboard of the bed and around one leg of the set of drawers. He connected the plug to the power cord of the record player and made sure this device was switched off before he took a record from the shelf below and placed it on the turntable. Finally, he set the needle on the record and turned the volume on the amplifier up to the maximum level.

Clever, shrewd Danyl. He tied the loose end of the extension cord around his ankle, making sure there was still plenty of slack, then he squeezed through the narrow gap between the drawers and the bookshelf until his head jutted into the adjacent section of the house.

The giant was facing away from him, sitting at the table eating muesli from a bucket. There was a power socket in the wall just above Danyl's head. Danyl lay prone on the floor, the corner of the bookshelf poking into his soft belly; he hugged his knee close to his chest and slipped the extension cord free of his ankle. He took a deep breath and plugged the cord into the power outlet.

The stereo speakers crackled and hissed. Danyl shrank into the shadows as the room filled with the deafening blare of 1970s French pop music, played at grotesque slowness as the player slowly picked up speed.

The giant leaped to its feet and began to shout, but it was drowned out by the slow-motion disco-pop. It spun about, its eyes moving over the darkened nook where Danyl cowered. It strode across the house and into the bedroom, while Danyl wriggled through the gap into the living room. Staying low, he scuttled across the floor and past the TV, past the couch and dining table. He was in the kitchen now, almost at the door: but then the sound of the needle lifting from the record tore the air. Silence flooded the room. Danyl crouched below the kitchen counter, the front door just before him. But reaching it would expose him to view. He took Eleanor's phone from his pocket and positioned it just above the rim of the counter, using the reflective black screen as a mirror to survey the room.

The giant stood by the record player, looking around in confusion. Then its gaze fell on his bed and it yelled out, 'What the hell?' and stepped towards it. It had seen the tableau Danyl arranged on the mattress: the woollen sock, pen and condom wrappers arranged in the form of a smiley face facing the record player. It lurched towards the bed then threw up its arms as its feet scrabbled on the pills. It wobbled, then vanished from view as it encountered the extension cord Danyl had strung across the bedroom at ankle level. The house shuddered with the impact of his fall.

Danyl gave a little squeal of triumph. He crawled to the front door, opened it, and fled down the path on his hands and knees, grinning and panting and giggling and free.

12

Verity's message

'Soup?' The bowl steamed, filling the air with the scents of chilli and mint. Danyl nodded and inhaled and sighed.

He was in the Sufi Soup Emporium, a place on Aro Street that sold Sufi Good Soup at Sufi Low Prices. The proprietor, a small round man with a long white beard and hypnotic brown eyes, set a bowl of steaming chickpea soup down on the table. He bowed and withdrew.

Danyl set the blue envelope beside it, unopened, and took Eleanor's phone from his jacket pocket. The display flashed at him: Message waiting.

Danyl was still shaken after his encounter with the giant. He'd taken a table facing the door of the soup kitchen—there were only three tables, crammed together between the bare concrete walls, the stainless steel serving counter and orange linoleum floor—so he could see the empty stretches of Aro Street through the windows. Every time he looked down at his soup he saw movement outside in his peripheral vision and thought it was the giant come to slay him, or Eleanor and her kitchen hands; but it was always just a bus passing by or a tree bending in the wind.

He sipped his soup and tried to relax. This café always played a type of mystical North African music: a fusion of cymbals, drums and chanting, and it had a calming effect on Danyl. After a few moments he felt safe.

He returned the blue envelope to his jacket pocket. He'd risked a lot to get it, but now he didn't need it: he had an actual message from Verity. Hopefully it would reveal her location. If she was lost he would find her. If she was in danger—and Danyl felt sure she was, even if Verity herself might not realise it—he would rescue her.

He picked up the phone, turned the volume back on and accessed the voicemail. There was a pause, then the sound of a bad line and Verity's voice, crackling and broken, saying, 'It's me.'

Verity. Danyl closed his eyes. The subharmonics of her voice—ethereal, mysterious; warm yet cruel—ran through him like a current. He'd found her. Oh, not literally. But he'd made contact. She was more than just a confusion of memories, a riddle from the past. She was real. He had her scent, or, at least a digital recording of it. He was close. Very close.

The message continued; she said, 'I'm leaving. You might never see me again. Goodbye.'

Danyl frowned. He swallowed a chickpea and reminded himself that Verity's message was meant for Eleanor. It was Eleanor who might never see Verity again. That might be a good thing, although the talk about leaving worried him a little.

'Before I go I want to tell you a story,' she continued. He heard footsteps in the background: she was calling from a cellphone and walking while she talked. 'I want to tell you about Simon.' Danyl licked his lips. Simon was the scientist who lived on the farm near Verity's childhood home. He'd played a mysterious and sinister role in her life ever since.

'You asked me how I found him but I never told you. I had this idea that it needed to stay secret.' She laughed mirthlessly. 'I had this idea,' she repeated. 'We both know, now, that our ideas are not our own. Our thoughts are not ours. Why did I keep that secret? Why am I telling you now?

'After we fought and you left to go into your monastery, I wandered. I drank too much. I lost myself. I spent a lot of time walking the streets of the cities I travelled through. I always took my camera with me, and I woke after week-long blackouts and looked back at all the pictures I took. I saw bars and houses I didn't remember, saw myself laughing with my arms around people I didn't know. But mostly I saw streets, buildings, squares. I saw cityscapes taken from impossible vantage points, or districts that couldn't be identified by anyone I showed them to. I wondered to myself, What are cities? Are they a human invention? Or are they a species of autonomous creature: unthinking, immortal which humans are doomed to perpetuate and service. Do we live in cities or do cities live off us, like parasites? Is that what's wrong with our species? We evolved as nomadic agrarians but we've been captured by this malign idea of urbanism, and now we're doomed to live and die in thrall to the perpetuation of cities, which will eventually merge to become one vast planetary city. And what then?

'But you know all this. One morning, one city, everything changed. I woke up on a gurney in a hospital ward with a backless hospital gown on and no memory of how I got there. A nurse gave me some clothes from the lost property bin and I wandered around the ward, and eventually found my way into a prayer meeting.

'It was a featureless, mostly empty room. A few quiet cancer patients. I don't remember what the priest looked like or even if he was a priest or an enthusiastic amateur. All I remember is that he was talking about the Tower of Babel, the old story from Genesis. You know how it goes, or at least you think you do. After the great flood of Noah, the people of the Earth spoke one language and so they attempted to build a tower reaching to the heavens. God saw this and took anger at their pride, and so he destroyed their tower and confused their languages. But at this point in the story, a voice from the back of the room called, "That's not what happened."

'I turned. A tall man with receding curly hair and a red beard stood at the back of the room. He wore a hospital orderly outfit with a raincoat over the top and a bag slung over his shoulder. I recognised him but I didn't remember from where. Someone I'd photographed? Someone I'd slept with? No, the memory was older than that. I knew him when I was young

. . . and then I realised. This was the man who lived at the farm near my childhood home. The man who changed my life. I stared but he didn't even see me. He was talking to the priest.

'He said, "The story you told is the way it's always told. People built a tower and God got angry. But pick up a copy of your Bible, any Bible." He gestured at the pile of King James Bibles stacked on the table by the door. "Read what's really written. The people built a city—the first city in human history—and a tower, but it was the city that angered God and the city he forced them to abandon by creating a confusion of languages. But why? We don't know. The Bible doesn't say. The real story isn't a parable about pride. It's a mystery."

'I can't remember what else he said, or if the priest replied. But his words shocked me. For months I'd been obsessed with cities, and suddenly this stranger from my past had reappeared in my life, and he'd talked about cities. How could this be? Then I realised he was gone. I ran to the door and saw him turn a corner at the far end of the hall. I followed him through the hospital to his workplace: a microbiology lab. I lurked around outside it for his entire shift, twelve hours, until he walked out through the security doors, unshaven and bleary, and I followed him home to his apartment in a tenement building near the hospital.

'It was Simon, of course. The poor man.' Verity laughed again. Danyl could hear rushing water in the background of her call, then the sound of her footsteps clattering over wood. 'Humans have always had an intuition about reality,' she continued. 'Everyone suspects it isn't what it seems, that you can pull back the curtain somehow and find the truth. Simon actually did it. For one brief moment, he stepped outside of existence and then he fell back into it again and spent the rest of his life trying to get out.

'By the time I appeared at his door, he'd given up. He was living in squalor, hiding under a false name, working at a dead-end job. He had no idea who I was. He didn't remember our first brief meeting. He barely remembered the farm and his laboratory hidden in a barn in its remote, overgrown reaches. That was just another failure in a lifetime filled with them. He barely listened as I introduced myself. He was shutting the door in my face until I told him that I'd crept onto the farm the morning after the police raid, before the bulldozers arrived, and looked inside the barn, and seen the mural he drew of a spiral, vast and incomprehensible, like the fabric of the world had torn itself apart. That picture destroyed my life, I told him. Fifteen years later it still throbbed and coiled inside my mind, taunting me, telling me that everything I saw was an illusion, that I could tear a hole in the world, if I could only figure out how.

'So I stood outside the door to his apartment and told him who I was. He listened, scratching his beard and thinking. Eventually he invited me into his room. I thought it might contain scientific apparatus, or holy books, or perhaps another mural of the spiral, but it was sparsely furnished. The only texts were a few news magazines. He locked the door and I felt my life closing in around me. I sat on his uncomfortable, food-stained couch, wondering if I would ever leave the room alive, and he perched at the end of his bed.

'He would help me, he announced. He would try to find a way back, make one last attempt. There was much he needed to tell me, many things to explain. Things were both simpler and more difficult than I could imagine. But first he needed one thing. One simple thing that I needed to fetch for him. A small vial of water from a certain pool. It was a kind of test, he explained, but also a vital step in the process. Then he smiled. "I'm getting ahead of myself," he said. "Let me begin at the beginning. I grew up in a place not far from here. A strange old place called the Aro Valley . . ."'

Verity broke off. The phone was warm against Danyl's ear. He listened to her breath; her footsteps as they crunched along a gravel path, the crackling of the line.

Finally, she said, 'We both know the rest. Or at least we think we do. We found what we were looking for. A path. A way beyond existence. The Real City. But of course when we found it, we saw that it wasn't what we really wanted, and that the pathway we'd spent our lives looking for merely led to another pathway. And where does the new one lead?

'That's what we've been trying to find out. That's what all this . . . madness has been about. But I think we've been doing it wrong. I think we've been tricked, Ellie. Lied to. I know you don't agree with me. And maybe you're right. I hope you are. But I have to find out.' There was another pause. More footsteps on gravel, then a series of dull clangs. Steps. Verity was climbing a flight of metal stairs. Danyl counted ten steps. Next he heard a key in a lock, the creak of a door, and Verity said, 'I'm here now. It's too late to stop me, even if you wanted to. I might never see you again. If I don't . . . I'm sorry. Goodbye.'

14

Music and silence and chickens

Danyl listened to the message three times.

The first time he was distracted by Verity's voice and the feelings it evoked. Loss. Sorrow. Rage. Did he still love her? Had she ever loved him? If she did, why had she left him?

The second time he listened to the actual words of the message. It answered some questions but asked many more. Who was Simon, really? Danyl thought he was just a biochemist, but Verity saw him as a kind of visionary. And where was this mysterious pool?

The third time Danyl tuned out the words and listened to the sounds beneath them. Verity was moving around the Aro Valley, talking as she walked. If he could pinpoint the background noises he could track her.

The message was nine minutes long. He took a scrap of paper from his satchel and wrote down markers at thirty-second intervals, then wrote the sounds as he identified them. At the start of the message was a garbled noise he could not identify. Then her footsteps splashing in puddles. The wind. About two minutes in, he heard metal scraping on concrete, and the wind died away. Perhaps she was walking along a sheltered path or an alleyway? Or inside a building somewhere?

Four minutes: the sound of running water. A gutter or even a stream.

Four minutes, thirty seconds: footsteps on wood, then the sound of water faded away. The wind again and Verity's footsteps crunching on gravel. Behind that an odd squawking noise he couldn't quite identify. He frowned, tried to tune out her voice . . . Chickens! Yes, definitely the sound of chickens. They weren't uncommon in the valley—few people in Te

Aro trusted the organic egg industrial complex—but still, a useful clue. For the last few minutes there was only wind and footsteps on gravel, ending with either a climb or descent of a long flight of steps, and then a door opening.

All good stuff, but the valley was a big place. Danyl really needed to identify the beginning of Verity's journey. Then he could track the subsequent sounds. He played the message a fourth time, pressing the phone to his ear, concentrating so intently his brain gave him a warning buzz. He ignored it and threw everything he had into deciphering the odd, faint noises in the background at the very start of the message.

Then Danyl laughed and slapped the table. He had her! The sound at the start of her call was music: cymbals; chanting. It was the mystical music playing in the soup kitchen. Verity had ended her call exactly nine minutes away from the same place he sat now.

'She's a little shorter than me. Thin. With dark hair, I don't know how she cuts it now, I haven't seen her for six months. Her name is Verity. She was talking on a phone when she walked out. You must know who I'm talking about.'

But the old man behind the soup counter shook his head again. 'I cannot help you, sir.'

'Sure you can.' Danyl reached into his pocket and peeled a note from the roll of cash he'd stolen from Eleanor's restaurant. He dropped it in the tip jar and leaned across the counter. 'Just tell me which way she went. Nod your head in that direction.'

'I cannot disclose anything. Sufi Soup places great importance on the privacy of its customers.'

'Ha!' Danyl pounced. 'So she was your customer! She was here. You admit it!'

'All of humanity is my customer.'

'Oh.' Danyl drummed his fingers on the counter, frustrated, trying to think of a way to outwit the wise and ancient soup cook. Nothing came to him, so he began to plead. 'Please, old man. I need your help. I need to find my girlfriend. Technically my ex-girlfriend. We might get back together. Anyway, she was here, earlier, and I need to find her. I think she's about to make a terrible mistake.'

'What kind of mistake?'

'I'm not sure, exactly. She said something about going beyond existence. Have you seen her?'

The old man was about to help. Danyl could see it in his eyes; they brimmed with compassion. But then they glanced sideways at the tip jar. The note Danyl had dropped inside it lay curled against the glass. Something about it seemed to displease the soup cook. His eyes turned cold, and he said curtly, 'I'm sorry. All I can offer you is soup.'

'Soup? Soup? What about your faith?' Danyl demanded, waving his hand at the painting of Rumi. 'Doesn't it command you to help the needy in their moment of need?'

'My faith is about obedience to God,' the old man replied. 'The prophets and sages are silent on whether I should help you find your girlfriend. But my common sense tells me to stay silent. You say you want to help her, but what if you intend her harm?'

'And so you don't get involved, just because you don't know what's going on? What kind of common sense is that? What if your silence leads to tragedy?'

'Silence is an ocean,' the old man answered. The bright yellow light mounted above the counter bathed him in an otherworldly glow. 'When the ocean seeks, do not flee into the river of words.'

It was raining again. Danyl stood outside the soup kitchen trying to parse the old man's cryptic aphorism. What did it mean? Nothing, he suspected. But perhaps it was wisdom, and Danyl simply wasn't wise enough to understand it. That was the problem with wisdom. It was only apparent to those who already had it. If you were ignorant and you really needed wisdom, it was useless to you.

He put the old man out of his mind, and looked up and down Aro Street. Verity's message was nine minutes long. She could have walked along the street in either direction. She could have turned off onto Epuni Street, or Devon Street, or walked through the park, or down any number of pathways. Still, there were the chickens. Chickens near a gravel path. And somewhere near the beginning of the message Verity had passed through a gate or doorway and then over running water. That was plenty to go on.

When he last saw Verity six months ago, she'd fled in a pickup truck driven—Danyl suspected—by Simon the mysterious chemist. They had gone west into the depths of the valley, so Danyl walked this way now. He kept his phone out and kept an eye on the time, and paced off nine minutes, then added on an extra sixty seconds to account for Verity's purpose-driven stride. This brought him out of the commercial area of the valley into a residential section of moderate prosperity. Many of the houses had cars parked outside them, and many of those cars had wheels. Danyl crossed from one side of the road to the other trying to identify gates or streams or gravel paths, and listening for chickens over the static of the rain.

There were a few gates. There were no streams and no chickens. There was gravel, but not enough. Verity walked up her path for at least three minutes, which was a long time to walk on gravel. Most garden paths took five to ten seconds. Her path was unusually long: he would know it when he saw it. It was nowhere in this part of the valley.

He returned to the soup kitchen and headed in the opposite direction. He detoured through the park. He investigated stairways. His shoes filled with water. He found chickens, eventually: a miserable clutch of fowl croaking beneath a leafless tree. They were confined in the back garden of a house bedecked with crystal wind chimes and daubed with astrological symbols, which the chickens themselves seemed to regard with contempt. Danyl searched this section of the valley for several minutes, peeking over fences and down driveways. There were no gravel paths. No steel gates. The chickens clucked to one another as he prowled about.

He continued his search. The streets were still empty, untravelled except for an empty bus that rumbled by. Where was everyone? The valley had a post-rapture feeling to it. Danyl surveyed the dark houses, the apartment buildings with their rows of darkened windows. He checked driveways. Down one of them he stumbled across three elderly men having sex on a muddy lawn. So not everyone was missing. Another drive led to a freshly painted, renovated house with an elegant sign beside the door advertising the Church of Real Economics, with a picture of a mushroom cloud beneath it. The sound of chanting came from inside. Interesting, but no sign of Verity and none of the sounds of her passage. He must have missed something.

He returned to Aro Street and stood under an awning, scanning the buildings. His eyes fell on the entrance to the alleyway where Joy had vanished.

Danyl hadn't looked inside the blue envelope yet. He'd been focused on Verity's message, but he was also a little scared. Everyone who opened a blue envelope vanished. Even Ann. But what if Verity had gone into the alleyway? Would Danyl have to look inside the envelope to follow her?

He crossed the road. The alley looked the same. Dirty and empty. No sign of Verity. No chickens. He checked the two branches where it forked behind the apartment buildings at the back. Nothing.

He was about to leave when he glanced down the narrow concrete steps that ran down the side of one of the buildings. At the bottom was a small landing and a door in the wall. The early morning rain had swept a flurry of leaves and rubbish to the bottom of the steps, where someone had opened the door, clearing a precise semicircle in the debris.

Verity? Possibly. Danyl descended the steps. He tried the handle. Of course, it was locked.

He consulted his timetable of Verity's message. A door opened about two minutes after the sound of the mystical music faded. He timed himself as he returned to the soup kitchen.

It took him exactly two minutes.

Danyl returned to the alleyway. He stood at the top of the steps and looked around, inspecting the area more carefully than last time. He noticed a sign attached to the wall of the alleyway, faded and weather-beaten into near invisibility. It read:

Ye Undergrounde Bookshoppe
Purveyors of Used Books and Finest Quality Darkness

An arrow on the sign pointed down the steps. Beneath the arrow, all but imperceptible, was an outline of the spiral.

Danyl took a deep breath and opened the blue envelope.

15

Ye Undergrounde Bookshoppe

A map. That's all there was inside the envelope. Just a map printed on bright blue paper. An odd map, though. Danyl turned it around, trying to figure out which was the top and the bottom. Half of it showed the valley: Aro Street, the park and other major routes and landmarks were clearly marked. The other half showed . . . somewhere else. A labyrinth of squares and wide roads. None of the areas on that side of the map were labelled. They weren't in the valley, Danyl knew, or any part of the Capital. Although the two regions were adjacent to each other there was only one crossover point between them. The steps in the alleyway.

According to the map there was a hallway beyond the door, and beyond the hallway a small square room, and after the room, the labyrinth: vast plazas with hundreds of paths connecting them. But Danyl couldn't get through the door. He held the map close to his face, reading the tiny words beside the steps:

*The First
Sign:
You must pay
to enter the
Real City
But
Your money is worth less than
ash*

The first part seemed pretty straightforward. Pay to enter the Real City. Which was, presumably, the labyrinth beyond the doorway. Easy. Danyl was a little confused about the last part, but maybe that would become clear. He tucked the map under his arm and faced the door.

How should he pay? He took the bundle of cash he stole from Eleanor out of his pocket, peeled off a ten-dollar bill, knelt down and slipped it under the base of the door. He listened. A soft scuffling sound came from the other side. There was someone there.

Danyl waited. The scuffling stopped. Then the ten-dollar bill reappeared. Whoever was behind the door had pushed it back. Why? Wasn't it enough?

Danyl looked down at the bill, confused. A wisp of smoke curled up from the crack beneath the door. Danyl blinked. A thin red line of fire crept along the note. He snatched at the money, then howled as the flames flared up and licked at his fingers. He blew on them, trying to save the ten dollars, which was enough money to live on for an entire week if he stole most of his food and found some nice doorways, but it was too late. The bill trembled in a gust of wind then dissolved into ash and drifted away, leaving only a tiny unburned corner between Danyl's thumb and forefinger.

He sucked at his scorched digits. Well, that explained the cryptic last line on the map. But it didn't help him get through the door. He spent a few minutes on his knees, whispering and pleading to the person beyond it. He didn't expect a reply, and he didn't get one.

Danyl sat at the top of the steps and tried to think.

What was going on? He'd been so busy seeking Verity and fleeing giants and finding maps that he hadn't stopped to ask that simple but important question.

People were disappearing. Ann. Her student. Joy. Steve. Verity. Some of them—maybe all of them—had gone through the door at the bottom of the steps, but to get through it you had to solve some kind of riddle. The riddle was the first sign; Joy mentioned others, one of which involved the fine structure constant of the universe. What possible explanation could there be for all of this? How could it make sense? It was hard to imagine, but Danyl was an imaginative guy. A writer. Imagination was his forte.

He stared into the sunken depths of the stairway and imagined with all his might. His thoughts drifted through empty streets and bitter memories: here was Steve's deserted house; there were Verity's unseeable photographs, her cryptic voice message, the spiral scrawled in her notebook. But his mind passed over all of these things lightly; it kept circling back to the soup kitchen, like a little dog tugging at the hem of his trousers. Here, it seemed to say. Something important happened here.

Danyl was dubious, but he gave his brain the benefit of the doubt and thought about Sufi Soup Emporium. Was it the soup cook? His cryptic aphorisms? The posters on the walls? He inspected them all for meaning and found nothing.

Although . . . there was something odd about the cook's behaviour. He'd been about to help Danyl, but then he glanced at the money in the tip jar and changed his mind. Why?

Danyl visualised the tip jar. It was empty except for the money he'd tossed in as a failed attempt to bribe the cook. The note had fallen against the side of the jar; the light mounted above the counter shone through the paper, casting the patterns in its design as a shadow against the back wall.

The shadow of a spiral.

He dug his hand into his pocket, pulling out the wad of cash he'd stolen from Eleanor's office. He sorted through the notes. They were all small denomination bills, but two of them looked odd. Discoloured. Inspecting them, he saw there was no value written on these bills: instead of a number, they read 'n+1'. He held one of them up to the light. It was fake.

In the middle of the bill, in the place of a face or an animal, was a complex interlocking spiral.

He slid the spiral dollar beneath the door at the bottom of the steps. The door shuddered, then creaked and swung outward.

A long, narrow hall was lit by a flickering white light. The light emitted a low hum. The hall ended in another door. The spiral dollar had disappeared, somehow, along with whoever had taken it.

The hallway was empty except for the far door and a tiny box on the wall beside it. Danyl made his way towards them, all the while expecting the door behind him to slam shut, trapping him. But it did not do this. If Danyl wanted to, he could turn and run away. The freedom to leave unsettled him even more than the door shutting, imprisoning him, would have.

As he drew closer he saw that the next door had no handle. A tiny scrap of paper taped to the centre of the door read:

This is a sign.

Beneath it was a numeric keypad.

Danyl already knew the code to open the door. It was the number he'd heard Joy muttering as she searched the alleyway. The secret constant, hidden in the deep structure of the universe. Before he tapped in the code, he hesitated. Was he doing the right thing? Did he want to disappear? Most sensible people avoided vanishing. But maybe it wouldn't be too bad? Maybe it was the best thing for him?

But when he reached out to tap in the code, his brain gave him a tiny little zap, like a warning. He started, afraid, but then he grew angry. What was he? A dog for his brain to shock whenever it disapproved of him? No, Danyl was a human. A man. A writer. He would go where he wanted, despite what his brain thought or did. He clenched his teeth and punched in the code: 1, 3, 7—the dimensionless number at the heart of existence, and a bell chimed somewhere in the distance. The light overheard went out and the door at the end of the hall slammed shut; the door ahead of him opened.

16

Things go really well for a little while

A squat male figure stood in the doorway; he stood aside and gestured for Danyl to enter the room beyond him. As he turned, his face met the light, revealing youthful pallid features ravaged by acne. It was Ann's missing student, Sophus the mathematician.

'Greetings, pilgrim,' Sophus said, bowing slightly.

'Hey, kid.' Danyl stepped past Sophus and looked around.

According to the blue envelope, the door at the end of the hall led to a vast labyrinth. The room Danyl found himself in was roughly double the size of a tennis court, but there were no other exits. Three of the walls were lined with empty bookshelves, with the slats of additional disassembled shelves leaning against them. The fourth wall was covered by a dirt-coloured curtain. There was a table beside the curtain and a second man stood at it. He had his back to Danyl. Open on the table before him was a plastic suitcase. Danyl couldn't see what was inside it.

The room was illuminated by candles. They were spaced along the shelves at irregular intervals. They lit up a dozen thin foam mattresses arranged in a grid in the centre of the room. Two of the mattresses were occupied—the first by a man dressed in black jeans and a black T-shirt, the second by a thickly bearded man wearing a red velvet dress. Both of them wore blindfolds. Both of their mouths were stained an odd blue colour. Neither of them moved. Danyl remembered the children's rhyme. *Hide me, blind me, or Gorgon will find me.*

'They have already made the crossing,' Sophus said in a low voice at Danyl's shoulder. 'You have many questions. We are here to answer them.'

And then the man at the far table turned. Danyl felt a shock of recognition. It was the goat-faced man he had met at the Free Market all those months ago and nearly fought with over a second-hand book. The goat-faced man was holding a syringe. Inside it was a bright blue liquid that seemed to glow. Its radiance pierced the gloom of the basement. It was a piece of sky inside a tiny tube.

'Don't worry,' Sophus said, his voice low, reassuring. 'There's no needle. We just squirt the correct dose into your mouth. Then you'll make the crossing to the Real City. This way, pilgrim.' Sophus tugged on Danyl's elbow, pulling him towards the mattresses. Danyl let himself be led.

What should he do? Why was the goat-faced man from the fair here? Why was Ann's student here? Where was the labyrinth? What was the Real City? Were they the same thing? And if Verity had come here but there wasn't any exit from this room, where had she gone?

The Goatman drew nigh with his syringe of glowing blue liquid. Danyl's brain gave him gentle, insistent shocks, warning him that he was in danger. *I know, dammit,* he thought back at it.

'Here's your blindfold,' Sophus said, applying a gentle pressure to Danyl's shoulder. 'It will keep you safe.'

Danyl either needed to push Sophus away and run for the door, hoping to escape, or to yield: let the goat-faced man squirt glowing liquid into his mouth and hope that everything worked out. But he couldn't decide; he couldn't think through the buzzing in his head, so he chose the last by default and let himself be guided down to a mattress.

'The first crossing is the hardest,' Sophus said, unfolding the blindfold, 'but also the most rewarding.'

Something in Danyl's mind clicked. He understood. He knew why the map leading to this room appeared in mysterious blue envelopes, and why the entrance was guarded by riddles and codes and mysterious spiral dollars. It was all artifice. A fake mystery. A lure; a trap to draw people here. But a lure by whom? Why? 'Stop!' Danyl batted Sophus's hand away. 'I need to think.'

'You can think in the Real City,' Sophus replied, and his voice was still soft, but with a hint of steel in it. 'You'll have all the answers there, all the time in the world.' Danyl tried to stand, but Sophus pressed down on his shoulder. Danyl braced himself. And then a buzzer sounded. The door to the hall swung open.

Everyone froze. Danyl on his knees; Sophus looming above; the Goatman with his glowing syringe. They all watched as a massive shadow filled the doorway. The shadow stooped to enter the room and boomed, 'I'm looking for my girlfriend?'

Danyl stared in horror. The giant wore huge blue jeans, a navy wool duffel coat and black leather boots with blood-red stitching. Its eyes were swimming behind thick, gold-rimmed glasses. It clutched a blue envelope in its massive hand. The giant must have seen the clues Joy left on her kitchen table. It had gone in search of her and found one of the blue envelopes, somehow, and now here it was, seeking answers.

'Your girlfriend. Yes.' Sophus released his grip on Danyl's shoulder and hurried across the room to meet the giant. 'I think I know who you mean. A very pretty girl. She is in here,' Sophus assured the giant. 'With us.'

'Who are you?'

'We are the Cartographers.'

'Are you some kind of cult?'

Sophus laughed. 'Of course not. We're scholars. Simple mapmakers.'

'Did you guys break into my house and booby-trap my bedroom?'

'Sir—' Sophus placed his palm on his chest, the picture of wounded pride. 'I'm a mathematician.'

'Did you though?'

'No.' Sophus drew closer to the giant and whispered to him. As the giant listened, Danyl sat on his mattress, watching, reassuring himself that the giant wouldn't recognise him. It hadn't seen his face, or heard his voice. It had no way of knowing that it was Danyl who booby-trapped its bedroom. Yet he had a sick certainty that he would do something stupid and reveal himself somehow. While he waited, trying not to attract the giant's attention, he gazed around the room.

He took in the two men beside him. Now that Danyl was close to them he could observe their blindfolded heads moving back and forth: tiny, jerking movements as if they were looking about for something. And he noticed something else.

The candles in the room were flickering, bowing away from the open door towards the dirty curtain on the opposite wall. And when the giant stepped into the room and closed the door, the flames danced then straightened and the curtain billowed then sagged back into place.

There was a hidden opening in that wall. A second way out of the room: a possible escape route. That must be where Verity had gone. Maybe the giant would create a distraction, somehow, and Danyl could slip away unnoticed. A perfect plan.

Then the giant said to Sophus, 'Give your blue compound to that guy first.' He pointed a massive finger at Danyl. 'I want to see it work.'

Sophus smiled. 'A sound idea, friend.'

Sophus and the giant stood over Danyl. He wanted to protest, to beg for freedom, or even to turn and run towards the curtain, but he was frozen in place by his fear of the giant, too terrified even to speak. His eyes shifted towards the goat-faced man who was closing in on Danyl, his syringe dripping fragments of sky, his yellow goat-eyes gleaming.

Then Danyl's gaze shifted again: the curtain at the back of the room billowed, like a drunken ghost; then it parted and three figures wearing camouflage clothes and black masks over their faces walked through it. Only Danyl saw them. Sophus, the giant and the Goatman were all oblivious; intent on Danyl, who sat motionless with fear, watching as one of the masked figures crept up behind the Goatman and touched a small rectangular object to his back. It made a clicking noise: the Goatman bleated in surprise and pain and dropped to the ground; the air filled with the smell of ozone.

As Sophus and the giant whirled around, the Goatman's attacker brandished a taser and cried out, 'Death to the agents of the Real City!'

17

Terrible things happen

The only sound in the room came from the Goatman's syringe, which rolled across the concrete floor in an arc. The arc began at Goatman's outstretched hand and ended just beside Danyl's mattress. Danyl huddled in the shadow cast by the giant.

'No one touch that.' The voice of the foremost masked figure rang out in the silence. He stepped towards the syringe then called over his shoulder to his comrades, 'Seize the suitcase.'

A second masked man hurried to the table. He closed the suitcase, snapped the latches shut and called out, 'Gassior. Blizey.' Danyl didn't know what that meant, and neither, evidently, did the first masked man, because his forehead, visible above his mask, furrowed in confusion. He looked backwards. That's when Sophus pushed past him and threw himself towards the suitcase. The man holding it turned around at the last second and gave a little cry of alarm, then pressed the trigger on his taser. Sophus ran straight into it and slumped to the ground, arcing his back in pain.

The first masked invader took another step towards the syringe, but this brought him within the shadow of the giant who stood with arms folded, watching everything with faint boredom, its glasses glinting in the candlelight. The invader stopped and took in the creature's scale—perhaps in the half-light he'd previously mistaken it for a pillar or giant statue—and the eyeholes in his mask went white with fear.

Sophus saw this. He rolled onto his side, pointed at the masked man and hissed, 'Him. Them.' He gritted his teeth against his pain. 'They broke into your house. They booby-trapped your bedroom. Stop them.'

'What? That's a lie! I didn't—' The masked man broke off

when the giant lumbered towards him; he fled towards the curtain but the giant crossed the room with a single mighty bound. It grabbed the man and flung him high into the air, then held him upside down by one leg and shook him. 'Who are you?' the giant asked in a reasonable voice. 'What's going on?'

The upside-down masked man did not reply. Instead he attempted to stun the giant with his taser but the giant merely extended one arm and the masked man flailed around in the space between them. Then he let his arms dangle below his head. 'Comrades!' he cried out. 'Help! A gigantic agent of the Real City has me!'

His comrades, standing back watching the scene unfold, were aware of this. They approached the giant, who turned to face them. The upside-down masked man gave a squeal of fear that dopplered into higher frequencies as the giant swung him about in a low arc, driving his comrades back.

'I don't want to hurt you,' the giant said. 'I don't care about your fight with those guys.' It tipped its head in the direction of Sophus, still prone on the ground. 'I'm just trying to find my girlfriend.'

'Gorgon's Cartographers have taken your girlfriend,' one of the masked men explained, keeping a wary distance. 'They've drugged her with DoorWay and imprisoned her in the Real City.'

The giant considered this for a second, then replied, 'I didn't understand a word of that. Make sense, please, or I will pull your friend's elbows out of their sockets.'

The third masked man stepped forward. 'There's no need for that.' He held the suitcase in one hand and stooped to pick up the dropped syringe in the other. His voice sounded familiar to Danyl. He tried to identify it but he was too confused. It was all he could do to watch the scene unfolding.

'Things are not as they seem,' the third masked man said. 'But there's no time for explanations. More Cartographers might arrive at any second. And this'—he held forth the blue syringe between thumb and forefinger—'will answer your questions.' The giant stared at the unearthly glow of the syringe, and fumbled as the masked man tossed it to him. Danyl saw a flurry of movement and cried out, but it was too late. The other masked man had crept up behind the giant and now he stunned it with his taser.

The giant grunted in pain. It spun about and struck its assailant, sending him flying across the room and crashing into a set of shelves. The man with the suitcase dropped it then lunged at the giant, striking its back. The giant stumbled, letting go of its upside-down captor, who fell and rolled to his feet, then plunged his own taser into the giant's armpit and shocked it a third time, then a fourth and fifth.

The giant roared and sank to its knees. Its foes darted about, shocking it then retreating. The giant covered its face and flailed about with its free hand. It gripped the jacket of one of his assailants—a green military surplus overcoat—but succeeded only in tearing off the pocket. Finally, another fusillade of taser strikes laid the giant low.

The masked men picked up the fallen suitcase, parted the curtain and left the room. Danyl glimpsed their torchlights dancing down a long tunnel receding into blackness. Then the curtain swung shut and they were gone.

The room was filled with bodies. Sophus was groaning in pain. He struggled to his knees and crawled across the floor to the Goatman. 'Get up!' he yelled, shaking him. 'They took the suitcase! They have the compound!' Then he doubled over, coughing.

The Goatman bleated. He and Sophus stood and dusted each other off while exchanging a series of angry whispers. Then they stumbled off down the darkened passageway, leaving Danyl alone with the giant and the two motionless guys with blue-stained lips. Danyl cowered on the floor as the giant clambered to its feet.

The giant glared around the room. It was like a lighthouse beaming out rage. Its gaze swept past Danyl and fixed on the wooden bookshelves against one wall. It bared its teeth and tore a crossbeam from the shelf and raised it up like a club: three long, bent nails gleamed in the half-light. The giant strode to the curtain and ripped it down with a contemptuous flick. Then it was moving through the tunnel. Its roars echoed out of the darkness.

OK. Time to flee. Danyl rolled onto his hands and knees and crawled towards the exit door. He wasn't thinking clearly. He had no plan except to get out—get away from the giant, the glowing blue liquid, the goat-faced man.

But he saw something on the floor. It was the patch of ground where the giant had fought with the masked invaders. A scrap of wool lay there: the pocket the giant had torn from his assailant's jacket. Screwed up inside it was a piece of notepaper covered in handwriting. Danyl picked it up and read:

The pocket of emptiness is deeper than the hand of wisdom

He looked at the door leading back to the alleyway. He looked at the piece of paper again. He turned and looked at the tunnel in the far wall. It was long and dark, extending far beyond the dimensions of the apartment building. Scattered lights danced in its depths. Sophus and the Goatman. The giant. The masked invaders, one of whom carried an incomprehensible aphorism about pockets in his jacket pocket. That could mean only one thing.

One of the fleeing points of light was Steve.

18

Splash

Danyl activated the display on his stolen phone. It lit the passageway with a ghostly radiance, revealing that the cinderblock walls beneath the apartment building had been replaced by decaying concrete joists patched with sections of brick. He was in the basement of another building. Still the tunnel continued. As he progressed, he passed entrances into unlit rooms. The ceiling lowered then raised again. He felt a blast of warm air from one doorway and heard the rumble of a furnace. Another apartment block. This passage connected to the basements of at least half the shops and tenements on Aro Street. But who built it? And why?

Danyl tripped. He caught himself and aimed his light down, revealing another wooden bookshelf tipped on its back. He played the light along the wall, revealing more shelves. Some were waist-high, others towered over his head. They were all empty. He ducked his head as he passed into the subterranean confines of yet another building.

He was moving deeper into the valley, travelling roughly in line with Aro Street. From far ahead came a faint but rising roar: the Waimapihi Stream; it went underground at the end of Holloway Road and ran all the way beneath Te Aro. He heard a flurry of shouting ahead of him.

As Danyl walked, he thought. What was the glowing blue drug? One of the masked men called it 'DoorWay'. When Danyl and Verity first met, they both worked for a wealthy lunatic who manufactured a mysterious drug, the formula for which was invented by a shadowy chemist. The same chemist, Danyl now suspected, who hid on the farm near Verity's childhood home. The name of the drug was DoorWay. It and the chemist were connected to all of this. But how?

The tunnel came to an end. It opened onto an underground passageway wide enough to drive a truck through. Most of it was taken up by the stream: dark icy waters flecked with foam, surging just below Danyl's feet. Narrow accessways ran alongside it on both sides. The roof of the tunnel curved overhead. The shouting came from upstream. Torchlight played against the walls. It shifted and dimmed; shadows moved against it.

Danyl crept onto the accessway. The shouts separated into distinct voices and almost audible words. He rounded the bend and saw two groups standing at opposite ends of a narrow bridge spanning the dark water. The bridge led to an opening in the far wall; its shadows suggested a stairway.

Two of the masked invaders stood in the opening. The third occupied the midpoint of the bridge which, as Danyl crept nearer, revealed itself as a large unsecured wooden plank. On Danyl's side of the bridge stood Sophus and the Goatman. The Goatman shuffled across the plank, which sagged under his weight, but he scurried back when the lead masked man menaced him with his taser.

Danyl inched along the wall until he was close enough to make out the shouting.

'Go away,' the masked man on the bridge yelled. 'Stop following us.'

'Give us back our suitcase.' That came from Sophus, who stood on the accessway some distance behind the Goatman.

'You have three seconds to go back,' the masked man replied. 'Or I'll kick this bridge into the river.'

'It doesn't matter. We'll still follow you.'

'Through that water? You're crazy. It's freezing.'

'Do you know where that suitcase came from?' Sophus demanded. 'What's inside it? Do you know who you're stealing from?'

'We're not afraid of Gorgon.' The speaker was another masked man. Danyl recognised the voice. The man stepped onto the bridge just behind his accomplice. Sophus shone his torch at him, lighting him up. The pocket of his woollen jacket was torn. It was Steve.

Steve. Suddenly Danyl had tears in his eyes. He'd been so lonely in the months since he'd left the valley, and he'd spent the last two days of his return in a state of perpetual confusion. Now Steve was here. Steve knew what was happening. Steve was stealing suitcases and shocking people with tasers and leading groups of masked men through secret tunnels.

Sophus shouted something but Danyl didn't hear any of it. He walked towards the bridge, his eyes fixed on Steve, desperate to reunite with his old friend. He opened his mouth to call to him, but suddenly a massive black shape detached itself from the darkness and pulled him down onto the cold concrete path. A voice hissed in his ear, 'Stay low.'

The giant had been hiding on the accessway just a few steps along from Danyl, who'd been too distracted to notice the huge patch of shadow adjacent to him. Now that shadow pinned Danyl to the ground and told him, 'Wait and listen.'

Danyl nodded to show he understood. He was overjoyed to see Steve but, now that he was unable to move, he realised that blundering into the middle of a stand-off on a narrow bridge involving angry people, tasers and a swift, dark stream might be a mistake. He craned his head and watched.

Sophus and Steve stood in the middle of the bridge, speaking in low voices. After a minute of this they both nodded and shook hands, then returned to their companions on the opposite banks. 'It's all right,' Sophus said to the Goatman. 'They've promised not to—' But the Goatman cried out as Steve kicked his end of bridge off the edge of the step. It splashed into the black water and the current swept it away.

'Hey!' he yelled across the stream. 'You vowed.'

'I don't make deals with traitors to reality,' Steve replied.

'You'll pay for this.' Sophus spat into the stream. 'We'll find you.'

'Perhaps,' Steve admitted, his voice cheerful. 'But it's a big valley and not all of it has fallen to Gorgon. Goodbye, Cartographers.' He turned, then paused on the bottom step and called out, 'You call yourselves Cartographers because you think you're discovering something. Exploring. Mapping new territory. But you're wrong. When you cross over to the Real City you're not exploring. You're not mapping anything. It's you who are being explored. You are the territory.'

Danyl lay on the concrete and the giant lay on Danyl, a vast warm bulk pressing down on him. It felt quite nice, actually: being pinned to the ground, face down, completely powerless. Not in a sexual way. It was more that while he was trapped beneath the giant Danyl didn't have to make any decisions about what to do or say. He felt safe.

Steve and the other masked men were gone. Sophus and the Goatman stood on the edge of the accessway arguing. Eventually Sophus took out his phone. 'I'll call the Apostle. She'll know what do to.'

'You won't get a signal down here,' the Goatman warned.

'There are relay sites all through the catacombs. Gorgon had them installed years ago.' Sophus held up a cautioning finger. 'It's ringing.'

Danyl waited eagerly. Yes, he thought, beaming encouragement into Sophus's brain. Call the Apostle, whoever that was. Explain everything to her. Unravel the mysteries of the basement and the Real City. And if there's anything we still don't understand, this giant will torture it out of you when we reveal ourselves.

These happy thoughts distracted Danyl from the sound of music, at first faint, then rising, now clearly audible over the roar of the stream. When he finally noticed it, it was because of the vibrating sensation coming from his left hip, which was also the source of the music.

It was the stolen smartphone in his jacket pocket. Eleanor's phone was ringing! Because Eleanor was the Apostle! They were calling Eleanor!

The giant rumbled, 'Is that you?' and shifted its weight.

Danyl could move again. He reached for his pocket to silence the phone before Sophus and the Goatman heard it. The name of the tune popped into his head: The Surprise Symphony by Haydn. Then Danyl remembered where he'd been the last time he'd heard that tune. He whispered 'Oh no' just as the giant growled in recognition.

'It was you!' Its hands seized Danyl and flipped him onto his back. 'You were in my house. You booby-trapped my bedroom.'

'I'm sorry.' Danyl tried to push himself up on his elbows but the giant was straddling him; two gigantic knees pinned Danyl's arms to his sides. 'I can explain everything.'

'That's good. Where's Joy?'

Danyl shook his head. 'I don't know that. I don't—'

'Oh.' The giant looked sad, disappointed. It drew back a fist, ready to drive it through Danyl's delicate skull. Suddenly a beam of torchlight illuminated its face. Sophus and the Goatman had heard the roar and were shining their torches at it. The giant shielded its eyes, dazzled; its knees pinning Danyl in place shifted, and Danyl seized his chance. He slithered between the giant's thighs. The concrete slab beneath him shuddered as a massive fist struck the ground where he'd lain a second earlier. Then he was free and there was only one escape route.

19

Stream of consciousness

He hung in the air for a second, the giant behind him, the black water beneath him, the beams of the torches cutting through the darkness, and he thought about Einstein.

Danyl wasn't scientifically trained, like Ann was. He didn't understand chemistry, or biology or physics. But he had recently spent a lot of time in a secure hospital ward where the only reading material consisted of either popular science magazines or the Bible. Danyl opted for the magazines, and a lot of the articles in them were about Einstein.

People used to think that time was a flowing river. Einstein showed that they were wrong. He proved that it was a fixed dimension intersecting with the three spatial dimensions to form a static four-dimensional block. Space–time. Space–time did not flow. If time was a river, it was a frozen one. Nothing moved. The flow of time was an illusion brought about by the way we perceived the world. It seemed as if time was passing as we lived, that we were making choices, that we were masters of our lives. Danyl learned that this was false, and that the future was already there, frozen in place: all the events in our lives were doomed to happen. From the very instant the universe collapsed into existence, long before Danyl was born, before the evolution of his race, before the formation of Earth and the nucleosynthesis of our sun, he was doomed to jump into the Waimapihi Stream. And he'd known it, somehow. As soon as the giant had entered the basement, Danyl knew the beast would unmask him and turn on him, and the instant he entered the tunnel and heard that muted roar in the distance, Danyl sensed that he'd end up in the stream. His choices weren't choices. He was trapped by fate, which carried him through fixed points of sequential space-time towards a doom that he was powerless to defy.

The last thing Danyl saw before he hit the water was the giant's hand grabbing for him. And then his head slipped under the water and he sank beneath the icy darkness.

This was hardly the first time Danyl had dived into a swift-moving body of water in a desperate bid for freedom. But this underground stream was colder and deeper than any of the other rivers, culverts or canals he'd plunged into recently. Colder and deeper and faster. He flailed about and righted himself; his feet found purchase on the streambed, but before he could stand up the current pulled him on, sweeping him away from the confusion of lights and angry faces above him. The next time he came up for air the light was gone.

Danyl swallowed and coughed. He closed his eyes. They stung from the terrible cold, and, anyway, there was nothing to see. The darkness was absolute. He drifted with the current for a minute then felt around with his arms and kicked with his feet, trying to find the walls. They were close. The tunnel had narrowed, and when he tried to stand his head collided with the concrete roof. The accessway was gone. He was trapped in a confined stormwater drain deep underground.

At least you escaped the giant, Danyl reminded himself. That was the immediate threat. He could probably survive in the water for several more minutes before his core temperature fell too low and his heart failed and he died. Everything was fine.

He lay back and let himself be borne by the current and tried to calculate his destination. Where did the stream resurface? It didn't come out anywhere in the Aro Valley. After leaving the valley it flowed beneath the Capital, but it didn't resurface there either. It ran all the way to the harbour. A distance of several kilometres. Probably not a survivable journey. He'd die of hypothermia long before being swept out to sea, if the roof didn't slope below the waterline and drown him first. Maybe, now that Danyl thought about it, drifting with the stream wasn't so smart?

He decided to turn back.

He braced himself between the roof and the wall. This was harder than it sounded because he had no feeling in his hands. He kicked out with his feet and found the muddy bottom of the tunnel, and after a little floundering and some minor drowning he stood in a cramped, squatting position. The water came to just below his nose and the current was strong. He waded against it, pressing his hands against the sides of the narrow space. Step by shivering, tentative step, he made his way back up the tunnel.

How long and how far had he floated downstream? He didn't know. His plan was to walk until he saw the torch lights of Sophus and the Goatman, and improvise from there. But progress was slow. Time passed, although whether it did so in seconds or many hours Danyl wasn't sure. He began to shake. He lost his grip on the wall and stumbled. Soon he'd be swept away. Was he close to the accessway? He must be. Should he shout for help? Was it better to freeze to death or be beaten by a giant?

He was struggling with this dilemma when he walked into the steel bars. He cried out and stood, hitting his forehead on a wooden beam overhead, which rattled from the impact. His cries of pain echoed around the tiny, dark space. He felt the bars with his numb hands and established that they were vertical. They were too narrow for him to fit through and there was a build-up of branches, leaves and organic matter on the other side of them.

He'd gone the wrong way, gotten lost in the darkness. He must have bypassed the accessway and continued up the stormwater drain. An easy mistake to make. It seemed unfair to Danyl that such a simple miscalculation would probably kill him in the next minute or two.

Because he'd stopped shaking. His body had used up all its available energy. He felt his heart beating, and each beat seemed slower and fainter than the last.

Danyl was dying.

So this was how it ended for him. Freezing to death in the mud and darkness in the catacombs beneath the Aro Valley. How fitting, he thought, calmer now that he accepted its inevitability. This was always going to be his doom. Always. And really, this wasn't such a bad way to go. Quiet. Peaceful. Numb. Those three words kept repeating themselves in his mind, and he sank down into the mud and felt himself drifting away.

Danyl dreamed about sex.

Warmth. Lips. Tongues. His thoughts drifted through a sea of sensual impressions, detached from any detail or time or place, until he half woke to find himself in a soft, warm bed, with a soft, warm woman beside him.

He reached out and touched her back. She sighed. It was Verity. Time and place returned to him. He was in their house on Devon Street. It was a few weeks after her exhibition opening. They'd had a terrible argument after Danyl broke open one of her cases during the party, but they'd made up and the exhibition was a critical and commercial success. Several reviewers insisted Verity's unseen photographs were so brilliant they caused nausea and migraines, and the gallery was doing a brisk trade in empty plastic cases.

Danyl rolled over and pressed himself against her, sliding his hand over her hip, inside her pyjamas. She sighed again and he pressed his palm against her thigh, and she said, 'I'm sleeping. Lemme alone.'

Danyl was half-asleep himself, still half-dreaming. He kissed her neck and embraced her, the sea of lips and tongues still ebbing in his mind. Verity muttered, 'Get. Off.' He kissed her neck again and fumbled with the buttons on her pyjama top and she turned and shoved his jaw, hard, then pivoted and pushed him with her foot. He tipped backwards and fell out of bed and knocked the top of his head on the corner of his bedside table.

'Ow! What did you do that for?'

'I told you to get off me.'

'I was just being friendly.'

'I know what you were doing.'

He felt the top of his head. 'My head is bleeding.'

'Good.'

'I think I tore open my scalp. Turn on the light.'

'Dammit, Danyl. It's 4 am. I have work today.'

'It's not my fault. You kicked me.'

Verity turned on her bedside lamp. There was a minor cut in Danyl's scalp. He sat on the floor, naked and miserable, holding a pillowcase to his head to staunch the bleeding while Verity went downstairs to find an ice pack.

He wiped a tear from the corner from his eye. This sorrow wasn't caused by only his injury. Danyl had been sad a lot recently. A minute ago he'd been sleeping and dreaming, and he'd been happy. Now he was awake and bleeding and miserable. The whole day stretched out before him: hours piled upon hours. Nothing but tedious reality.

He looked around the bedroom. It was piled with life's debris. Almost everything belonged to Verity except a pile of Danyl's dirty clothes in the corner. The furniture, the books, the pictures hanging on the walls were all Verity's. Now his eyes settled on a photo sitting on the top shelf of a waist-high bookshelf.

It was from her first exhibition; it was also, he recalled, the picture that Eleanor had found in a magazine, causing her to leave her monastery and seek out Verity in the Aro Valley. It showed a near-derelict house atop a slope dotted with ruins.

The house looked like a post-war construction. It was two storeys, with a deck along the front looking out over the slope below, and a stairway with broken and missing steps leading up to the deck.

Looking at this photograph compounded Danyl's misery. People had lived in that house once. Slept in it. Dreamed in it. Tried to love in it and then bled on its floors. Now they were probably dead and gone, and their house was falling apart. Just like the house Danyl and Verity lived in now would one day crumble and fall. A tear ran down his cheek.

'Danyl?'

He looked up. Verity stood in the doorway. She held an ice tray wrapped in a tea towel, which she handed to him. 'What's wrong?'

He sighed. 'I was just thinking that it all seems pointless. Life . . .' He started to gesture towards the photograph, but found he didn't have the energy. He'd been feeling down for a while now. A terrible sadness had invaded his life, and it was gathering in intensity. He hadn't written anything for weeks. Where did it come from? What was wrong with him?

'Obviously life is pointless, if you think about it,' Verity replied. 'The trick is not to think about it. Distract yourself. That's what art is for.'

'So your art is just a distraction from the real truth?'

'Partly,' she admitted. 'Mostly.'

'And when you and Eleanor left home to search for something, you were just distracting yourselves from reality?'

Verity's smile died. 'No. That was . . . different. That was about escaping it altogether.'

'How?'

'It doesn't matter anymore. The way out wasn't what it seemed.' She blinked. 'I'm going back to sleep.' She climbed under the blankets and reached for her light. Danyl's gaze returned to the photograph.

The house in the centre of the frame was in focus. But

there was something in the foreground of the picture. A pool. Although it was blurred. Danyl could see that it was small and round, sunken into the ground and edged by mossy paving stones. The water had an odd blue tinge to it. He'd seen the picture before, many times, but he'd never noticed the pool before.

'Goodnight, Danyl.' There was a click as Verity turned out the light. The picture vanished.

But Danyl still thought about it. There was something else about the picture, something odd, and just before he fell asleep again he realised what it was. The picture was from Verity exhibition of Te Aro photographs, yet he'd never seen that house or those ruined buildings anywhere in the valley. He couldn't even imagine where they'd be.

He lay in the darkness of the blocked stormwater drain, his warmth and life bleeding out of him. He was almost completely numb now. His only physical sensation was the pain in his head from knocking it on the wooden beam.

And soon that would be gone. All he needed to do was lie there: to sink into the mud and dissolve into nothing. That was the smart move. After all, what was the point of doing anything else? All these thoughts came from a voice inside his mind, a voice he'd always thought of as himself—but now that he lay in the mud, remembering, close to death, he realised it was the voice of his sickness. The depression. Unmedicated Danyl. It came into his life two years ago: it spoke to him and through him that night when he lay on the floor, bleeding. It went away when he went on the antidepressants, and in the last few days it had returned. Danyl's brain had been buzzing at him and he'd ignored it but—he realised now—the buzzing wasn't the sickness, but rather his brain trying to warn him against its approach. And he'd ignored his brain, mocked it—and now the sickness was triumphant. It had lured Danyl down here into the mud and darkness. It had manipulated his thoughts and led him here to die, and now it spread its wings above him, casting all his thoughts into shadow. It had won.

Danyl accepted this without bitterness. Without regret. Without pain. He was beyond that. Soon even the pain in his head would be gone.

Although it was odd, wasn't it? Why was there a wooden beam overhead for Danyl to hit his head on? Wasn't he encased in concrete? And why was he lying in mud and not water? He thought about this, knowing that these thoughts might be his last. Was the beam above him like the plank in the accessway? A makeshift bridge? If it was a bridge, what did it connect with? Entrances and exits from the tunnel?

It doesn't matter, the sickness replied, soothing, calm. Lie down. Be at peace.

But Danyl was curious. Groaning, he pulled himself out of the mud. He could stand. He wasn't in a drain anymore but some sort of tall, narrow maintenance area, probably for clearing away the debris lodged against the bars. He clawed his way up the wall and gripped the plank and pulled himself onto it. After a few seconds of agonised fumbling, he found the wall, the ledge the plank rested on, and the bottom of a flight of steps.

Yes, they're steps, the voice of the sickness conceded, but they are steps to nowhere. There's nothing out there. There's no escape, just a delay of the inevitable. And the voice was right. Danyl accepted that. But, inevitability aside, he did want to know where the steps led. So he crawled up them, each occasional beat of his heart like a hammer-blow to his chest. Each narrow stone step that he collapsed on felt as if it would be his last, yet somehow he continued on. After an unknown length of time, he realised he could see his hands. The darkness was no longer total.

Danyl looked up and saw stars.

20

Threshold

He stood in a culvert. It was a deep depression in the ground with rough steps cut into the mud leading up to the surface level. Wooden boards were fitted into the steps to stop them from eroding.

The tunnel behind him, which he'd just crawled his way out of, was a large round pipe sloping downwards, deep into the earth. Looking closer, he saw the stubs of thick bars jutting from the roof. They'd been sawed through.

A stream had once run into the hole, probably where the steps were now, but someone had diverted it and turned the flood tunnel into a secret route. But a route to where?

He made his slow, painful way up the steps. The beauty of the night sky glowing with stars filled Danyl with joy and silenced the voice of the sickness, temporarily at least. But dressed as he was in soaking wet clothes, and pretty much dying of hypothermia, he was still too weak to walk. He needed to get inside and get warm, fast. His plan was to crawl to the nearest house, pound on their front door and throw himself on the mercy of whoever answered. He scrabbled up the last few steps and out of the hole and looked around.

He wasn't sure where he was. Somewhere in the valley: the familiar hills rose up on either side of him. But which street? The roadway swept up a steep slope past rows of buildings, all of which were dark. Not a single light shone on the hillside. Not even a street lamp.

This was a disappointing and possibly fatal development. What had happened? Had civilisation collapsed while Danyl was underground? Or was there a power cut?

He climbed to his feet and stumbled towards the road.

The intensity of the starlight made the scene look like a photo negative. The street was a white ribbon winding through black fields, with bright white paths and driveways intersecting it. Danyl reached it and lurched towards the nearest building. It was a townhouse: four homes with separate driveways and entrances combined into a single construct. There was something strange about it, though. Something missing, something wrong—but in Danyl's exhausted state, it took a long time to figure out what it was.

There weren't any cars parked outside. Nor, now that his barely conscious brain noticed it, were there any mailboxes. Or fences. Or gardens. The hillside simply consisted of shadowy buildings surrounded by empty lots filled with weeds. That was weird. And spooky. What if Danyl had somehow crossed over into some alternate version of Te Aro? He remembered the cryptic message carved on Verity's door, echoed by Steve when he stormed the basement. *Death to the agents of the Real City.* Was this the Real City?

Then he saw the billboard. It stood in the middle of an empty section. Huge words were printed in bright black letters against the starlit background:

*Te Aro Threshold Development! Experience life
as it's meant to be lived—at the Threshold!*

Beneath this was an artist's rendition of a series of handsome townhouses foregrounded by a picture of a half-naked man and woman lying on a bed, smiling towards the sunrise. The bottom third of the billboard showed a tree-lined driveway winding through landscaped gardens followed by the slogan *Come LIVE . . . beyond the Threshold!*

The Threshold development was part of Te Aro lore: one of the great mysteries of the valley. It was a housing project planned back in the 1970s. When it was announced that a large, wooded section of the valley would be bulldozed and subdivided to make way for dozens of townhouses offering modern solutions to inner-city living, Te Aro rose up in open revolt. There were protests, candlelit vigils, Sanskrit prayers chanted in the paths of bulldozers, naked demonstrators screaming anarchist slogans dragged away by bewildered police and, finally, a legendary, drug-fuelled dance party held amidst the fallen trees beneath a luminous full moon.

After that, the trees were hauled away. Construction on the townhouses began, and then, suddenly, stopped. No one knew why. Huge fences went up around the half-developed land; guard dogs prowled the unsealed roads and unfinished buildings. The Threshold protests entered into legend but the location of the place itself slipped away, forgotten. No one even knew where it was anymore. Danyl had stumbled into the one place in the valley where there was no one to help him. Even if he had the strength to cry out, no one would hear, no one would come. He'd reached a dead end.

He crumpled and fell face down on the road. He used his last flicker of strength to roll onto his back. Each breath was a little shorter. Each heartbeat a little weaker. In a voice that wasn't triumphant at all but rather friendly and sympathetic, the voice said, See? This dying business isn't so bad. It's just darkness and numbness and silence, and what's so terrible about that? Danyl was inclined to agree.

There wasn't absolute silence, of course. There was the wind. The trees. Water dripping. The rush of cars on distant roads. And there was another sound beneath all those. An odd babble, almost voice-like. It surged briefly when the wind died down, then another gust swept it away.

Danyl put it out of his mind. He didn't have to know everything.

It's nothing, the voice agreed. Hush now. Close your eyes.

Danyl closed his eyes. He breathed out. He did not breathe in again.

The water dripped. The trees rustled. The starlight poured

down on him as he lay on the gravel road, his arms outstretched, his face at peace. And then the wind died away and the sound came back, sharp and clear in the frozen air.

The soft, nervous clucking of chickens.

21

Dawn

Danyl's arrival caused quite a stir amongst the birds. The half-finished, half-ruined townhouse was three storeys high with a peaked roof, built in the Victorian style with fake shutters next to the windowless frames and fake plaster arches over the three front doors. When he first crawled around the back of the building and discovered the coop—a row of straw-lined cardboard boxes set against the rear wall of the townhouse—the chickens rushed over to Danyl and clustered about him, clucking and burbling as he crawled through the weeds and mud, heading towards the nearest door.

Because the chickens meant life. They meant someone lived in the unfinished building, or at least nearby, and they could save Danyl. Or, alternately, if there wasn't anyone around he could use the chickens themselves for warmth. He cast an appreciative eye over their plump, feathered bodies as they milled about.

The chickens also meant Verity was near. Danyl may have been mentally ill and very close to death but he wasn't stupid. He knew that the gravel path and the clucking chickens of Threshold were the same gravel and chickens he'd heard on Verity's voice message. He'd figured that out, eventually, and that had spurred him to start breathing again, roll over and crawl his way up the hill. Now that he'd rounded the back of the townhouse he saw further evidence of habitation. There were bloated rubbish bags stacked in a pile, and a makeshift washing line strung up between two trees midway to the next building, with sheets and clothes forming motionless black shapes suspended in the air.

Three more doors along the back wall were at waist height

above the ground with no steps leading to them. The door Danyl crawled towards had a small pile of rocks beneath it. He slithered over the rocks and pulled himself onto his knees, fumbled at the doorknob and fell forward as the door swung inwards.

The interior was almost as black as the tunnels beneath the valley. The starlight cast a vague wash of illumination across a smooth concrete floor. At the periphery of the light was a woman asleep on a mattress piled high with blankets. Her head was turned away, facing the darkness.

Danyl moaned with relief. He'd made it. He'd found someone. He pulled himself through the doorway and rasped in his dying voice, 'Help me.'

The woman did not move.

Danyl decided to make his plea a little louder. He shuffled closer and croaked, 'Hey! I'm dying.' She still did not respond. His wet clothes left a damp trail on the ground as he crawled to the mattress and shook the woman's shoulder. Her head rolled to face him and he gasped.

It was Joy. The woman Danyl had met in the alleyway. The giant's girlfriend. She was blindfolded. Her lips were stained bright blue. There was a mattress beyond her with another sleeping form in it, and as Danyl's eyes adjusted to the gloom, more blindfolded forms materialised. They were spaced a few metres from each other, and the bodies receded into the darkness.

Danyl had never been so happy to find a vast room filled with blindfolded comatose bodies. He stripped off his soaking clothes and dried himself with a blanket. He found the two largest men he could find and tugged their mattresses together, then slipped under the blankets between them. His plan was to lie there tucked up with the men until they raised his core temperature. He'd wait until his teeth stopped chattering and his heart worked properly again instead of skipping beats and madly fluttering as if were trying to wriggle free of his ribcage. After that, he'd make his escape.

He woke with a start. It was day. The room was lit by shafts of sunlight coming in through cracks in the walls.

Danyl had dreamed of a black river and a derelict house filled with bodies; he took a few seconds to sort out that those dreams were actually memories and that he was inside a huge house and surrounded by drugged, unconscious people.

He wriggled free of his companions, sat up and looked around. The interior of the townhouse was a vast continuous space. Most of the internal walls and the floors of the higher storeys were just supporting beams, so he could see all the way to the far end of the building. Rows of regularly spaced windows admitted identical shafts of grey light; they illuminated dozens of mattresses, each occupied by a motionless sleeper buried under a pile of blankets.

The floor was freezing. Danyl stole a pair of socks off one of the men he'd spent the night with and then prowled around stealing bits of warm clothing off different people until he was properly dressed. None of the sleepers had shoes on. He found all their footwear piled in a remote corner of the townhouse and picked out a pair of sneakers in his size.

All this time, the chickens watched him from the doorway. He walked over to them and found a makeshift kitchen set up against the back wall. There was a stone jug filled with water, a camping stove on the windowsill, and on the floor was a box containing tea bags, instant coffee, sugar sachets and milk powder. He boiled water and made tea. He sat on the porch and watched the sunrise. The chickens gathered around him, and he felt as though they were celebrating his survival. It had been close.

The light behind the low grey clouds intensified. The

darkness shrank into shadows and the desolate landscape of Threshold revealed itself. It was a wide slope ringed by tree-lined ridges and enclosed by a high wooden fence. The top of the slope was hidden in a bank of mist. The other unfinished townhouses loomed over the patches of weeds and pools of mud that lay between them. These spaces were littered with abandoned building materials: rusting girders, piles of stones. Narrow muddy paths criss-crossed the wasteland.

The road swept back and forth across the slope, passing out of sight into the mist. As Danyl peered up into the bank of fog he saw a faint yellow light shining somewhere high above, its source concealed in the grey haze. There was someone up there. Someone was home.

He remembered Verity's voice message: the timeline of background sounds. She'd walked past the chickens, along the gravel road for several minutes, then up a flight of steps. There were no steps around here. Verity must have gone up the hill: towards the light.

Danyl looked back over his shoulder at the building filled with sleeping bodies. He looked up at the light again. Then he looked at the chickens, shook his head and said, 'I'm not going up there. It's not worth it. I almost died down in those tunnels. I shouldn't even be here. I'm leaving this valley. I'm going back to my medication. My doctor.' The lead chicken tipped its head to one side. Danyl held up his hand. 'I know what you're going to say. That if I leave now I'll never understand anything. The blue envelope. Gorgon. The Real City.' He gestured at the rows of bodies. 'This place. I'll never know what happened to Verity. And you're right. But I can live with not knowing if it means I get to live. So—goodbye.'

The chickens warbled sadly. They followed Danyl to the edge of the building, some of them running on ahead, and it was the change in intensity of their clucking that warned him something was wrong. He knelt down and peeked around the corner.

A procession of people in shabby, ill-fitting clothes emerged from the ground at the base of the hill, springing forth like flowers in stop-motion footage. They were coming out of the culvert. They were coming from the catacombs.

The procession reached the road. It moved slowly. Each pair carried a stretcher between them. On each stretcher was a body. They were too far away for Danyl to make out individual features of the bodies, but he could see blue stains around their mouths: fragments of sky amidst the mud and drifts of mist. One of the bodies had a thick beard and wore a red velvet dress.

The procession ended with a final, lone figure emerging from the tunnel. This person wasn't carrying a stretcher. She was dressed in a chef's outfit with a plastic raincoat over it. It was Eleanor.

22

Flee!

Danyl hid behind the far wall, silencing the chickens with a finger to his lips. He knelt in the grass and looked back down the hill. The procession turned off the gravel road and made for the nearby townhouse; all except for Eleanor, who continued up the hill, heading for the vague patch of light in the mist.

Danyl couldn't stay here. It was too exposed. And he couldn't circle around and go back into the catacombs. Who knew what lurked down there. Cultists? Giants? It was too dangerous.

He made his way to a row of low trees and lay in the grass behind them. He would watch and wait. When things were quiet again, he'd make for safety.

The gravel road wound down the hill and out of sight, heading towards two large tree-covered ridges. Danyl recalled a remote section of Raroa Road with a tall wooden gate stretching between two steep spurs, with hills on both sides. That had to be the exit, where the track came out and the Threshold development connected with the rest of the valley. He'd break for the gate, climb over it and flee Te Aro itself—forever.

The procession reached the townhouse. Danyl watched them through the windows. The first pair entered, laid their stretcher down and transferred its drugged occupant to a mattress. When the pair had finished, they turned to face the back of the building. Danyl recognised them. Sophus and the Goatman.

He cast his mind back to the chaotic scenes in the catacombs. What did Steve say before he kicked the plank into the stream? Something about maps. Explorers . . . Cartographers. He'd called Sophus and the Goatman 'cartographers'. And that's how they referred to themselves. Sophus had referred to 'The Apostle' just before he called Eleanor's phone. And their leader was Gorgon—whoever or whatever Gorgon was.

The Cartographers went about their business. The rest of their procession unloaded the bodies from the stretchers. They stripped their lower bodies; removing trousers and underwear; next they tore open gigantic bags of adult nappies and tugged them on to their half-naked victims. They did the same to the rest of the comatose forms spaced out across the room, moving from mattress to mattress, tugging soiled nappies off and putting clean ones on. Danyl could hear their expressions of disgust chiming out through the still, misty air of the dawn.

Then one of them cried out in surprise. Danyl couldn't see why: his view was blocked. The rest of the Cartographers were moving towards the section of the building where Danyl had slept the night before. Then the Goatman stepped into view, holding up the damp, torn clothes Danyl had discarded when he'd crawled into the townhouse. Sophus hurried over to them. He held a trouser leg to the light, inspecting it. He shouted and gestured to Cartographers, pointing at the exits. The Cartographers dropped their soiled nappies and obeyed.

Danyl backed away through the scrub, keeping to his hands and knees until he figured there were enough trees between him and the townhouse to mask his escape. Then he ran.

It was no good heading towards the gate. The Cartographers would guard it. He'd have to head up and try to make his way over the hill. He found a trail through the trees heading in the right direction. The shouts of his hunters rang out. They sounded far away.

Danyl ran on through the trees, heading up the slope to where he hoped the fence would intersect with the ridgeline. Something glinted through the foliage: coils of wire. The fence! Freedom. He ran towards it.

The fence was made of wooden vertical slats and steel poles

and topped with rows of barbed wire slanting outwards at a diagonal angle. It wasn't going to be easy to climb over. The best way would be to climb a tree and jump from a branch to the fence-top.

Danyl looked around for such a tree. He clambered up a small bank adjacent to the fence, trying to get a good view, and from it he looked up to the plateau at the top of the hill. This was a level expanse of weeds, about the size of a single car park, and in the centre of the expanse was a large wooden cross sticking out of a rectangle of freshly churned mud. It looked an awful lot like a grave.

Danyl thought back to Verity's message to Eleanor, her final words: *I might never see you again. I'm sorry. Goodbye.*

He looked back at the fence. Not far from him was a sturdy-looking tree with a branch leading directly to it. He could climb it now. Run down to Aro Street. Jump on the next bus. Be free. But what if that grave was Verity's? Could he live the rest of his life never knowing if she had died here and now lay in a shallow grave in the forgotten wilds of Te Aro?

He jogged up to the plateau. It looked out over a region of sunlit mist. A wind had sprung up and it drove the drifts of vapour back and forth across the hillside, concealing then revealing the entire expanse of Threshold. Six derelict buildings staggered up the slope. A group of Cartographers milled about at the bottom of the hill. They were tiny and distant. They hadn't seen him yet.

Danyl approached the grave. It was a makeshift affair. A rough pit in the clay. The cross stood at a crooked angle. Something was carved on the crossbeam. Two words. A name.

Danyl drew closer.

And then a huge gust of wind shook the trees and drove the mist apart, revealing the top of the slope which terminated at the bottom of a stone cliff. A house sat at the base of the cliff, looking out over all of Threshold. Danyl had seen that house before. It was in the photograph of Verity's that had hung on the wall of their bedroom.

The house looked older than it did in Verity's picture. The front deck had gone and so had the steps leading up to it. There was now a large scaffolding on the house, and the wooden boards laid across it formed a stairway leading to the front door. Two Cartographers stood guard at the base of the scaffolding.

And there was Eleanor, a tiny figure in a chef's outfit and raincoat, almost at the top of the gravel road. Danyl watched as she made her way past the guards and up the scaffolding steps. The front door opened and a woman emerged. She was small, stooped: she walked with a cane. Her hair was white and tangled. A dog—a great beast of an animal—trotted out onto the scaffolding and stood beside her. The dog was almost as tall as the two women. It looked around the valley, and its eyes seemed to settle on Danyl.

His first instinct was to run. It's just a dog, he told himself, and it's a long way away. Neither of the women had noticed him, and the dog didn't bark. It just stared.

Danyl turned his back on the dog and the vast and desolate Threshold development. He approached the grave, squinting his eyes, trying decipher the name on the cross. The words were tiny. They seemed to blur . . .

Then he cried out in pain. Something had stabbed him! He clutched at the wound and looked down. A needle-tipped dart about the size of a matchstick was embedded in his chest.

Whimpering, he pulled it out. The tip of the needle was coated in a thin, sticky, sky-blue residue, mixed with his blood. It was the same luminous blue substance he'd seen in the basement.

Leaves rustled. Danyl looked towards the sound.

The Goatman. His yellow eyes were gleaming; he grinned in triumph with his broad buck teeth. He held a dart-gun in his stumpy, hairy hand. He tugged at the pump on the back of the gun, re-coiling the spring. He took another step towards

Danyl, aimed, and fired. A second dart slammed into Danyl's belly, which quivered under the shock of the impact.

Danyl staggered backwards. He needed to run; perhaps he could outdistance the Goatman and get to the fence? He could still escape, dammit. But his legs weren't working, weren't responding to commands from his brain. Or was his brain at fault? He wasn't wasn't sure. He tried to turn, but his balance was gone. He toppled sideways, landing on his side in the soft soft mud. He couldn't move. Couldn't speak. There was something something wrong with him. His brain wasn't working working properly properly anymore. He'd been drugged drugged by the mysterious blue blue substance.

The Goatman loomed in Danyl's vision. His voice was a distant echo. Danyl heard scattered words. 'The Spiral. Gorgon. The Real City.' The voice surged to a roar then faded to nothing.

Reality drained away like raindrops down a window, and Danyl saw what was behind it.

PART II

23

The applicant

It was the last day of summer. The morning sun shone on the happy crowds bustling about Aro Community Hall. The children in the crèche were running and laughing. A group of them held hands and danced around a tree singing the Gorgon song, then fell to the ground shrieking with mock fear. Another cluster of toddlers squatted around the vegetables in the vegetable garden, urinating on them with abandon; their teachers had taught them this fed the crops.

The applicant stood outside the council offices. He smoothed the front of his shirt, which was buttoned up to his collar. He checked his reflection in the window. It showed a bald man with a neatly trimmed beard, a dimpled smile and too-bright eyes. He bared his teeth at the glass to make sure there wasn't any food stuck to them. He repeated an inspirational aphorism, reminding himself that he could achieve his dreams because he was made of stardust, then he slapped himself in the face and warned his reflection not to mess things up. This was too important.

He knocked on the door.

It was opened by a man dressed in tan pants and an open-necked business shirt who—at first glance—appeared impossibly handsome: slender with smooth tan skin, a strong jaw, dark jewelled eyes; but on closer examination he was oddly proportioned. His head was too large for his body; his arms too short. He looked like a figure in a digital photograph that had been improperly resized. He blinked at the applicant then held out his hand.

'Welcome,' he said, 'I am the Te Aro Council secretary. Very pleased to meet you, although I must add that this statement is not an endorsement of your application. I must remain strictly neutral towards each candidate.'

'How many candidates are there?'

'Just yourself,' the secretary replied. 'But the principle remains.'

The applicant said, 'I appreciate that.'

'Your appreciation is appreciated.'

'Thank you.'

'Thank you for thanking me.'

The applicant hesitated, tempted to thank the secretary again, curious to see how many times he could compel the secretary to go on thanking him for thanking him. How deep would he go? But something in the man's smile spoke of a gentle willingness to stand on the doorstep engaged in a nest of infinitely recursed pleasantries. So the applicant said nothing, and the secretary stood aside and waved him in to the council offices.

'We're in here,' he said, leading the applicant past the desks to a meeting room. A plastic table with a fake oak weave took up most of the space. A whiteboard on one wall was covered with plans and dates and diagrams, with 'Te Aro Council Election' written at the top.

'Only two months to go,' the secretary said, gesturing at the whiteboard. 'You won't be involved in the election,' he added. 'If you get this job. And I'm not saying you will or won't. But for the rest of us it is very exciting. It's been a troubled time at Te Aro Community Council.'

The applicant knew all about the troubles. They began with the Holloway Road incident six months ago. When police investigated a disturbance in an old house way up the remote end of the valley, they found an elderly Satanist who'd died of a heart attack, a fortune in lost gold and a naked, mentally ill writer named Danyl. There was a scandal and for several terrible weeks at the end of that summer the eyes of the world and the attentions of the authorities settled upon the hitherto untroubled community of Te Aro. Marijuana plantations were found and burned. Cult headquarters were raided and their fanatics deprogrammed. Anarchist cells were broken up; revolutionary demagogues returned to their anxious parents. Much-loved tenement buildings were deemed unfit for human habitation and condemned; their inhabitants were dragged blinking and screaming from their lightless interiors by child welfare agencies. It was a disaster for the culture and economy of the valley.

The old Te Aro Councillor—a merry, gnomish old man known only as the Sheriff—did everything in his power to stop the raids, but he was thwarted by one of his own staffers: the former treasurer. This treasurer was a human rights lawyer who had long despaired of the grip that illegal drugs and obscene cults wielded in his community, and he seized the moment. It was he who informed the police that the Church of Divine Laughter, a respected doomsday sect, did not have planning permission to build their gigantic medieval siege weapons, and he who revealed the location of Ys—a shipping container, buried beneath the allotments in Tanera Park, which housed an LSD laboratory rumoured to pre-date the Swiss scientist Albert Hofmann's discovery of the drug and which was dug up and destroyed before a crowd of weeping onlookers. The Sheriff fired the treasurer then went back to his desk and suffered a massive stroke. He died, as the officiating druid at his funeral pyre said, of a broken heart.

The secretary hired a new treasurer. But the Councillor was not so easy to replace. A general election was needed, but according to the Te Aro Charter, elections in Te Aro could only be held on certain dates: Matariki, the seasonal equinoxes, or Walpurgis Night. Fortunately, the secretary explained, the autumn equinox was only two months away and then Te Aro would have a Councillor again.

Until then, the routine business of the council went on. 'Let me introduce our new treasurer,' the secretary said, indicating a woman with dark hair seated on the far side of the fake oak table. The applicant waved and gave Ann a cheerful smile. She inclined her head slightly in his direction.

'And here is the most important member of the interview panel,' he continued, as the door opened and another man entered. 'The Te Aro community archivist. He's who you'll be reporting to, if your application to become assistant archivist is successful, and I cannot indicate at this point whether it will or will not.'

The applicant stood and shook the newcomer's hand. The archivist, who was middle-aged and of medium height, wore a tweed jacket with worn elbows over an Iron Maiden concert T-shirt. He had large front teeth, a triangular face with a goatee beard, and gleaming yellow eyes. He looked a bit like a goat. He sat down, indicating to the applicant that he should remain standing, then he belched. The sound suggested that the archivist's interior spaces were larger than his body could encompass.

'So you want to be an archivist?' he said.

'Very much so.'

The archivist looked the applicant up and down for a minute before he spoke again. 'It is a great privilege to work in Te Aro Archive. The pay is low but the prestige'—he drew out the end of the word—'is considerable.'

'I understand that,' the applicant said.

'And the requirements for this job are very special. *Verrrrry* special.' He fluttered a piece of paper. 'The advertisement. It reads: "Entry-level position in local government. Successful applicant must be hard working, a fast learner and illiterate."'

The applicant nodded. 'That's right. That's me.'

'You're really illiterate?'

'I literally cannot read.'

'Then how,' the archivist smirked, 'did you read the ad?'

The applicant replied, 'A friend read it out to me.'

'What's this friend's name?'

'Immanuel.'

'How do you spell that?'

The applicant saw the trap. He smiled. 'I don't know.'

'Very good.' The archivist smiled back. He peered at the applicant down his round, goat-like nose and said, '*Verrry* good.'

The treasurer spoke up. 'Can I just say that an apprentice archivist who can't read makes no sense. Can I get that on the record?'

'So noted.' The secretary looked at the archivist. 'I've been wondering about that myself, but I didn't want to overstep my bounds. The Te Aro Charter clearly states that the archivist has sole discretion over the appointment of their apprentice. But I would also strongly advise against employing an illiterate archivist. What say you to that?'

'I say . . .' The archivist tapped his long, pointed fingernails on the table. 'That this illiterate is hired.'

'Magnificent isn't it.' The archivist led the applicant—now, officially, his new apprentice—into the shadow cast by the archive. It was a squat, windowless, concrete building on the far side of the square from the council offices. 'All of Te Aro's history is in here. All of its secrets. Its mysteries. Ten decades of stony sleep look down upon us.' The archivist sorted through the ring of keys that dangled from a chain on his belt. 'Some would die for the chance to glimpse inside these walls. One or two,' he added with an ominous look, holding up a key, 'would kill for it.'

He turned the lock.

Then he leaned his shoulder against the heavy wooden door and pushed, grunting. The door inched open and a cascade of papers and folders poured through the widening gap, spilling down the stairway. The door stuck. 'Don't just stand there,' the archivist snapped at the apprentice, 'help me.' The apprentice bent his shoulder to the task. Together they forced the door open and stood in the entrance to Te Aro Archive.

It was a long, gloomy room with a low ceiling. A faint, fouled light came in through a pair of dirty skylights. It lit up dozens of white metal shelves piled with boxes and books, which rose like cliffs from a sea of pages and cardboard. The sea of paper began just beyond the arc of the doorway, ankle deep, rising like a great wave to the back of the room where it towered over the shelves themselves.

'It needs a bit of a tidy-up,' the archivist explained. 'That's why you're here. There are a few too many rats' nests. We can hear them rustling and squeaking all the way over in the council buildings. The secretary is afraid they'll chew through the wiring and start a fire and burn the building down. I've stalled him for years, but now the new treasurer agrees with him. You know how women are about rats and fires. You've her to thank for the funding for your job.'

The archivist returned his attention to the pile. 'There are cockroaches too, and beetles. So everything in here needs stacking or trapping or poisoning. Be careful. And above all, be on guard for the archivist's greatest enemy.'

'Moths?'

'Researchers.' The archivist spat out the word. 'Journalists. Historians. Filth. This room'—he gestured at the boxes and mounds of papers; a sleek brown rat nosing along a shelf stopped as if to listen—'might contain anything. Anything at all. So long as no one knows what is in here, all things are possible. This is what gives archivists our power. But researchers *catalogue*.' He clasped the apprentice's arm, wrapping his strong, hairy fingers around it. 'They document. They publish. They rob the archive of its mystery, and diminish our power by increasing their own. Never let them in. Never.'

'You don't want anyone to read anything in this archive?'

'That's right.' His grip loosened. 'That's why I hired you. That's why I'm trusting you with the key to this building. 'Because of your special'—the archivist cupped the apprentice's chin with his thumb and forefinger, tilted his face up and beamed at him—'qualities, your blessed illiteracy, my archive will remain inviolate. Its secrets will remain secret. Its mysteries will remain mysterious. Let no one in here. Do you understand?'

'I do.'

'Then set to work. I'll come check on you in a week. Ah—' He stopped halfway through the door. 'What's your name?'

The apprentice told him. The archivist nodded and repeated the name. Then he was gone and Steve was alone with the rats and the beetles and the wave of paper rising out of sight into the gloom.

24

The plot against reality

At last.

Steve drew a deep breath into his lungs. He savoured the damp, rat-urine-scented air, then he let it all out with a primal grunt of triumph. He twirled and bowed at the duo of rats observing him from the shelf.

At last. Te Aro Archive. After all this time.

Steve's long journey here had begun when he first arrived in Te Aro. Back then he was just an undergraduate. He had taken a job at the university library over the summer, and his experiences there set him on the path to the forbidden world of Te Aro Archive.

Steve's first task that summer was to stocktake. He had to count all the books in the library, level by level. He started on the top floor—history and geology—and began counting. Book by book. Shelf by shelf. Row by row. But by the time he reached the second row, Steve was bored. By the third row, he was mutinous. How dare the librarians delegate such a dull, mind-numbing task to a man of Steve's unique gifts? What a waste of his phenomenal potential. It was an outrage. He wouldn't do it.

He couldn't tell the librarians that, of course, because then they wouldn't pay him. No. Instead he'd estimate the number. Simply count the books in a shelf, multiply that by the number of shelves in a row, the number of rows in an aisle and the number of aisles on a floor. That would give a roughly accurate estimate in a fraction of the time. Steve could spend the rest of the day sleeping in a toilet cubicle.

His plan did have one flaw. Steve also got bored counting the number of rows and aisles, and in the end he just guessed them too. So when he reported to his supervisor at the end of the day, his voice cracked and eyes bleary from his seven-hour nap, she compared his guess for the top floor with that of the previous year's stocktake, and found that it was out by several thousand.

'It's obvious what's happened here,' Steve replied, rolling his head to unkink his neck. 'This is a daunting task and last year's stocktaker obviously wasn't up for it. They must have guessed a number, so of course it doesn't match up to the actual count.'

'I did the stocktake last year,' the supervisor replied. Then she leaned forward and lowered her voice to a conspiratorial hush. 'You're right. I did just guess the numbers.'

Steve reflected on this as he walked home that night. Libraries were repositories of knowledge, of information. Yet they couldn't obtain basic information about the nature of the knowledge they held. It was impossible to count all of the books. Even if someone did so and the number was accurate, there was no way to know it. It would have to be verified, and any verification would surely be wrong. Steve nodded thoughtfully to himself as he absorbed this insight. He had learned something important about the world.

It was a lesson the Head Librarian herself had failed to master. She was a large woman with short hair and dangly earrings. Every Monday morning she addressed the staff with an inspirational speech impressing upon them the importance of their work. Human knowledge was a tapestry, she told them, and libraries were the thread knitting the tapestry together, connecting all the wisdom into a vast and beautiful whole. Steve shook his head in disbelief at her hubris. A tapestry of human wisdom? This woman couldn't even count her own books.

Steve finished the stocktake in record time, so he was promoted to the collection and cataloguing department. His responsibility was postgraduate publications. When students submitted a completed thesis or a doctorate to the library,

Steve entered it in the catalogue and shelved it.

Steve did not care for these postgraduate students. So proud of themselves and their accomplishments; so smug about their contributions to human thought. What became of all their endeavours? Nothing, Steve decided. To prove this point he carefully misspelled the names and titles of every piece of work submitted and he misshelved every item in the remotest reaches of the library. If knowledge was a tapestry it was tattered; a thing of scraps and holes.

Eventually the summer came to an end. Steve's contract was not renewed, despite his excellent performance record: the library's administrators had determined that the vast shortfall in books over the last year pointed to large-scale theft of texts, and they reallocated the funds to improve security. This too pleased Steve, although he was disappointed to lose access to the toilet in the closed stacks, a cosy room that no one else visited, where he could doze for hours listening to the rumble of the central heating, feeling the vast number of books in the uncountable shelves all around him and knowing that they represented both wisdom and entropy, knowledge and disinformation.

One of Steve's psychology courses that year involved fieldwork. 'Go out into the community,' the students were told. 'Find people who have been diagnosed with mental illnesses. Hear their stories. They have much to teach us.'

So he wandered around Aro Valley, pestering its homeless population and asking them to talk to him, or at least sign a form saying that they had so he could get course credit. But it was hard. Most of the vagrants in the valley were already the subjects of academic studies by sociologists and economists and anthropologists, and they'd signed non-competition clauses. Only one vagrant was unattached: a friendly but occasionally violent drunk called Strawberry. He was a ruddy-faced man with shoulder-length blond hair. He wore an orange hooded sweatshirt that reached down to his knees, and a pair of jandals. He lived beneath a stairway outside an abandoned shop, in an area he'd partitioned off with a wall of discarded amateur artworks: paintings of storm clouds and dead trees and melting children; giant dolphin sculptures.

'I don't sign contracts,' he told Steve, waving away his course form. 'But I can teach you a thing or two about life. Here.' He reached for Steve's hand. 'Put the tip of your finger between my teeth.'

Steve withdrew his hand and stepped behind a rusting trolley. 'Maybe later,' he demurred. 'Why don't you tell me your story first?'

'Smart kid.' Strawberry grinned, revealing a row of teeth filed down into fangs. He sat on the bottom step and began to talk.

He'd once had a job, Strawberry explained. And a house. A family. A life. He was a journalist right here in Te Aro. But he asked the wrong questions. Angered the wrong people.

'What happened?' Steve asked him.

In response, Strawberry pointed down the valley. 'You see that building?' He indicated a squat concrete structure on the far side of the park. 'That's Te Aro Archive. Everything that's happened in this valley is recorded in there. Every election. Every crime. Every secret. There are places like the archive everywhere. Libraries. Halls of Record. Bureaucracies. Data warehouses. They have dossiers. Databases. Files. They're supposed to contain information about the world, about us.' He swept his arm towards the buildings, the road, the valley, Steve himself. 'All of this. But somewhere along the way, the relationship reversed. The information no longer describes us. Now *we* describe *it*. If it changes, reality changes. You might think you own your own house, but if your bank's information about you changes'—he snapped his fingers—'you're out on the street. And if all our information disappears . . .' He lit a cigarette and uncrossed his legs, revealing that he wasn't wearing any shorts or underwear beneath his baggy sweater. 'Well, we disappear. That's what happened to me.'

Strawberry was right, Steve thought, as he made his way home to type up his interview notes. Information about reality dictated reality. His experiences in the library proved that. But if Steve could manipulate the university library, what was to stop some individual or group doing that on a massive scale? To cities? Nations? Countries? All of reality itself?

Nothing. It had happened. Steve knew, therefore it was happening; now, all around. And he might never prove that this conspiracy was real. By its very nature there would be no evidence; indeed, the lack of evidence was irrefutable proof of this conspiracy's existence.

Steve decided to search anyway. The next day he went looking for Strawberry to find out more about his nonexistent past. But Strawberry was gone. The official story was that he had gone into the Capital and bitten off a policeman's fingertip and was then committed to a secure psychiatric unit but Steve knew the truth. He'd been locked away because he knew too much.

Next, Steve tried Te Aro Archive. A sign on the door read 'No Admittance to Anyone Under Any Circumstances'. Steve phoned the council and spoke to the archivist, many times: the archive was always closed, and there was always an excuse: earthquake strengthening, asbestos, radiation leaks.

Steve continued with his studies. He finished his honours degree and began his doctorate. But he never forgot Strawberry, or the archive, or the plot against reality, which was everywhere and nowhere. He made a list of all the thinkers and visionaries who might have known about the plot. They could never say anything out loud, of course, but they hinted at it in their works. Painters. Poets. Psychics. Steve had his contacts at the library set alerts on books by these individuals. Anyone reading certain combinations of these texts would be flagged to Steve's attention.

Then, about a year ago, Verity's name tripped one of these alarms. Steve made contact with her hapless boyfriend, Danyl. He gathered intelligence about Verity. He went to her house while she was out and watched daytime TV with Danyl. He ate her leftover food. He went to the opening of her photography exhibition, and when he heard her describe her work, all of Steve's suspicions were validated. Verity was involved in a plot against reality.

Shortly after this discovery, Steve's life was rocked by a series of catastrophes. Verity vanished. Danyl was taken into custody and sent out of the valley. The cult that Steve was studying for his doctoral work disintegrated, and Steve himself was dismissed from his department, his enemies on the university ethics committee picking their moment to strike while Steve was distracted by all this turmoil.

That's how Steve found himself in the faculty office, flanked by two security guards waiting to escort him from the campus, while an associate dean gave him career advice. Steve's teaching methods were unacceptable, the associate dean explained, but the university had generously decided not to file a police complaint, so Steve could still consider a career as a secondary school teacher, and the faculty would provide a reference. Was he interested?

Steve was not. He wasn't listening to the associate dean. His eyes had drifted to the noticeboard outside the glass office, and an ad in the Situations Vacant that began 'Illiterate Wanted'. The ad bore the logo of Te Aro Community Council.

And here Steve was, at long last. He waited for the archivist's footsteps to die away. Then he picked up a large cardboard box and blockaded the door with it. Best to take precautions.

He picked up a random folder from the pile at his feet, blew the dust and mouse droppings off it and read: 'Minutes of Te Aro Council Meeting: All Hallows Eve, 1982.' He sighed a deep satisfied sigh and began to read.

Steve wasn't sure what he was looking for. He knew there was something wrong with the world, something rotten at its core. He'd been lied to; everyone had. But he wasn't sure who had lied about what, or why. But there were answers in the archive and he would find them.

He spent the first week cleaning. Before he could learn anything he needed to impose some order; teach the rodents and beetles who was boss. He worked his way through the sea of papers to the first row of shelves, sorting and stacking and poisoning as he went. The archivist checked on him from time to time, monitoring his progress, but these visits became less frequent. In the second week they stopped altogether.

That's when Steve's research began. He smuggled pens and notebooks into the building. He read minutes and reports. He scoured boundary maps. He studied the findings of property inspectors, engineers and dowsers, all commissioned by the council for various reports over the years.

He learned many things. He learned that the geology of the Aro Valley was very different from that of the surrounding region. The bedrock beneath most of the Capital was composed of strata of recent volcanic rock, but the earth beneath Te Aro consisted of ancient crystalline basement sediments laid down in the Precambrian Era. This meant that the Aro Valley was one of the last surviving parts of Vaalbara, the Earth's mysterious and sinister first supercontinent. No one knew what had happened to Vaalbara, or how and why the fragments of it comprising the bedrock below the valley had survived the tectonic shifts of the eons. Was this related to the plot? Or was it just a distraction? He marked the geological surveys as suspicious but interesting, and moved on.

Steve also discovered who owned most of the property in Te Aro. Although the area was slowly gentrifying, most of the houses, still old and poorly maintained, were owned by slumlords. The wealthiest of these slumlords had died many years ago, Steve learned, but his death was kept secret because the mad old man bequeathed all of his estate to a handsome cabbage tree not far from the public toilets on Aro Street. Did that mean the public owned the land? No one knew. What happened if the tree died, or was killed by its angry tenants, of whom there were many—for, in truth, the tree was an indifferent landlord. No one knew the answer to that, either, and as property values in the valley soared, the tree grew ever more wealthy and powerful.

Much else that Steve read was dull. Lists of expenses. Transcripts of councillors bickering over what to name public benches or alleyways. Trivia. And none of it, not even the revelations about the cabbage tree or the Vaalbara supercontinent, brought Steve closer to what he was really looking for. Proof of the plot against reality.

By the end of his third week as apprentice archivist, he was halfway across the room and the frozen wave of papers and folders stood at head height. It needed to be barricaded with boxes and braces jerry-rigged from broken shelves. It creaked and groaned as Steve laid out grids of documents across the floor beneath its shadow, trying to make sense of the chaotic bureaucratic intricacies of sixty years of community business.

He learned about feuds. Love affairs. Pacts and betrayals. Yet he was no closer to the secret. It was in here, somewhere. Hidden in some box, sunk deep beneath the paper sea. But he had yet to find a hint. Or maybe he'd found it and passed it over? Maybe there was a story here, but it was too scattered to read.

Steve rearranged the papers into chronological order. Year by year. There were a few ancient, yellowed documents from the 1940s. Then two large piles from the fifties. With the sixties came an explosion of documentation. And the early seventies were even worse.

By then Steve was into his fifth week. His fingers were

lacerated with paper cuts and mouse bites. His lungs rattled with mucus—an infection from breathing in the mould that layered the papers at the bottom of the great wave. Steve was on the verge of giving up, of abandoning his dream, when he found his first clue. Or, rather, didn't find it.

1974 was missing.

It manifested as a great gap. A pile of papers from 1973. An even greater pile from 1975. From the year in between: nothing. Not even a community newsletter.

That was strange. Maybe the entire year waited in the great unsorted pile beyond the barricade? But Steve doubted it. Perhaps the secret he was looking for was not information, but the absence of it. Now that he thought back through the tens of thousands of pages and millions of words he'd read since he entered the archive, there were many inexplicable gaps. Pages cut from reports or newsletters. Maps with sections torn from them. Minutes redacted.

Steve had thought this was just random entropy. Mice. Insects. Bureaucrats. Time. But now he saw a pattern. There were clusters of spaces. Someone had gone through and deliberately erased traces of . . . something. Whatever it was, it began in the early 1970s, and peaked with the redaction of an entire year.

He kept searching, invigorated. A forgotten secret was one thing, but a deliberately concealed secret—a mystery—was the best secret of all. He climbed the barricade. He fought and destroyed the last and greatest of the rats' nests. He found tiny clues: sentences that weren't quite blacked out; shreds of maps; indexes to destroyed reports. Gaps within the gaps. He began to piece things together.

Something had happened in Te Aro in 1974.

It involved a man named Matthias Ogilvy. Ogilvy was a property developer. Politically connected. He bought a large tract of land somewhere in the valley. He worked with the government in the Capital to make great changes to Te Aro.

Widen the roads. Build a commercial district. State housing. Tenement buildings. A commercial development on his land. He would upgrade the entire infrastructure to support it all. There was outrage—town meetings, protests—but the plans went ahead anyway. Then, in late 1974, something happened. Someone vanished. Ogilvy cancelled his plans. The government abandoned its urban renewal scheme and the valley remained the way it was.

And there the record ended. Steve continued to search for that one clue that would explain everything or, at least, tell him where to search next. Finally, in his seventh week at the archive, with winter drawing near and rain dripping through holes in the roof, he found it.

It was a box. It had gotten damp at some stage and then dried, and the bottom was wrinkled and warped. Steve could tell just by lifting it that the box was empty.

He opened it anyway and looked inside. There were ink stains on the base, and just at the edge were words transferred from a wet document. Steve turned the box around, trying to make them out, but they were too blurred, too faded. All he could make out were a few words. It was a news story written by a man named Jacob Strawberry, about a place called Threshold.

25

The secret archive

'Is there a second archive? A secret archive?'

'Eh?' The archivist frowned. He sat at his desk in the council building, smoking pot from a cheap plastic bong and watching moon-landing conspiracy videos on the internet. It was late afternoon. The shadows were long. The only other council staffer left in the building was the new treasurer, whispering with her horrible young mathematics student. Steve lowered his voice and leaned closer to the archivist.

'A woman knocked on the door to the archive today,' he said. 'A historian. She wanted to do some research.' He held up his hands as the archivist's bloodshot eyes went white with fear. 'Relax. I told her we'd sprayed the interior of the building for bugs, that it couldn't be re-entered for thirty-six months.'

The archivist relaxed back into his chair. 'Good lad,' he murmured. 'Quick thinking.'

'But then she told me, "The documents I need are in the second Te Aro Archive." That got me to wondering if we had some kind of . . . I don't know . . . second archive?'

The archivist tugged at his goatee. He asked, 'What did this woman look like?'

'Medium height,' Steve replied. 'Inquisitive. Persistent. Troublesome. Brown hair.'

'What documents did she want?'

'She wouldn't say.'

'Did she mention—?' The archivist hesitated. He scrutinised Steve's face, obviously speculating how far he could trust his apprentice. Steve adopted his most cheerful, oblivious grin. Reassured, the archivist asked, 'Did she mention anything about reality?'

Steve's face remained impassive. 'Reality. Reality. Let me think. She did . . . talk about existence a little bit.'

'Aha.' The archivist snapped his fingers. 'You were right to bring this to me. Alert me immediately if you see this historian again. And tell no one else of this.'

'Of course.' Steve glanced over at the treasurer then leaned close to the archivist. 'Is it true then? Is there a second archive?'

The archivist licked his teeth and said, 'Of course not.'

Darkness. Rain. Steve.

He hid in the shadow cast by the climbing frame that loomed over the crèche's non-competitive playground. Waiting. Watching.

It didn't take long. The door to the council offices opened and the archivist emerged. He looked about: suspicious, paranoid—but he didn't see Steve. He scuttled over to the Councillor's Chamber and looked about again before slipping a key into the lock. He opened the door and entered.

Steve nodded to himself in grim satisfaction. His theory was correct. The documents missing from the archive hadn't been lost, or destroyed. They'd been hidden in a second, secret archive, and the archivist's fear of Steve's 'inquisitive historian' had led him right to it.

The archivist wasn't supposed to be in the Councillor's Chamber. No one was. According to the Te Aro Charter, the chamber was inviolate until a new Councillor was elected at the end of the week.

Like most psychologists Steve could move through the darkness without making a sound. He slipped over the crèche fence and across the quad to the lit window. The curtains in the chamber were drawn but they had huge holes in them where moths had eaten their way through, so Steve looked directly into the room.

It had wood-panelled walls and a polished wooden desk.

The archivist stood in the corner next to a large closet. He was trying one key after another in the lock. None of them worked. His angry muttering was audible through the glass. Eventually he found the right key and opened the closet, revealing a row of cowboy outfits and, below them, a filing cabinet with a combination lock. He twirled the dial a few times and tried to open it. It didn't budge. He neighed to himself in satisfaction then locked the closet.

Steve slipped away. He walked home, thinking, planning; his hyper-accelerated brain considered all the possibilities. By the time he'd splashed his way down the muddy path to his front door, he knew what he had to do.

Next morning he was late to work.

The archive was now a neat, orderly place. The giant wave of paper was gone. Everything had been arranged: assimilated into the shelves or the great piles of boxes between them. In the centre of the floor was a clear space where Steve had partially assembled a giant aerial map of Te Aro.

He blockaded the door, as always, then set to work. He was trying to complete the map then link the property lots to the location of the land that Ogilvy had once owned. That way he could pinpoint the location of the legendary Threshold development.

This wasn't easy. Everything to do with Ogilvy had been erased or moved to the secret archive. But Steve was finding patterns in the gaps: properties that existed during the 1960s then vanished in the early seventies. He pieced the maps together: yellowed faded aerial photos intersecting with bright satellite imagery. Gradually the entire valley emerged—except for a blank space high up the valley where tree-covered hills crowded around a sloping field that wasn't there, and a remote section of Aro Street that vanished into nothing before reconnecting with another photo and winding up into the gloomy eastern hills. Whatever Threshold was, and whatever happened in it, it was all in that gap; that absence in space and time.

Something moved in the recesses of the archive.

Steve froze. His senses were attuned to the rustling of rodents and insects, but they were all dead now. This was something larger. It came from the far corner.

The archivist materialised out of the gloom and walked towards Steve, who sat cross-legged beside his map. The archivist walked across it, his feet crunching on the ancient papers and photographs.

'Well, well.' He stood before Steve and folded his arms, waiting. Steve smiled pleasantly and said nothing.

The archivist filled the silence. 'Nobody knows about the secret archive. The Sheriff knew, but he never breathed a word of it to anyone before he died. The secretary knows the combination to the filing cabinet, but he doesn't know what's in there. So I asked myself, "How would some historian know of its existence?"'

'There was no historian. I made it up.'

'Ha!' He pointed an accusatory finger at Steve. 'You admit it. You lied. I've been checking on you, lad.' He circled Steve, who remained stationary in his cross-legged position. 'While you've been in here researching'—he spat out the word—'I've done a little research of my own.' He whipped a piece of paper from the pocket of his blazer and shook it in Steve's face. 'In the resumé you submitted to the secretary when you applied for this job, you claim to have worked at the The Royal Library of Ashurbanipal. I tried to call them to ask about you, and learned that it was destroyed by a Babylonian army in 700 BC.' He flipped to another page. 'You supplied a reference from the Antarctic Museum of Indigenous History. I phoned them too, and they'd never heard of you. You're a fraud, Steve. And you can read. You're a stinking, reading literate. Admit it.'

'It's true.' There was little point in denying it. The archivist clenched his fists and his teeth at Steve's confession.

'You are dismissed from your position as my apprentice archivist,' he said. 'You are banned from this building for life, and after the election when we have a new Councillor, I will make it my goal to gain access to the secret archive and burn every document inside it.'

Steve listened to this speech with good-tempered patience. Then he said, 'I'm sorry I was late this morning.'

'I don't care about that.' The archivist's yellow eyes flashed. 'Didn't you hear what I said? You're fired.'

'Don't you want to know why I took so long to get here?'

'I don't give a damn.' The eyes narrowed. 'All right, why?'

'I was talking to the council secretary. Going through the paperwork.'

'What paperwork?'

Steve took a photocopied document from his jacket pocket. The archivist snatched it from his hand and scanned it, his eyes flicking back to Steve, until he reached the midpoint of the letter. His pale pink ears flattened against his skull and his nostrils flared. 'No,' he whispered. 'You can't.'

'I'm afraid so,' Steve said. 'I'm standing for council. And I'm running unopposed. I'm going to be the new Councillor of Te Aro.'

26

The campaign

But Steve did not run unopposed. Two more candidates announced their campaigns later that day and that year's battle for Te Aro Council was the fiercest in living memory.

The first of Steve's opponents to declare was Kim, an eminent imaginary languages poet. Kim was a jolly spherical man with shoulder-length grey hair combed very straight and a long, neatly kept moustache and beard worn in the manner of Confucius. Kim was an eloquent speaker in many languages, but none of them were English or, indeed, any other language or dialect known to anyone else on Earth. His campaign posters consisted of Kim's beaming face with the slogan 'Procks! Terples Mas exterples!' below it in Gothic red lettering.

Steve was confident he could beat Kim. He spent a whole day touring the local businesses, promising them lighter regulations and tax relief, promises he intended to keep if the council ever gained the power to tax or regulate local business. That evening, he gave a speech in Aro Park. It was well attended by many pigeons and several people.

'People of Te Aro,' he called across the park. A pigeon cooed and a couple having sex under a nearby tree halted their coitus to listen to him. 'I promise you something wonderful, the one thing that no one else can possibly offer.' He hesitated; a gaggle of curious passersby who had stopped to watch waited as he held up his hand and drew out the silence. 'I give you . . .' He touched his fingertips to his chest. 'Myself. Steve.' Successful political campaigns had catchy slogans, and now Steve's voice rose to a roar as he ended his speech with his carefully crafted phrase. 'I promise you a sensible, friendly Steve for a sensible, friendly future.'

Scattered applause. Steve bowed and stepped down.

After the speech he talked to a group of young men who were members of a libertarian commune. They were worried about religious persecution. Steve pledged that under him the council would protect them, but if they voted for someone else he could not guarantee their lives. They shook his hand and pledged their votes and moved on.

A good day. Steve felt confident. He would defeat Kim and become Te Aro Councillor. He would see inside the secret archive.

There were four more days until the election.

He had the rest of his campaign mapped out in his head. Tomorrow he would meet the editor of the Te Aro Community Volunteer Newsletter for coffee and tell them—off the record— that Kim was involved in the Holloway Road scandal that inflicted so much damage on the valley. This wasn't true—in fact, Steve was heavily involved in the scandal himself—but Kim's inability to speak English left him defenceless against a smear campaign. Steve rubbed his hands together with glee.

On his way to the Community Hall to see if the secretary had set a time for the election debate, he stopped outside the council offices. Mounted above the doorway was a board listing the date of the election and the names of the candidates. That morning only Steve's name was there. Kim's name had been added at lunchtime. And now there was a third name on the board. A third contender for council. A new opponent.

They called themself Gorgon.

'It's an outrage!'

Steve leaned over the secretary's desk. The secretary sat in his swivel chair, his face a few centimetres from Steve's. He was unruffled. 'I don't understand your concern, Steve. Gorgon is a legitimate candidate.'

'She's not real,' Steve argued. 'She's a myth. A monster from the valley's collective unconscious. The parents of Te Aro use it to frighten their children. "Do your pranayama breathing meditations or Gorgon will get you." The candidates for Councillor have to be actual living people. It says so right there in the Charter.' He pointed to the document hanging on the wall behind the secretary's desk. The seventh clause clearly prohibited fictional or imaginary beings from standing for office.

'But Gorgon is real.'

'Did Gorgon come to this office? Produce a birth certificate? What did they look like?'

'I didn't handle that registration,' the secretary replied. 'The archivist did.' He pointed to the goat-faced man, who sat at his desk watching the exchange, his hands behind his head, his long thin tongue poking out between his teeth. 'And he verified Gorgon's existence, didn't you, archivist?'

'That's right, Mr Secretary.' The archivist turned to Steve. 'Gorgon is real. Verrrry real. You have roused it to anger. Prepare yourselves,' the archivist warned them both, 'for fates you cannot imagine and suffering beyond comprehension.'

'You see?' The secretary clapped his palms on his desk. 'Everything's fine. It's a choice of visions. A contest of ideas. Democracy!'

Steve needed backers. Powerful allies. He went to the Earthenware Café and entreated with the owner, a powerful member of the valley's gay and lesbian community, to seek her support.

'I'm sorry, Steve.' She set an espresso down in front of him and shook her head. 'I don't know anything about Gorgon except their name. But in Greek mythology, Gorgon symbolises primal darkness. Mystery. Devouring sexuality. These values speak to my community's everyday values.'

'I stand for all of those things too,' Steve pleaded. 'And I also stand for balanced budgets and sensible solutions.' But the café owner did not reply. She was pro-Gorgon.

Three days until the election. Steve got up early. He reminded himself that in politics image was everything, so he brushed his teeth, shaved and dressed. His plan was to go around the local businesses again. Warn them that Gorgon was a radical who would cripple them with regulation, bureaucracy and red tape. There weren't many business owners in Te Aro, but they were pretty much the only people who actually voted in the elections. So long as Steve had them on his side he'd be fine.

But when he turned onto Aro Street the first thing he saw was a small crowd gathered around the video store admiring a black spiral spray-painted on the side of the building. Beneath the spiral, dripping black letters spelled: GORGON.

Steve saw the owner of the video store on the edge of the crowd. He hurried over to him.

'It happened last night,' the owner explained, pointing at the graffiti. He was a thin man with a bowl of light brown hair hanging down over his face.

'It's illegal advertising,' Steve said. 'Why don't you clean it off?'

'People seem to like it.' The owner gestured at the crowd. 'Maybe it'll be good for business. Maybe this Gorgon knows what they're doing.'

'Nobody even knows who Gorgon is,' Steve protested. 'Does Gorgon even exist?'

'I grew up here in the valley,' said an older woman standing beside them. She had grey hair and wore a fake fur coat over a sundress. 'When we were kids, we sang a rhyme about Gorgon. *Hide me. Blind me. Or Gorgon will find me.*'

'What does it mean?' Steve asked.

The woman creased her brow. 'It was something to do

with someone who disappeared a long time ago, down in the catacombs.'

'Who disappeared? When?'

'A girl, I think. I don't remember when. I'm pretty drunk.'

'So what is Gorgon?'

The video store owner said, 'When I was a kid, we thought Gorgon was a terrible monster that destroyed everything it encountered. Now, I don't know much about politics,' he admitted, 'but maybe that's the kind of leader Te Aro needs right now.'

Steve went home and spent the rest of the morning designing leaflets on his laptop. Decency. Family. Values. These were things that mattered to voters, even in Te Aro. So he Photoshopped a smiling image of himself onto a picture of laughing children and typed beneath it in a large, friendly light-blue font: *Safer Sensible Friendly Communities*. He had forty pieces of paper left in his printer and no money to buy more, so he printed out forty copies of his image and spent the afternoon wandering the valley looking for houses where families probably lived and slipping his pamphlet into their letterboxes.

The next morning there were leaflets in every mailbox in Te Aro. Nobody had seen who'd delivered them. They were totally black on both sides. The paper itself felt oddly heavy and cold, and all who touched them experienced headaches and dizziness. Everyone knew they'd come from Gorgon.

Steve spent most of the day at home. The Te Aro Community Volunteer Newsletter had run a vicious smear story against him alleging his involvement in the controversial Holloway Road scandal. The allegations were sourced to 'senior staffers' in the Gorgon campaign.

~

Election day.

It was the autumnal equinox. There was early-morning frost; ice in the puddles. A chill mist hung about the valley. People saw malign, ominous shapes in the fog, and everyone agreed that this was a good omen for Gorgon.

Steve spent the day getting the vote. He toured all of the cults that were friendly to him and reminded their leaders to command their disciples to vote Steve, and to do so multiple times. 'Make them stagger their votes throughout the day so the scrutineers don't get suspicious.'

Then the sun set behind the western hills and the polls closed. Steve watched as the council secretary ordered the ballot box to be sealed and led the Grand Druid and the Chief Executive of the Te Aro Anarchist Organisation into his offices to count the votes. Anxiety ate at him. He'd done everything he could to win and committed voter fraud on a massive scale—but would it be enough to defeat Gorgon? He just didn't know.

By midnight the Community Hall was filled. A sea of people stretched from wall to wall. Steve and Kim sat on the stage waiting for the result. Gorgon's chair remained empty.

Then the council secretary forced his way through the crowd, which hushed when he stood on a chair and waved his arms for silence. He flourished a piece of paper in his hand. 'The votes have been counted and checked,' he shouted. 'And the results are decisive. This was not a narrow win. This was not a comfortable victory. This was a landslide. The new Councillor of Te Aro Community Council is'—he glanced at his piece of paper to double-check—'Gorgon!'

Before the crowd could react, a sudden, savage gust of wind shook the building. The double doors at the back of the hall boomed open. The lights flickered and died, plunging the crowd into darkness.

A red light flared up in the square outside. A man screamed and the whole hall gasped. The stench of smoke and gasoline filled the room as sheets of flames criss-crossed the square, casting a hellish glare on the crowd. From his vantage point on the stage, Steve could see that the fire on the square had a pattern.

A spiral.

There was another long moment of shocked silence, then the archivist appeared beside the doorway. The flames danced in his yellow eyes; he gestured at the doorway and the darkness and fire beyond it. 'Residents of Te Aro,' he cried out, 'I give you—Gorgon!'

The flames surged. The crowd cheered.

27

Clues

Steve took his crowbar from the pocket of his overcoat. He stood on tiptoes and gently smashed in a window in the back wall of the Councillor's Chamber.

Steve did not believe in defeat. Yes, he'd lost the election. Technically, if you wanted to split hairs, Gorgon had 'defeated' Steve. But why had Steve fought in the election in the first place? To get access to the secret archive. And he could still do that, just not by democratic means. And what better time to act than now, in Gorgon's moment of triumph when the rest of the council staff were distracted by the post-election celebration and the bonfire in the quad and the screams of people whose hair had caught on fire? Steve cared about knowledge, not political power. Now he would obtain that knowledge, and once he had it he would use it to bring down Gorgon and seize all that power for himself.

Steve's crowbar was his most prized possession. It was made of high-carbon steel. It gleamed with a silver-coloured enamel coating. It was the length of his forearm and able to be slipped into the pocket of his overcoat; it was very light, but strong enough to snap doors from their frames like kindling. No psychologist had a better friend than their crowbar. Steve had, in a moment of extravagance, etched the name of his crowbar into its shaft, in an elegant flowing script. *Lightbringer.*

He used the curved hook of Lightbringer to clear the last few shards of glass from the frame, then he threw a scrap of carpet over the rim and hauled himself into the chamber.

He kept low. Holes in the curtains looked directly out on the quad, where celebrating Te Aro residents danced around the spiral-shaped fire, howling and screaming with abandon.

He crawled across the dusty carpet to the corner of the room. He wedged Lightbringer between the closet door and its frame and gave an expert twist. The door popped open, revealing the cowboy uniforms. He could just make out the bulge where the filing cabinet was hidden. Lightbringer would make short work of its lock: then the secret archive would be his, and finally, he would have answers. He'd solve the mystery of Ogilvy. Of Threshold. Of the plot against reality. And he'd know what happened in 1974.

He parted the cowboy outfits. The cabinet was there, but the steel around the combination lock was buckled. It had been forced.

Steve was too late. The filing drawers were empty. The archive had already been stolen.

The secretary frowned. 'Stolen by whom?'

Steve stood in the door to the Councillor's Chamber, looking at the broken window and the smashed, empty filing cabinet. Steve stood behind him. 'Stolen by the archivist,' he replied.

'The archivist? Impossible. He knows the Charter forbids entry to this room.'

Steve whispered in the secretary's ear. 'I saw him. I happened to be wandering behind the building, and I witnessed the archivist smash the window with a crowbar and climb inside. That's when I came to get you.'

The fire in the quad was out and all the revellers were gone. It was just Steve, the secretary, and Kim, the other failed election candidate, who stood beside Steve and said sadly, 'Bretec quagnet.'

'I don't understand this.' The secretary looked tired. Lost. 'Why would the archivist break in through the window? He has a key.'

'That's the genius of it,' Steve countered. 'If he'd used the key to get in, we'd have known it was him. He didn't, so we don't, and that's how we can be sure it was.'

'Yes, that makes perfect sense. But what did he take?'

'A secret archive,' Steve explained. 'Documents removed from the old archive and hidden in the Councillor's cabinet. I believe these documents are proof of a sinister plot within this valley.'

'But he's the archivist,' the secretary replied. 'Why would he steal the secret archive? And why tonight?'

'Let's find out,' Steve replied. 'We'll hunt him down.'

'I can't hunt anyone down. I have to stay here and wait for Gorgon. He or she is now the rightfully elected Councillor of Te Aro.'

'There is no Gorgon.'

'What?'

'Vertek?' Kim looked astonished.

'It's a conspiracy,' Steve explained. 'A plot. The archivist is in on it. So was the old Councillor. Something happened in this valley in 1974. All evidence of it was removed from the archive and hidden in here. The archivist knew I was looking for it, and that if I won the election I'd uncover the plot. So he created a fake candidate to run against me and used Gorgon's strong brand recognition as an evil mythological creature to trick the people into voting for it. That's why Gorgon hasn't appeared to celebrate its victory. Because it doesn't exist. So let's search the archivist's desk.'

The secretary looked bewildered. 'For what?'

'I have no idea,' Steve replied. 'But whatever we find is bound to be incriminating.'

The drawer sprang open in a shower of wood splinters.

Steve used the tip of his crowbar to search through the debris inside it. The secretary gave Lightbringer a funny look. 'Why did you have that in your pocket?'

'I'm a psychologist,' Steve explained. The drawer contained pens, a stapler, a bag of pot, obsolete computer peripherals. 'And what's this?' He picked up a thick roll of cash tucked in the back corner. 'That's a lot of money for someone on an archivist's salary.'

The secretary peered at it. 'That's not real money,' he said. 'Look. The denomination is n+1. And the symbol on it is a spiral.'

'An alternative system of currency,' Steve breathed. 'This conspiracy is more diabolical than I thought.'

'What do you mean?'

'I'll show you. Do you have any cash?'

The secretary produced a five-dollar note. Steve held it next to the spiral dollar. 'Which of these is worth more?'

'The real one.'

'Why?'

'It's a form of social contract,' the secretary replied. 'The note is worthless, but we all agree to believe that it's worth something because it's a very convenient symbol of value.'

'It is a symbol,' Steve agreed, disappointed that the secretary's answer was so cogent. 'It's a pointer to other things, like value and trust, and they point back to money. That is what reality is. A network of symbols and pointers. Masks behind masks. These people,' he flapped the spiral dollar, 'the archivist and his co-conspirators, they want to attack those symbols. They want to attack reality itself. We have to stop them. But first we have to find them.'

'Blet,' said Kim, behind them. 'Klo bey blet reware.' He was flipping through a large hardback book that he'd picked up from beside the archivist's computer monitor. He opened it to the inside cover and displayed it to Steve and the secretary.

'Tnex.'

It was a book on counterfeiting. There was a large black stamp beneath the title on the first page:

Beneath the stamp was a picture of a spiral.

'The symbol of Gorgon,' Steve said gritted his teeth and spoke in a low growl. 'Proof of the archivist's complicity. This election was a fraud. And, according to the Te Aro Charter'—he indicated the document on the far wall—'as runner-up, I am the rightful new Councillor.'

'Actually,' the secretary gave an apologetic cough, 'Kim was runner-up. He came second. You came last.'

Kim said, 'Blego!'

Steve took a second to absorb this unhappy news, then said, 'But Kim abdicates his position to me. Right, Kim?'

'Ea.' Kim shook his head vigorously, frowning, and made a slashing motion with his hand. 'Kanb ea!'

'There,' Steve said. 'You see? Now, as de facto Councillor of Te Aro, I order you both to accompany me to the nameless alley.' He slapped his crowbar against his open palm. 'It's time to do a little book shopping.'

28

Gorgon

Steve kicked open the door to the bookshop and stepped through it, Lightbringer raised, ready to swing at any archivist or bookshop clerk who came at him.

But the entrance wasn't guarded. Beyond the door was a small clear space with a table, cash register and rocking chair; beyond that were wooden shelves stretching from the floor to the low, dimly lit ceiling and radiating out into the unseen reaches of the room. It was impossible to tell how large the space was, or if any enemies lurked out there in the darkness. Sound in the room was muted: their footfalls on the bare concrete were swallowed by the thousands of books.

Steve's hearing was far more powerful than that of most humans. He listened, tuning out the sounds of Kim and the secretary, who had followed him; he tuned out the hum of the lights overhead, water hissing in distant pipes, the central heating of the building. And out there, just at the edge of the audible spectrum he heard something: voices in the distance and between the voices an odd sound: a repetitive thumping, like the beating of the bookshop's dark and musty heart.

He whispered to Kim and the secretary. 'This way.' He led them into the shelves, towards the sounds, his senses on high alert. The thumping grew louder. Steve came to a fork in the path through the books. He turned left, then cursed as he tripped and fell. He landed on something soft. A person? He wasn't sure, so he bit into it. The thing did not scream. And it didn't taste like a person. He unclenched his jaw and pushed himself up onto his knees.

A mattress. He'd fallen on a mattress. No—a whole pile of mattresses. Thin, foam ones; dozens of them. And beyond them lay another pile, and another.

Steve clambered over them and stepped onto another path through the shelves. He was very close to the thumping noise now, and he could hear the voices. Two women: a low murmur back and forth. The thumping sounded like something being dropped, picked up and dropped again, over and over.

He turned and signalled to Kim and the secretary to go down the other row, circle around and come at the voices from the opposite side to Steve. They gave the thumbs-up sign and crawled over the mattresses to him, ignoring his gestures while he waved at them and mouthed, 'No! No!'

They refused to turn back, and the group continued on down another row of shelves stocked not with books but with large cardboard boxes. Steve paused under a fluorescent light and checked the box labels. Some of them were filled with blankets. Others contained syringes and adult nappies. The final shelf in the row was empty except for three plastic trays filled with hundreds of blue envelopes packed in together neatly. Steve opened one of the envelopes. Inside he found a map, half of which showed the Aro Valley, the rest of which depicted a vast and bewildering labyrinth.

The thumping came from just beyond the last shelf. Steve took a breath. He nodded at Kim and the secretary. He stepped out into the light.

It was an open space extending to the concrete walls at the back of the room. There were boxes everywhere. The thumping echoing through the room was the sound of two women taking books from the shelves and dropping them into the boxes. They stopped when Steve appeared. He looked them up and down and said to the closer of the two, 'Verity?'

'Steve?'

'Well,' said Steve. 'Well. Well. Well.' He strolled towards the women, twirling his crowbar like a ringmaster menacing a troupe of mutinous clowns. 'So the conspiracy is revealed.'

'What are you doing here?'

'Why, I'm looking for Gorgon.'

'Gorgon?' Verity cast a concerned glance at the second woman, who gave a tiny shrug. Verity turned back to Steve and said, 'She's busy.'

'She?' Steve looked amused. 'Tell her she has official visitors.'

Verity sat back on her knees. She looked hot from her work. She picked up a bottle of water and drank from it. The second woman spoke; Steve recognised her now. It was Eleanor, Verity's friend who owned the Dolphin Café. 'We're busy too,' she snapped. 'Beat it, deadbeat.'

'You have to go,' Verity added. 'Now. Please.'

Steve refused to acknowledge her absurd request and snapped, 'There is no Gorgon, is there? You and the archivist made it all up. You faked her.'

Verity looked genuinely confused. 'Why would we do that?'

'You know why.' The stolen archive was probably right here somewhere, hidden in one of the boxes, Steve thought. But which one? There were hundreds. 'You have something,' he said. 'Something we want. Something very valuable.'

Verity and the archivist both glanced towards a mound of boxes stacked against the wall. Steve calculated the intersecting angles of their gaze and identified an ordinary box on the top of the pile. So: that was the secret archive. It was smaller than he'd expected. And, now that he inspected it, he noticed a faint blue glow emanating from a tear in the cardboard. Why would the secret archive glow?

'We don't have anything for you, Steve. And you're trespassing. Get out. The bookshop is closed.'

'Oh, but I'm not trespassing. I happen to be the new Te Aro Councillor. I can go anywhere I want and do anything I want.'

'That's not true,' the secretary said quickly. 'The role is mostly ceremonial.'

'What's more,' Steve continued, raising his voice to drown out any future unhelpful comments from the secretary, 'I can impound property and belongings. All of these boxes are now the property of the Te Aro Council Subcommittee for Public Safety.'

'The what?'

'So either we search through all of these boxes until we find what we're looking for,' Steve said to Verity, 'or you turn the secret archive over to us now and we all find out whatever big mystery is hidden inside it.'

'What secret archive?' Verity looked even more confused, but Eleanor did not. Comprehension was dawning in her eyes. Steve pointed at her. 'Ask your accomplice there. She knows.'

Verity turned. Eleanor hesitated, then said to her, 'About ten years ago, Gorgon ordered the old Councillor—the Sheriff— to destroy all the records . . .' She licked her lips and glanced at Steve. 'The records of what happened at Threshold. Last week we learned that the Sheriff disobeyed. Instead he hid the records in a safe in the closet in his chamber.'

Verity looked wary. 'And now they've vanished? Where are they?'

'I don't know,' said Eleanor nervously. 'The archivist didn't take them. He's at Threshold.'

'Well if he didn't steal them, and this idiot didn't take them' —Verity flicked her hand at Steve—'that only leaves . . .'

An expression of dread came over Eleanor's face. 'The Adversary.'

Steve said, 'The who?'

Verity nodded. 'And now the Adversary knows about Ogilvy and Threshold. They'll figure out what's beneath the valley.'

'Hey? Hello? Excuse me?' Steve tapped his crowbar against a shelf. The sound rang out in. 'Remember me? Are you saying you don't have the archive? You expect me to believe that?'

Verity turned to him. 'I know it doesn't look like it'—she gestured at the boxes of books—'but what we're doing down here is the most important thing in the whole world right now. Someone is trying to stop us. We don't know who they are;

we just know they're very smart and very ruthless. They are the Adversary.'

'I'm your Adversary!' Steve pointed at his chest with his thumb.

'Oh please, Steve. Our real Adversary is dangerous. Competent. We need to find out who they are before they ruin everything. You can help us.'

'Help you? I don't think so. You're in a lot of trouble, Verity. First you vanish mysteriously. Now you're down here operating a bookshop without a permit.' Steve ticked off crimes on his fingers. 'Stacking mattresses in violation of Te Aro bylaws. Boxing books in an unsafe manner. Whatever you're doing down here . . .' He stopped, frowned. 'Where's that eerie music coming from?'

Everyone listened. At first there was nothing; just the subterranean silence of the bookshop. But the rest of them soon heard it too: distant music, notes rising and falling. A child's tune played on a wind instrument like a flute or a recorder. It came from somewhere deep underground, beyond the walls.

'It's her,' said Eleanor. 'She comes.'

'Her who? Who comes?' But Steve already knew the answer. Gorgon. He looked around the room again and this time he saw the curtain. A thick fabric hung over a shadowed section of the wall. Steve's keen senses detected subtle shifts in the fabric and micro-changes in air density. There was a hidden passageway there.

'Steve.' Verity said. 'You need to go. Now. Run.'

Steve thought about it. Should he run? He analysed Verity's physiological signals: the fluttering at her temples, the moistness of her eyes and the stress in her voice. She was frightened by whatever was making that music and coming towards them down the passageway. Maybe he should run? Or could he use Verity's fear to his advantage?

He turned towards Kim, who was closest to the blanket draped on the wall. 'Kim!' he called out. 'Tear down that

181

curtain!'

'Blas,' Kim replied. He loped towards the curtain with an obedient grin. Verity and the archivist chorused, 'No!' and ran to intercept him. Over this din of voices and footsteps the music came again, very close, just behind the curtain; the same haunting childhood tune. *Bind me. Blind me. Or Gorgon will find me.*

Steve took advantage of the chaos to run towards the glowing cardboard box. Maybe Gorgon was real. Maybe this mysterious Adversary was real, and maybe the Adversary took the secret archive, or, maybe it was all a lie and the archive was right here, within Steve's grasp. Well, he would find out. He sped towards the box and raised his crowbar. Verity reversed and tried to intercept him but she was too slow and far too late.

He swung. The box caved inwards, revealing that it didn't contain the secret archive after all, but rather countless vials filled with a glowing blue compound, which now exploded into millions of fragments of glass and radiant droplets. These rained upon Steve, soaking his clothes and splattering his face.

Verity slid to her knees. She scrambled backwards, away from the glowing blue liquid. Her mouth was opening and closing but no sound came out. Maybe there was something wrong with her? Steve didn't know. He turned to watch Kim and Eleanor struggle. Their thrashing bodies tore the curtain from its hooks: it draped itself over them, revealing a long, dark passageway receding into the distance. There was a woman moving down it, coming towards the bookshop. She moved with an odd lurching gait. A wild tangle of hair surrounded her head. Another step, and she would emerge into the light.

And then all the luminance and all the shadow in the room drained away; reality dissolved, and Steve found himself in the Real City.

29

The Real City

It went on forever.

Steve was in the exact centre of a vast circular plaza. The ground was a muted grey, the colour of a cloud backlit by sunlight. Radiating out from the plaza were countless pathways seamlessly joined to it, all fashioned from the same dull substance, all stretching out into the fathomless distance. Overhead was a cloudless, sunless, starless void.

Where was this place? What was it? Steve didn't know. After a few moments of intense, powerful thinking he decided that, wherever he was, it wasn't real.

Did that mean he was dreaming? No. Steve was an accomplished dreamer. A professional. He knew the difference between a dream and waking life. In a dream the space you occupied was mutable, shifting: but he'd stared at the vast, impossible space around him for several minutes now and it remained the same. This was no dream. It had to be the result of the glowing blue stuff hidden in the box he'd smashed open. It was obviously some kind of mind-altering drug.

Did that mean that the vast impossible landscape around him was a hallucination? Steve had never taken any hallucinogenic drugs. His brain was a precision tool. It operated at the elite outer bounds of human thought. He didn't believe in mistreating it. But he was almost a doctor of psychology. He knew how hallucinogens worked. They interfered with the brain's ability to interpret sensory data. They altered your perception of reality. Steve wasn't perceiving reality at all. Reality was gone. He'd never heard of any drug that did that. The glowing blue substance was something new. A class of compound that contemporary psychology hadn't encountered before.

Why had Verity manipulated Steve into exposing himself to it? To get him out of the way, clearly. They'd plotted against reality and they'd neutralised the only man who could stop them, tricking him with the old hide-the-drug-in-the-glowing-box-and-manipulate-Steve-into-smashing-it-with-a-crowbar routine. And he'd fallen for it. Like an amateur. He thought back over the last confusing moments before he lost consciousness. Who was the woman in the dark passageway? Gorgon? Why didn't Verity want anyone to see her? How was she connected to Ogilvy and Threshold? He vowed to find out when he returned to reality.

If he returned.

He looked around again and gave a little snort of disgust at the monotony of the landscape, or mindscape, or drugscape, or whatever kind of scape he was imprisoned in. He was equidistant from all of the many pathways branching into infinity, so he picked a side of the plaza at random and moved towards it.

How far did he walk? It seemed like a long way, a long time. He was inside his mind: why couldn't he simply materialise wherever he wanted? Or cause this vast, dreary place to vanish entirely? He couldn't even perceive his own body. Trying to think about it was like handling something slippery: if he tried to command his brain to look down at his legs, the thought dissolved before he could fully form it.

After an unknowable amount of time he reached the edge of the plaza. The ground continued on, seamless and matte, transforming into a bridge projecting into nothing, spanning an impossible distance until it intersected with another bridge, which stretched from one side of the horizon to the other.

Steve shuffled towards the edge and looked down. Nothing. An endless blur. What would happen if he stepped off? Would he wake, or fall forever?

He stepped onto the bridge and continued on. Eventually it intersected with another bridge, and this led to another circular plaza with ten bridges branching off in different directions. He picked another direction at random. This led to another featureless plaza with more featureless bridges, and he continued on and on with no aim or destination, moving from nowhere to nowhere.

Until he saw the Spiral.

At first it was just a tiny dot in the distance. An imperfection in the otherwise uniform void, a dead pixel in the sky.

He tried to approach it. Sometimes the pathways doubled back and it disappeared, and he was forced to backtrack, find new routes, but gradually it grew larger: a malevolent black polestar guiding him towards nothing but itself.

The Spiral consisted of black spidery cracks, like fissures in the fabric of space. They formed a dense, complicated three-dimensional structure, coiling in the air, motionless but charged with a terrible potential energy. The Spiral could have appeared one second ago, tearing apart the very fabric of things, but it also looked like it had hung there for countless billions of years. The outer tendrils of the Spiral arced down towards a plaza. A single bridge connected to this plaza on the side opposite Steve, telescoping off into infinity.

So Steve could, in theory, find his way through the maze and touch the Spiral. That might be a bad idea—the object radiated an awesome sense of malice, power and doom—but Steve was not one to be cowed by any of these things. He laughed at power and doom! He moved on, heading in the general direction of the Spiral.

He was making progress, he thought. The Spiral was getting larger. Then something moved across the foreground of his vision. A sudden flurry, gone almost before he noticed it.

What was that? He looked around. The plaza he stood in was empty. Changeless. He was utterly alone.

Then he saw it again: a formless shape darting across his gaze. Steve concentrated, focusing on it, bending his mind towards this task.

Reality shifted into view.

At first he could see only moving blurs. Lights. Vague shapes. But the more he concentrated, the clearer things became, and he realised he could see the bookshop; that he was lying on his side on the floor, staring at the rows of boxes while people walked back and forth in front of him. Everything was vague, insubstantial, like a watermark behind a page of text. It reminded Steve of the hours he'd spent looking at the cobwebs and flecks of blood vessels that drifted around inside his eyeballs. He focused on the bookshop and tried to move his body, or even be aware of it. But there was nothing. Even seeing the world required intense concentration, and the instant his concentration lapsed, the ghostly outline of reality dissolved and Steve was left with the concrete unreality of the Real City.

Interesting. Steve wasn't unconscious: instead, the drug was somehow interfering with the input from his senses, imposing the City over the top of it. Or . . . Steve had a troubling thought. Why did Verity refer to this place as 'The Real City'? Was she being ironic? Or, what if reality was really a hallucination and the Real City was really real? What if the blue drug was an antidote to the mass delusion that the world existed?

Steve drove these thoughts from his mind and continued on, trying to find the path to the Spiral. Next time he checked in with his body—days later? Weeks?—they'd moved it.

He'd gotten a bit lost, and while retracing his steps he wondered what was happening back in reality—whatever that meant—so he struggled to refocus and discovered that he was back inside his house, in the gully on Devon Street, lying on his lounge floor. They'd laid him sideways on a foam mat and draped a blanket over him. Which was nice, he supposed. More than you would expect from people who drugged you and imprisoned your mind inside a maze. There were two more people lying on mattresses within Steve's field of vision, but he couldn't make out their faces. They were too ghostly.

He let them fade.

He explored the City. He found his way back to the vast plaza he'd initially arrived in and tried each of the 136 paths radiating out from it, hoping that one of them would lead to the Spiral. But none of them did.

He continued to monitor his body to see if they'd moved it again, but his viewpoint stayed the same. Sometimes when he refocused, it was night and he couldn't see anything. His glimpses of reality became fewer as the search for the way to the Spiral became all-consuming. He tried to map the City in his mind, but it was too vast. He formed theories of the City and tested them; none of them were sound.

Then something changed. Steve found his first dead end.

It was a plaza with only one path connecting to it. He retraced his steps but the plaza he returned to had more pathways than when he'd left it. The Real City was changing.

He took a new pathway to a plaza he'd never seen, and then another, and another. Soon the Spiral loomed in his vision. He was getting closer.

And then he woke up.

30

Back to reality

It happened quickly. The City flickered off and on like city lights in a storm. Then it was gone and he was huddled on the mattress in the dark of his lounge.

Steve hadn't felt anything while he was in the Real City. No fatigue. No pain. Not even anger or fear. Now that he was back he could feel things again, and feeling things sucked. He was tired and cold. His throat hurt. His head hurt. He tried to turn his neck: it was like rattling a key in a long-rusted lock.

Also, he smelt bad. As he lay there, he parsed out the components of the stench. There was body odour, obviously, but stronger than that was the smell of bleach, and stronger even than the bleach was the urine. It came from under the blanket. Steve flexed his fingers: they radiated little stabs of pain up his wrists, along his arms and into his brain, but his willpower was strong. He ignored the agony and peeled the blanket back. He was naked from the waist down except for a swollen adult nappy fastened around his midsection. He poked it and a tiny trickle of urine pooled around his fingertip.

This was intolerable. They'd drugged him. Him! That was bad enough. But to toss him aside, abandoned, soaking in his own urine? His anger rose. Verity had done this to him! Verity and Gorgon! And who were they? Nobodies. Verity was just an artist, and Gorgon was only a terrifying myth. Steve was a scientist who had almost completed his PhD. He was the rightful Councillor of Te Aro. Sort of. If anyone was going to be drugging people and leaving them unconscious in their own urine, it should be him. He trembled with fury and cold. Mostly cold. He needed to get dressed and get away. Then he could wreak his vengeance.

Gritting his teeth, he forced his neck to turn. There were other mattresses distributed around the floor, all of them occupied by motionless blanket-covered forms. Steve was near one of the walls. The door to the hall was above his head and to the left.

He stretched his legs and waited as the inevitable cramps and spasms wracked his long-unused thigh muscles. The pain was extreme: enough to drive an ordinary human mad. Steve bore it in silence, and when it finally ebbed to a state of moderate agony he rolled onto his side and sat up.

He recognised Kim and the secretary. They lay on adjacent mattresses; their lips stained a brilliant sky blue. On a shelf in one corner were dozens of empty plastic syringes, all discoloured with the same blue liquid.

So that's how they kept them imprisoned in the Real City. They re-drugged them. But why?

A door banged. Voices and torchlights. Steve fell backwards, covering himself with his reeking blanket and closing his eyes to slits. 'Take up positions in the doorways.' It was Eleanor. 'Stay alert. Some of them will wake soon.'

Steve waited, counting footsteps as Eleanor and her accomplices moved through his house. He listened, gathering intelligence on his enemies and preparing to strike. One of them stood in the entrance to the lounge. A man. He played a torch over the bodies and called out, 'When will we have more compound?'

'It's about an hour away,' Eleanor replied.

'What went wrong, Apostle?' Another man from a different region of the house. 'How did we run out?'

'We've been too successful,' said Eleanor. 'We sent too many maps and spiral dollars into the community and brought too many pilgrims across to the Real City. We ran out of compound to keep them all there. I've assigned more Cartographers to the lab to increase product—' She stopped. 'What was that?'

Steve heard it too: a low moan from half-a-dozen mattresses

away. Someone else was awake. Through his nearly-shut eyes he perceived a dim form shaking off its blanket and struggling to its knees. The torchlights converged on it and two people ran across the room. The figure saw them approach and said, 'Hi there,' and then screamed as they set upon him. They struck him with small rectangular objects and the man collapsed back on the mattress. Tasers, Steve realised. His captors had tasers.

'This guy stinks. They all do.'

'We need to change them,' Eleanor ordered. 'And hydrate them. They're no good to us if they die. From now on I want someone stationed here permanently.'

'Apostle? Why are these pilgrims even here, in this hovel?' asked one of the voices. 'Why not keep them all at Threshold with the others?'

'This place is our insurance policy. The Adversary knows about Threshold,' Eleanor explained. 'If they attacked it, somehow, and woke all the pilgrims, we'd lose everything. We'd never find our way through the Real City.'

'I can help you find your way!' This pained cry came from the man who'd woken up. There was another buzz and he screamed, then continued pleading. 'Stop! I'm a mathematician. My name is Sophus. I can help you find the way through the City. It isn't what you think. Its underlying structure is mathematical. You're trying to reach the Spiral, right? But it's not even a spiral. It's technically a cardioid. There are algorithms. Hidden . . . Arghh! Stop that, damn it, I'm trying to help you!'

One of the men stunning him with a taser spoke, and Steve recognised the voice of the archivist. 'The Real City is a spiritual artefact. A sacred place. And nothing that some smooth-talking mathematician—'

'Arggghhh.'

'—says will help us comprehend it.'

'You're partly right,' the mathematician gasped. 'The City might be spiritual. But logic and reason aren't the opposite of spirituality. They're components of it. They alone cannot explain the City, but it cannot be explained without them. Please don't shock me anymore. Arrrgghhh.'

'Wait,' Eleanor called. The screaming stopped. 'Pick him up.'

'What?' The archivist was incredulous. 'Surely you're not taken in by this charlatan.'

'He may be of some use. We have hundreds of pilgrims in the City, and still we're no closer to our goal. Perhaps he can help. Can you walk, mathematician?'

The archivist helped Sophus to his feet. The ugly young student wobbled, then tipped forward. The archivist grabbed his arm. Eleanor said, 'You'll have to help me carry him.'

'Carry him where?'

'To Threshold. We're taking him to Gorgon. Kurt'—she addressed the second man—'you stay here. Watch the pilgrims. If anyone wakes or moves, stun them. I'll be back with more compound.'

Steve plotted his escape.

It wouldn't be easy. One Steve, unarmed and weakened, against a healthy opponent armed with a taser. All Steve had was a blanket and a urine-soaked nappy. That would have to be enough.

He needed a distraction. He kept still, waiting for one of the other captors to regain conciousness. Eleanor said that the drug was wearing off. That's why Steve woke up. So, logically, someone else would wake soon and distract the guard long enough for Steve to strike.

So he waited.

But no one else woke. Steve didn't have a lot of time here. He needed to get away before Eleanor returned with more compound. He needed to act.

The Cartographer called Kurt stood on the far side of the

room, scanning the sleepers with a torch. Steve waited until the beam was off him then he slowly unfastened the adhesive straps of his nappy. Next he tugged a thread from his blanket and fashioned a noose with it. Finally he cast the noose with a flick of his wrist, flinging it towards the adjacent mattress. It hit its target, landing on the outflung hand of the woman beside him. Steve tugged and the noose slipped around the woman's wrist and tightened.

The rest was easy. All Steve needed to do was groan, luring Kurt towards him. The Cartographer played his torchlight over the floor, trying to spot which captor was waking; Steve tugged on his thread and the arm of the body next to him flailed about. Kurt's torch locked onto the moving limb. He hurried over to it, leaned down and zapped the senseless body.

Steve struck. He sprang up behind Kurt and forced the bloated nappy over the unwitting Cartographer's head. He fastened the sticky tabs and fixed it in place, blinding him. Kurt gave a muffled scream and tried to tear it off, but he wasn't quick enough. Steve grabbed his flailing hand and twisted his wrist and the taser fell to the floor.

Tasers weren't Steve's favourite non-lethal weapon, but years of laboratory work had made him an expert with the devices. He picked it up, pressed the probes against Kurt's back and depressed the trigger. Kurt arced and fell, spasming, to the floor.

Steve staggered towards the table in the corner. He had pins and needles in both his legs. He wove back and forth across half the room before he reached his destination. Then he fumbled with the syringes, scraping the residues of blue compound into a single tube, taking great care not to let any of the compound touch his skin, which was tricky because his knees were still weak, bowing like saplings in a gale, but he did it. When he had enough compound he staggered back to Kurt, who was trying to sit up. Steve pushed the Cartographer down and squirted the luminous drug into his mouth. Kurt's eyes went white with fear and rolled back and around, before centering. They fixed on Steve's face, but Steve knew that they gazed upon the Real City.

He lay down. Agony racked his body, surging up and down his legs and through his spine. But Steve knew that agony was just a signal from the nervous system to alert the brain that the body was in pain. He ignored it and eventually the agony ebbed, then died away.

Now he could escape: flee out the door, hide in the valley somewhere, plan his revenge against Eleanor and Verity. And Gorgon, whoever or whatever she was.

But he couldn't defeat them alone. Steve needed backup. Muscle. An elite strike force. He picked his way around the room, inspecting the faces and torsos of all the comatose captives. He wanted troops who were fast. Strong. They'd be quick-thinking and utterly obedient to Steve. He identified several candidates and tried to wake them by jostling them, poking their cheeks, and shouting 'Attention', but no one responded.

Then he heard something. He crouched, listening. Footsteps. Someone outside, coming down his steps and across the mire of his front yard. He heard his front door open, then Eleanor's voice calling, 'It's just me. I forgot my phone.'

Steve crept to the door. The hall was lit by a shaft of daylight from the back door. Eleanor stood midway down the hall, backlit. Beside her was the shelf where Steve had kept his self-help books. But now the shelf was empty—except for a black cellphone on top of it. Eleanor picked it up and said, without glancing at Steve, 'Everything OK here?'

'Everything's fine, Apostle.'

Eleanor looked up. Saw him. Saw the taser in his hand. She turned and ran for the back door. She pulled it open but stumbled over a rubbish bag lying in the doorway. Steve tasered her: she stiffened and then fell, landing face-down in the unbroken expanse of mud.

The war for the Aro Valley had begun.

31

The Subcommittee for Public Safety

'Aren't you afraid?'

Steve stood in the torchlit darkness of the Waimapihi Tunnel. He was at the mouth of a passageway, one foot on the plank of wood that spanned the swift, dark waters. The stream was high, surging along the culvert. At the other end of the bridge was Sophus.

Two weeks had passed since Steve had awoken from the Real City. It had taken him days to fully recover, but after a brutal regime of pasta-eating and power-sleeping he was back at the height of his powers. And he was in total command of his strike force, the Subcommittee for Public Safety.

Steve had rescued his shock troops from his house and they'd recovered alongside him. For the past few nights they'd scouted the catacombs: the network of tunnels beneath Te Aro. They'd discovered an alternate entrance to the network via an abandoned sub-station on Epuni Street: a rusty ladder fixed into the rock led down to a narrow corridor that joined with the passageway connecting the basements of the Aro Street apartment buildings. They ventured as far as the stormwater tunnel, but that seemed to be a thoroughfare for the Cartographers. Dozens of them regularly passed back and forth along the accessway beside the stream; some carried bodies on stretchers, others lugged boxes along the platform. Steve and his subcommittee kept out of sight. They lurked in the darkness, spying, eavesdropping. Piecing together the Cartographers' evil plan.

During the early hours of the morning the Cartographers distributed blue envelopes and fake spiral dollars around the valley. The denizens of the valley found the dollars and the maps and the clues, and followed them to the bookshop, which was now something even worse than a bookshop.

It was a trap.

The bookshop was the crossing point to the Real City. Those who made their way there were drugged and taken away through the tunnels to an as-yet-unknown destination.

Why? What was the point of Gorgon's plan? Steve didn't know. What he did know was that he needed to stop it; cripple Gorgon's organisation. Strike at the weak point. And he'd succeeded. His raid on the bookshop had captured a suitcase full of DoorWay compound while simultaneously stopping Sophus and the archivist from snaring more victims.

Unfortunately, one of the victims they'd saved back there was a confused, angry giant, and he'd hurt Steve quite badly and delayed their getaway, allowing Sophus and the archivist to recover from the attack and chase them down the tunnel. Steve led the subcommittee right past the ladder leading up to the sub-station—they'd never make it up there in time—and down to the underground stream. They ran alongside it, through the roaring darkness. Now he stood on the plank bridging the Waimapihi. At his back was a narrow flight of steps leading to regions of the catacombs unmapped by Steve.

'We're not scared of Gorgon,' he called out to Sophus, who stood on the opposite side of the stream, one foot on the plank.

'Then you're a fool.'

Steve smirked behind his mask. 'Would a fool do this?' He took his stolen suitcase filled with DoorWay and held it over the rushing stream. Sophus gasped and took an involuntary step across the plank, his arms outstretched.

'Uh-uh.' Steve held up his hand. 'That's far enough, Cartographer. Either get back off this bridge and stop following us, or I throw Gorgon's precious vials into the water. What'll it be?'

Sophus stepped back. He addressed Steve in a low, trembling voice. 'You can't take our compound. You don't understand what we're doing here. How important it is—'

'I'm not here to understand things,' Steve snarled. 'I'm here to stop you.'

'I understand your anger,' Sophus said. 'I was once like you. They tricked me and trapped me in the Real City. But then I woke up and they explained everything.'

'They brainwashed you.'

'They told me the truth.'

'Ha! What do mathematicians know about truth? Get off the bridge or your precious compound goes in the water!'

Sophus licked his lips. 'All right. But let's make a deal. We need this plank to cross the stream, for our work.' He swept his torchbeam over the plank. 'If we promise not to follow you, will you promise to leave it in place? As a gesture of good faith.'

Steve considered the offer. 'All right,' he agreed, covertly placing the toe of his shoe beneath the plank. 'Good faith.'

Steve and his subcommittee reached the top of the steps when they heard someone scream, followed by a loud splash.

'Sounds like one of the Cartographers is mapping the stream,' said Steve. His shock troops laughed.

Steve glanced back at his troops, remembering their escape from captivity. After he'd stunned Eleanor with the taser, he hurried inside and scraped together a syringeful of DoorWay to drug her with. But she was tougher then she looked. By the time Steve returned, she'd picked herself up out of the mud and escaped. She would go for reinforcements, he knew. Return with hordes of Cartographers and try to recapture him. He needed to get out. Fast.

But then he'd heard a groan from the lounge. Then another: a cry for help. Two voices. Two captives were awake. If Steve was lucky he could rescue them both; drag them across the yard and into the trees, out of sight. Get them somewhere safe, then train them up.

That's what he did, and now those two handpicked soldiers trotted along behind Steve as they made their way through the catacombs. The first one said, 'I wonder if these tunnels are gazetted in the Te Aro Charter?' and the second replied, 'Piperfant cunang.'

Steve would have preferred to go into battle with someone other than the Council secretary and Kim, Steve's former opponent in the election campaign. Anyone else, really. But great military leaders worked with the elite strike force they had. And they had acquitted themselves well against the giant.

'I wonder if the legitimacy of our subcommittee extends down here,' the secretary continued. 'Are we still in Te Aro? Do you think we've exceeded our authority?'

Steve did not reply. He was concentrating on getting them back to the surface. They came to a fork in the tunnel. Steve believed in making irrational decisions based on intuition and instinct—it made him unpredictable to his enemies—so he swerved to the left without stopping and continued downwards, noting, briefly, that the other passageway sloped up.

Something nagged at him. He felt he'd seen something important back in the bookshop, some detail or clue, but he didn't know what. His powerful subconscious urged him to stop and think about it. But they didn't have time. They needed to flee. Meanwhile the secretary continued to muse aloud. 'The legal principle here, I think, is *Cuius est solum eius est usque ad coelum et ad inferos*. Whoever owns the soil it is theirs all the way to heaven and down to hell,' he translated. 'But that is a principle of property law, not government, and even so I've never been happy with it. Does the council's authority extend all the way through the Earth's core to the surface on the opposite side of the planet? Preposterous. And, since it mentions heaven and hell, what about the Real City? Does our authority extend there?'

'Of course not,' Steve replied. The tunnel he'd chosen seemed to be leading deeper into the earth, and he wondered if they should turn back, pick the other direction. No: he couldn't second-guess himself in front of his troops. If they lost confidence in him, the entire subcommittee could fall apart. 'Pick up the pace,' he called, and they hurried down into the dark behind him.

'Why wouldn't we have legal authority over the Real City?' the secretary demanded. 'It's a legal territory accessed and located within the Aro Valley.'

'The Real City isn't real,' Steve explained.

'Why not? We all saw it. The exact same spiral-haunted labyrinth, down to the smallest detail.'

'We only saw it because they drugged us.'

'You only hear radio broadcasts if you intercept the waves with a conductor. That doesn't mean they aren't there.'

'Taking DoorWay is like reading a novel,' Steve explained. 'The words are real, just like the drug. But when people read they experience profound hallucinations, and the hallucinations are the same, but that doesn't make the contents of the book real. Destroy all the physical books and the contents are destroyed. That's what we're going to do to the Real City. We defeat Gorgon and destroy the drug and the City vanishes.'

The secretary frowned. 'By that logic, if we stay within these caves and seal off the outside world so that we can never reach it, does the outside world cease to be real?'

'Yes,' said Steve.

'Larlet,' said Kim.

'Speaking of the outside world, we seem to be moving away from it. Are we lost?'

'We are not lost,' Steve assured him. 'We're just exploring alternative routes.' He paused when they came to another fork in the tunnel. He chose a direction at random and said, 'This way has a good feel about it.' He led his troops down it.

The downward slope became steeper. The air seemed colder. Eventually the secretary said, 'We're not in an access tunnel anymore.' He played his torch over the walls. They were stone, roughly hacked. The floor was smooth. 'There used to be a quarry in Aro Valley, back in the late nineteenth century,' he continued. 'It was mostly open cast, but they dug a few tunnels looking for ores, and this must be one of them. How interesting. And what do you think that terrible stench is?'

Steve had noticed it too: an alien yet oddly familiar smell that grew stronger, more pungent the deeper they went. His powerful nose identified the odour of brine along with complex aromatic compounds. Whatever was down there was metallic and old.

Then they came to the end. The tunnel terminated in a wall of bricks. Diagonal wooden beams braced the wall, set against the hard stone floor. The three men swept their torchbeams over the structure.

'The tunnel keeps going past this wall,' the secretary said. 'You can feel the breeze.' He held his hand up near the roof of the tunnel. 'And you can see the gaps around the edges.'

'What's that?' Steve directed his beam of light to the side of the tunnel. There was something scratched into the stone. Words. Names carved into the rock.

'Elizas McKenzie.' The secretary read them aloud. 'Augustus Conway. Loyal Smith. Victorian names. Probably the masons who carved the tunnel.'

'Qlip.'

'This wall isn't Victorian, though.' Steve rested his palm against it. The bricks were dry and cold. He saw something gleam in the darkness at its base and knelt down to find a wooden clipboard hanging from a rusty nail. There was a single piece of paper on the board; time and the dry air had curled it into a scroll. Steve took a latex glove from his jacket pocket, snapped it on and gently flattened the page. The edges crumbled at his touch.

It was an official form from the Department of Works and Engineering. The underlined heading read 'Completion Sheet'.

Beneath that, 'Building or Structure: Underground Reinforced Wall'. Beneath that: 'Note name of senior inspecting engineer, time, date and any comments.' Beneath this were columns corresponding to those headings, but the page was blank except for a single entry. 'M. Ogilvy. 16/08/1974'.

'Sutala,' said Kim. He nudged Steve and pointed up at the roof.

The tunnel above their heads was curved, and rent by fissures that swallowed the light. Between these were smooth planes covered with carved pictures: stick figures, some standing, most of them lying down; above the figures were vague sketches: lines, vast shapes. A wave of fear ran through Steve's heart. He knew now that they were looking at a rough depiction of the Real City. Looming over the sleeping stick figures and the plazas and bridges of the City was a shape, half concealed by the brick wall: a brooding, malignant pattern.

The Spiral.

'Daylight!'

'Pluqentoil!'

Steve saw it too. A faint wash of blue colouring the dark. They all cried out and stumbled towards it.

They'd wandered the tunnels for many hours, until Steve had begun to doubt his own leadership skills. Now he felt vindicated. He hadn't led them to a lingering death in the darkness after all.

The tunnel sloped upwards, narrowing. As they trudged on, the light resolved into a series of faint blue outlines illuminating a pile of bulky, square boxes blocking the exit.

The secretary climbed to the top of the pile, throwing up clouds of dust. 'It's someone's garage,' he called down. 'I don't think anyone's been in here for years.'

They cleared a path through the boxes and emerged into a double garage filled with rusting car parts, garden tools and obsolete electrical appliances. The garage's roller doors were shut. Sheets of Perspex in the roof admitted a murky, underwater light.

Steve picked his way through the debris covering the floor, knelt by the doors and tugged it up.

He recognised his surroundings immediately. Central Te Aro. Boston Terrace. The sun was hidden behind dense cloud and the shadows were vague. Steve estimated that the time was 9.28 am.

'The Cartographers will be looking for this.' He held up the stolen suitcase filled with DoorWay. 'They'll watch the streets. We need to hide until dark.' He gestured at the garage littered with rusting lawnmower blades, the air heavy with the stink of petrol and paint-thinner. 'This seems like a good place to hole up. Everyone get some rest.'

'What about food?' the secretary asked.

'Vlay,' added Kim.

'What about it?'

'We haven't eaten in about sixteen hours. We're pretty hungry.'

'Hunger is just a very powerful physical craving,' Steve explained. 'Try to ignore it.' He frowned at Kim, who was heading towards the roller doors. 'Where are you going, soldier? You have your orders.'

Kim pointed at something. Steve squinted in the light and stepped closer.

There was a blue envelope taped to one of the doors. Kim tugged it free, inspected it and held it out to Steve. 'Baal chring.'

Steve's name was on the envelope.

32

It's a trap!

Dear Steve,
Gorgon wishes to meet with you. Today. Te Aro Archive.
12 pm. Come on time and come alone, with no companions
or substitutes or tricks, or everything you care about will be
destroyed, utterly.
Yours,
A Friend.

'It's a trap,' said the secretary.

Steve agreed and was about to say so, but the secretary wasn't done. 'Look there,' he said, pointing at the note. 'It tells you to meet Gorgon at 12 pm. But that's impossible. There's no such thing as 12 pm.'

'Isn't 12 pm twelve noon?'

'No.' The secretary shook his head, saddened by Steve's ignorance. 'PM stands for post meridiem. After the meridiem. But twelve is the meridiem. How can you have a time that is both the meridiem and past the meridiem? You can't. It's a logical impossibility.'

Steve turned his back on the secretary and showed Kim the note. 'I think this is a trap,' he said. 'However, if we know it's a trap then it ceases to become one.'

'Kanb.'

'And if we go and spring this trap we can get something to eat on the way.'

'Ere kanb.'

'Then it's decided.' He rubbed this hands together. 'I'll do exactly as this note says. I'll go to the archive all right. Alone, with no tricks or substitutes. But with one slight, subtle twist.'

~

Steve sat cross-legged on the roof of the Community Hall, watching Kim and the secretary approach the archive.

The park and the Community Hall were deserted. Clouds hung low about the hills. No one had entered or left the archive in the two hours Steve had it under observation.

Kim and the secretary neared the entrance. The doorway was recessed into the wall of the concrete bunker, atop a short flight of steps. Steve's troops hesitated before it. They looked back at him; he gave them a cheerful thumbs-up and flapped his hands, urging them into the darkness.

Kim tried the door. It opened. Steve sipped his soup, which he had purchased from Sufi Soup on his way to the meeting. He'd promised Kim and the secretary soup of their own if their mission was successful. Hunger will sharpen your wits, he assured them.

He'd worked out a series of signals with the secretary. 'If you enter the archive and it turns out to be a trap, which it will, scream "It's a trap" and try to run away,' Steve instructed. 'If someone drugs you with DoorWay, scream "I'm drugged". If someone electroshocks you with a taser, scream "I've been electroshocked with a taser". Or just scream. If Gorgon herself is inside, scream twice. Got it?'

'I have,' the secretary replied. 'But there's a problem. Gorgon is still, technically, the legal Councillor of Te Aro. I work for her. If she's in the archive then I can't betray her by signalling you.'

'I see your problem.' Steve thought for a moment. 'I have it. If Gorgon's inside, come back out but don't signal. You're not betraying her by not signalling, are you?'

'Isn't not signalling a form of signal? Wouldn't that still be a betrayal?'

Steve sighed. 'Just signal then. Why does everything have to be so complicated?'

'I won't betray the rightful Councillor,' the secretary declared. 'I won't signal.'

'Then not signalling will be the signal. Now go. Hurry!'

Steve waited as his troops shuffled closer to the archive entrance. While he waited, he wondered who had left that note for him in the abandoned garage. Gorgon or one of her lieutenants? How had they known Steve would end up there? There were many secret entrances to the catacombs, and Steve had chosen the path to the garage at random. Impossible to predict. Yet they had. How?

Also, why set a trap in the archive? If they could predict his movements then why not set a trap for him back in the tunnels? And why make it so obvious? Did Gorgon underestimate Steve's leadership qualities? His tactical brilliance and willingness to sacrifice his entire team by sending them directly into an ambush? Or was something else playing out here? Schemes within schemes, plans within plans?

Something else nagged at Steve. He'd seen something during his raid on the bookshop: something significant, but he didn't know what. His subconscious needled him. He tried to think, to focus. It might be important . . .

Then he heard the first scream.

It was Kim. A series of nonsense words tapering into an incoherent cry of terror which hung in the air for a moment then died away. Steve drank some more soup and waited. Kim's cowardly howls could mean anything. Steve was relying on the secretary to transmit meaningful information.

Then the secretary appeared. He emerged from the shadows of the archive doorway and stood, blinking in the sunlight. He looked up at Steve. Steve chewed his bread and looked back.

The secretary did not make a signal. Steve nodded to show that he understood. Then the secretary pitched forward. He landed face down, a dart embedded between his shoulder blades.

Did that mean Gorgon was inside? Or just that the secretary

couldn't signal because he was drugged? Steve didn't know. The secretary had botched the operation. Typical. At least they now knew that the archive was a trap.

Sipping his soup, he planned his next move. He'd remain here on the roof, out of sight, and see who emerged from the archive. Next he'd follow Gorgon, or whoever it was, back to their lair. Then he'd rescue some more pilgrims from the Real City, somehow, and train them up as shock troops. Good ones, this time. Then he'd strike a decisive blow of some kind.

Steve waited. Minutes crawled by. He looked at the secretary sprawled on the concrete. Why didn't they move him? Were they using him as bait? Did they think Steve would break cover to rescue his fallen comrade? Were they that naive?

Then he noticed movement in the corner of his vision. There was someone in the park. He ducked down behind the peak of the roof.

It was a giant, loping through the trees. The same giant Steve had encountered yesterday in the bookshop. It stopped in the middle of the great lawn, took something from its pocket and looked at it, then corrected its direction, heading for the Community Hall.

Watching the giant, something plucked softly at Steve's memory. The elusive thought that had been nagging him returned. *You saw something*, it whispered. *Something in the bookshop. Something important.*

Steve cast his mind back to the raid, replaying the scene. They burst into the room. Stunned Sophus and the archivist. Grabbed the suitcase. Fought with the giant. Fled into the labyrinth. Steve's memory recreated each instant with eidetic detail. He was attacked by the giant, hauled up into the air. Interrogated. Then dropped . . .

There! Steve froze the moment in his mind and zoomed in. He was lying on the ground while Kim and the secretary fought the giant. And in the periphery of Steve's vision was a second man, kneeling on a mattress in the giant's great shadow; one of the so-called pilgrims lured into the bookshop to be drugged and trapped in the Real City. The man's face was partially obscured by an outflung hand but Steve could see that his mouth was open; the man was clearly stunned by the violence exploding around him. Steve flipped through more images in his mind, trying to find a clearer picture of the man, and when he did he gasped.

The man kneeling on the mattress next to the giant was Danyl.

Danyl. Poor, sad Danyl. He was supposed to be far away in a facility somewhere: medicated, shuffling around in a daze, performing basic menial tasks: mowing lawns, cleaning toilets. Yet he was here in the valley finding his way into sinister bookshops and fraternising with giants. He'd broken free. Steve felt a surge of pride for his old friend, tempered with concern. Where was Danyl now? Trapped in the Real City? Or wandering the streets of Te Aro, helpless and vulnerable and afraid? Steve needed to find him.

He called out to the giant. 'Hey there!' The creature ignored him. It strode past the council building, and Steve waved at it and called out again. No response. It strode up to the archive, glanced at the secretary on the ground, and then called into the darkness beyond the doorway, 'Joy?'

Joy? Who was Joy? Steve had to stop the giant from entering the archive. He grabbed Lightbringer. He slid down the rooftop, lowered himself from its edge, and dropped. He landed on the ground and rolled, sustaining moderate injuries to his left ankle, both legs, his right hip, lower back and left shoulder. Then he was up, limping after the giant, commanding him to stop in the name of the Subcommittee for Public Safety.

But he was too late. The giant stepped over the secretary's body and through the doorway into the archive. The door swung shut behind it. Steve heard it call out 'Joy?' again, and this was followed by a terrible roar and loud crashing that sounded to Steve like bodies being tossed against shelves, followed by running footsteps and desperate screams. The noise lasted for about thirty seconds. There was a final scream of 'Joy!', a final patter of footsteps, then silence.

Steve approached the building. He stood outside the entrance and listened. His powerful ears heard birds. Insects. Distant cars. But nothing from inside.

He opened the door and entered the archive.

PART III

33

Danyl unchained

Danyl woke.

He lay on a cold floor. A blanket was draped over his body. He craned his neck and looked around.

He was in a large sunlit room. The floor was tiled. The tiles continued halfway up the wall: they'd been white once, but were now stained and chipped. The ceiling was high overhead. There were no windows. The light came in through a glass skylight which was cracked and mottled with mould.

He tried to stand and was disappointed to learn that he couldn't because his left wrist was chained to a pipe. The pipe protruded from the wall and ran to a stainless steel bath at the far end of the room. There was a door nearby. The air smelled damp. It was very cold.

Where was he? Danyl tried to think. He remembered . . . Ye Undergrounde Bookshoppe. The catacombs. Stumbling out of the culvert. The Threshold development, and the ruined townhouse filled with bodies. Fleeing from the Cartographers. He remembered the house from Verity's photograph. The grave. Then the goat-faced man shot him with a dart-gun; reality drained away and he found himself in the Real City.

Once Danyl recovered from the shock of reality disappearing and being replaced with something utterly alien, he examined his surroundings. It appeared to be a vast plaza. He counted the pathways branching off from it. There were 136 with a blank space where the 137th should have been. When he stood before it, he could make out a tiny black spot in the far distance.

The Spiral.

He headed towards it. The Spiral grew larger, but then he passed through a succession of plazas that took him further away from it until it was out of sight. He tried to retrace his steps; he wandered down immeasurable paths until suddenly the Real City faded and the world knit itself together in front of his eyes, and he found himself lying in this decaying bathroom, handcuffed to the plumbing.

It was good to be back in good old reality again, even if he didn't know quite which bit of reality he was imprisoned in. One of the half-finished townhouses at Threshold, he guessed.

Well, Danyl figured, now that he was awake he should probably try to escape. He inspected the steel handcuff, tapping it with his fingertips and rattling it against the pipe. It looked exactly like a handcuff in the movies. The steel seemed very strong.

What about the pipe? One end led to the bath, the other to the wash-basin. He stood and tugged with his cuffed hand, theorising that he could tear the pipe out of the wall. It did not move and the cuff bit into the flesh of his wrist. It really hurt.

Escape was clearly impossible. Danyl decided to wait and see what his captors had in store for him. He leaned against the wash-basin, crossed his legs and made himself comfortable, then patted his belly, wondering when a Cartographer would be along to feed him.

Someone grunted.

The sound came from the bath. Danyl craned his neck and tried to see over the rim. There was a green wool blanket inside the bath, covering something bulky. Another grunt. The blanket shifted. There was someone underneath it.

Danyl called out, 'Are you OK? Can you hear me? I can't help you. I'm chained to a pipe.'

The only answer was more grunting. And maybe it was the acoustics of the room, but it sounded like the grunting of a very large man. The blanket shifted again and Danyl watched in transfixed horror as the blanket rose to the top of the bath, slipping back to reveal an enormous black leather boot with blood-red stitching, which came to rest on the rim.

Danyl recognised that boot. It was the giant's. The creature must have been drugged, just like Danyl, and dumped in the bathtub, and now the drug was wearing off. Danyl's thoughts became very calm and very focused. He had to get out of this bathroom. The beast might wake any second.

Danyl examined the cabinet below the wash-basin. The pipe entered it through a hole in the side. He opened the cabinet door. The pipe attached to a mixer unit where it joined a second pipe, which disappeared into the wall. All Danyl needed to do was disassemble the mixer, pull the pipe out of the cabinet and slip his handcuff loose.

He lay on the floor in an L-shape, his head and torso inside the cabinet. The pipe was bolted to the mixer and did not shift when Danyl twisted it with his fingers, so he tugged off his belt, laid the metal clasps of the buckle flat against the top of the bolt, wrapped the strap around it and pulled.

The bolt gave. Water spilled out from the join between the mixer and the pipe. Danyl pulled again; the pipe jolted and came loose, sending a high-pressure stream of water gushing into the confined space of the wash-basin. It was difficult to wrestle the pipe out through the hole, since Danyl's mouth and eyes were filled with very cold water, but he managed it. Once it was free of the cabinet, he forced it down to the floor and the handcuff slipped off.

Free Danyl! He picked up his belt and looped it through his pants, regarded himself in the mirror and rewarded his reflection with a triumphant thumbs up, then splashed across the rapidly spreading pool of water to the door. Which was locked from the outside.

That made sense: Danyl was a prisoner, after all. But, he reasoned, it couldn't be too hard to break the door down. If it was impregnable then his captor wouldn't have bothered to cuff him to the pipe. Danyl shoved at the door. It shuddered a little, but held firm. He kicked it. Nothing. He waded to the opposite wall—the water was already ankle-deep and rising fast—and ran at the door, slamming into it with his shoulder. He bounced off it and fell into the water, sending waves splashing against the walls.

He climbed to his knees, his clothes soaked. He looked around the room looking for something, anything that could help him escape.

There was the wash-basin. The pipe. The toilet. The bathtub, with the blanket and the massive boot with the blood-red stitching, and the groans getting louder. Danyl forced himself to keep calm, think rationally. He waited for inspiration as the water rose to his knees and then his waist. But nothing came, and the water reached the rim of the bath and spilled into it. The groans from inside the bath transformed to roars. There was no way out of the room and the giant was waking. Its massive legs kicked in the air, then its boots found purchase on the side of the bath. It began to rise.

Danyl panicked. He let out a roar of his own and flung himself at the blanket and rained blows upon it.

34

Old friends

The first thing Steve saw when he stepped inside Te Aro Archive was the comatose body of the giant. It lay sprawled on the floor just inside the entrance, its eyes wide open, unseeing. Its chest was rising and falling and a dozen darts were embedded in its torso. Books and papers were scattered everywhere. Some of the shelves were tipped on their sides. Others were broken beneath the bodies of unconscious Cartographers who'd been hurled into walls or shelves or onto burst cardboard boxes by the giant's wrath. The whole building stank of DoorWay: a rich organic brine. Shards of broken glass glittered in the light. Stains of sky blue soaked the floor.

Steve wasn't going back to the Real City. Not by being shot with a dart gun, and not by stepping on contaminated broken glass. He needed protection. He knelt and laid Lightbringer on the ground. Working quickly, he unlaced the giant's boots and wrenched them off its terrible feet. They were large enough to fit over Steve's own shoes. He slipped them on.

Someone coughed.

The sound came from the back of the archive. Steve made his way towards it, glass crunching underfoot.

Eleanor lay on the floor, propped against a fallen shelf. One side of her face was bruised. She looked up at Steve, coughed again and said, 'So. It's you. I underestimated you.' She grimaced from the pain. 'But Gorgon isn't here. Your trap failed.'

'My trap?' Steve sneered. 'I didn't set a trap. The only trap that failed was your trap to trap me, because I knew it was a trap.'

Steve's logic was so powerful that Eleanor did not even acknowledge it. Instead she nodded her head at the fallen giant.

'Sending him in was a masterstroke. We didn't anticipate it. Very clever.'

'Thanks.' Steve smiled.

'How did you get him to attack us?'

Steve did not reply because that was actually a pretty good question. He remembered the giant striding towards the archive clutching something in its hand. He held up a cautioning finger and said to Eleanor, 'Wait there please.' Then he returned to the fallen beast.

There was something in its grasp. Something blue.

Fortunately Steve had Lightbringer. He prised the giant's fingers apart with it. Hidden inside them was a blue envelope. Steve tugged it free, took the letter from the envelope and read:

Dear Giant,
If you want to rescue Joy, you'll find her at Te Aro Archive at
12 pm today.
Yours,
A Friend.

The writing was identical to the note Steve had found in the abandoned garage. He returned to Eleanor and held it out to her. She read it and sighed. 'We've been set up.' She let the note slip to the floor.

'Me? Set up? Impossible.' Steve thought a bit more. 'Set up by who?'

'By Verity.'

'Isn't Verity on your side?'

'She's betrayed me. Betrayed Gorgon. And you. Everyone.' She shifted position, grimacing again, and drew something from her pocket. Another blue letter. She fumbled, dropping it on the floor, then picked it up and held it out. 'See for yourself.'

Steve took the letter and positioned it under the light.

Ellie,
I know who the Adversary is. They'll be at the archive today
at 12 pm.
Verity.

The writing was the same.

Steve was confused. He asked Eleanor, 'What does this mean?'

'It means this was a distraction. A ruse to get me and the Cartographers out of the way while Verity does something very foolish.'

'What?'

'Something that puts our universe at risk. You wouldn't understand.'

'Maybe not.' Steve squatted down to Eleanor's eye level. 'But you're going to tell me anyway, prisoner.'

'Prisoner?'

'That's right. You're wounded. Your Cartographers are beaten. And there's no Gorgon to save you. You are mine.'

Eleanor smiled through her pain. 'You've got it the wrong way around, Steve. It's you who is my prisoner.'

Steve smiled back. She was obviously bluffing. Right? He tightened his grip on Lightbringer and glanced over his shoulder, checking to see if reinforcements had arrived. But there was no one around. Just him, Eleanor, the drugged giant and the unconscious Cartographers. The broken shelves and drifts of paper.

But then, reality—the boxes, the shelves, the entire building—flickered like a reflection in a briefly lit window, and Steve glimpsed something else behind it; something very familiar: a plaza, pathways, an endless void.

He whispered, 'No.' He said it again, more firmly. Then he glanced down at his hand holding the blue letter. It was damp. His fingers were stained a faint blue.

He dropped the paper and it floated to the floor. But it was

217

too late. He could feel feel the drug drug working already. Eleanor had trapped him after all: tricked tricked him with the old drugged drugged letter trick trick. And he'd fallen for it it it.

Eleanor's voice was distant; an echo of an echo. 'So long, Steve,' it said, 'I'll take good care of this universe while you're gone.'

He walked through the now familiar plazas and pathways of the Real City, its Spiral pulsating in the distance, and while he walked, he thought.

Eleanor said that by betraying Gorgon Verity was putting the universe at risk. Which implied Gorgon was saving the universe, somehow. Which was absurd. And even if she was, that didn't change anything. Gorgon had stolen the Te Aro election and her agents had drugged Steve. Twice. She was going down. Te Aro would be Steve's, and the rest of the universe would have to take care of itself.

And what was Verity's role in all this? Why did she lure Steve, the giant and the Cartographers to the archive at the same time? Whose side was she on? And where was poor Danyl? How did he fit into the puzzle? And who was the mysterious Adversary?

Then Steve noticed something odd. The Real City had changed since he was here last. A minor alteration, barely noticeable, but his powerful and all-seeing subconscious had picked it up and alerted him.

He stopped wandering and looked around. He stood in a plaza with four bridges connecting to it. The Spiral hung overhead in the medium distance. Everything else was void, the colour of rain.

What was it? What had Steve's non-rational mind seen? He rotated about, trying to figure it out. It was something to do with the number of pathways in the plazas . . .

He was just about to grasp it, when he woke.

~

He lay on a hard surface. Some kind of scratchy fabric covered his face. The light was murky. Was he back in his own reality? Or another, different reality? Steve needed to be careful here. He'd read mid-twentieth-century science fiction so he knew that once you started switching realities you ran into problems with nested levels of existence. Which one was real? How could you tell?

Also, which way was up? He groaned and shifted position. He was wrapped in some sort of thick fabric and was confined on three sides by a cold, hard surface. Wherever he was, it was very noisy: there was a rushing sound, like torrential rain, interspersed with occasional thuds. The thuds grew louder, then came the sound of someone running through water, a louder thud still, then a pitiful whimper followed by nearly inaudible sobbing.

Steve tried to roll over but something pulled tight at his ankle. His leg was handcuffed to what looked like a metal handle. He pulled at the fabric covering him: it was some sort of blanket. He fumbled at it for a few seconds but this only tangled him further. Relax, he reminded himself. Be very calm. Take deep breaths. Remember the awesome power of your own mind. You can unlock that power and untangle yourself from this blanket, but you must remain calm and in control.

He took another deep breath and felt his muscles relax and his mind fill with peace. That's when the water breached the rim of the bath and flooded over it.

Steve leapt to his feet, hyperventilating from the cold. He was still in shock when someone leapt on top of him, screaming.

It had been a while since Steve last fought off an attacker while he was blinded and chained and half-submerged in freezing water. He spluttered as his face was forced underwater; he fumbled weakly against his assailant to no effect. Then his cunning returned: Steve went limp, he let his attacker push him down; he held his breath and offered no resistance, relying on his superior lung capacity to keep him conscious.

The trick worked. Within a few seconds the attacker relaxed his grip and Steve struck back, struggling to his feet and lashing out blindly through the blanket. He struck something solid and heard a loud splash, following by howl: 'My cheekbone!'

He knew that voice! He tore the blanket off his head. He saw now that he was in a tiled bathroom filling with water. An ill-kempt bearded man bobbed in the water, clutching the left side of his face. His eyes widened when he saw Steve, who cried out, 'Danyl!'

35

What Danyl did

'I put the giant's boots on to protect my feet while I stormed the archive.' Steve was coming to the end of his long and partly accurate story describing the election and its aftermath and his war against Gorgon. 'But the forces of the Cartographers overwhelmed me.'

Danyl nodded. That made sense. He felt a surge of affection for Steve. All this time he'd been looking for Verity, but it was Steve who was his true friend. Steve! Danyl felt relaxed. For the first time since he'd returned to the valley, he felt that things were going to be OK.

Steve looked around the room. It was still filling with water. He asked, 'What's the sitstatrep?'

'The what?'

'The sitstatrep. Situational status report. Where are we? What's going on? C'mon, buddy.' Steve clicked his fingers in Danyl's face. 'Quick.'

'I've never heard anyone say "sitstatrep" before. Please stop clicking your fingers at me.'

'Give me your sitstatrep stat and I'll stop.'

Danyl felt his affection for Steve ebbing away. 'Our sitstatrep is that we're in a room that is filling with water,' he explained. 'That's actually a good thing because that door is locked, but up there'—he pointed at the ceiling—'is a skylight. So my plan is that we just wait for the room to flood and float to the ceiling and escape.'

'You really think Gorgon will let us get away that easily?' Steve gave a bitter laugh. 'No, we're locked inside a room filling with water for a reason. A diabolical reason.'

'I don't think—'

'I know what it is.' Steve clicked his fingers in Danyl's face again. 'Water torture.'

'No—'

'Let me explain. Last night I stole a suitcase filled with DoorWay from Gorgon's Cartographers. Because of that she doesn't have enough DoorWay to keep all of her captives imprisoned in the Real City. She needs the compound in the stolen briefcase back, so she's trapped us in this room and flooded it to get us to talk. Classic Gorgon. She's watching us right now.'

Danyl shook his head. 'No. Firstly, water torture is where they tie you down and drip water on your face.'

'That's one type. This is another.' Steve looked around the room. 'Hello, Gorgon!' he called out, addressing the featureless walls. 'We know you're there. Why don't you show yourself?'

'She's not watching.'

'Of course she is. Why else am I chained to this bath?' Steve pointed at his foot. Danyl peered into the surging water. A handcuff, identical to the one still attached to Danyl's wrist, connected Steve's leg to a handrail inside the tub. 'If Gorgon wasn't watching, waiting for me to talk, then the water would keep rising until I drowned,' he said patiently. 'And what would be the point of subjecting me to such a horrible death? No, she's there all right.'

Danyl stared at the handcuff in horror. What had he done? The water was up to their chests now, and rising quickly. He looked up at Steve's smiling, confident face. Should he tell him the truth? No. Why confuse him? 'I can stop the water,' he explained. 'There's a broken pipe.' He decided not to waste time explaining that it was his fault the room was flooding. Danyl would just reattach the pipe to the mixer beneath the sink and everything would be fine. He turned and headed for the wash-basin, which now fully submerged, but Steve grabbed his arm and pulled him back.

'You can't stop the water,' he insisted. 'Only Gorgon can

do that.' He called out, 'This isn't working, Gorgon! You can't break us. We stand together. United. Indivisible. Hey!' Steve stumbled as Danyl wrenched free of his grasp and half ran, half swam across the room. He took a deep breath and dived.

The pipe was hard to manoeuvre back into place. The water pouring out of it at high pressure made it difficult to thread it back through the hole in the side of the wash-basin; it required concentration, and the burning in Danyl's lungs, the maddening pounding of his heart and the buzzing in his brain as he flailed about underwater were all very distracting. Eventually he resurfaced to breathe.

The water was now up to his chin. Steve was splashing about, screaming at the walls. Danyl doggy-paddled for a moment, gasping in lungfuls of air, then he dived again.

He seized the pipe and pressed it to the mixer under the sink. He remembered he needed the bolt to fix it in place. Where was it? It must have fallen someplace. He ran his hand over the dark, drowned bottom of the basin, found the bolt and slid it onto the pipe, gave a victory pump with his fist and then hit his head on the top of the basin. He cried out in pain, coughing and choking as he swallowed water. He rose to the surface for air.

Steve's arms were waving but his head was almost entirely underwater. Only his chin and the tip of his nose was visible.

Danyl gasped for a few seconds then dived again. He swam to the basin and gripped the pipe. He jammed the pipe back into the inlet on the mixer and spun the bolt into place.

The room exploded.

A wave slammed Danyl into the cabinet and dragged him backwards. A series of cracks louder than gunshots boomed through the churning water. He scrabbled at the floor tiles, trying to get a grip on something. A giant bubble of air rose and burst open. Danyl bobbed to the surface and looked about in utter confusion.

A sucking, gurgling sound bubbled up from below. The

water was draining away. Danyl's feet found the floor. The water was at his chest; seconds later it was down to his waist.

The lower half of the room came into view. The toilet at the far end of the room had pitched over. Beyond the toilet loomed a jagged gap between the wall and the floor. Water drained through it. The tiles around the gap were shattered. Danyl inched towards it and looked down, and realised what had happened.

Beneath the tiles lay the skeleton of the building: massive wooden beams that had been twisted and split apart by the weight of the water, which had dragged the entire floor down on an angle as it burst through. The gap opened onto another room directly below. It looked like a kitchen—or, rather, it was supposed to be a kitchen before construction was abandoned, long ago; before the unfinished fittings decayed and it was filled with drugged prisoners splayed out on mattresses, then flooded.

The space was long and narrow with a concrete bench running along the centre and stacks of discarded construction materials piled against the walls. Bobbing amidst them were dozens of bodies, all blindfolded with their lips stained blue. A row of windows bracketed by aluminium strips looked out over the desolate waste of Threshold. A door in the far wall led deeper into the house.

Steve coughed. 'Sitstatrep,' he croaked. 'Sitstatrep!'

'In a minute, dammit.' Danyl squeezed himself through the gap and dropped down. He landed on a decaying pile of concrete blocks and sheets of Perspex. He splashed his way through the bodies and floating mattresses and called out, 'We're in one of the Threshold townhouses.'

'What?' Steve was still chained to the bath. Danyl returned to the spot beneath the hole in the ceiling, trying not to look at the people he was stepping over.

'We're in this abandoned housing development,' he hissed up at Steve. 'Threshold. It's a hideout for the Cartographers.'

'Please, Danyl,' Steve hissed back. 'I know all about Threshold.'

'Oh? That's great. What happened here?'

A short silence. 'That's classified. What's important is that you get me out of this bath. Fast. We'll need tools. Bolt-cutters or an acetylene torch. They won't just be lying around. You'll have to search the entire complex for them. It will be incredibly dangerous. If Gorgon's agents see you, try to lead them away from me. Now, quickly, buddy. Go!'

Danyl waded towards a wall, keeping a lookout for any acetylene torches. The door opened onto a foyer with a rough concrete floor. There were no bodies in here. An archway in the opposite wall led to a large unfinished room with plaster walls. A concrete stairway climbed to a landing on the second floor. A door to Danyl's right led outside.

He inched it open and peered through the gap. Dozens of Cartographers were running back and forth in the medium distance. They were moving along the road that wound across the hillside. Some of them carried bulky laboratory equipment; others moved in pairs carrying stretchers bearing bodies.

Danyl shut the door and backed away. He hurried through the archway, moving with a new sense of urgency. There was some sort of crisis happening out there. Perhaps that was why no one had come for Danyl and Steve, or even to investigate the sound of the bathroom floor collapsing. Perhaps they could use the chaos to escape? But how could they evade all those Cartographers?

The next room was empty except for a pair of wooden planks leaning at an angle against the wall, forming a ramp that led to the window. The planks were spattered with dry muddy footprints. The window itself was boarded up, but one of the boards had been removed and the light flooding through gave the room a hushed cathedral quality.

Danyl stepped onto the planks and looked outside.

Now this was an escape route. The bank sloped away from this end of the house, but someone had stacked broken chunks of concrete in a pile below the window. Beyond this lay a field of weeds hidden from view of the rest of the Threshold development. And across the field, just a short sprint away, was a thick cluster of trees. Danyl could climb out, run and be free of Threshold in a matter of minutes.

But what to do about Steve? He was chained to the tub, which they couldn't even move from the bathroom let alone fit through this window or lift over the fence. His situation seemed hopeless. If escaping with Steve was impossible, did that mean Danyl should just leave without him? Steve would see it as a betrayal, but if doing the right thing was impossible, didn't that mean that doing the wrong thing was the right thing to do?

Danyl put his hands on the window, ready to pull himself up; he stopped when something fluttered at the edge of his vision. Taped to the wall was a piece of yellowed paper with curled edges. It read:

Simon—
We've gone to get some food. Back tonight.
E & V

A cold wind blew through the room.

Danyl knew that handwriting. Verity had left him countless messages written in that same elegant hand, on their kitchen table or stuck to his forehead while he slept.

He ripped the note from the wall. The ink was faded. It had been here a long time.

E & V. Eleanor and Verity. And Simon, the chemist.

This was where they'd come when Verity left Danyl and vanished from the world. They came to Threshold to do . . . what? Take DoorWay? Cross to the Real City? Seek the Spiral?

What had happened? What went wrong? Where did Gorgon come into it?

Danyl didn't understand any of it. He stood in the centre of the room, staring at the page as light flooded through the broken window. Then he folded the letter in half and slipped it into his pocket and went back to help Steve.

36

Teamwork

Steve woke from his light doze when Danyl poked his head through the gap in the bathroom floor and said, 'The sitstatrep is that we're getting out of here.'

Steve was still in the bath. 'Excellent,' he said. 'How?'

'With this.' He held up his hand. A band of steel gleamed in the sunlight.

Steve grasped. 'Lightbringer! Where was it?'

'On the floor downstairs, by the main door.'

Steve reached for his crowbar, then caught himself. 'But no crowbar can cut through a handcuff,' he protested. 'Not even Lightbringer.'

'We don't need to cut through the handcuff. The bath you're chained to is fixed to the tiles beneath it. So we'll use this'—he swung Lightbringer like a golf club; it made a whooshing sound as it cut through the air—'to smash those tiles, then we slide the bath across the floor and drop it through the gap. Once we're downstairs we'll have to carry the bath out the front door, but if we run we might make it to the side of the building without being seen. Once we're there we can dash into the trees and make it to the road, somehow. Once we're away from Threshold we'll find a way to cut you free.'

Steve scratched at the stubble on his head. He contemplated the collapsed bathroom floor. 'You want to drop the bath through there? Won't that be dangerous?'

'Not really. Oh, wait. You mean dangerous for you?'

Steve nodded.

'I guess so, yeah. Very. But we can pad the bath with blankets and lay mattresses on the floor where you'll land. That might reduce the risk of death or serious injury.'

'What about the bathroom door? Why don't we just force it open with the crowbar?'

'The bath is too wide. It'll never fit through.'

Steve drummed his fingers on the rim of the bath, trying to think of a way to improve the escape plan by somehow transferring the risk of injury away from himself and onto Danyl. Getting hold of a blowtorch or some bolt-cutters was still the best option. He'd have to manipulate Danyl into going out and searching the rest of Threshold.

But then Steve looked at his poor, unfortunate friend and felt a sense of—not shame, exactly, because Steve didn't believe in the evolutionary utility of shame or guilt; no, what he felt was pity. Danyl had nothing. He'd lost his girlfriend, his book. Even his sanity. All he had left was Steve's friendship—and Steve, who had everything, was plotting to send him into great danger. Gorgon was a monster. She'd deliberately chained Steve to the bathtub and flooded the room, trying to drown him. Danyl was no match for her. What was he thinking?

All of these thoughts flashed through Steve's mind, and he smiled at Danyl and said, 'It's an excellent plan. Proceed.'

Things went well. At first. Danyl smashed the tiles fixing the bath in place then Steve lay inside it as he slid the tub down the sloping floor. It picked up speed, but midway to the gap Steve lost confidence in the finer details of the plan.

'This is madness,' he screamed. 'We have to find another way.' But the tiles were slick and the bath was heavy. It sped onwards while Danyl tried to grab it and Steve tugged at his handcuffed leg, howling. The bath hurtled towards the jagged gap in the floor and came to a shuddering halt when the rim slammed into the base of the wall. Steve fell back and Danyl breathed a sigh of relief just as the buckled and waterlogged floor gave way with a series of sickeningly loud cracks, collapsing under the weight of the bath, which see-sawed for a few seconds then pitched forward and fell.

The impact on the floor below made a sound like a church bell: a deep, pure, solemn note that hung in the air. Danyl peered through the gap, coughing and waving away the clouds of plaster and dust, to see the bath intact and a spiderweb of cracks radiating out from it. Steve lay in the bath, his arms crossed over his chest. When he saw Danyl he smiled and gave a thumbs up.

The best way to carry the bath, Steve explained, once Danyl climbed down and joined him, was to set it on its side. That way Steve's handcuffed leg could reach the ground and he could stand and walk. Then they could just slide the bath along the floor to the front door. 'Old-school style.'

They chatted as they worked. Steve told Danyl about Gorgon's operation, and he smiled patiently as Danyl recounted his own feeble efforts to understand what was happening in the valley. They slid from the kitchen to the entrance hall, opened the front door a crack and peered through it.

Outside was a muddy slope dotted with weeds. To their left was a brief, slippery dash along the side of the house. Their escape route lay around the corner. Directly ahead of them was the driveway zigzagging back and forth across the incline, and beyond that lay a cluster of townhouses. There were at least thirty Cartographers moving about, some of them singly, most in groups.

But they still had a chance. A group of a dozen people were carrying boxes past their house, heading downhill. They'd have their backs to Danyl and Steve, and they'd block anyone else on the hillside from seeing them. Hopefully. 'We'll have to lift the bath off the ground,' Danyl said. 'If we drag it we'll make too much noise, and take too long.'

'Affirmative,' Steve whispered back. 'Get ready.'

They squatted down and gripped the bath, waiting for the perfect moment. The Cartographers shuffled down the driveway; when they were in position Steve hissed, 'Go!'

They hurried through the door, carrying the bath between them, gritting their teeth under its awkward weight. They turned left and slipped their way across the slope. Steve expected to hear a shout ring out at any second. All it would take was one person to glimpse them and get suspicious about a bathtub floating across the hill and they'd be caught.

But the shout never came. They reached the corner and steered the bath around it, then they were out of sight behind the house. They sank to their knees, grinning and gasping for breath.

'We made it.' Steve gripped Danyl's shoulder. 'You did well back there buddy. Much better than the shock troops I've been working with. Amateurs. Imbeciles.'

'Thanks. We're still not free though. We should—'

'Oh, we're as good as free. We did it. Mostly me, but you helped and I won't forget that. Nothing can stop us. We're a team.' Steve held out his hand and Danyl shook it, and that's when the dog attacked them.

37

Danyl and Steve match wits against a dog

She came at them from downwind, with the afternoon sun behind her. She ran with an easy loping gait. She did not bark.

There were two males. They'd emerged from one of the houses which Dog was Not Allowed Inside. They carried a large bath and one of them was chained to it. They hobbled towards the trees, stopping and resting every few steps. They stank of sweat and weakness and shame.

The male chained to the bath was being punished for something, Dog decided, and the other one must be his master: his pack leader. She would take the master first. She would sink her teeth into the soft, weak flesh of his leg, laming him, and then do the same to his underling, and then she would leap around them, shouting and snarling while they cowered and cried and submitted to her strength, and then Dog's own pack leader would come and see her works and praise her and know that Dog was loyal and brave, and kept the pack leader safe. Dog's heart filled with joy, and she ran faster, head down and ears flat.

Now the males saw her. They picked up the bath and ran, but made it only a few steps before they dropped the bath and fell over. They yelled at each other and the enemy pack leader leaped to his feet and tried to run for the trees, abandoning his inferior, but the other male grabbed his feet and brought his master crashing to the ground. Now they howled at each other and the stink of their terror reached her, carried on the breeze, and intensified Dog's joy. As she sprinted across the last stretch of open ground, she vowed: *I will make you proud of me, pack leader.* She opened her mouth and locked her eyes on the enemy pack leader's thick, flabby calves.

But what were they doing? They'd stopped howling. They were lying down on the ground together. Were they mating? Or prostrating, submitting themselves to Dog? Fools! Did they think she would spare them? She growled with joy; her mouth flooded with drool.

They were doing something with the bath: scratching at it, pushing it. And now it lifted and Dog saw their cowardly plan. She put on an extra burst of speed and barked at them, warning them to stand their ground and fight, but they disobeyed and crawled inside the bath then tipped it down again just as she reached it.

She circled it, snarling and shouting, furious at her enemies' cowardice but also at herself. She pushed at the bath with her snout, but it was solid, impregnable. They were safe inside. She circled it, looking for an opening, listening to the cowardly babble of their voices.

'Great. We're trapped inside again.'

'We're outside, Steve. We're just inside the bath.'

'That's what I said. We're inside.'

'But the bath is outside.'

'The house was outside. Does that mean that when we were inside the house we were really outside?'

'That's stupid.'

'Stupid? You wouldn't dare talk to me like that if my shock troops were here. Why, they'd—' The underling broke off and screamed. Dog had dug a small hole in the mud beneath the bath and forced her snout through it, and now she growled and snapped at his pink terrified face. Both males recoiled, knocking the bath backwards off the hole.

'Get off me!'

'Stop kicking, Steve. Calm down. Listen. We don't have long. That creature will dig its way in, or someone will hear it barking and find us. We need to think our way out of this.'

'You're right. What should we do?'

'We should come up with a plan.'

'Your plan is that we come up with a plan?'

'Hush, Steve. I'm trying to think.'

'Hush? Hush? How dare you.'

Dog ignored them. She had problems of her own. Should she go and get help? There were dozens of people on the other side of the house, and they would come running if she barked loud enough. But then they would take these enemies to the pack leader. Dog wanted the joy and ecstasy of delivering these captives herself: laying them before the pack leader in a bloody, defeated pile.

She sat back on her haunches and panted a little. This sometimes helped her think. Should she go and find the pack leader? She would be in her house at the top of the hill. Dog was not allowed inside this house either, but she could run up to it and bark outside. Maybe even rest her forelegs on the floor inside the door if it was open? Then the pack leader would come and follow her down and see that she'd trapped these enemies and vigorously scratch her ears. But what if they returned to find the enemies gone? No, she'd have to deal with these disgusting creatures herself.

And then Dog broke off her thoughts and leapt to her feet. The males were doing something. They'd been whispering to each other; now the bath lifted an inch or two off the ground. Dog trotted towards it. It moved! She leapt back. She growled as it slowly crawled across the muddy ground, back towards the house. It rounded the corner and headed for the front door.

So that was their plan! They knew Dog wasn't allowed inside the House and they thought they'd be safe if they made it back inside. Well, they were wrong about that. Why, she would follow them right in and drag them out again! And they had to reach the House first. She pushed her snout at the gap below the bath and tried to push it up to tip it over. She snarled as the stench of fear and weakness grew stronger, and her enemies howled and babbled and the bath moved even faster. But it was too heavy for her to lift with her snout, and she withdrew and danced away again, snuffling at the trail of scent they left behind. Dog could smell the dye in their clothes, the glue in their shoes, the blood in their veins. She could smell their sour bladders and the yeasty contents of their bowels and, in the sweat that now soaked their backs, the components of their last meal. And she could smell the Old Smell. The complex and frightening smell that she had never smelt before she came to this valley.

Dog had arrived in Te Aro ten winters ago. Her memory of life before that was vague: she remembered vast planes of concrete, loud noises that made her bristle and whimper, terrible loneliness. How much happier she was at her new home! She loved the cool shade beneath the trees, the fields of long grass and hidden rabbits, the screams of occasional trespassers when Dog fell upon them, her teeth flashing in the sun. But she didn't like the Old Smell. How to describe it? Salty and metallic, half-organic, very very old. It came from the old house on top of the hill but it also bubbled up from flooded rabbit warrens when it rained in the spring, and it was strongest outside the culvert at the bottom of the hill, which led into the tunnels beneath the valley.

Dog's job was to protect the pack leader's territory. Dog Was Not Allowed inside the crumbling old buildings staggered up the hillside, or inside the tunnel, or inside the pack leader's house at the top of the slope. She patrolled the territory during the day, and at night she greeted the pack leader when she emerged from the tunnel and escorted her up the hillside to her house.

At first the door to this house was reached by a flight of rotting steps, but shortly after Dog arrived, the pack leader ordered her underlings to tear them down.

The underlings came from the tunnel: a pale, weak-limbed gaggle. They replaced the steps with a scaffolding made of vertical steel poles and horizontal wooden planks. The planks formed a makeshift stairway which the pack leader climbed every evening. Dog would scramble up behind her.

Then the pack leader cooked dinner in the kitchen while Dog waited at the door. Sometimes putting one foot inside the hall, sometimes snuffling. Not trying to be obtrusive, just letting the pack leader know she was still there. Finally the pack leader would finish cooking and would sit on the scaffolding next to Dog, swinging her legs over the side and letting Dog eat bacon or chops or potatoes off her plate.

When the plate was licked clean, Dog rested her muzzle on the pack leader's knee and sniffed her extensively. She smelled of tunnels and darkness, and books, but beyond that she smelled of the old house and the hill where Dog lived.

The pack leader had been a pup here. She'd lived here a long time, far longer than Dog's lifetime. She owned the territory, and every night Dog communicated her fealty with a sequence of snout-pushes and eye-rolls. The pack leader understood and scratched Dog's ears. Then she went inside and slept in her bedroom while Dog slept in the small shelter at the end of the scaffolding, in the snug warmth of her blanket.

For many seasons their days were the same. Then, at the end of last summer, things changed.

It was a baking hot day. Dog spent the morning investigating the mouse and butterfly situation in the lower meadow, then she retreated to the cool shade of a beech tree by the driveway. She dozed—it was hours before the pack leader would return— but woke when she heard voices.

It was a man and a woman. Dog watched as they climbed over the fence. They were wearing backpacks and carrying bags filled with groceries. The wind carried their scents: the usual medley of human smells, but also the Old Smell. Dog was about to charge them, send them running, bite them if they defied her; but then she parsed out the man's scent. He smelled of this place and the house on the hill. He smelled like

236

the pack leader. He was of her litter. Did that mean he was allowed to be here?

The woman shouted. She'd seen Dog. The man knelt and rummaged in his pack. He brought out a package of sausages, tore it open and whistled at Dog, then clicked his fingers and pointed at them.

Dog was noble and proud and fierce. When newcomers invaded her territory she would fight them or die. But this man was of the pack leader's kin; this was his territory. Also: sausages. So she trotted forward and greeted them. The man patted Dog and the woman praised Dog's beauty. Dog accepted these compliments then ate the sausages with quiet dignity. Eventually the woman said to the man, 'Let's get out of sight.'

They set off up the driveway. Dog trotted after them.

The man carried a box filled with paper, and a briefcase. Inside the case was crushed ice. Beneath that, barely detectable to Dog's nose, were hundreds of glass vials with rubber stoppers. Inside them was a liquid that smelled of the Old Smell.

They picked one of the abandoned houses halfway up the hill. Back then the buildings were all uninhabited, boarded up, but the man and woman circled around and found a loose board hanging from a window. They piled rocks and built a stairway up to it. The man prised the board away, then he and the woman disappeared inside.

They stayed there all day. When the pack leader returned from the tunnels, Dog greeted her and indicated the presence of the newcomers via a sequence of jumps and snorts and tail motions. 'There are two people living in one of the abandoned buildings,' Dog explained, bounding along beside the pack leader. 'A male and a female. They gave me a sausage! The man is of your kin. I'm guessing the female is his mate although she did not carry the stink of his seed in her loins. Maybe they're going through a tough patch? I think he can do better than her. Anyway, because the male is your kin, I let them stay. Was that cool? If it wasn't, I can chase them away or take you to

237

them, or we can just sit on the scaffolding outside your house and watch the sunset, and eat bacon. Your call.'

They sat on the scaffolding and ate bacon.

The next day the pack leader went into the tunnel as usual. Dog spent the day waiting below the window of the abandoned townhouse, her tail thumping on the dry grass, wondering if the newcomers had any more sausages. They did! The female emerged in the mid-morning, stinking of the Old Smell. She saw Dog and tossed another sausage at her. She climbed down the pile of bricks and hurried down the driveway, climbed over the gate and disappeared. She returned late in the day with another female, taller than her with ink patterns carved around her ankles, and they went up into the house and spent the night there.

And so Dog's life went on for several months and many sausages. The days grew shorter. The autumn winds blew up and the shadows of clouds raced across the fields of grass. An owl moved into a tree near the pack leader's house and defied Dog's command to move on. But the lives of the pack leader and the male and female went on much the same. Until late one afternoon.

Dog had been sleeping. There was a pile of concrete slabs in the top meadow and they soaked up the heat of the sun. Dog decided to guard these slabs. She lay upon them, her paws outstretched, the rough warmth toasty on her belly, and she dozed. She had a frustrating dream in which she chased large butterflies made of meat across a drowned meadow and her legs got stuck in the mire. She woke snarling, her footpads damp with sweat. The air was contaminated with the scent of an invader.

Dog stood and sniffed deeply. The invader was a human female. She smelled strange: very clean but contaminated in some indefinable way. Dog could tell that she'd entered the development by climbing the gate at the bottom of the hill, then she'd made her way up, searching the derelict townhouses before arriving at the building where the man and the woman slept. That's when her smell became close enough to wake Dog.

Dog sped towards the townhouse, and as she ran her nose detected movement below. The invader was heading back down the hill. She stank of blood.

The information was in the air but Dog was too excited to make sense of it. She charged down pathways, under bushes and over puddles. By the time she reached the townhouse the invader was halfway to the bottom of the hill. She was fast but Dog was faster. She could reach this invader before the invader reached the gate.

But Dog hesitated. The smell of blood flooding out from the townhouse was overpowering. It came in great drifts, mixed with urine, stress hormones, the Old Smell. Someone had been hurt; hurt badly. It was the man. The pack leader's kin. Dog concentrated and the sequence of events written in the air became clear to her. The invader had come into the townhouse and attacked the male while he slept.

Should Dog pursue the invader or go inside and help the wounded man? She could lick his face and nuzzle his fingers until he got better. Or—and now that she thought of this, she realised this was what she must do—she could alert the pack leader. Summon her and tell her everything. The pack leader would know what to do.

She raced to the culvert at the bottom of the hill. When she passed the last townhouse she caught a glimpse of the invader. They were a long way away and Dog's eyes weren't very good: what she saw was a blur of motion as the invader approached the gate. The invader held a cardboard box under her arm and a club in her free hand, and she tossed them over the gate before clambering over herself. The box carried the wounded male's scent. Is that why the invader had invaded? To steal the box?

Dog reached the culvert. Beyond it lay the network of

tunnels which Dog Was Not Allowed Inside. But she knew the network well. She could smell the stream, teeming with its tiny sightless aquatic life. Beyond that the bookshop, with its acidic aroma of paper, ink and glue. Deeper down was the old quarry. These tunnels were all blocked off, but traces of what lay beyond filtered out through the gaps in the brickwork and wound its way to Dog's warm, damp, powerful nose, and troubled her brain with incomprehensible sensations. There was something down there, Dog knew. Something deep. Something strange. Something very, very old.

It was the Old Smell in its deepest most pure essence. But closer—much closer—was the warm mixture of the pack leader's scent. Dog sat at the mouth of the tunnel and barked. She explained what had happened and took full responsibility for the lapse in security. She explained about the sun-warmed blocks and promised not to sleep on them again. She described the invader—bipedal, female, mostly hairless—and her attack on the man in the townhouse and the theft of the box.

And the pack leader was coming! Dog leaped about for joy, jumping and barking. The pack leader! The pack leader! And then she was there! Dog forgot—for a moment—everything that had happened, and continued leaping for joy, until a scream rang out. It came from the townhouse halfway up the slope. The woman had awoken and discovered the man. The pack leader hurried towards the townhouse.

Dog led the way. By the time they arrived, the woman had emerged from the house. She had the man's blood on her, and she clutched a stick like a club and trembled with fear. She was sobbing and breathing in deep ragged gasps. When she saw the pack leader her terror deepened. She raised the stick and stepped backwards and said, in a voice drowned in fear, 'Gorgon.'

~

The bath crashed into the edge of the doorway. The males inside it cried out, adjusted direction and tried again.

Dog watched, amused. As soon as they were inside she would follow them. If they tried to stop her or shut the door, or poke any of their limbs out from beneath the bath, Dog would grab them and pull them outdoors and run around them, barking. Fools.

They were halfway through now. Dog scratched at the bath, ready to rush inside. But what was happening? The bath rose to block the doorway. They were shutting her out! They'd tricked Dog! She threw herself against the upturned tub, but it held firm.

She would have to go get help. The pack leader's house was too far away but her servants were nearby. They would do.

She headed towards the road. Several servants were coming up the hill. They carried strange instruments, all of which reeked of the Old Smell. Dog would get them to follow her.

She was halfway to the road when something struck her flank. She snarled and spun around. A stone! Someone had hit her with a stone! Who dared?

There was a flash of movement from the side of the house. One of the enemy males: the master, the one not chained to the bathtub. It had found another exit. And now it thought it could stand there and toss stones at Dog with impunity! Her head clouded with rage. She charged at him and he fled, his stupid bald arms flying about his soft weak bald body. She rounded the corner of the house and saw him scrabbling up the concrete stacked against the wall—the same one the man and the woman once used—leading to an open window. He jumped through and Dog gave chase, racing up the steps.

But just as she reached the top a new smell reached her. There was another person in Threshold. Someone who wasn't supposed to be here. They were around the other side of the townhouse, coming up the hillside. Someone Dog had smelled before.

The invader.

Dog knew what she had to do. Leave these absurd males. Find the invader and destroy them. But it took a second for Dog's brain to process these thoughts, and while she thought she continued to run up the steps, carried on by rage and instinct. Beyond the window was a dark room with a long drop to the floor. Once inside, Dog wouldn't be able to get out. She needed to stop. Turn back!

But she was moving too fast. Dog leapt into the darkness.

38

No!

Danyl ran.

The room was lit by a shaft of light from the window. He was almost at the door when the light vanished, blocked by the head and body of the shaggy wolf-sized dog he'd deliberately enraged.

It bounded into the room. The light returned, casting the dog's monstrous shadow on the wall. This shadow looked up, growled and leapt. Danyl stumbled backwards then remembered that the actual dog was behind him. He reversed direction and ran for the archway.

This was all his idea. Five minutes ago he'd been trapped beneath the bath with Steve while the dog's fanged, drooling snout pushed under the rim millimetres from his face. They were screaming at each other until Danyl clutched Steve's wrist and said, 'We're friends, remember? We're a team. We can beat a dog.'

He'd laid out his plan. They would scuttle back to the house using the bath as protection, then use it to blockade the door. Steve would hold it in place while Danyl ran back through the house, climbed out the back window, got the dog's attention and tricked it into chasing him back inside. Danyl could then run to the front door, by which time Steve would be ready to slam it shut the instant Danyl ran through, thus trapping the dog in the building.

It was a great plan, Steve had said, nodding with approval. And yet, Danyl wondered, as he sped towards the entrance hall jumping over piles of construction debris like a nimble but terrified steeplechase pony, was any plan in which a drooling beast chased him through the darkness towards a remote exit really, truly great?

He jumped on a pile of boards, then jumped off it and sailed through the air, his legs pedalling in space. Before he landed, his brain gave him a series of gentle zaps. Danyl blinked them away, trying to concentrate. Be quiet, he thought at his brain. I'm handling this.

His brain had a point, though. Danyl was supposed to avoid stressful situations and here he was being chased by a monster through a ruined building. Maybe he'd chosen poorly. Should he have abandoned Steve after all and fled when he had the chance? No. That thought was unworthy. Steve was Danyl's friend: saving him was the right thing to do. It was nice to think he'd made one good choice in his life.

But once he'd trapped the dog and escaped from Threshold, Danyl would need to leave the valley immediately. Go back to his former tranquil life. Become Medicated Danyl again. He would never solve the mystery of the Real City, or the Spiral, or Verity's disappearance, but if the price of knowledge was being eaten by a dog, then it was a price he was not prepared to pay.

He landed with organ-bruising force. The dog was right behind him: he heard its paws scrabbling on the tiles. But he was in the entrance hall. He was going to make it. There was the door, a rectangle of sunlight. There was Steve, silhouetted. There was a shape behind him. Danyl couldn't make it out; the light was too bright. But he could see Steve's face: the smile lines around his eyes, the stubble on his head. His lips were moving. Was he saying something? Danyl couldn't hear over the tide of blood pounding in his ears.

And then the room dimmed. The light was going out. Why? A solar eclipse? No! The door was closing! Steve was shutting it, trapping Danyl in the house with the dog!

Danyl couldn't even scream. He didn't have the oxygen. He met Steve's eyes and mouthed his name, and the beam of light tightened. The shape behind Steve swam into focus like an object in a telescope.

It was Ann, the treasurer.

The light vanished and the door clicked shut.

39

Steve thinks hard

Steve closed the door, kneeled down and leaned against it, blockading it.

The door was wood. It was warm from the sun. From the other side came footsteps. Barking. Furious screams. Behind him Ann was saying something. Steve ignored these distractions. He was trying to think. Some combination of thoughts had turned a key inside his mind and he remembered what he saw on his second journey to the Real City.

Danyl and Steve had discussed the Real City before escaping the townhouse and being attacked by the dog. What was it? What were the pathways? What was the Spiral and where did it lead? Was the Real City another reality? Or an ultimate reality? Was it, Danyl had wondered, a more real reality?

Steve insisted that there was no ultimate reality. There was no face behind the mask of appearance. It was all masks. Everything was a symbol for something else. A pointer to a pointer. But you couldn't explain that to Danyl. He refused to believe there was nothing to believe in. You couldn't make him understand that there was nothing, ultimately, to understand. Steve focused on what mattered. What happened here, in Te Aro, not some alternate or ultimate reality, or whatever the Real City was or was not.

But Gorgon cared about the Real City and Gorgon was Steve's enemy. Anything that might help defeat her: any clue, any weakness, any scrap of intelligence could be vital. Steve's subconscious had noticed something and the act of locking Danyl inside the townhouse with the savage dog had somehow unlocked the memory.

The paths in the Real City had changed.

There wasn't much to see in the City. Plazas. Pathways. Void. The Spiral. That uniformity made it difficult to map. Everywhere looked the same, and not even Steve's powerful intellect could chart it. If he'd been allowed to wake every day and document his path, then take a different one the next night, he could have done so. That's what Sophus and the rest of the Cartographers did.

Why? They wanted to reach the Spiral, obviously. But why were they keeping all those so-called pilgrims captive in the City? Why lure more prisoners into the bookshop? Why not just chart the City themselves? During his first imprisonment, Steve had observed that the number of pathways connecting to each plaza was always an even number. When he returned to the Real City today, his subconscious noticed that this had changed. Some plazas had three pathways, and some pathways led to dead ends, meaning that the plaza at the terminus had only one pathway.

Interesting, but what did it mean?

This wasn't the best time to be trying to figure that out, to be honest. Steve was deep in enemy territory, chained to a bathtub, alone, having just locked his only ally in a house with a savage dog, and with a lot of generally stressful stuff going on around him. But Steve's intellect was like a runaway train. It had momentum. He couldn't just think about something more pressing, like Danyl screaming from behind the locked door, or why Ann the treasurer was here, her hands cuffed behind her back, or even what he was going to do about the goat-faced archivist holding a syringe filled with DoorWay to Steve's throat. No, his mind bore down on the problem of the Real City.

It had changed. Why?

Was it because the number of people trapped in the City had increased? Was the act of observing the City generating a pathway through the maze? Had that been Gorgon's plan all along—to imprison enough people in the Real City to bring a route through it into being, then travel to the Spiral herself? That had to be it. It explained everything. That was the reason Gorgon was so furious at Steve. His operations struck at the heart of her scheme. That was why she'd imprisoned him in a room flooding with water. When that failed, she'd sent her top lieutenants to capture Steve and bring him before her, and that's why Steve was now kneeling beside his bathtub with Sophus on one side of him and Eleanor on the other, and the archivist behind him holding a syringe filled with DoorWay, the tip of the needle pressing against Steve's cervical artery.

However, it didn't explain the presence of the treasurer. Ann's face was smeared with mud. Her expression was one of silent fury.

Eleanor regarded them both with evident satisfaction and said, 'Take this idiot'—she indicated Steve—'and this treasurer'—she nodded at Ann—'to the top of the hill. Take them before Gorgon.'

40

Danyl tries to out-think the dog

Danyl crashed into the door and bounced off it. His jaw and genitals sustained most of the impact, and he pivoted and stumbled directly towards the dog who was astonished to see the door slam shut and her target reverse direction. Her claws scrambled on the smooth tiles and her hindquarters swung as she pitched over into a controlled slide, snapping at Danyl's legs as he leapt over her in a desperate but successful star-jump.

He landed and ran towards the kitchen. When he reached the doorway he turned and screamed, 'Steve?'

Steve did not reply. The dog clambered to its feet and snarled at Danyl.

'Steve!'

The dog lunged. Danyl fled. He jumped onto the long bench running down the centre of the room. His plan was to sprint to the end and leap for the jagged hole in the roof then pull himself up into the bathroom and cower in terror until Steve rescued him. But the dog anticipated all of this. It ran to the end of the bench, easily outpacing Danyl, and stood on its hind legs with its front paws on the countertop, grinning at him.

Elevation. He needed elevation. Fast. He backed away from the dog while it watched him with glistening brown eyes. It thought Danyl was trapped. If he jumped off the bench it would run him down in seconds. There was nowhere else to go.

But there was. Danyl feinted to the left. The dog dropped down and ran to the left side of the counter, so Danyl jumped to the right. He splashed his way across the floor, over the half-submerged, staring bodies of the blue-lipped pilgrims, to the pile of concrete and sheets of Perspex stacked against the wall. He clambered to the top of the pile. The dog tried to jump after him but Danyl pulled a wobbly sheet of Perspex out from under him and held it up as a shield. The dog's snout collided with the sheet in a smeared tableau of fangs and nostrils and drool. It fell back and jumped up again, but Danyl's shield held firm.

The dog paced back and forth. She did not look worried. She knew Danyl was trapped on top of the pile, that he had nowhere to go. She sat, looked up at him and panted happily.

Danyl smiled back. This dog thought it was better than him, but she was probably wrong. Danyl could use reason and symbols and tools. All the dog could do was run fast and crush his bones between her jaws.

He gripped the Perspex and wobbled it. He looked at the hole in the roof, which was about three metres away. The sheet of Perspex was about three metres long.

Danyl wasn't an engineer or a materials scientist. He was just a writer trapped by a dog. But he was pretty sure there were building codes and minimum standards for construction materials such that any discarded Perspex left lying around should be able to bear the weight of an adult male crawling through mid-air above a savage animal. So he shifted his grip on the Perspex and, grunting with effort, manoeuvred the far end into place and slid it through the hole. After that it was a simple matter of inching along the sheet while it bent under Danyl's weight and the dog leapt high into the air and grabbed the hem of his trousers in her jaw and tried to drag him down. His face pressed onto the Perspex as he gripped its edges with both hands, and he saw it begin to crack; flaws were appearing millimetres away from his face and spreading out with a cascade of tiny crackling sounds, then the fabric of his trousers ripped and the dog dropped back down to the floor and uttered a frustrated, sorrowful growl as the sheet sprang up again, waves wobbling along its disintegrating length.

Danyl scuttled forward, his screams rising and falling with

the undulation of the sheet, and then he was through the hole in the roof, his arms clutching the twisted beams, pulling himself up into the wet, sunlit bathroom where he lay on his back and panted in time with the dog's loud panting below and his heart thrashed in his chest like a suffocating fish.

After a while his breathing calmed and his heart slowed. He was lying on something hard and sharp that was digging into his back. He sat up and discovered he'd been lying on Steve's crowbar. They must have left it here when the bath collapsed through the floor. Finally, a lucky break.

It took a few minutes of precision jimmying and smashing to force the bathroom door open; eventually the wooden joints crackled and gave way. A block of timber was jammed between the door and the floor on the other side. Danyl forced the crowbar through the gap and poked at it. It gave, and the door opened.

The room beyond was empty except for three single mattresses on the floor. The light came in through a window in the east wall, looking out on the trees rising up the flank of the hill. A second window faced the Threshold development, but it was boarded up. There was another door in the far wall. It opened onto the landing: stairs leading down to the foyer. Danyl closed it hurriedly. He didn't know much about dogs, but he was pretty sure they could climb stairs.

As he moved towards the window, his shoes made a crackling sound, like slow tap-dancing. There was something sticky underfoot. The floor was littered with screwed-up pieces of paper and dozens of empty plastic vials, all embedded in a dry brown pool radiating from one of the mattresses, which had a dull reddish stain at one end. Danyl knelt and touched his fingertips to the floor then sniffed them. Blood.

He picked up a vial. It was the size of his little finger, empty, with a blue residue.

Three people had lain in here taking DoorWay. Travelling to the Real City. One of them had been wounded while they lay. They'd lost a lot of blood. Danyl remembered the freshly dug grave atop the plateau.

He wondered what happened to your mind if you died while you were in the Real City.

He picked up a piece of paper and unscrewed it. It shed a rain of brown flakes like insect skins, revealing a map: a scrawled diagram of the Real City. The other side of the page was covered in dense, printed text. It was hard to read through the creasing and the blood. Danyl held it up to the window and the letters swam into focus.

It was a page from his book.

41

Sophus and Ann

They formed an odd procession. Eleanor led them across the patch of weeds to the road. Ann followed, her hands cuffed behind her back. She glanced back at Sophus as if she were about to speak, but shook her head and resumed her trudge up the slope, heading towards the house at the top of the hill.

Sophus carried the front of Steve's bath. Steve was behind him and the archivist took up the rear. Progress was slow. The bath was heavy and the driveway was steep and muddy. Each time they stumbled the bath slipped from their fingers and fell in the mud, and Steve had to brace himself to stop it from sliding back down the hill and dragging him with it. And each time this happened Ann glanced back at Sophus, and Sophus looked at her, and then at Eleanor, and his expression grew grim.

Steve's training as a psychologist told him that something strange was happening. Why was Ann here? Why was she being taken to Gorgon? He decided to investigate. To probe, subtly. He called out, 'You there, treasurer. Why are you here?'

'She's not just a treasurer,' Sophus snapped. 'She's Professor Ann Day. Show some respect.'

'Who?'

'You've never heard of Ann Day? The brilliant mathematical philosopher?'

'No. Should I have?'

Sophus shook his head in disbelief. 'She's an international superstar of differential topology. The queen of sympleptic geometry.'

'Not anymore,' Ann interjected, her voice weary. 'I used to be those things, but I gave it all up. I retired. He's right—I'm nobody now. Just a simple treasurer.'

'Why did you retire?'

'She won't tell you,' Sophus said. 'She won't tell anyone. She was at the highest vertex of the polyhedron of her career, and she stepped down. She said she was done with mathematics forever, then she disappeared.'

Steve asked, 'Why?'

'She won't tell you,' Sophus repeated, and Ann bowed her head.

'How do you know so much about her?'

'I studied her work when I was a graduate student,' Sophus replied. 'I read her final, baffling paper on Gaussian curvature in higher dimensional spaces. It was brilliant, but also disturbing. It seemed she was moving towards a final breakthrough. Something that would change everything we think we know about curves. But it also seemed that she was holding something back. She was hiding something, some key insight. And then she announced that her career was over, and she vanished. I decided to find her.

'I tracked her here, to Te Aro. I moved here to learn from her. But she rejected me. Oh, she gave me a scholarship and a hovel to live in while I finished my thesis, in exchange for my silence. But she refused to discuss her work, or why she abandoned it. Instead she warned me about the peril of new ideas. Her work was dangerous, she claimed. A threat to civilisation. Possibly to all of existence!

'I was furious with her. What kind of world would we live in if thinkers refused to publicise our ideas simply because they are incredibly dangerous? Little did she know that her refusal to share her insights would lead me to an even greater discovery.

'One night, after we fought, I went out and walked the streets of Te Aro. That is when I discovered the clues that lead me to the most important discovery in the history of mathematics. The Real City.'

'The Real City isn't what you think it is,' Ann replied, her voice a wretched mumble.

Steve asked, 'What is it?'

'It's an artefact of pure mathematics,' Sophus said. 'It's a solution to the oldest unsolved problem in philosophy. The problem of mathematical reality. My work on the topology of the City goes beyond anything Ann dreamed of. And we haven't even reached the Spiral yet, which is technically not even a spiral, but a geometric curve called a cardioid.'

Eleanor snorted. She'd listened to their conversation while she led them up the hill towards Gorgon's house, and now she rounded on Sophus. 'Do you still think the Real City is some kind of geometry problem? An equation you can solve? That if we reach the Spiral you'll be able to publish some meaningless proof? Go ahead and believe that if it makes you happy. But the City is only a means to an end. It and you are part of Gorgon's work to free humanity from the tyranny of the world of forms and change. Once her work is finished and we reach the Spiral, you won't care about mathematics, or philosophy. Everything will be explained, and nothing will be explained. All will be both light and darkness, wisdom and mystery. That is the Real City.'

Then Ann said in a quiet, miserable voice, 'You're both wrong. The Real City is a trap.'

And she told them her story.

42

Lacunae

Danyl watched the procession make its way up the hill. The window looking out over the wastes of Threshold was boarded up, but someone had drilled a circle in the board at head height. A spy-hole. Danyl spied through it now, watching as Steve, Sophus and the archivist wrestled with the bathtub. Eleanor turned to address them, and Ann, looking miserable, replied.

What was Ann doing there? Why was she being taken to Gorgon's house? Danyl didn't know, but he knew he had to rescue her. And Steve. But how? The group was guarded. The hillside swarmed with Cartographers. And Steve was still chained to the bathtub. Impossible.

Danyl stepped back from the spy-hole, avoiding the pool of dried blood on the floor. He looked at the bloodsoaked mattress and shivered.

Whose blood was it? Surely it belonged to whoever lay buried in that crude grave on the distant, windswept plateau on the other side of Threshold. The note Danyl had found downstairs mentioned three names: Eleanor, Verity and Simon. Eleanor was still alive. She was right outside, being evil. He didn't know where Verity was, but she was still alive a day ago, and whatever had happened here had clearly happened a while back. Weeks. Months. An air of abandonment hung about the room. That just left Simon, the chemist. Was he dead? Rotting in that grave? Who killed him? Eleanor? Verity? Gorgon?

He looked at the bloodstained page from his book. When Verity and Simon disappeared, they'd taken the only manuscript of Danyl's novel with them. Why? It was bound up in the mystery somehow: DoorWay, the Real City. And where was the rest of it?

He folded up the page and slipped it into his pocket, then rounded the mattress. There was a triangular gap in the edge of the blood pool. Something had sat on the floor here. A medium-sized box.

Just after Verity broke up with him, before he was exiled from the valley, Danyl found an empty vial of DoorWay in the pocket of Verity's old dressing gown. It was circumstantial proof that she'd drugged him with small amounts of the substance while he was writing his novel. Why? Danyl knew the answer now. To test the drug. She'd given him minute traces: not enough to send him to the Real City, just enough to contaminate his book, somehow, which Verity then read looking for proof that DoorWay worked. He remembered Verity's art exhibition: the black cases, the patrons experiencing dizziness and disorientation. Were the photos inside the cases coated with DoorWay? And what of Eleanor's restaurant? Danyl recalled a prominent food critic accusing the Dolphin Café of giving him food poisoning. The seafood noodles, he'd claimed, caused him to pass out and experience vivid hallucinations of an endless, sprawling city. Did that have something to do with all of this?

Danyl suspected that it did. They'd been testing the drug. Clinical trials. And when they had the right dosage they'd stolen Danyl's book, closed down Eleanor's restaurant and disappeared. They came here, bringing a supply of DoorWay with them. They hid here, mapping the Real City and trying to find their way to the Spiral. But something had happened. Simon the biochemist was killed. After that, Gorgon appeared. Her Cartographers lured people to the bookshop and trapped them in the Real City. And Eleanor and Verity helped her, until yesterday, when Verity left that message on Eleanor's phone then vanished.

A shout came from outside the house. Danyl returned to the spy-hole. The procession hadn't moved far. Sophus and the archivist had slipped in the mud and dropped the bath.

Ann was talking to Steve and Sophus, and they were trying to pay attention while they wrestled with the mud-stained tub. Eleanor was shouting at them and pointing up the slope to the old house. Its scaffolding gleamed like teeth in the sunlight.

And suddenly Danyl had a plan. He tucked Steve's crowbar into the back of his pants, climbed out the window and lowered himself down. As he kicked around with his foot, trying to find a toehold, an odd thought struck him.

Back when Verity and Danyl were living together, a lunatic had broken into their house and tried to burn it down, all to destroy Danyl's book. According to the lunatic, the book was contaminated and the ideas within it would infect and destroy the universe. Or something like that. It was late at night and there had been a lot of petrol and screaming.

Back then, Danyl hadn't paid much attention to the lunatic but now he wondered. He recalled the deranged screams and he thought about the DoorWay compound and the Real City, and he wondered some more. If Verity had drugged Danyl while he was writing his book, then where did the ideas in his book come from? If they were inspired by DoorWay, and DoorWay led to the Real City, then, logically, the ideas had come from the Real City. But what did that even mean? And, if the ideas in his book came from there, then were the rest of the thoughts that ran through his head contaminated too? The decision to stop his medication, to return to Te Aro, to look for Verity, to rescue Steve? Where did the thoughts that made him do those things come from? Why did he think them? And why was he thinking this now?

His brain buzzed at him impatiently, and he found himself climbing down the side of the townhouse, his thoughts about his own thoughts scattered and abandoned. Maybe his brain was right, Danyl thought: rescue Ann and Steve now, then escape. Think about thinking later.

He let go of the window ledge and landed in the mud.

43

Ann's story

Ann said, 'Like most children, I would lie awake at night and wonder about the world. Why did it have three physical dimensions but only one time dimension? What would our lives be like if it were the other way around? If we could move back and forth through time but were stuck travelling in one direction through space? Of course, later, when I went to pre-kindergarten and taught myself to read, I understood that if there were fewer spatial dimensions, then there would be no gravitational forces between masses. Everything we see'—she pointed at Steve—'would simply drift apart. And if there were more time dimensions then the elementary particles of matter would be too unstable. They'd simply decay into nothing. But that just made things worse. I worried about what would happen if the structure of our reality suddenly changed, and I and my parents and my doll's house and sandpit instantly dissolved into a quantum vacuum.'

'I worried about the exact same thing,' Sophus said. 'I guess most kids do.'

'When I started school,' Ann continued, 'my teachers took me out of the normal classes and let me study whatever I wanted. Of course, what I wanted was mathematics, and I began to read Lobachevsky.'

'Ah!' Sophus gave a blissful smile. 'Lobachevsky!'

This was why Steve hated mathematicians. He liked to think he knew pretty much everything about everything. Oh, sure, there were tiny areas of academic interest where experts knew more than he did about, say, specific species of beetles or ancient Mayan literature, but in general Steve knew everything important. Mathematicians attacked his sense of omniscience.

They didn't know any of the things Steve knew, like the fact that humans evolved from cannibalistic apes addicted to eating each other's brains or that Jesus was a woman who moved to India after he died. Instead they viewed history as the grand sweeping progress of mathematical thought, while art and philosophy and empire ebbed and flowed about it. And he disliked the way mathematicians celebrated great thinkers whom Steve had never heard of, like this Lobachevsky guy. So he said, 'Lobachevsky? Hasn't he been debunked?'

'Oh, no.' Ann shook her head, visibly shocked by this heresy. 'Nikolai Lobachevsky was one of the greatest mathematicians of all time. When he was an astronomer at the University of Kazan in Russia, he developed non-Euclidean geometry, and in so doing he challenged one of the most basic intuitions about reality and the way we think about it.

'Philosophers once believed that Euclid's Axioms were such basic, obvious truths about our universe that we were born with this mathematical model of reality, in which parallel lines remained at a constant distance even if extended to infinity, and that its truth transcended logic or deduction. No one questioned this until Lobachevsky. It's impossible to overstate his influence on Minkowski and Einstein, and because of that lineage we know that the universe isn't the way it seems at all. It's a four-dimensional hyperbola that can only be described using mathematics pioneered by Lobachevsky.

'I remember sitting in an empty classroom,' Ann continued, 'and looking up from his equations and staring at the world around me and wondering, What else is wrong? What else about our reality do we think is so self-evident we never question it, but if we did it would reveal amazing new truths about our existence? And how do you make a breakthrough like that?

'But then, years later when I was a postgraduate student, I read deeper into Lobachevsky's work and found something . . . disturbing. At the same time as Lobachevsky, a mathematician called János Bolyai, working in Hungary and totally unknown to Lobachevsky, was working on the exact same idea. At first this seemed like an odd coincidence but then I learned that two other mathematicians, Carl Friedrich Gauss and Friedrich Karl Schweikart, also worked on the same idea at the same time, all independently of one another. How could this be? An idea which had remained unthinkable for two thousand years suddenly manifests itself in four minds simultaneously? Impossible, surely. Yet it happened, and reading their four papers I was struck by the notion that I was reading the work of a single author, a unique individual intelligence somehow working through the separate minds of the four mathematicians. But who or what could this author be? Where did mathematical innovation come from? Was all progress in mathematics over the last several thousand years the result of a singular intellect developing its thoughts through a succession of individuals? Why did almost all mathematical discovery all around the world suddenly stop for 800 years, from 300AD to 1100AD? Is it because whatever directed these discoveries was blocked?

'These questions haunted me. Perhaps our species was merely a tool for the development of mathematics. But who was the developer and what was their goal?

'At first, all this was just wild supposition. I couldn't publish anything on it. My career would be destroyed. So I set out to prove my theory. I built models charting and predicting mathematical progress throughout history. Again and again I saw previously incomprehensible concepts suddenly manifest themselves through mathematicians, and those ideas proliferated out in the world, giving birth to technologies, systems, new societies. And they weren't limited to mathematics. I also looked for the emergence of certain abstract mathematical structures in songs, paintings, even novels.

'And I found them. Hundreds of instances throughout history of inexplicable, emergent breakthroughs. But what I really needed was a contemporary example. I wanted to examine the circumstances behind one of these breakthroughs. I wrote computer algorithms that would search songs, books, academic writings, architectural blueprints—all the intellectual outputs of our species—trying to find an outbreak, a radical change in the pattern. Evidence of something incomprehensible. Something alien and new.

'And after months of searching, I found it. A series of routine articles published in a biochemistry journal fifteen years ago. The author's name was Simon Ogilvy. There was nothing interesting about the papers themselves, but embedded deep within the words and the graphs were radical new ideas in symmetric geometry, ideas that didn't appear within the mathematics community until a decade after Ogilvy published his work.

'Who was Ogilvy? More importantly, what happened to him? I learned that he'd been fired from his university, but no reason was given publicly. Then his name was mentioned in a police raid on a remote farm near an isolated seaside town. He was suspected of operating a clandestine laboratory. But he vanished just before the raid; the police never caught him. And after that there wasn't a trace of him. Simon Ogilvy, suspected conduit for revolutionary ideas from an alien dimension, had vanished. So I learned about his past. I learned that he grew up here, in the Aro Valley, in a place called Threshold.'

They were at the house now. The scaffolding served as a stairway to the front door. Eleanor went first, then turned to watch as Steve and the Cartographers manoeuvred the bath onto the first plank, and grunted and strained as they lifted it up the makeshift steps, one by one. Sophus frowned; he looked troubled by Ann's words.

They were halfway to the top when the archivist, exhausted and panting, fumbled and dropped the bath. Steve squawked as it fell backwards, dragging him with it back down the steps, until Sophus grabbed the bath by the rim with one hand and clutched at one of the poles with the other, gritting his teeth with the effort. Steve grabbed on to a wooden slat to stop himself from sliding off the side of the scaffold. The structure swayed.

'We need to rest,' Sophus told Eleanor, once they'd pulled Steve back up and got their breath back.

'Don't be absurd,' she snapped. 'We're nearly there. Gorgon awaits.'

'She can await a while longer,' Sophus replied. He and the archivist wedged the bath between two poles and squatted down on the plank, breathing heavily and rubbing their hands. Sophus nodded at Ann. 'Finish your story.'

'There's no time,' Eleanor barked. 'Gorgon demands—'

'Gorgon demands? Or you demand?' He turned to Ann again. 'Finish.'

'I took leave from my university,' Ann continued, 'and I travelled to this country, and made my way to Te Aro, where I took a room in a boarding house on Aro Street. I tried to research the past of Simon Ogilvy, this mysterious biochemist, but the people who lived in Te Aro were hard to reason with. I tried to search the town archive but the archivist told me there was a radiation leak, and the archives were closed for a thousand years.' The archivist gave a low, throaty chuckle. Ann went on. 'After two weeks I made no progress, but I sensed that the key to my search was here, somewhere in the valley. I quit my job and used my savings and the money from my prizes to buy my house. I took a job at the Community Council to meet my living costs, and help me in my quest. But after months of searching I was still no closer to Simon Ogilvy or his connection with another reality. Oh, there were hints. Signs. Snatches of children's songs. Graffiti on fences. I knew there was something here, somewhere. That something had happened in this valley. But what? When? Why?

'I reread Ogilvy's work. The mathematics in his papers seemed to describe a specific space. A mathematical graph with edges and vertices.'

'The Real City,' Sophus murmured.

'I didn't know that then. I designed an equation to measure the constants of that space. In our universe we can measure the ratio of a circle's circumference to its diameter to find the number pi. The Ogilvy-Day equations measure this value in the non-Euclidean geometry of the Real City. What shocked me is that, six months ago, the values in these equations changed.'

'Impossible,' Sophus protested. 'They aren't physical values. They're like the properties of a circle, or the sum of angles of a triangle. They're fixed. They can't change.'

'That's what I thought,' Ann said. 'It took weeks of investigations followed by three solid days of calculations to understand what had happened. The values changed when someone took the DoorWay compound and entered the Real City. They observed the City, and the act of that observation changed the deep structure of that reality. Not by much; just a little. The Ogilvy-Day constants fluctuated for a few months, then it returned almost to zero. Then, this winter, they shot up. They've been skyrocketing ever since. The more people who observe the Real City, the more the values change. That's why Gorgon and her Cartographers are drugging people and kidnapping them.' She turned to Steve and said, 'I know you're not a mathematician. But you understand the relationship between pi and Gaussian curvature, right? You're not a moron.'

Steve chose not to respond.

'If Gorgon traps a few more people in the Real City, this value will reach its maximal rate in a matter of hours.'

'Then what happens?'

'I don't know,' Ann admitted. 'I fear that whatever exists beyond the Real City will cross over into our world. And then—'

Eleanor interjected. 'That's enough.' She stood on the steps above them, her taser raised. 'Pick up that bath.'

~

They made their way up the steps. The old house loomed over them. It was old, crumbling. The windows were dirty and the curtains were drawn. Grass sprouted from the gutter running along the roof. An empty doghouse sat at the end of the scaffolding. The cliff behind it ascended into mist. A sharp wind blew up from the slope; the scaffolding trembled with each gust.

Eleanor reached the top of the steps. Ann was behind her but she'd fallen back to exchange whispers with Sophus. Footsteps clattered on wooden slats; the bath chimed as it knocked against the beams. Then Eleanor, Ann, Sophus, the archivist, Steve and the bathtub were at the top of the scaffolding, outside Gorgon's front door.

Eleanor crossed to the front door and knocked. She bade Sophus and the archivist to wait with a flick of her hand. 'Gorgon comes,' she announced.

Steve cursed. He kicked out his leg, feeling the cuff bite into his ankle. He didn't want to wait and let Gorgon take him. He wanted to struggle. To fight. To win! But his captors were armed with tasers and syringes, and he was handcuffed to a bath. Even Steve had his limitations.

He drummed his fingertips on the scaffolding and looked out over the vast sweep of the Threshold development. The hill fell away in a patchwork of weeds and mud, ending in a row of pine trees. Beyond that was the valley proper. Steve gazed out at it. He loved Te Aro: its dark narrow roads, the gardens with rusting camper vans, the parks filled with sleeping vagrants. Was he seeing it now for the last time? Would he spend the rest of his days in the Real City, a place where rusting vans and vagrants didn't even exist?

Someone jostled him. Steve did not resist. His time was up. But then there was a cry of pain, a flurry of movement. He looked around.

The archivist lay on the planks of the scaffold, twitching. Someone had stunned him! Steve flinched as Sophus pushed past him, heading for Eleanor with his taser humming in his hand. Eleanor turned, eyes wide, and shrank towards the door, waving her syringe to ward Sophus off. 'What's the meaning of this?' she asked him. 'Are you betraying Gorgon to side with these heretics?'

'Ann isn't a heretic,' Sophus replied. 'She's just questioning the assumptions behind our beliefs.'

Steve said, 'That's the definition of a heretic.'

'Shut up, Steve.' Ann pushed past him and began to say something to Eleanor, but she broke off when a blast of wind shook the scaffolding. They all lurched and swayed. When it was still again, Ann said, 'I just want to talk to Gorgon. Ask her why she's doing this.'

'Gorgon doesn't answer to you.'

The scaffolding shook again. Eleanor dropped her syringe. She reached for it, but Sophus darted forward and stepped on it. Eleanor reeled back, eyes flashing. She gave each of them a glance of pure hatred and then ran through Gorgon's front door.

'Look.' Ann pointed at the buildings further down the valley. Some of the Cartographers below had seen what was happening on the scaffolding and they were running up the slope, yelling and pointing. 'We'd better get out of here.'

Sophus glanced around. 'Back down the steps. We'll make for the fence.'

But Steve knew that running for the fence was a terrible idea. Ann and Sophus might make it, but Steve was chained to the bath, which was too heavy to lift over a high fence. Their plan would put Sophus and Ann in the uncomfortable position of having to abandon Steve, and he didn't want to subject them to that. So he blocked the scaffolding and said, 'We can't leave now. This is our chance to capture Eleanor and Gorgon. They're trapped inside that house and we outnumber them.'

Ann and Sophus paused. They looked uncertain. Typical intellectuals, Steve thought, trying to think things through, to consider consequences and risks. But he would not give them the chance. 'Quick!' He rattled his handcuff. 'Sophus—grab that syringe. Move in. Secure the first room. Ann! Help me shift this bathtub over to the doorway.'

He was thrilled to see them obey his orders without question. Eleanor took the other end of the tub and together they progressed along the scaffolding, heading for Gorgon's front door. The Cartographers were coming closer, but they were still minutes away. By the time they arrived, Steve and his allies would be blockaded inside Gorgon's house. Gorgon would be his prisoner, and Steve could question her. Finally, he'd get some answers.

The scaffolding trembled again; Steve gripped the rail to brace himself against the gust but, in the midst of his glee, he noted that the wind had died down but the structure was still shaking. That was odd, he thought. Then the entire scaffolding broke away from the side of the building, its steel framework screaming as it broke apart.

44

The great escape

Danyl twisted the last bolt from the cross-section of the scaffolding and tossed it aside. The entire structure swayed back and forth. It was ready to fall.

It was a desperate, crazy plan, but it was all Danyl had. He couldn't abandon Steve and Ann to Gorgon. But he was unarmed and alone. There was no way he could take on Eleanor and her Cartographer thugs. Collapsing the scaffolding was the only way. With luck, Ann and Steve would tumble gently to the ground and not be horribly injured by the fall or the crashing poles and huge wooden planks.

He stepped backwards to shelter beneath the overhanging second storey of the house. He should be safe there. His plan might be insanely dangerous, but there was no sense putting himself at risk. He pressed his back against the wall and took a wide stance. He raised Lightbringer and swung, and in the space before connection with the supporting beam, between the action and the consequence, he heard Steve's voice high above him, shouting orders. He said something about Gorgon and Eleanor but the rest of his words were engulfed by the shattering thunder of Danyl's escape plan as the crowbar knocked the beam loose and the scaffolding came apart in a howling orchestra of steel on steel and splintering wood and terrified screams.

When Danyl conceived of his plan he'd imagined it much like a scene in a cartoon. The scaffolding would fall in a brief rain of debris and collapse in a cloud of dust, and the survivors would stumble out of the cloud coughing and dazed. Danyl would grab his friends, they'd thank him for saving them, and they'd all flee amidst the confusion.

But it wasn't like that at all. Instead of disintegrating neatly into its components, the scaffolding broke in half and sagged away from the wall, producing a hideous groaning sound as the poles twisted and bent against each other. The people on top of the scaffolding also screamed, and slid back and forth across the planks. The noise rolled down the hillside. Further down the slope, the Cartographers gaped at this spectacle while more doors in the townhouses opened and more Cartographers poured out. All of them began to run towards Gorgon's house.

Danyl muttered, 'No. No. No.' But he couldn't run away. Bits of steel and wood were breaking and falling to earth directly in front of him. A pole impaled itself in the mud, and Danyl tried not to think about what it might have done to his internal organs. Half of the structure tipped forward and crashed to the ground. He thought he glimpsed a bathtub in the rubble. Should he rush into the danger zone and drag his friends free? Or kneel down, close his eyes, tuck his head between his knees and cover his neck with his hands and repeat his own name over and over again?

Definitely the second option. Danyl cowered for about a minute, waiting for the worst of the din to die.

When it did, he opened his eyes again. His face was pressed against the brick wall that made up the lower storey of Gorgon's house, and he found himself looking through a ventilation hole in one of the bricks into the dim subterranean room beneath it. Gorgon's basement.

This was a mostly empty space with bare rock walls and a clay floor. It was lit by tiny beams of light admitted through the wall. They illuminated a wooden flight of stairs and a cot, made up with blankets and an old patchwork quilt, in the centre of the room. There was someone in the bed.

Was it Gorgon? Was this where she slept? The face was just outside one of the light beams. Danyl angled his nose and eye socket into the hole in the brick, straining to see . . .

A hand grabbed his shoulder and pulled him about.

It was Ann. She was bleeding from a cut in her forehead and holding up Sophus with one arm. The young mathematician wore a dazed expression on his face that Danyl immediately diagnosed as concussion, a side effect of many of his escape plans.

Ann demanded, 'What did you do?'

'I saved you from Gorgon.' He gave a jaunty grin and added, 'I scaffoiled her.'

Ann didn't laugh at this hilarious joke. She stared back with disbelief and said, 'We saved ourselves, Danyl. Sophus switched sides. We were about to storm Gorgon's house and capture her. Now . . .' She pointed at the door high above their heads. 'We can't even get to her. You almost killed us.'

'Let's not argue about who almost killed whom,' Danyl replied. He pointed at the mob of Cartographers rushing up the hill towards them. 'We need to get out of here. Quick.' He took her arm and pulled her through the rubble. Sophus stumbled along behind them.

'Where are we going?'

'Don't worry. I've thought it all through.' He led them to the bathtub, which lay top-down in a pile of rubble. 'We'll escape in this.' He flipped it onto its side. Steve lay beneath it, unharmed and smiling.

'Oh, hey buddy. Can you put the bath back where it was? I'm hiding in here.'

Danyl turned the tub onto its back, flipping Steve onto his side with a startled squawk, and waved at Ann. 'Get in.'

Ann frowned at the mob of Cartographers. They were now gathered at the bottom of the path that led from the driveway up to Gorgon's house, and they were looking up and pointing, not at the ruined scaffolding or Danyl and Ann, but over their heads.

Danyl looked up. The ruined house loomed. The front door opened into empty air and a small figure appeared: it was a female with long, tangled grey hair and a scarf tied around her head, covering her eyes. She held something in her hands: a recorder. A child's musical instrument. Danyl watched, bewildered, as she raised it to her lips and played a tune, the same haunting song the children of Te Aro sang. *Hide me, blind me or Gorgon will find me.*

'Get down!' Steve pulled Danyl into the bathtub. It clanged as a dart ricocheted off it and landed in the mud.

'The darts are tipped with DoorWay.'

Another dart embedded itself in a broken piece of wood beside them. Danyl said, 'Into the bath!'

Steve lay in the bottom of the tub. They shoved Sophus on top of him, then Ann and Danyl pushed the bath down the muddy slope, aiming away from the mass of Cartographers. The bath gathered speed and began to move by itself. Ann jumped inside and held out her hand to Danyl. 'Get in!'

But they weren't going fast enough. Danyl kept pushing: the bath slid through the mud. They reached a steep section of the slope and the bath sped up so quickly it was difficult to keep up; he tripped in a patch of weeds.

As he stumbled he took Ann's hand and she pulled him onboard. The bath wobbled and righted itself as the slope and weight of its cargo drove it onwards. The Cartographers had moved to intercept them, but the bath was moving too fast, and their enemies scattered before them. Danyl screamed with joy as they hurtled towards freedom.

45

Danyl's plan works perfectly for several seconds

The tub flew down the slope, its prow throwing up sheets of muddy spray. Its non-concussed occupants all cheered as they left the mob of Cartographers far behind, but their cheer turned into a scream when the bath hit a large stone and tipped over on its side. It was still travelling downhill at a thrilling speed, but now Danyl's face was millimetres from the ground. Specks of cold mud and gravel strafed his cheeks and forehead while blades of grass lashed at him like a cat-o'-nine-tails. He lost his grip on Steve's crowbar and it slipped into the mud. Steve lunged for it, crying out, 'Lightbringer!' The others held him down as the crowbar cartwheeled out of sight.

Gradually the slope levelled out. The tub passed over the gravel driveway and came to rest not far from the culvert. Danyl crawled free. He wiped the mud and blood from his face and looked back up the hill. A long, bath-shaped trench led directly from Gorgon's house, now far above them, to their current position. A horde of Cartographers were running down the hill, following the trench.

Ann said, 'What now?'

'We flee,' Danyl replied.

'How? Sophus can't walk, and Steve's chained to the bathtub.'

'Relax. I've got everything all figured out.' Danyl glanced around while he said this, trying to figure things out. He pointed and said, 'Thataway. Down the culvert and into the catacombs.'

It took them several minutes to wrestle Steve, Sophus and the bathtub into position and to make their way down the steps at the base of the culvert, into the darkness of the stormwater drain. By the time they reached the bottom they could hear the tread of boots behind them.

But Danyl wasn't worried. They passed through an antechamber filled with supplies: stretchers, planks, torches. He grabbed a torch and lit up the tunnel, which was narrow and twisting. The edges of the bath scraped against its walls. They grazed their fingers trying to force it through. The footsteps behind them grew louder.

And then the walls were gone; the roof curved away into darkness. They were in the accessway. A narrow plank stretched to the platform on the far side. The black Waimapihi surged beneath them, its torrents flecked with white foam. They'd made it.

Danyl called to Ann, 'Quick! Toss the bath into the stream then jump in.'

'You want us to jump in there? That stream must be teeming with bacteria. That's your plan?'

'At least I have a plan.'

'I had a plan,' Ann snapped. 'A rational plan, which you ruined.'

'Oh, really?' Danyl stuck his hands on his hips, ready to snap back, ready to put Ann in her place, when he realised she was right. He had ruined her plan. He couldn't admit to that though. He'd look like an idiot. Instead, he reached out and pushed her. She stumbled backwards into Steve, who toppled, dragging the bath with him, into the stream. Sophus, still half dazed, had been leaning against the bath, and he fell too, and Ann gasped and clutched at him, and then she tipped and fell. Danyl switched off his torch and jumped after them. As he hit the water he heard the Cartographers burst into the accessway. They poured across the narrow bridge, shouting and waving torches. Danyl and his companions bobbed away from them, calm and unseen in the familiar safety of the ice-cold deadly black stream.

He floundered about in the darkness until he found the

bath and Steve bobbing beside it. He held it in place against the current while he located Ann and Sophus. Once they were all inside the bath, they floated downstream. The shouts of the Cartographers echoed through the lightless halls.

Eventually they came to rest in a tributary that diverted off the main stream. The bath was dangerously low in the water. The stream lapped at the rim and they lay together, soaked and cold, drawing heat from one another's bodies.

'We made it,' Ann said. 'What do we do now?'

Sophus spoke up groggily. 'There's an exit near here. It comes out behind the sub-station on Epuni Street.'

'That's near my place,' Ann said. 'We can hide there. My goodness, listen to them.' They paused to take in the remote howls of the outraged Cartographers.

'We'd better wait down here for a while,' Danyl said. 'We can't fall into their hands again. Gorgon won't give us a second chance. Then we need to go to ground. To think. To plan. And then—'

Steve asked, 'Then what?'

'Then we need to go back.'

'Back to Threshold?' Ann asked.

Danyl nodded.

'To stop Gorgon?'

'To rescue Lightbringer?'

'Partly,' Danyl said to Ann. 'Not really,' he said to Steve. 'I have to go back because just as the scaffolding came down I saw inside Gorgon's basement. There's a bed there with a person in it. Someone with a blue-stained mouth and wide-open eyes.' He paused, then said, 'It's Verity.'

PART IV

46

The council of Danyl

'The Real City is a conduit,' Ann explained. 'The Spiral leads to another universe. Any questions?'

They were sitting around Ann's dining-room table. They were warm and safe and dry. They'd made it to her house—a sunlit bungalow on Marama Crescent and the cleanest place Danyl had ever seen—by creeping through the catacombs to the exit behind the abandoned sub-station, then dashing across the empty street and through the gardens of deserted houses to Ann's backyard.

She'd found some bolt-cutters in her toolshed and cut Steve free of the bath. Then they'd all stripped off their sodden clothes and formed a miserable queue for the shower.

When they were clean, Ann lit the fire in her lounge. They sat around it drinking tea, dressed in whatever clothes she could find that would fit them. They talked about their dazzling escape, with a minimum of recrimination and blame, then lapsed into a comfortable silence, until Ann suggested they make a plan to defeat Gorgon and protect reality from what lay behind the Real City. That's when Danyl, dressed in pale purple trackpants and a tight low-cut T-shirt advertising a numerical analysis software company on the back, asked what the Real City was and received her brief but confusing answer.

'But,' he asked her, still confused, 'how can there be other universes? They talk about alternate universes in science fiction, but this is reality.' He knocked on the table. 'Isn't the universe everything there is? Isn't it infinite?'

Ann and Sophus exchanged glances, amused by Danyl's naiveté. 'Our universe appears infinite to us,' Sophus explained. 'True, our observable universe is limited to about 46 billion light years in each direction, but outside that perimeter it extends forever, repeating every possible combination of matter infinitely, including infinite identical replications of ourselves sitting around this table right now, and an even larger infinity of copies of ourselves with minor variations, all separated by unthinkably vast gulfs of space-time. But to outside observers, our universe is finite and quite small. It's obvious once you think about it.'

'So there is something outside our universe?'

'Not to us,' Sophus said. 'But yes, of course there's something outside it.'

'What?'

Ann sighed. 'We'll have to go back to basics,' she said to Sophus. 'Let's start with the beginning of time.' She pointed at the table. 'Let's say this tablecloth is the universe.'

Everything in Ann's house was either black or white. The tablecloth was white and made from fine linen. She scrunched a section of it into a ball and said, 'At the beginning of time the universe was just a false vacuum with no matter or radiation in it. But the vacuum was filled with a powerful, repulsive gravitational energy, and that caused it to expand very quickly to a space far larger than our universe in less than a billionth of a second.' She smoothed out the scrunched-up section of tablecloth. 'This inflationary vacuum was highly unstable, so almost every point in the vacuum'—she pointed at the countless tiny gaps in the tablecloth's weave—'collapsed into stable universes, each of which expanded at the speed of light and appear infinite to observers inside them.' She pointed to two adjacent black teacups and stirred them both. The detritus of tea leaves swirled around in spirals. 'But not every point in the inflationary vacuum collapses. Some tiny points of it remain, and of course those points expand at a rate many times faster than the speed of light, so all the countless infinite universes become impossibly tiny remote islands in the vast sea of the vacuum.' She moved the teacups apart, their tea still swirling, and pointed at the gaps in the weave between them. 'And then almost all the points in that new vacuum collapse into more infinite universes, which then fly apart. And so it goes, on and on, forever and ever, worlds without end.'

She shrugged. 'That much is trivial. Here's where it gets interesting. Each universe will have different properties inherited from random quantum fluctuations in the inflationary void. Different particles. Different fields. Different physical constants. A different value for the fine structure constant. Most of these universes will probably be voids. Nothing. Eternal darkness, clean and beautiful and perfect.' She sighed wistfully and picked up a black china sugar bowl filled with cubes of white sugar and set it down next to her teacup. 'Others will be seas of plasma. Incompatible with biological life and even atomic structure, but they may have other stable structures we cannot imagine. Or,' she said meaningfully, 'structures we can imagine. Points, lines, integers, rational numbers. In our universe we have atoms and they combine to form structures: gas, suns, planets, organisms, eventually intelligent life like ourselves. A mathematical universe would be capable of similar complexity. At least some of its structures would be intelligent. Self-aware. Perhaps all of it. The entire mathematical universe could be one infinitely vast sentient being that's entangled itself with our universe, somehow, across the vast abyss of the inflating vacuum. Mathematicians perceive tiny fragments of it and think they're glimpsing eternal truths. Their insights transform our world. But they're seeing what the sentient mathematical universe wants them to see. If true, then our entire technological civilisation is based on secrets whispered to us from another universe by an incomprehensible being.'

Ann picked up a sugar cube from the bowl and dropped it into her tea. It dissolved.

'What is the Real City? As I said, I believe it is a conduit. It's like an airlock: a way for signals to pass between our universe and that of the sentient mathematical reality. I suppose there are many such conduits, that the mathematical universe trails them through higher dimensional spaces, like strands from a spider's web, hoping to hook some sentient bait and gain access to another reality.

'Why?'

Ann picked up her teacup and looked at Danyl. 'I don't know,' she replied. 'Maybe it's an old universe and is moving towards thermodynamic heat death, and it's figured out a way to save itself by outputting its entropy into our reality. Or maybe we can't know. Its motives might be incomprehensible. But we do know that it's not working in good faith. Its engagement with our species is covert. Disguised. We know that it tempts us with the promise of truth, of insights into the nature of reality, but behind each truth is another mystery. It wants us to enter the Real City. It wants us to reach the Spiral and open the way. And that will happen very soon. According to the Ogilvy-Day equations, the Gaussian curvature of the Real City is almost at its maximal value. If Gorgon and the Cartographers imprison a few more pilgrims in the City, the way will open. The sentient mathematical universe will have direct access to our reality. And then . . .'

She raised her teacup to her lips and drank, emptying the cup with a soft sipping sound.

47

The plan

'What's in here?'

Steve had been sitting at the table, half listening to Ann talk and bicker with Danyl and Sophus about what to do next. Rescue Verity? Rescue the pilgrims? Raid the Threshold development? Save the universe? It was all so boring. So he got up and drifted out into the hall. He liked to know the layout of whatever building he was in, in case of attack, so he tried all the doors. One led to Ann's bedroom. Another to the toilet, a windowless room which was also a laundry. Another to a study which was mostly empty except for a small wooden desk with a laptop on it. And a fourth door at the end of the hall, which was locked.

Steve rattled the handle and called out, 'Ann? This door won't open. What's inside it?'

He heard Ann's chair scrape on the floor. Her footsteps. She stuck her head into the hall. 'That's the spare room. That door is stuck.'

'Help me get it open.' Steve pressed his shoulder against the door and pushed. The wood creaked.

'Stop that. Excuse me. Don't do that.' Ann hurried across the hall. 'That carpentry is original. Late nineteenth century. Made by skilled artisans at a time when people cared about hygiene and individual freedom.' She took Steve's arm and tugged him back towards the lounge. 'There's nothing in that room. And we need your help. We're drawing a map of Threshold. It must be precise. An exact representation.'

Steve allowed himself to be led. He did have a very powerful spatial memory. If they tried to map Threshold without him they'd be lost. He glanced back when they reached the lounge and noticed that there was a gap between the locked door and the wooden floor. In the gleam of the highly polished floorboards, Steve saw tiny flashing lights: red and green, reflections from the interior of the locked room.

Sophus said, 'An attack on Threshold is hopeless. Unthinkable.'

The completed map of the development lay on the table. It showed the fenceline. The culvert leading to the catacombs. The driveway and the gate leading to Aro Street. Gorgon's house, and a shaded area where Steve believed his lost crowbar had fallen from the bathtub.

'Just tell us everything you can about Gorgon and the Cartographers,' said Danyl. 'Let the rest of us do the thinking about what is and isn't unthinkable.'

'What do you want to know?'

'Start from the beginning,' he replied, then added quickly, 'Not the beginning of time, just your involvement with Gorgon and the Cartographers.'

'You already know most of it,' Sophus said. 'It started one night after Ann and I fought, bitterly, about incompleteness and incomputability. Each of us was so sure the other was wrong. I stormed out and walked the streets of Te Aro, and I stumbled across the clues the Cartographers had laid about the valley and followed them to Ye Undergrounde Bookshoppe. The archivist was there. He offered me the DoorWay compound, promising me answers, revelations. I refused so he punched me in the belly and squirted his syringe into my mouth. I passed out and woke up in the Real City.

'When I woke some weeks later in a disgusting hovel, I convinced Eleanor—Gorgon's so-called Apostle—not to send me back. I told her I could find the way through the City to the Spiral.

'Eleanor led me back to the bookshop and through the catacombs. They were filled with Cartographers carrying boxes filled with books through the tunnels to the Threshold.

Ann asked, 'Where did they take them? What do they do with the books?'

'They take them to his building here.' He pointed at a rectangle on the map. 'Gorgon's laboratory. The books are the raw material used to synthesise DoorWay. Something to do with the wood pulp. The acid in the paper. This is where DoorWay is manufactured. They've been working non-stop to synthesise a new batch ever since Steve stole most of the last one. I know what you're thinking.' He glanced at Danyl and Steve. 'Destroy the batch, and the pilgrims in the Real City will wake. But the lab is guarded by armed Cartographers. Gorgon knows that's the first place you'll strike.'

'What about the pilgrims?'

'They're here.' He pointed to more rectangles lower down the slope. 'And here. These buildings weren't guarded before, but they will be now. And all of the Cartographers have phones. Alert them and the rest will come running.'

'Who are the Cartographers?' Danyl asked. 'How many are there?'

'There are about thirty,' Sophus replied. 'Mostly workers from Gorgon's bookstore. Others are former waiters and bartenders from Eleanor's café, or just postgraduate students and drifters. They sleep here, in shifts.' He tapped the map.

'Not tonight,' Ann said. 'Gorgon is close to her goal. She'll have the Cartographers finish their batch, administer it to the captives and bring new pilgrims in through the bookshop.'

'Tell us about Gorgon,' Danyl said to Sophus. 'What does she look like? What happened when you met her?'

Sophus continued his story. 'Eleanor led me up past the other buildings to Gorgon's house. We climbed up to the front door, knocked and waited, while that gigantic dog sat on the scaffolding, watching us. Then someone called for us to enter. We opened the door and found ourselves in a living room filled with junk. Two Cartographers with tasers sat in this room, guarding the entrance.

'Eleanor motioned for me to sit on a threadbare couch. I obeyed. She opened a door in the far wall, revealing a second room. It was dark in there. A creaking sound came from inside. I dimly made out a figure in a rocking chair, rocking back and forth. I had the sense there was a second person in that room, behind the chair. Neither of them spoke.

'Eleanor told me to talk about the Real City. So I did. I explained that it was a planar graph. That you could eventually visit every plaza by taking a bridge you hadn't taken before, which meant that the City was solvable, and a pilgrim to it could eventually reach the Spiral. I postulated that the City was a sphere, and that if you travelled far enough you'd travel around it and arrive at the Spiral, which is visible from the entrance plaza. When I was finished Eleanor thought for a moment, then got up and entered the dark room.

'There was a murmured conversation. Two voices or three? I couldn't tell. I could only make out a few stray words. Adversary. Spiral. Universe.

'Then Eleanor returned. "You'll join us," she said to me. "You'll work in the bookshop, helping to bring the pilgrims across each night. Afterwards you'll make the journey to the City itself. Map it. Observe it. Report your observations back to me.' Then she gestured to one of the guards and said, "Take him to the archivist."

'That's how I became a Cartographer. By day I helped my fellow Cartographers hide spiral dollars and blue envelopes around the valley. By night we accepted pilgrims into the bookshop and drugged them, and the rest of the Cartographers took them to Threshold. You all know the rest.'

'You must know more,' Danyl said. 'Why is Gorgon doing all of this? Does she really want to destroy the universe?'

'I don't know,' Sophus admitted. 'I only glimpsed her that one time. She never leaves her house. And I was just a hired hand. A mathematician they thought might be useful.'

He thought for a moment, and added, 'They talk about an Adversary. Someone evil and dangerous. Someone who wants to stop them. They're terrified of this person.' He thought for another minute then said, 'I'm sorry. I don't know who Gorgon is. I wish I knew more.'

He indicated the map again. 'You can see it's hopeless. There are only three of you. You can't hope to raid the laboratory or rescue enough pilgrims to make a difference. And you can't rescue Danyl's ex-girlfriend. You'd have to go in through the tunnels or over the fence, then make it to Gorgon's house without being seen. Then you'd need to get inside, even though Danyl tore down the scaffolding. Then get past the guards and Gorgon herself. Get into the basement and carry Verity all the way out again. It's impossible.'

'Difficult,' said Danyl, 'but not impossible. We can rescue Verity and defeat Gorgon—if we have a plan.'

Ann looked at him, surprised. 'And do you have such a plan?'

He hesitated. Danyl did, actually have a brilliant and intricate plan. It had come to him while Sophus was talking; it had simply unfolded in Danyl's mind as if it had been there all along, waiting to be discovered. Where did it come from? His brain, obviously—but Danyl didn't entirely trust his brain. And it acknowledged this: I don't trust you either, it thought to him, giving him a gentle zap to emphasise its point. But if you want to rescue Verity and save the universe, this is the only way. You have no choice.

So Danyl picked up the pen and began to make markings on the map, and said, 'Listen carefully.'

48

Combinations

Friend! Neighbour! Dreamer!

Are you afraid of radiation? Do you oppose secret government plans to build dehumanising superhighways through your community? Do you think advertising and the mainstream media are manipulating your thoughts to make you paranoid?

If you answered YES to these QUESTIONS then YOU are one of the rare freethinkers LEFT alive on GAIA and you MUST attend:

The global people's WORLDWIDE moment of TRUTH.

To be held: In Ye Undergrounde Bookshoppe at 10 pm tonight. (Please follow attached map, enter the code 137 to gain admittance, give the attached spiral dollar to the person who greets you and do not attempt to discuss these issues with anyone, for reasons of operational security. Do not deviate from these instructions. Take extreme precautions. Bring a friend.) FREEDOM!

'Do you really think this will work?'

Danyl rolled up another leaflet, bundling it with a copy of the map to the basement and some spiral dollars, and slipped it into the letterbox of the first house on Ohiro Road. 'It'll work.' He continued on to the next box and repeated the task. 'People see the residents of Te Aro as pot-addled, new-age dreamers. But that's just a lazy stereotype. Only about sixty or seventy percent of the population falls into that category. They're the people Gorgon has captured. The rest of the people in the valley have jobs, families, lives. They probably haven't noticed anything strange has happened at all. The streets seem a bit emptier, that's all. These notes will grab their attention.'

'But why do we have to lie?' Ann demanded. 'Why don't we just say there's an evil group at work here, drugging people and trying to destroy the universe?'

'These people don't really care about the universe,' Danyl said, 'but if you tell them someone's building a road through their community, they'll riot.'

Ann accepted this. She crossed to the opposite side of the road and began leafleting.

It was early afternoon. The sun made occasional, indifferent appearances through the clouds. They had half an hour to deliver leaflets before meeting Steve and Sophus for the next phase of the plan. It felt good to just wander along the roadside engaged in a simple, routine task for a few minutes and not have to escape from anyone or worry about the fate of reality.

The slope on Danyl's side rose into a hill too steep to build houses on, so he crossed the road and walked with Ann. 'What will you do when all this is over?' she asked. 'If we succeed, I mean? Will you stay here in Te Aro?'

'I don't think so. This valley isn't good for my mental health. No, I'd like to live in the country, or maybe by the sea. Write another book. Grow vegetables.'

'Vegetables are a big responsibility.'

'I know. I want chickens, too. I feel comfortable around them. But I'm not sure I'm ready.' He looked at her sideways. What will you do?'

'I don't know. I can't go back to mathematics. Not after all this.'

'Maybe you can join me in the country and count my chickens.'

'That sounds nice.'

They were silent for a moment; they walked on to the next cluster of letterboxes. Ann asked, 'And what about Verity?'

'Things ended awkwardly with Verity. What with my

breakdown and her stealing my book and vanishing, we never got the chance to talk things out. I don't know if we have a future together.'

Ann said nothing. The steep unoccupied slope on the other side of the road was replaced by a row of modern houses built into the hillside. She crossed over to them and the two of them distributed the rest of their fake leaflets in silence.

Te Aro Archive was deserted. The shelves destroyed during yesterday's brutal confrontation still lay where they'd been thrown. Papers and files soaked with congealed DoorWay lit up the floor in pools of glowing blue. The giant lay where he fell, sprawled inside the door, his eyes wide open.

'He's in the Real City,' Sophus said. 'We shot him full of darts tipped with DoorWay. But we couldn't move him. So . . .' He gestured. 'Here he is.'

'How long will he be out?'

Sophus shrugged. 'He's been here for roughly eighteen hours and a typical dose of DoorWay sends a captive to the Real City for two days. He got more than an average dose, but we've never drugged anyone this size before. He could wake up right now.'

They all took a step back. The giant did not move.

'OK. Let's get to work.' Danyl clapped his hands. Everyone started at the sound. 'I'll watch the door. Steve, you search the giant's pockets and find his house keys.'

Steve considered this then replied, 'No.'

'Why not? You're not scared of a little giant, are you?'

'Why don't you search him?'

'Me? I came up with the plan.'

'So you're the best person to execute it.'

'We don't have time to argue about who is the best person to do what,' Danyl said. 'We're here to save the universe. Step one is to get inside the giant's house. The longer we stand here and argue, the greater the chance the giant will wake and kill us all. So let's stop squabbling and just search his pockets and get his keys. The fate of all existence relies on us working together as a team.'

Danyl and Ann stood behind the giant's house. Danyl pointed at a window and said, 'Let's break that one.'

He picked up a large rock and approached the window. He covered his face with one arm and used the rock to break the glass in the window leading into the giant's bathroom. Next, he went around the frame tapping at the remaining shards.

Ann said, 'This makes me uncomfortable.'

'Why?'

'I'm a public servant. I'm supposed to uphold the law. If we break into someone's house and steal their stuff, then what makes us any better than Gorgon?'

Danyl took off his jacket and laid it over the window ledge. 'You can't save the universe without breaking a few windows,' he said. 'Help me in.'

The giant's house was empty. Someone had tidied it up since Danyl had booby-trapped the bedroom and fled out the front door.

Danyl crawled under the bed and over to the lock box fixed to the floor beneath it. The lid was down. He tried to open it, then crawled out from under the bed and returned to the bathroom window. 'Climb through,' he told Ann.

'Why?'

'There's a problem with the lock box.'

'What?'

'It's locked. I didn't anticipate that.'

'What do you want me to do?'

'To open it, you need to type in a code on a numeric keypad,' Danyl explained.

'So?'

'Numeric. As in, numbers.'

'I know what numeric means. What do you want me to do?'

'You're a mathematician,' Danyl replied. 'Can't you do some mathematical stuff to figure out the code?'

Ann frowned. 'Like what?'

'I don't know. Just come and look.' He tugged on her arm. Ann allowed herself to be pulled through the window.

They lifted the bed and moved it to one side, revealing the box. It was made of steel and was the size of a hardback book. Ann knelt beside it. 'I can't tell you how to crack the code,' she said. 'You'll have to do that by trial and error. But I can estimate how long that'll take.' She pressed a few numbers at random. The keypad made a soft beeping sound. She pressed the UNLOCK key. A red light flashed and a lower, harsher beeping sound rang out.

She pressed a few more numbers and hit UNLOCK again. A harsh beep, and the red light stayed on longer this time. She pressed some numbers on the keypad and it didn't beep.

'OK,' Ann said. 'It takes about one second to press each key. Let's assume that this box has a four-digit PIN. It might be longer but let's start there. That means there are ten thousand possible combinations. If each combination takes five seconds, then it'll take just under fourteen hours to try them all. But there's a problem. Each time you enter an incorrect sequence, that red light flashes and the keypad times out. With each subsequent incorrect sequence, the timeout period is exponentially longer. So to try all possible four-digit combinations would take about'—she paused for a second, calculating—'one times ten to the seventeen seconds.'

'How long is that?'

'Long enough for our sun to have exhausted its fuel then expanded and enveloped the Earth.'

'The giant will have woken up by then.' Danyl stared at the keypad, thinking. 'What if the code was just one number?'

290

'A one-digit combination?'

'Yeah.'

Ann shrugged. 'Well, then the number of sequences is just one times ten.' She looked at Danyl's curious, expectant face and explained to him, 'That equals ten. So twenty seconds to type them all in, plus the exponential time-outs add up to about 400 seconds. Six point six minutes. But—'

'That's more like it.' Danyl knelt down and pressed 1 and then UNLOCK. He looked disappointed when the red light flicked on, but waited, hopeful and patient. When it went off after a few seconds he looked hopeful again. He pressed 2, then UNLOCK. The red light came on and he deflated.

'Danyl.' Ann's voice was gentle. 'The combination isn't going to be one digit. We need another plan.'

He grimaced. She was right. He ran his hand around the edge of the box. It was bonded to the wooden floorboards with some sort of glue. Maybe they could saw through the floorboards, take the box and force it open back at Ann's house? That would be faster than waiting for the sun to envelop the Earth.

He said, 'You're right,' just as the red light went out again. He pressed 3 anyway. The red light came back on.

Ann's phone rang. She took it from her pocket, glanced at the screen and said to Danyl in a worried voice, 'It's Sophus.'

Sophus and Steve were back at the archive, keeping a watch on the giant's body. Their job was to phone and warn Ann and Danyl if the giant woke. Ann held the phone to Danyl. He took it and answered.

'Hey, buddy.' It was Steve. He sounded happy.

Danyl asked him, 'What's wrong?'

'Do you have the drugs yet?'

'No. We've hit a small problem, but we're making progress.' The red light went out. Danyl hit the number 4 and pressed UNLOCK. The red light went on again. 'Why?'

'Because the giant is moving.'

'OK.' Danyl rubbed the bridge of his nose. 'We need a few more minutes. Try and stall it.'

'I'll be honest here, buddy. By moving I mean he's moved. He got up and left.'

'What? When?'

'Hard to tell. I wasn't super-awake when it happened.'

'You were sleeping?'

'Of course not. I was power-napping.'

'Where was Sophus?'

'I sent him to buy soup. He's back now though. He says hi.'

'How long since you last saw the giant? How much time do I have before he gets here?'

'I'd say you've got at least ten minutes,' Steve said confidently. A key rattled in the giant's front door. 'Maybe five minutes,' he conceded. 'Absolute worst-case scenario.'

Danyl hung up.

Ann hissed, 'Let's go.' Danyl started to stand but then the red light on the keypad blinked out. Danyl instinctively pressed number 5, and then UNLOCK. The light flashed green. The lock clicked. The box opened.

Ann whispered, 'No way. Five? Their secret code was five?'

Danyl flipped open the lid, revealing a trove of pills and vials and sachets of powder.

The front door opened. The floor shook and the pills rattled in their cases as the giant entered the building.

'Stay low,' Danyl told Ann, shovelling drugs into his pocket. 'Move fast. Now! Run!'

They ran. Around the bed. Towards the bathroom door. They passed the entrance to the lounge and a roar broke out. The giant had seen them.

Ann reached the bathroom first. She climbed up on the toilet and pulled herself through the window. Danyl was right behind her. He skidded a little on the broken glass but caught himself. He stepped on the toilet bowl, gripped the sides of the window, and hauled himself through head first. He was out! Free!

And then a mighty hand closed around his kicking leg and dragged him back inside. Ann reached for him. She gripped his hand for a second, and the giant tugged him back, and Danyl was gone.

49

A new ally

Steve did not drink coffee. Or tea. Or anything with caffeine in it. His mind functioned on the outer extremes of human thought and he refused to handicap it with drugs or stimulants. Especially not now, with half of the valley captured and drugged, and Gorgon on the verge of triumph.

That's why Steve had had that power nap in the archive. Sleep was vital to cognition. It supported learning and positive energy and it cleared waste products from the brain. What was more important than that? Watching some giant sleep, or keeping Steve's brain—their most precious strategic asset—in peak operating condition?

When Steve woke and saw that the giant was gone, he alerted Danyl as a courtesy, then ate some of the bagels Sophus had brought back from the soup place. Then he and Sophus strolled up Epuni Street to the giant's house.

When they arrived they learned that Danyl had done something to enrage the creature. Which was typical. But Ann had calmed the savage beast, and now Ann was standing in the giant's kitchen with it, drinking black coffee and explaining the Real City and Gorgon's plan while the giant leaned against the bench holding a bucket of coffee in one hand and Danyl in the other. Suspended by his throat, Danyl was dangling and kicking and occasionally giving a feeble slap at the giant's arm, but most of his attention was focused on gasping for breath.

'So that's what's happened to your girlfriend,' Ann was finishing up. 'The Cartographers have drugged Joy and trapped her mind in the Real City. They've taken her body to Threshold.'

'Threshold?'

'It's a vast abandoned housing project with a sinister past. It's too well guarded for a direct assault. But we have a plan. Help us, and we can save Joy.'

The giant swished its coffee around in its mouth, thinking. Its massive brow furrowed like a stately building cracking in an earthquake. Eventually it said, 'What you're talking about here is Platonism. The Real City is an abstract mathematical object but the DoorWay compound lets us perceive it directly, as if it were real.' It scratched its armpit, still thinking. 'And the act of perceiving the City changes it. Like the wave function collapse of a quantum superposition.'

'Well, we don't know the mechanism of the change,' Ann replied. 'But we think that's the motive behind Gorgon's plan. If enough people observe the Real City it will open up the pathway to the Spiral. This will happen tonight if we don't stop her.'

'All right,' said the giant. He lowered Danyl to the floor, where he collapsed to his knees and panted like a dog. 'Little thief,' the giant warned him, 'if you free my girlfriend then we will be even. If not . . .' A silence, brief yet heavy with implied violence, filled the room. 'Do you understand?'

Danyl nodded. The giant clapped its hands together. 'Good, then.' It turned to Ann. 'What now?'

'We need drugs. That's why we're here. To raid your girlfriend's supply.' She knelt beside Danyl and turned out his pockets, holding up vials and plastic tubes for the giant's inspection. 'We want a powerful stimulant and a powerful sedative.'

'Sedatives are very popular around here. This one is good.' The giant indicated a small vial filled with a milky liquid. 'And stimulants . . .' He peered at their drug haul. 'There's this.' He pointed at another vial filled with flakes of silver grit.

'What is it?'

'It's called Ragnarok. Joy sells it to students during exam time and biker gangs during gang wars.'

'Perfect.'

'You'll need to go easy on it, though. It has odd side effects, especially if combined with other drugs. And the dosages must be perfectly measured.'

Steve took the jar from Ann. He tossed it in the air, watching it glint in the light. 'We can't get each dosage exactly right,' he said, 'but too much Ragnarok never hurt anyone.'

Steve stood in Ann's lounge, facing the window and watching the sun set behind the hills to the west.

Everyone else was asleep. Ann was in her bedroom. Danyl slept on a single bed in her guest room. Sophus dozed on the couch in the lounge. The giant was sprawled out in the hall.

The next phase of their plan would begin when the sun finally slipped behind the depthless hills and the valley was steeped in darkness. Then Steve could slip through the streets and over the fence into Threshold. If he succeeded, the rest of his allies could wake in a few hours and join in the final assault. If he failed . . .

The sun fell from sight and the unnatural red colour drained from the clouds.

It was time. Almost. Steve had one last little job to do. He crossed to the kitchen and searched the cutlery drawer until he found a butter knife. He made his way down the hall, stepping over the sprawled-out body of the slumbering giant. Outside the locked door with the flickering lights beneath it, he paused. He pushed against the door and slipped the blade of the knife into the crack. Ann might have been a brilliant philosopher whose work gave glimpses into other realities and other worlds, but Steve was a psychologist and he knew that old-fashioned bolt locks in late-Victorian homes like these were laughably simple to open.

The knife caught against the bolt. Steve twisted it and the lock clicked open. He stepped through the door and closed it behind him.

The yellow lights came from a stack of computers. Eight black boxes were mounted in a rack fixed to the wall, emitting a low hum and a wash of noise from the fans. Adjacent to them was a small desk with a monitor and mouse and keyboard. The air in the room was very warm.

Steve twitched the mouse and the monitor flicked into life. It queried him for a user ID and password. He suspected that breaking into Ann's secret computer would be a lot harder than breaking into her spare room, so he turned his attention to the tall wooden shelves in the corner.

These were filled with cardboard binders. Hundreds of them, each with an alphanumeric notation on the spine. Steve pulled one out and flipped through it. Graphs. Charts. Mathematical equations. Incomprehensible nonsense. He dropped it on the floor.

Stacked on top of the bookshelf were two cardboard boxes. He stood on tiptoes and tugged the closest one towards him. It was battered and stained and muddy. It didn't weigh much. He pulled it off the shelf and set it aside, revealing the side of the second box which was labelled in black marker:

Te Aro Sheriff's Secret Archive. Sheriff's Eyes Only, partner.

50

Meant to be

Something woke Danyl. Sounds. A door closing. Footsteps. He sat up in bed and parted the curtains. The sun had set and the moon had not yet risen. The stars looked like fake jewels.

A shape darted between the pools of light from the streetlights. It ran across the road and slid across a car bonnet, then ran back across the road and slid across the bonnet of a second car.

It was Steve. Danyl frowned. Steve was supposed to have left just after sundown. Now it was—he checked the alarm clock on the bedside table—almost 9 pm. Why had he left so late?

The bedroom door creaked. A voice whispered, 'Danyl?' It was Ann. 'Are you awake?'

'Steve woke me.'

'He's late.'

'I know.'

'Can we trust him?'

Danyl thought about this. He said, 'No.' Then he thought about his old friend some more and added, 'Definitely not. But if he fails it will be spectacular, and that might cover us while we make for Gorgon's house. And having the giant on our side will help.'

Ann gestured at the end of Danyl's bed. 'Can I sit there?'

'Sure.' Danyl shifted and she sat beside him.

'Things are very uncertain,' she said. Her voice was low. She spoke quickly, nervously; she did not look directly at him. 'If we fail tonight, the universe might end. If we succeed you will rescue Verity. Everything will change. Our future is a complex non-linear system. It cannot be determined. I hope you do not find me too forward in saying this.'

'Not at all,' said Danyl.

'I must say what I want to say now, before things change, or cease to be.' Now she looked up and gazed into his eyes and said, 'Danyl. I have feelings for you.'

'Feelings?'

She nodded seriously. 'Strong feelings. Romantic feelings. I know these feelings do not make sense. You have many undesirable qualities. Poverty. Psychological instability. Slightly lower than average intelligence. But I don't care.' Her eyes shone. 'Although my feelings cannot be calculated logically, they are real. I can feel the feelings. I know them to be true. Do you also experience them phenomenologically for me?' She did not wait for Danyl to answer. Instead she shifted across the narrow reach of moonlit bed and kissed him. The kiss was inexpert but enthusiastic. Danyl responded and took her into his arms and then they fell back on the bed together.

It had been a long time since Danyl had been touched by someone who wasn't trying to hurt him. It felt nice. But did that mean he had feelings for Ann? He didn't know. His brain seemed indifferent to what was happening. Go ahead, it told him. Have sex. Or don't. Do you think I care? Danyl checked in with his lust, usually a powerful and indiscriminate lobbyist in these matters, but it was hesitant. You've been dosing me with antidepressants for six months, it warned him. Things are still shaky. I can't promise anything.

Did Danyl like Ann? He didn't know. All his thoughts of late had been of Verity. Finding Verity. Revenging himself on Verity. Rescuing Verity. Defeating Verity. Maybe his heart was like an airlock and his feelings for Verity needed to be drained so they could admit strong tender romantic feelings for someone else. He continued to kiss Ann and simultaneously purge himself of Verity, but instead of ridding himself of feelings for his ex-girlfriend the purging process stirred them up, and his mind was flooded with visions of her.

Verity shifting furniture into their new house. Verity walking along a sunlit path. Verity talking about her art. Verity leaving him, vanishing into the depths of Te Aro. Verity.

Somewhere in this deluge of memories, he'd stopped kissing Ann and now she pulled back from him. 'So.' Her voice was flat, cold. 'I have my answer. My feelings are real for me, but not for you. No.' She held up her hand. 'Do not apologise. Your heart is with your ex-girlfriend. I understand. She is worldly. Sophisticated. Elusive. She treated you cruelly, and your heart wants what it cannot have. Maybe,' she added with a bitter smile, 'if *I* were mysterious and cruel and you could not have me, then you would want me.' She was trying not to cry. She stood. 'I'll leave you alone now.'

Danyl said, 'Ann—'

'Don't.' She held up her hand again. 'There is nothing to say.' Her voice cracked at the end of the sentence, and she turned and hurried from the room.

Danyl sat up. He pressed his palms into his eyes. He groaned. What was he supposed to do? Go after her, he supposed. Say something about friendship and respect. He felt awful. Ann was a brilliant, honourable person. She'd never steal his book, never turn on him for incomprehensible reasons. Why didn't he care for her? What was wrong with him?

He glanced at the clock. They were almost out of time. They needed to get into position for the next phase of the plan. He needed to talk to Ann now. Apologise. Try to make her feel better about him rejecting her. It would be a shame if the universe were destroyed just because she couldn't control her feelings.

He got up and entered the hall. It was dark. Ann had returned to her bedroom at the far end. He could hear her pacing around in there. The quality of light coming into the hall changed as she moved.

He approached her room, dreading every second of the upcoming conversation. He picked his way over the massive limbs of the giant. The creature's chest rose and fell, and Danyl felt the air pressure in the hall fluctuate in time with its deep, gentle breaths. They were lucky to have won this creature to their cause. That was Ann's doing, Danyl reminded himself.

Her shadow flickered across the opposite wall, then disappeared, illuminating the door to her spare room. Which was now ajar. That was strange, because Ann had told Steve that the key was lost. Why was it open?

He could hear Ann sniffing. Blowing her nose. Muttering to herself. He should go to her. But instead he stepped back over the giant, almost losing his balance as he spanned the creature's belly, and entered the spare room.

He saw the rack of computers. The desk. The bookshelves. There was a row of cardboard boxes stacked atop the shelves, with a space in the centre—a large, box-shaped space.

There was a large box on the desk.

Danyl looked through it. Papers. Newsletters. Something to do with Ann's job at the council, perhaps? It meant nothing to Danyl.

He examined the folders in the shelves. They were filled with mathematical notes. So this was Ann's library. But why had she lied about it being filled with junk, the key being lost? What was she hiding?

He stood on tiptoes and pulled down another box. It was filled with cables and spare computer components. He heard another sniff from Ann's bedroom. He really shouldn't be in here. If she caught him searching through her house she'd be angry. Justifiably so. He put the box of computer components back on the shelf, then frowned when he noticed the side of the another box. It was a battered and muddy. It looked very, very familiar.

On tiptoes again, Danyl used his fingertips to pull the box over the edge of the bookshelf then lowered it down. He unfolded the lid and looked inside.

It was filled with paper. Hundreds of pages. The top few

were ripped, screwed up, matted with dried blood. The rest were undamaged. Tens of thousands of words. Plots. Ideas. Worlds.

It was Danyl's novel.

Why was it here? What did this mean? He tried to think. Verity had stolen Danyl's book and taken it to Threshold with Simon and Eleanor. Then someone had murdered Simon and taken the book. And now here it was.

Did that mean that Ann killed Simon Ogilvy? That she did so before the Cartographers began drugging people and kidnapping them? If so, then she'd known about Threshold and Gorgon before she recruited Danyl to find out what had happened to Sophus. Why?

Danyl needed answers. They couldn't attack Threshold without knowing what Ann knew; what her real motives were. She needed to explain herself. He picked up the box and walked into the hall just as Ann emerged from her room. She was zipping up her black raincoat, a determined expression on her face. Danyl wondered at her. Who was she, really? Had she really killed someone? She looked poised. Self-confident. And brilliant. One had to respect the power of her mind. His eyes ran over the contours of her black jeans that outlined her hips.

She started when she saw him. Danyl held up the box and said, 'We need to talk.'

Her eyes flicked from the box to Danyl's face and then back again. 'All right.' She nudged the giant's flank with her foot. The giant grunted.

'Did you know this was my book? You must have. My name is on the title page.'

'I knew,' Ann replied. She smiled. She had a beautiful smile—why hadn't Danyl notice before? She nudged the giant again, harder.

'Where did you get it?' Danyl asked. 'Threshold? Did you kill Simon Ogilvy? I'm sorry about what happened before, by the way. I've been confused. Medicated. I think I'm better now, but my thoughts are all scattered. I think I might have tender feelings for you. But—' he indicated the bloodstained box. 'I do need an explanation for this. And we don't have much time. Steve is out there. We need to go soon.'

Ann's smile widened. 'We need to go soon,' she replied, indicating the giant and herself. 'But you won't be joining us.'

'I don't understand,' Danyl said.

'That's right. You don't.'

The giant's massive eyes opened. It groaned, sat up and looked at Ann. She pointed at Danyl and said, 'He's betrayed us. Our universe. Your girlfriend. Everything. Destroy him.'

51

What Steve found in the secret archive

The fence around perimeter of the Threshold development was made of tall wooden slats topped with barbed wire that jutted out at an impossible-to-climb diagonal angle. It was designed to keep people out.

Ordinary people. Not Steve.

He slipped through the barbed wire, sustaining only minor injuries to his face. Then he was inside Threshold, moving through the darkness, more shadow than man.

He'd entered Threshold at the point closest to the laboratory where the Cartographers manufactured their DoorWay. And there it was, dead ahead through the trees: a dark bulk against a dark sky.

He drew closer. He circled the two-storey building until he came to an area with lights in the windows. The hum of voices. The Cartographers were on the ground floor in the rooms adjacent to the road. There was a sentry, a lone male Cartographer who stood outside the main entrance with his hands in the pockets of his black wool jacket, stamping his feet, his breath steaming. Steve watched. After a few minutes the sentry did a circuit of the building and returned to his post.

Rudimentary. Really this was almost beneath him. If the fate of the universe wasn't at stake, Steve probably wouldn't bother at all. But it was, so he faded back into the trees and took up position overlooking the lightless, unoccupied back of the laboratory. He waited for the sentry to pass.

While he waited, his gaze drifted from the laboratory townhouse to the road zigzagging up the hillside, to the lit windows of the house at the top of the hill. Gorgon's house. The wreckage of the scaffolding had been cleared away. Now a ladder led from the base of the house to the front door high above. It would take several minutes to get Steve's entire team up that ladder. And they'd be exposed: vulnerable to attack the entire time. He reached into his pocket and made sure that the giant's drugs were still there. If everything went to plan, they could all climb up to Gorgon's house without a care in the world. There would be no Cartographers to attack them.

He shifted his gaze to the lower storey of Gorgon's house. The basement. It was where Danyl had claimed Verity was being held. Even if she wasn't, the basement was still their ultimate destination. The key to the mystery of Gorgon and the Real City lay within it.

Steve had learned much from the secret archive. He'd learned about Matthias Ogilvy. The man was a wealthy property owner who'd built huge tracts of land in the Aro Valley and used his political connections to push through a plan of urban renewal. Larger roads. Huge tenement buildings. Massive changes to infrastructure. He began the Threshold development in anticipation of Te Aro's transformation from a bedraggled village into a modern urban utopia. There were protests. Battles pitched on the construction sites. But Threshold went ahead, and the skeletons of the townhouses rose above the Aro Valley mist.

Then, in August of 1974, everything changed.

Most of the front page of the 13 August 1974 issue of the Te Aro Community Volunteer Newsletter was taken up by an editorial pledging the Aro Valley's military support for the Communist government of North Vietnam, but a smaller story at the bottom of the page was headlined 'Monster's Children Vanish Mysteriously'.

Police and search experts are combing the hills and gullies around Te Aro after the two children of loathsome property

developer Matthias Ogilvy were reported missing from his Aro
Street lair. Ogilvy has accused opponents of his horrible urban
so-called renewal plans of kidnapping the children. However
the Detective leading the investigation revealed that Ogilvy
and his children had fought shortly before their disappearance.

The children had been locked inside the basement beneath
Ogilvy's property as punishment, and the detective believes
they have escaped and are hiding somewhere nearby.

The detective did admit bafflement as to how the children
escaped the basement, which could be exited only via a narrow
internal stairway accessed by a solid wooden door which
Ogilvy assured him was never unlocked.

The police urge Te Aro residents to contact them immediately if
they see Simon Ogilvy (age five) or Georgina Ogilvy (age ten).

But, as Steve learned, what had begun as a simple story of
two children disappearing from an evil property developer's
locked basement turned murky when, three days later, the
children were found. They were rescued from the catacombs
by a police search team, who found them terrified and
hypothermic. Simon Ogilvy was unharmed, but his older sister
Georgina had suffered terrible injuries to her head. Something
had gouged out the child's eyes.

Were Matthias Ogilvy's sins as a property developing
capitalist the reason for his little girl's horrible mutilation?
The subsequent edition of the Te Aro Community Volunteer
Newsletter felt that they were. 'Not that we're calling for little
girls to be mutilated,' the editor insisted. 'But if they are, then
sadly urban development is often to blame.'

What had happened to the children? How did they get
from the locked basement of Ogilvy's house at Threshold to
the stormwater tunnel several kilometres away? What attacked
them? The newspaper did not answer these questions, nor

did the minutes from the confidential council meetings with Matthias Ogilvy that took place a week after his children were recovered:

7.45 pm: MR OGILVY requested that Te Aro Council abandon its infrastructure development plans, keep the roads at their current width and capacity and preserve the sewers and stormwater systems beneath the valley in their current state in perpetuity.

7.50 pm: TREASURER FOWLER reminded the council and MR OGILVY that the council has spent substantial sums on the planning and consent process for Te Aro's planned infrastructure upgrades, that these have been done at MR OGILVY'S insistence, and that to abandon the work will mean writing off all of these costs.

7.55 pm: COUNCILLOR MCNAUGHTON declined MR OGVILY'S request and announced that the infrastructure projects will proceed.

8.00 pm: MR OGILVY requested that he be allowed to address the council in confidence. The council approved this request.

8.05 pm: RECORD HALTED.

9.15 pm: RECORD RESUMED. The Council has agreed to halt all infrastructure projects and approved the construction of walls within the stormwater maintenance system for the purpose of blocking access to the tunnels of the old quarry and other natural cave networks beneath Te Aro.

There was more. Steve found the articles of incorporation for 'The Threshold Reservation'. These were drawn up by

Matthias Ogilvy's lawyers and signed by him on 28 August 1974. They established the site of the former property development as a nature reserve. 'The site must remain untouched,' the articles insisted. 'The buildings within its boundaries must be neither completed nor destroyed, and must remain uninhabited. No excavation of any kind must ever take place within Threshold. Its secrets must remain buried.'

The reservation was administered by the Threshold Trust. Matthias Ogilvy was its director. On the event of his death, the trust would be run by his daughter, Georgina. If she was not of age, or died, or violated the aforementioned laws of the reservation as determined by the secretary of Te Aro Council, then administration of the site would pass to Te Aro Council.

Steve was interested in that last point. Very interested. Ogilvy's poor, mutilated daughter Georgina had obviously grown up to become Gorgon, and she now ruled the Threshold development, or reservation, or whatever it was. But legally she had voided her right to do so. Hadn't she built tunnels connecting Threshold to the rest of the valley? Filled the uninhabited buildings with Cartographers and captors of the Real City? Didn't that mean that ownership of Threshold should pass to the head of Te Aro Council? And wasn't that Steve?

The answer to all of these questions was yes. Ergo, Threshold should belong to Steve. From here he could rule the entire valley, while covertly excavating deep below the reservation and uncovering its buried secrets, because what was the point of ruling from a reservation with buried secrets if you didn't excavate them?

So Steve's mission had changed. He wasn't here to save the universe. If Danyl and Ann and the giant wanted to save it, then that was fine. Steve wouldn't stop them. He had no quarrel with the universe. No, his mission was Gorgon. He needed to take her down, rescue the Council secretary from the Real City and have him strip Gorgon of her titles and lands. Then Steve would rule in her stead. And if the universe got saved along the way, so much the better.

Movement. Footsteps. Steve froze, held his breath and watched as the Cartographer made his way around the back of the townhouse. As soon as he was out of sight, Steve broke from the darkness, heading for the lab.

52

Second thoughts

Danyl fled into Ann's bathroom. He shut and locked the door behind him. Ann rattled the handle and screamed, 'Stop him! He's betraying the universe!' The house shook as the giant approached.

Danyl thought quickly. Was he betraying the universe? If Gorgon was trying to destroy it and Ann was trying to stop her, then yes, sure, he was betraying the universe. But, according to Steve, Eleanor argued that Gorgon and the Cartographers were saving the universe, and that her mysterious Adversary was trying to destroy it. And Ann was obviously that Adversary, right? She'd killed Simon Ogilvy, and stolen Danyl's book, and kept all of that a secret and manipulated Danyl all along. So if Ann was trying to destroy the universe and Gorgon was saving it, then Danyl's brilliant plan to cripple Gorgon's plot and defeat the Cartographers might not be such a great plan after all. It might actually end up destroying the universe.

So he had to stop Steve. Or alert Eleanor and the Cartographers, and they could stop him. But first Danyl needed to escape. He looked around Ann's bathroom and laundry, which had no other exits, no windows and only a small skylight with an extractor fan built into it in the roof high overhead.

This would be Danyl's third dramatic escape from a bathroom within twenty-four hours. Only this time it wouldn't be a simple case of leaping through the window or flooding the room until the floor collapsed. No, he needed something ingenious and fast.

He opened the cupboard beneath the wash-basin. It contained spare rolls of toilet paper, a toilet plunger, a bottle of bleach and an aerosol can of room freshener. That could be the answer. Danyl knew that if you mixed some common household items together you could make explosives, deadly gases, napalm. He didn't know what those items were, or how to mix them, but maybe he could stir the toilet paper, bleach and aerosol spray in the sink together, get lucky and blow a hole through the wall?

'Danyl.' Ann pounded on the door. 'Open up, now, or the giant will take the door off.'

Danyl ignored her. Improvising a deadly explosive inside the bathroom was a last resort. What else was there? He stood up and opened the washing machine, which was fixed to the wall by two steel braces. He was greeted with the smell of wet, dank laundry. He closed the washing machine and opened the dryer, which rested on the floor underneath it. It contained four large, dry, fluffy towels.

Interesting. Danyl looked up at the skylight. A wooden crossbeam ran beneath it, holding the extractor fan in place. There was a narrow gap between the crossbeam and the fan and, Danyl noticed, the skylight also had hinges at one end. It could be opened.

He looked from the skylight to the towels to the bottle of bleach to the sink and back again. Tie the wet clothes and towels together and escape through the roof? Or mix the chemicals and see if they blew up? Both plans had their strengths and weaknesses but Danyl went for the skylight. He dumped the sheets and clothes in a pile on the floor, squatted down and started to thread them together.

'Little man. Don't make this harder than it needs to be.'

Danyl knew from experience that you can't just tie towels together then climb up them and expect them to hold. Fortunately, he also had the wet clothes to work with. Working quickly, he used sodden socks and bras to knot the towels into a long chain. He tied one end of the chain to the toilet plunger. He anchored the other end to one of the braces that fixed the washing machine to the wall.

'Little man?' The door trembled as the giant drummed his fingers against it. 'Open the door.'

'Smash it in,' Ann commanded. 'Quickly. He's up to something.'

Danyl took careful aim and threw the toilet plunger up at the skylight. It toppled over the crossbeam and fell back down, tumbling over and over in slow motion. Danyl caught it and pulled himself into the air, swinging across the room until his feet found purchase on the mirror above the wash-basin.

The door burst open and the giant's vast form darkened the doorway.

Danyl climbed faster: if he could reach the crossbeam he'd be out of the giant's grasp. But there was no way to make it in time. The giant looked almost bored as it approached. Danyl kicked off from the wall and swung to the other side of the room, landing on the washing machine, which shuddered under his weight.

The giant filled his field of vision; its massive arms telescoped towards him.

And then it all fell away. Danyl felt a terrible pain in his shoulder muscles as he was wrenched up through the air, out of the giant's deadly reach. The room filled with noise, then silence. Danyl looked down.

He was high above the floor now, adjacent to the crossbeam, in reach of the skylight. He looked down and saw the giant glaring up at him. On the floor at its feet lay the cracked and broken washing machine. The other end of the chain of towels was still attached to one of the wall braces, which had snapped off under Danyl's weight.

Ann stepped into the bathroom. She held her golf club in one hand. She saw Danyl dangling beneath the skylight, traced the path of his rope and ordered the giant, 'Undo it.'

The giant knelt down and his massive fingers fumbled with the slender chain of towels and clothes. He was too slow.

Far too slow. Danyl let go and grabbed on to the crossbeam beneath the skylight. He unlatched it and gave it a mighty shove. It swung open, admitting the cold wet night. He gasped in a lungful of rainwater and air.

Ann screamed with rage. Danyl winced as something that felt like a thrown golf club struck him in the back. But he didn't fall, and then he was through the skylight and lying belly-down on the roof of her house.

The night was black, the clouds were low and the rain was thick. Excellent conditions for running and hiding. He skidded down the slick tiles, jumped onto the roof of Ann's garage then over the fence into her neighbour's garden, which was a tangled, overgrown slope leading down, down towards Aro Street, where he could see the distant, mist-haloed lights of the apartment buildings above the bookshop.

With luck he could still stop Steve, and save the universe.

53

Plenty of time

Steve hung suspended in mid-air, the laboratory beneath him. He held the vial of Ragnarok between his teeth.

The makeshift laboratory was in a large room on the ground floor, but the ceiling had long since rotted away, so it extended up into the second storey of the crumbling Threshold townhouse. The space was lit by lamps mounted on tripods, like on a film set. They lit up six workbenches laid lengthways across the room, where dozens of Cartographers dressed in pale green lab coats, red latex gloves, surgical masks and oversized plastic eyeglasses busied themselves at a complex biochemical assembly line.

The benches were crowded with glass beakers, benchtop water baths, centrifuges and dozens of other glowing, beeping, bubbling devices and things. The first bench groaned under the weight of a large vat filled with books soaking in a vile-smelling translucent yellow liquid. Steve watched as the Cartographers pulped the books and spun them dry, diluting the run-off with a boiling hot black paste. The paste was subjected to a series of concentrations, washes and tests, then poured into large beakers and left to cool on the final bench in Styrofoam containers filled with ice, where it slowly changed colour into the pure, radiant blue that Steve knew and hated.

Sophus had described what he knew of the DoorWay synthesis process to Steve, explaining which stage should be tampered with if their plan was to succeed. But Steve was running a little late. The Cartographers had already brewed up four beakers of DoorWay. Steve needed to contaminate both the process and the finished batch.

That's why he'd climbed into the rafters high above the

lab. The tripod-mounted lamps cast bright lights but also deep shadows. Like a large, brilliant spider, Steve clambered above the bustling, oblivious heads of the lab-workers. He positioned himself above the beakers at the end of the table, distributing his weight across a number of intersecting beams. Next he took the jar of Ragnarok from his mouth and unscrewed it. He estimated the distance to the beakers, the wind speed of the drafts and eddies in the laboratory, the mass and aerodynamic qualities of the flakes of Ragnarok. He positioned the vial and tipped it over and tapped its base.

The flakes separated into a fine silver dust, which drifted down into the light, twinkling like cheap computer-generated special effects. It settled over the beakers. Steve watched as the dust dissolved into the blue liquid, vanishing without a trace. He repositioned himself over another workbench and repeated this procedure, emptying the last grains of dust into a bubbling water bath, where tubes filled with steaming book-pulp run-off were bobbing about. As he did so, the empty vial slipped from his fingers, but it landed in the clutter of equipment beside the beakers.

He'd done it. Another triumph for Steve. Soon Threshold would be his. He crawled back through the rafters and climbed down onto the mezzanine overlooking the laboratory.

A door opened below. The archivist entered, his goat-eyes gleaming. He was flanked by two burly Cartographers wielding tasers. One of the lab-workers stepped forward to meet him, removing her mask and goggles. It was Eleanor.

The archivist said, 'I've just come from the bookshop. Something's wrong.'

'Do we have any new pilgrims?'

'We have dozens of new pilgrims. Hundreds. They're queueing up the stairs and down the alleyway.'

'Do they have spiral dollars?'

'More than we've ever printed. Someone is forging them. Do you think it's the Adversary?'

Eleanor made a clicking sound with her tongue. The sound rolled around the room, echoing through the darkness to where Steve lay.

'Maybe,' she said. 'But maybe this is just the Tao of the Spiral. We're close now. Very close. This could be enough people to open the path.'

'So we bring them all across? Do we have enough compound?'

Eleanor smirked. 'We've been working hard.' She gestured. A trio of Cartographers were decanting the beakers of contaminated DoorWay into plastic tubes and stoppering them up. 'We have enough compound for every pilgrim in Threshold for at least a week. How many doses do you need?'

'Fifty?' the archivist guessed. 'Maybe a hundred?'

Eleanor raised an eyebrow. 'The Spiral provides,' she said, gesturing to a lab-coated Cartographer, who loaded a briefcase with glowing vials and handed it to the archivist.

'Guard them well,' Eleanor commanded. 'Gorgon thinks the Adversary will try to seize our stocks of compound again. Be alert and prepared for ambushes. Call me when you make it through the catacombs.'

'Aren't you coming?'

She shook her head. 'Gorgon wants me here. Close to her.'

Steve waited for the archivist and his bodyguards to leave. Eleanor supervised the distribution of more vials of compound, and teams of armed Cartographers marched out into the night, bound for the different buildings scattered across Threshold and the hundreds of pilgrims held captive in the Real City.

Steve still had business to attend to. He made his way through the darkness of the upper storey, through unfinished walls, over black pits and gaping stairwells to the far side of the building.

He still had the second vial from the giant's stash. It was filled with sedative, and it was bound for the meal currently being cooked in the Cartographer's kitchen. They would eat just after 10 pm, and by glancing up at the stars through a ragged gap in the clouds Steve determined that it was 9.47 pm. He had plenty of time.

He made his way through the windswept darkness, heading for the building where the kitchen and communal dining area were. He was halfway there when he noticed a lone figure trudging up the road, parallel to his own path.

Eleanor.

He checked the stars again. 9.53 pm. Taking out Eleanor wasn't part of the plan, but if Steve could incapacitate Gorgon's most trusted lieutenant then Danyl would have a much better shot at defeating Gorgon herself and rescuing Verity. And Steve felt generous. He felt like helping out his friend. He drew his taser from his pocket, switched it on, and closed in on Eleanor.

54

No time at all

Eleanor. Danyl had to get to Eleanor. If he could make it to the bookshop and tell the Cartographers there to phone her and warn her that the new batch of DoorWay was contaminated, then everything would be fine.

Things weren't hopeless. But they weren't great, either. He took an indirect route from Ann's house to Aro Street, climbing over fences and crawling through backyards and along muddy ditches. When he reached the bottom of the hill, he saw a car crawling along Ohiro Road with its headlights off and its windows wound down, and Ann's sharp eyes peering out into the darkness.

He needed to stay out of sight. Unfortunately he also needed to cross Aro Street. He reached a house adjacent to the street and crept through the garden, using a bed of flowers to muffle his footsteps. He crouched behind a fence and peered through its ricketty rails.

It looked good. The street was clear, and there was the alleyway leading to the bookshop, just across the road and down a little.

Danyl was about to vault the fence and sprint for the alleyway when he noticed a huge black shape beneath a shop awning. It was the giant, lurking in ambush. Danyl shivered as its head swivelled and those impossibly huge eyes swept over him. But nothing happened. Danyl was hidden in the shadows. The giant's gaze travelled on.

There was a bus stop halfway between Danyl's hiding position and the alleyway. It was just close enough for him to make it there before the giant turned his way again. He readied himself, waiting until the giant's gaze passed over him; then he vaulted the fence and sprinted for the bus stop. He threw himself to the ground behind the bench and waited, listening for the sound of the giant's feet crashing through puddles. The sound never came.

Instead, Danyl heard screaming. Faint, distant. It was a mixture of male and female voices: no words, just wild, inchoate yells growing louder.

What now? Life wasn't difficult enough, what with Ann and the giant and his mental illness and maybe an alien universe —now there had to be a bunch of people screaming? Danyl peeked around the bench.

The giant had emerged from under the awning. It stood in the middle of the street, staring towards the alleyway, which Danyl now realised was the source of the screams. It had its back to Danyl and it was talking on its phone, probably to Ann. Danyl snuck across Aro Street and crept through the shadows, closer to the entrance of the alleyway. He paused in the darkness, watching the giant. Then, just as it tossed its head and spoke into the phone, Danyl slipped around the corner and into the safety of darkness. The screams were very loud, echoing out of the stairway that led to the bookshop. They drowned out Danyl's footsteps, his thoughts, the sound of the rain.

The door at the bottom of the steps was open. Danyl hesitated. He had to go in, but something about a crowd of people screaming insanely in an underground space unsettled him.

But he had no choice. Ann and the giant might enter the alleyway at any second. He descended the steps then fell backwards when the archivist burst through the door. His clothes were torn, his shirt hung from his shoulders in rags. He ran straight into Danyl's arms and flailed about in panic. 'Don't go in there,' he neighed. His yellow eyes strained towards the end of the hall. The door was swinging shut. Danyl had a vague impression of movement beyond it, then it closed. 'Don't go in there,' the archivist moaned again, his breath hot on Danyl's face.

'Call Eleanor,' Danyl urged him. 'You have to warn her. Ann might be the Adversary. We have to stop Steve.' But the archivist was hysterical; deaf to Danyl's commands. So Danyl patted at his muscular, furry body, trying to find a pocket to see if he had a phone on him.

The screaming beyond the doorway ebbed for a second, and Danyl heard footsteps on the steps. Voices. Ann and the giant were coming.

He found the archivist's phone hidden in the damp warmth of his shirt pocket. He pressed a button on the screen to bring up the list of recent calls. Eleanor's name was at the top. He pressed it.

55

Ragnarok

Eleanor's phone rang. She took it from her pocket and lifted it to her ear but before she could speak Steve struck her from behind with his taser. She cried out and fell to the ground, stunned.

Steve rested his foot on her inert body. He took a moment to savour his victory.

When the moment was over, he wondered what he was going to do with Eleanor, now that he'd defeated her, utterly. Put her on trial? In Aro Park? Presided over by Steve, dressed in a judge's elaborate black robes? Lit by flickering torches? Watched by jeering crowds? Yes, that was the simplest option. He'd tie her up, conceal her body, defeat Gorgon, then come back for her.

Eleanor's phone lay in the mud. A tiny disembodied voice squawked from the speaker, calling her name, warning her that the new batch of DoorWay was contaminated. The fool on the other end was too late. Danyl's plan had worked, and that wretched creature babbling into the mire was powerless to stop it. Steve hung up and tossed the phone onto Eleanor's comatose form. He picked up her legs and dragged her through the mud, heading for a silent, unlit townhouse nearby. She groaned, and he shushed her. He pulled her up the path to the front door. He was just about to open it when the screaming started.

It was coming from one of the buildings further down the hill: a single man's voice bellowing into the night. What was he saying? Was he crying out in fear? Pain? Joy? Steve couldn't tell.

Then another scream joined the first. A woman this time. Steve closed his eyes and triangulated the sounds. They came from different buildings. One down near the lab, another higher up the hill. He used his photographic memory to recall Sophus's sketch of the development. The screams came from two of the buildings where the Cartographers kept their pilgrims, drugged and blinded, trapped in the Real City.

Only now they were waking. They'd been administered doses of the contaminated DoorWay compound, and they were waking and screaming, presumably out of joy at returning to life, and outrage at what had been done to them. The Ragnarok was working!

More and more cries rang out. A chorus. A symphony! Steve pumped his fist in triumph, but as the screaming grew louder and more horrible, more animalistic, his fist-pumping slowed and then stopped. Something was wrong.

He decided to investigate. He gave Eleanor another gentle stun with the taser then made his way down the hill to the next row of townhouses. The windows were lit up. Muted white light shone through the plastic covers. He made out dim shapes flitting about inside.

He crouched beneath a window, reached up and tore a hole in the plastic. He stood and looked through.

No! Steve whipped his head away from the window and staggered backwards. He knelt again in the wet grass, hyperventilating, trying to erase the scene inside the townhouse from his brain. But he couldn't. Steve's memory was too powerful. It remembered everything. So he concentrated on his breathing, calming it, taking control of his autonomic nervous system.

That was better.

Then something inside the building slammed into the wall. Steve jumped with fright, tripped over, then stumbled to his feet and ran back up the hill.

What should he do? He checked the stars. He still had time to execute the second stage of Danyl's plan: infiltrate the kitchen and drug the Cartographers' food. But after seeing what the Ragnarok had done, he wasn't sure he could go through with it. Maybe he should meet up with Danyl? Talk about what to do next? Yes, that would be best.

But first he'd deal with Eleanor. He hurried up the hill towards her body, but tripped over something and fell. He cursed as he landed in the mud and weeds. Then his fingers closed around something cold and hard. He picked it up. A flame of steel gleamed in the starlight.

Lightbringer. It must have landed here when it flew from the bathtub during their escape. Steve thought it was lost forever but now, against all odds, he'd found it again. It was a good omen. A sign. Luck was on Steve's side. Whatever foes he faced—Cartographers, Gorgons, sentient mathematical universes—Steve would overcome them.

He tucked Lightbringer under his armpit and returned to Eleanor. He dragged her over to the door of the townhouse. He unhooked the handle of the front door with his foot and it swung open. There was a snarl; a sudden flurry in the darkness. Claws clicking on concrete.

Dog leapt into the air, slamming into Steve, knocking him to the ground.

56

On the electrodynamics of moving bodies

It was the largest orgy Danyl had ever seen. The noise and the smell inside the bookshop beat down upon him like gusts of a thrusting, disgusting wind. He gripped the door and willed himself not to turn around and go back up the steps. Ann was coming. Ann and the giant. He had no choice but to go on.

The bookshop was filled with people. All of them stumbled about, insane with lust, their eyes black with madness, their genitals purple and red and engorged, their lips stained blue by the contaminated DoorWay compound.

Danyl guessed there were about a hundred people having sex in the basement, most of them spaced across the floor, utilising the foam mattresses, coupling in little groups that numbered between one and five; other groups of two and three were propped up against the walls. But there could have been half that many, or twice that. They were all naked, their clothes swept into shredded piles, and the groups merged and divided, amoeba-like, absorbing lone individuals and then splitting apart. Two Cartographers stood in a corner, barricaded behind a table, clutching broken chairs and fighting back a mixed-gender horde of naked, visibly aroused assailants. They were yelling something, but Danyl couldn't hear them. The carnal screams of the orgy drowned out everything.

So Danyl didn't hear the giant's approach—he felt it. The floor trembled. Danyl glanced down the hall and he saw a vast shadow darken the steps. He had no choice but to enter the basement. It was the orgy or death.

His world became a labyrinth of moans, rolling eyes, gaping, inflamed orifices, dripping penises and clutching hands. Halfway across the room, he looked back and saw Ann and the giant at the end of the hall, scanning the crowd. Ann saw Danyl and pointed. The giant strode towards him.

But the beast's size attracted attention. Naked bodies flung themselves upon it, tearing at its clothes. The giant slowed then stumbled, trying to pry its assailants away, first losing its T-shirt and then one of its pant legs as the screaming, mindless horde surged about. Danyl fled. It was too dangerous to stand, so he dropped to his knees and crawled towards the tunnel at the far side of the room. He made rapid progress even as his hands and knees slipped on the wet floor and the rutting, tumbling figures clutched at him.

He was almost at the tunnel when a hand emerged from a thicket of limbs and grabbed his ankle. Ann's face appeared. Her jacket was ripped to shreds; her eyes glowed. 'I've got him,' she screamed into the crowd. 'He's over here!' and the giant rose out of the carpet of flesh and stomped towards him.

Fortunately Danyl's ankle was slick with sweat—mostly sweat—and he slipped out of Ann's grasp and rolled aside as she swung at him with her golf club. The club ricocheted off the concrete where his head had been. He fled into the tunnel.

It was dark. Scattered torches were rolling on the floor, illuminating yet more grunting, copulating couples. The beams of light picked out rolling eyes, webs of undulating flesh, contorting orifices. He stumbled through it all, falling over unseen forms, struggling to free himself as they clawed at him; all the while the giant and Ann coming closer and closer.

Danyl knew where he was going. Sophus had drawn them a map of the tunnels, and he was following the route to Threshold. But what would he do when he reached it? He could stay ahead of the giant while he was weaving about in the darkness, but once he was out in the open, with nowhere to hide, he'd be in trouble.

He wriggled out from underneath a thin but very strong woman who was trying to straddle his head, picked up a torch and dashed down a side tunnel. It was mostly empty.

The few rutting fiends Danyl encountered were dazzled by his torchlight. They covered their eyes as he passed and then returned to befouling each other in the darkness.

In the catacombs, the sounds of the great orgy were muted. Danyl could hear the roar of the underground stream in the distance. He headed towards it. His breathing was ragged. His legs were heavy. The giant's footsteps were drawing closer.

And then he was running along the accessway. He found the steps leading to the culvert and fled up them. He was outside in Threshold now, the slope stretching into the darkness above him, his breath steaming in the torchlight.

Onwards. He puffed his way up the hill, heading for the lights and the screams of the nearest townhouse—the same building he'd stumbled into only two days earlier, frozen and near death. Now Danyl was alive, but not likely to remain so for long. He looked back. The giant was clear of the culvert and approaching fast. Not even running, just striding up the slope, his huge gait closing the distance.

Danyl reached the townhouse. He ran through the door and into yet another orgy. The sounds and the stench of body odour, copulation and stale urine sent him reeling. All of the pilgrims were awake now, clawing at each other with vile abandon. Someone grabbed at Danyl. He fell and landed on a trio of copulating men. He skidded across their hairy, sweat-soaked backs and came to rest on a mattress.

The giant stooped and entered the room. He saw Danyl and came after him, scattering the men before him like fleshy pink leaves.

Danyl fled through the crowd. He wasn't running blind anymore. He was looking for someone, checking the face of each moaning, thrusting, blue-lipped demon, peering over and poking his head inside tangles of limbs, pressing his face to the ground to identify each person he passed.

But it was no good. These faces were all unfamiliar, and the giant was too fast. Finally, he wrapped his hand around

Danyl's leg and hauled him high into the air, ready to dash his mind out with his head-sized fist. Just then, upside-down Danyl glimpsed what he'd been looking for: the delicate elfin face and almond eyes of Joy, the giant's girlfriend.

Danyl saw her for only a second before she was eclipsed by a mound of thrusting white buttocks, but it was enough. He slapped at the giant's arm and cried out, 'Stop! I see Joy! I see Joy!'

The giant looked amused. 'Enough lies, little thief.' It prepared to strike. Danyl twisted himself in mid-air and pointed, screaming. 'It's no lie. I swear! She's right there!'

The buttocks parted again and Joy's face appeared, her lips curled back in savage ecstasy. The giant gasped. He lowered his arm and ran towards Joy, dragging Danyl behind him. He picked up several men and tossed them through the air, uncovering the pale slender frame of his girlfriend.

The giant raised Danyl before his face, and his voice broke. 'Thank you, little man.' Then he tossed Danyl aside and clutched his girlfriend to his chest, sobbing.

Danyl rolled onto his side and lay on a mattress for a moment, panting. His head was buzzing: probably from the stress of being chased through an orgy by a giant. But he was safe now. Unless Ann caught him. He climbed onto his knees and looked around for her. He found her standing directly behind him in the act of swinging her golf club towards his head.

Danyl was too exhausted to duck. Instead he tipped his head back and the tip of the club grazed his forehead. He yelped. Ann swung again, but her foot slipped in one of the pools of semen on the floor. Her swing went wide and the club connected with the leering, bestial face of a bald, bearded hairy man who had been creeping up on Danyl from behind. The man fell backwards, screaming, still masturbating, and landed on a flock of women who swarmed over him in an instant. Ann was off-balance now. Danyl stepped forward and shoved her. She screeched and tipped over as two men fellating each other rolled into the back of her knees. Her golf club flew into the air and a tide of heaving flesh carried her away. Danyl staggered to the exit.

He emerged into the fresh night air. The rain had stopped. A gap in the clouds revealed a small, bright moon. It lit up the pathway winding up the hill. The lights were on in most of the buildings and the screams of the orgy floated through the air. But the path itself was empty. The way to Gorgon's house was clear.

Danyl reached the roadway and headed up the hill. He wondered what had happened to Steve.

57

Lightbringer

Dog was strong. She was fast and well trained and intelligent. Her jaws were powerful. She lay on top of Steve, pinning him to the ground, his left arm gripped between her teeth.

The grip tightened whenever he moved. His taser was gone. He'd dropped it when he fell. He'd lost Lightbringer too—it had spun off into the darkness when the dog took him.

Steve hated to admit this but he was no match for the dog. Not in a straight fight. His superhuman reflexes were no good when he was trapped beneath a heavy, panting, sharp-fanged beast that could crush his forearm and tear out his throat. No. Steve needed to trick the dog. Outwit it. And he'd have to do so quickly.

A low groan came from the muddy darkness beyond the open door. Eleanor was recovering from her taser shock. Steve had only a few minutes to act before she was able to stand and stagger up the hill and call for help.

He turned his head and looked into the dog's huge brown eyes. What was she thinking? What was thought even like for a dog? Human cognition worked in terms of language and static images, but dogs had no language and their eyes had evolved to track movement, not to perceive their surroundings. They thought in terms of sound and smell and motion: when they thought about the future, they formed dense imaginary tapestries of scents and noises and objects in flux. That was how the dog thought and that was how Steve would defeat her.

He slid his hand down the side of his body. The dog heard this: tiny muscles in her erect, furry ears twitched and the ear closest to the noise rotated towards it, monitoring the sound; but the dog did nothing. The movements were too slight to be an escape attempt or a prelude to violence.

Or so she thought. Steve's fingers reached his trouser pocket. His questing fingertips found the vial containing the sedative. He pulled it free, keeping his breathing very slow and measured. Steve had powerful finger muscles: it was a simple matter for him to uncap the vial without moving his arm. The dog's ears twitched and its damp nose quivered in response, but it took no action. The odd scent of the drug and the tiny motions of its quarry didn't combine in its mind to form any immediate threat.

Now Steve raised the vial. The dog saw the motion. Her grip on Steve's arm tightened slightly, her fangs pressing through the black fabric of his jacket; she made a low, growling noise in her throat. Steve froze. The vial occupied the mid-point between the dog's face and his own.

A fit of coughing erupted from Eleanor. She rolled onto her hands and knees. Steve took advantage of this distraction to tip the vial. The liquid dripped out and soaked into the sleeve of his jacket, already wet with drool. The dark pool of the drug permeated his sleeve, disappearing into the region of his arm enclosed by the dog's hot, wet mouth.

The dog, thinking it had defeated him, was hyper-salivating with pride. Uptake of the substance through its tongue and gums would be quick. Steve's eyes flicked to Eleanor, who was now kneeling: she'd fished her phone out of the mud and activated it. She dropped it again when another coughing fit struck.

How long would the sedative take to subdue the dog? Steve performed a lightning calculation: he didn't know what the drug was, but the giant had estimated it would knock out about twenty Cartographers—many of them adult males—within about five minutes of them ingesting it. The dog was only one dog and she was about half the weight of a male Cartographer, but she was absorbing the drug through her gums instead of eating it. So, assuming the drug was a classical benzodiazepine, roughly ten millilitres administered, about half of which had soaked into his coat, and the rest mingled with the rainwater . . .

Steve estimated it would knock out the dog in ten to fifteen seconds, which was roughly the time he'd spent performing that calculation. And, indeed, the dog's eyelids were sinking, her grip on his arm loosening. He felt the heavy body lying atop him go slack, the force pinning him transforming into a dead weight.

He sat up and tried to push the animal aside. Immediately her eyes flicked open, great gouts of steaming dog breath shot from her mouth and nostrils, and her jaw clamped down on his arm. Steve bellowed, outraged that the creature had defied his biochemical calculations and also distressed by the incredible pain in his forearm as the dog slowly crushed it.

The screaming distracted Eleanor. She'd come to her senses in a daze. She remembered walking up the path towards Gorgon's house; she'd heard a sound behind her, turned, and then—a flurry of movement. Pain. Darkness. And now she was halfway across the hillside and covered in mud. There were screams coming from almost every building on the hillside. Horrible screams coming from hundreds of screamers. Something had gone wrong.

Then Steve's yelling drew her attention. That imbecile was here. And he was wrestling with Gorgon's dog. An empty vial lay on the grass beside them. And then she understood everything. She remembered seeing an identical vial in the laboratory: right next to the beakers filled with compound. That idiot had done something to the new batch of DoorWay and now the pilgrims were waking. Disaster.

Eleanor had sought the Spiral for most of her life. It was the gate to all mystery. The way which was not the way. And Verity was her companion in that search. Ever since that childhood morning, many years ago now, when the two girls had crept onto the abandoned farm: past the police tape, the farm house, the empty fields, the trees with huge dew-lined spiderwebs floating between them like ghosts. Finally, they'd arrived at the barn. Eleanor remembered it as if it were yesterday.

The tin walls caught the light of the sunrise, and walking towards it was like approaching a sheet of cold flame. Then they were inside, in the darkness. The floor was dirt. There were wooden benches piled high with incomprehensible tools and instruments. Bottles of chemicals. Vats. Water baths. There was a strange smell in the air.

There were books on one of the benches. Reference texts. Chemistry manuals. Beside them was a photograph in a cheap plastic frame. It showed a hillside dotted with half-built buildings, with a house at the top of the slope. Three figures stood in the foreground. A man, a girl about the same age as Eleanor and Verity, and a young boy.

Then a tree creaked outside and both girls were afraid. What were they doing in such a dangerous, lonely place? What if the scientist came back? Or the police caught them? Would they send them to prison? Eleanor almost ran but then the sun reached the window and a watery light flooded the room, illuminating a huge diagram sprawled across a wall of the barn.

The Spiral.

The girls stood transfixed, staring. It was vast and impossible and alien. The man who lived here must have drawn it, they agreed. But no human could ever have imagined such a sacred and monstrous thing. He must have rendered it from life; must have seen it somewhere. But where? Verity took her journal from her pocket and sketched a crude reproduction of the thing. A copy of a copy. She was almost finished when they heard the rumble of an engine outside. Men's voices. Eleanor dragged her gaze from the Spiral and ran to the window.

The police were coming. They had a bulldozer. Beside it, a dozen policemen walked along the dirt track, carrying rifles. They were here to destroy the barn.

Eleanor grabbed Verity and dragged her to the far door. They fled just seconds before the huge metal plate of the bulldozer tore through a wall and the building collapsed behind them. They made it to the safety of the trees and looked back. No one had seen them. A broken fragment of the Spiral poked from the ruins, then the bulldozer nudged the debris and it crumbled apart.

They sought the Spiral for almost ten years. But they had almost nothing to look for. An impossible image. A man's name: Simon. A half-glimpsed photograph. Eventually they fought, and Verity abandoned the search. Abandoned Eleanor. Abandoned herself, losing her identity in drinking and drugs.

Eleanor turned to meditation. Mysticism. Faith. She continued to seek the Spiral, but it was Verity who found it, and who brought Simon Ogilvy back to Te Aro.

Simon had spent decades trying to synthesise the DoorWay compound. But with the help of Eleanor and Verity he finally succeeded, and the three of them reached the Real City. They hid in one of the Threshold buildings, unseen by the occupant of the house at the top of the slope. They spent several blissful months mapping the City, trying to find a path to the Spiral. But all that ended one sunny afternoon when Eleanor left Simon and Verity alone for a few hours and returned to find Simon in a coma, the side of his head smashed in. An old woman with tangled grey hair stood over them, the gigantic dog that patrolled Threshold at her side.

'He's in a coma,' the woman explained. 'The Adversary attacked him.'

'He's dying,' Eleanor said. 'We need to get him to a hospital.'

'We can't take him to the hospital,' the woman replied. 'The way is opening.'

'What?'

'His mind is trapped in the Real City.'

'How do you know? Who are you?'

Then Verity, kneeling on the floor beside Simon's battered form, looked up. Her hands were soaked in blood, her face streaked with tears. 'We've been wrong about everything,' she said to Eleanor. 'Everything we thought about the Spiral. About the Real City. Everything Simon told us. It was all wrong.'

'Wrong?' Eleanor snorted. 'That's nonsense. We've been seeking the Spiral all our lives. How could we be wrong? Who is this?'

Verity pointed a trembling bloody finger at the white-haired woman. 'This is who Simon warned us about,' she whispered. 'This is Gorgon.'

Eleanor swore as she unlocked her new phone, tapping through the unfamiliar interface. Her old phone had vanished a few days ago. She thought she'd merely lost it; but maybe that too had been part of the Adversary's evil plot? The device beeped cheerfully; she pressed the number to dial the laboratory. Hopefully someone would answer. Hopefully there was still time to prevent the contaminated DoorWay from going to all the pilgrims. Hopefully she could still save the universe.

Steve shouted again. She turned her back on him. The dog had that idiot under control. The phone was ringing. Would the laboratory even pick up?

Then the phone connected. Someone answered. One of Gorgon's former clerks from the bookshop. He sounded terrified. There was screaming in the background. He babbled at Eleanor, but she silenced him. 'Stop. Listen. Do what I say.' Then she dropped the phone and collapsed into the mud, twitching and seizing. She'd landed at a right angle to Steve, who lay at her feet. The drooling, half-drugged body of the dog lay atop him. Steve's outstretched hand found his taser. He clutched it to him.

He pulled Eleanor's jacket off her and used it to tie a tourniquet around his half-eaten arm. Then he tugged the drugged dog and the stunned woman through the double doors, into the darkened building he'd escaped from with Danyl and a bathtub only a few hours earlier. The pilgrims were gone. Someone must have cleared them out after the flood.

He took his torch from his pocket, switched it on and set it on the floor with the beam aimed at the ceiling. He tugged a length of power cable out of the wall, braced with his feet and yanked it loose. He used this to bind the dog's paws. Next he tied up Eleanor. Finally, he switched off his torch and stood in the darkness. The pilgrims' screams were distant now. Muted by the walls. He could hear water: it dripped from the jagged hole in the ceiling, pattering on the concrete floor.

Steve rubbed his mutilated arm. What was he to do? He couldn't storm Gorgon's house. He'd never make it up the ladder. Should he leave Threshold, go to an all-night pharmacy, get a rabies shot, some anti-bacterial cream and some bandages on his arm? No, that was the coward's way out. He could go and look for Danyl. But searching Threshold in the dark and the rain while it was crawling with armed Cartographers and sprawling orgies would be dangerous, even for Steve.

He stood and thought, and listened to the dripping water and the panting of the dog, and the distant screams. After a few seconds his heightened pattern recognition abilities noticed that the dripping produced an irregular echo. When a drop of water dropped, the sound sometimes repeated itself a few seconds later.

Steve switched on his torch again and entered the kitchen.

When he and Danyl had escaped from the upstairs bathroom by collapsing the floor, all the water had poured down onto this level of the building. But now it had drained away. The water dripping from the jagged gap in the ceiling dripped onto the shattered concrete. Steve stood beneath the gap, lighting up the beads of moisture with his torch. He tracked them as they fell. Some drops of water landed on the broken region of the floor where Steve had crash-landed in the bath. Little rivulets of water ran down the shards of concrete then dropped into the darkness, producing a second dripping sound.

Steve knelt over the cracks and held his hand above them. He felt a strong, cool breeze. He thought about the stipulation in Ogilvy's will: *No excavation of any kind must ever take place beneath Threshold. Its secrets must remain buried.*

On impulse, Steve turned off his torch. A faint, ghostly blue glow radiated up from below.

58

Gorgon's lair

Danyl sat on Gorgon's toilet eating a bean salad.

He'd made it. He'd walked up the road that wound through Threshold, numb and dumbstruck after the horrors he'd escaped. Screams still rent the air, and Cartographers ran back and forth along the hillside, but they paid Danyl no mind. He was just a lone person stumbling through the dark.

Then he reached the ladder. It stood amidst the debris of the scaffold, luminous in the moon's glow, rising to the front door of Gorgon's house. Behind the house loomed the clifftop: a region of bare stone pitted with scrub; above that were the southern hills, a dark mass rising and rising.

Danyl climbed the ladder. He opened Gorgon's front door, took his torch from his pocket, and switched it on. He saw a disappointingly ordinary lounge with several doors.

He stepped inside.

The first door opened onto a small laundry which smelled of laundry. After that was the kitchen, which smelled of cabbage. It was cramped. A hot plate sat on a bench, surrounded by mounds of miscellaneous rubbish. A tiny table piled with more debris sat in the corner. There was only one chair. An empty footbath sat on the floor before it.

Danyl turned left. The beam of his torch danced about. He flinched every time the house shifted in the wind or a horrible scream rang out from the development below. He should have brought a weapon. But Steve had their only taser and he'd insisted on taking it.

Where was Steve? He was supposed to rendezvous with Danyl at the foot of the ladder. That was the plan. Danyl had waited for him for a few minutes, hissing Steve's name into the darkness, then he'd given up. Maybe Steve had already entered the house? Or been captured? Or just gotten bored and distracted, and wandered off somewhere else? All of these were strong possibilities.

Danyl opened the next door. He was greeted by the scent of disinfectant. It was the toilet. The room next to that was a bedroom. It contained a single bed and a dresser with no mirror. An old-fashioned cassette-player was on a shelf with hundreds of cassette tapes in giant piles beside it.

There was one door left at the far end of the hall. It opened onto a narrow flight of stairs leading down.

This was it. Gorgon's basement. Was Gorgon waiting down there in the darkness? Of course. Was Danyl ready to confront her? No, he decided. Not quite yet.

He was afraid. He was also hungry. He backed away from the stairs and returned to the kitchen. He rummaged through the fridge, found half a bowl of bean salad and retreated with it to the toilet, which seemed like the most defensible room in the house.

And now he sat in the dim light, eating beans. The wind howled. The salad had some kind of vinegar marinade that tasted really good. The rain started again; a roar of white noise on the roof overhead extending into infinity.

What would he find in the basement? Answers? More questions? Verity? If she was still there, how would he rescue her? Carry her up the stairs through Gorgon's house and down the ladder, then down the slopes of Threshold and back through the tunnels? Well, that would just be really hard work. It would take hours. It would be exhausting. And yet, Danyl reflected, that was the best possible outcome. Whatever happened when he reached the basement would probably be far worse.

He finished his beans and stood, his mind weighed down by grim thoughts. Then he made his way through the empty house. He descended the steps. A cold breeze blew up from the basement, carrying with it a rich organic scent. It was the smell of DoorWay. The stench of other worlds.

The basement stretched the length and width of the house. Its dirt floor was wet with puddles. Three of the walls were concrete. The back wall was bare stone: the base of the cliff. Danyl's torch lit up a cot in the centre, piled high with blankets. He hurried to it, his feet splashing in the deep puddles. He pulled back the blankets and sobbed as he ran his hands over the blank face staring back at him.

Verity! It was Verity! Danyl had done it! He'd outwitted Gorgon. Eleanor. The Cartographers. Ann and the giant. And possibly an evil sentient mathematical universe. He'd found Verity.

He kissed her forehead. He grasped her warm hand. 'I'll get you out of here,' he whispered. Yes, it would be a major drag carrying her all that way, but it was worth it just to see her. He wondered when she'd wake up. She obviously hadn't been dosed with the new batch of DoorWay. Maybe she'd walk some of the way herself? That would be nice. Danyl couldn't do everything.

He lifted her arm and draped it over his shoulder and stood, lifting her off the bed. He lurched towards the stairway. He was leaving. He felt, for a brief, impossible second, that he was going to make it.

It was then that he heard the music. The keening notes of the recorder, rising and falling. A child's tune, mocking his plans, killing his hopes. He turned and shone his torch towards the sound. It lit up a fissure in the rock. It looked like a patch of shadow, but it was an entranceway. A tunnel leading deep into the earth. The walls of the fissure gleamed and dripped in the torchlight. They curved downwards out of sight, leading directly into the heart of the ancient stone hills that loomed high over the Aro Valley. A figure detached itself from the darkness and moved into the light.

It was Gorgon.

59

Gorgon's song

'How far down does this go?'

Gorgon turned and squinted at him. 'Eh?'

Danyl raised his voice. 'I said how far DOWN DOES THIS GO?'

'Aye.' Gorgon nodded. 'It goes down.'

The walls of the tunnel were close and slick. The floor descended in an odd natural stairway consisting of irregularly spaced, shallow steps. They'd been descending for a long time. The tunnel seemed to curve in and down like the interior of a nautilus shell. Where did it end?

And who or what was Gorgon? Danyl still didn't know. He'd expected an evil genius or an insane monster. He was even prepared for an unimaginable alien intellect peering out through a human's eyes.

What he wasn't prepared for was a mostly deaf elderly lady who laughed a lot for no obvious reason. She walked behind him, a tiny bent-over creature with a large head topped with bright white hair. She carried a cane and had a limp, but walked briskly. She hummed as she walked: the same strange, tuneless tune she'd played on her recorder. Sometimes she broke off her humming to cackle. She kept up her speed on the slippery descent.

She didn't even answer to the name Gorgon. When she'd first appeared in the basement, standing inside the fissure in the wall, her hideous music flooding the room, Danyl had turned towards her, still straining to hold Verity up, and he'd said, 'Take me, Gorgon. But let Verity go.'

The music stopped. She lowered the recorder, tipped her head to one side and said, 'Eh?'

Danyl repeated his offer.

'Eh? Take who?'

'TAKE ME, GORGON.' His voice clattered in the darkness; the echoes of echoes. Gorgon shook her head.

'No, no. Me brother called me Gorgon, but he's passed, see. The Adversary took him. And he had them all call me that at school, like. A long time ago now. And with all these young people runnin' around the property, they all call me that.' She touched her fingertips to her chest. 'But you can call me Georgie.'

'Georgie?'

'Aye. Is that your girl you've got wit' you there?'

Danyl held Verity close to him. 'Yes. Well, sort of. We broke up. I might still have feelings for her. I'm not sure. You know how it is. Anyway,' he injected a note of steel into his voice, 'I'm taking her out of here, Gorgon.'

'Georgie.'

'Sorry, Georgie.'

'You can't leave with yer wee girl,' she said. 'She's in a bad way.'

'She'll be fine once she's free of this place,' Danyl said. 'She's been drugged with DoorWay.' He pointed at her lips to show Georgie the blue stains, but Verity's lips were untouched.

'She's not taken the compound,' Georgie said. She stepped out of the tunnel. She wore baggy polyester trackpants and a wool overcoat. The skin around her eyes was heavily lined, and her lids were shut. She looked like she was blinking but the lids never opened. She was blind.

She said, 'If your girl took my brother's compound that they brew up in that lab, she'd be awake again by now. No. Yer young lady got into my house a few days ago. Got past the guards. Got in while I were fast asleep. Got down here and then went down there.' Georgie tipped her head in the direction of the tunnel. 'Where it all began. When she went down there, she crossed over to the City. I found her and brought her back

341

here, to keep her close to me and look after her.'

'How do I wake her up?'

'We don't. We wait,' Georgie replied. 'She's trying to reach the Spiral, and when she gives up she'll come back to us.'

'Verity's been searching for that Spiral for her whole life,' Danyl said. 'What if she reaches it?

Georgie chuckled. 'She can't. The way is sealed. The only way she could reach it is if all the other pilgrims trapped in the City all woke up somehow. Imagine that!' More chuckling. 'That would be a terrible thing. A terrible thing. Everything would be lost. But don't worry, lad. That'll never happen. Your girl will come back to us eventually.'

The sweat on Danyl's back had cooled. Now the cold seemed to seep inside into his body, chilling his blood. He said, 'What would happen if all of the pilgrims woke?'

Georgie pulled her head back like a surprised bird. 'All woke? No, no. The Cartographers and all will make sure they don't wake. Don't be minding that. It's horrible that they keep all those poor souls trapped in that City, against their will. But if they all woke while Verity was there, why, then the way would open. She'd reach the Spiral. She'd pass beyond it. And with no one else in the Real City, the way would be open. The terrible thing beyond the Spiral could pass through the City and into Verity. And that'd be the end of us. Of everything. But don't you worry about that. Everything's fixed and runnin' smoothly. Pop your girl back down in the bed, there's a lad, and we'll have a cup o' tea and I'll explain it all, calm and simple like.'

'Hurry up ahead there,' Georgie urged. 'We've no time. Run. Run!'

Danyl was trying to run, but Verity was heavy. A dead weight. He had to walk sideways through the narrow tunnel while carrying her along with him. She was still unconscious.

And if what Georgie had told Danyl was true, she might never wake up, and if she did, something unthinkable might happen.

But there was a way to save her from the unthinkable thing. That way lay somewhere far below, at the end of the tunnel. Danyl was unclear about what that was, or what lay ahead of them, or what the unthinkable thing that might happen was.

'You'll see when we get there,' Georgie replied to all his questions.

'Where is *there*?'

'There is the Chamber of the Great Sponge.'

'Great Sponge?'

'Aye.'

'What is the Great Sponge?' But Georgie did not hear him. She continued on down the tunnel, and with much shouting and cackling and cryptic mumbling in the darkness, she told Danyl her story.

One day when she was a young girl, Georgie fought with her father. He punished her by locking her and her brother in the basement. They were down there for hours, and eventually, when they stopped crying and looked about in the meagre light from the tiny windows, they discovered a discoloured patch on a wall. It wasn't stone, like the rest of the cliff that the house was built up against, but some kind of brittle crystalline material with a dull blue sheen to it. The girl and her little brother picked up tools from their father's workbench and chipped away at the patch of blue. It broke off in clumped fragments, revealing a tunnel that led deep into the earth. They took a torch and ventured in.

The tunnel was a long, curving spiral that descended into the hill. After walking along it for a while, the children got scared and turned back, but when they reached the entrance, they found it blocked. The brittle blue material had grown back. It was damp and sticky with jagged edges. They could see their father's tools through the tiny cracks where the wall hadn't closed, but they couldn't reach them, and they couldn't break their way through without them.

They called for their father—they screamed—but he didn't reply. Maybe he couldn't hear? Maybe he did hear but did not come.

So Georgie told her brother to stay at the mouth of the tunnel while she went back down to look for another way out. She followed the spiral down, deeper and deeper, until she came to a chamber.

It was huge. The beam of her torch couldn't reach the far side. It revealed other passageways leading out again, but Georgie ignored them and approached the pool in the centre of the chamber. It was filled with a liquid that looked almost like water, except it seemed to glow with a faint blue light. She knelt by the pool and dipped her little finger into it, then she raised it to her tongue.

She woke in the Real City.

'Then what happened?' Danyl demanded. Georgie had fallen silent.

'Eh?'

'What happened when you saw the Real City?'

She sighed. 'I walked about for a bit. Then I saw the Spiral and walked up to it and touched it.'

'What happened then?'

'Once I touched it, the City just disappeared. Melted away, like. Just like that. And I saw what was beyond it.'

'What?'

'Somethin' horrible.'

Georgie lapsed into silence. Danyl tolerated this for several seconds then demanded. 'What, specifically? Horrible how? What did you see beyond the Real City?'

'Something old,' Georgie replied. 'Somethin' old and mad that's always been scratching at the edge of space and time, tryin' to get into our world.'

'Was it the evil sentient mathematical universe?'

'Eh? I can't hear ya. You'll have to speak up.'

'EVIL SENTIENT MATHEMATICAL UNIVERSE?'

'Eh?'

Danyl gave up on questioning her and let Georgie tell her story.

She'd glimpsed the thing beyond the Real City for only a brief second, she explained. She'd been exposed to only a tiny quantity of the liquid in the pool and she woke up on the cold dirt floor of the chamber to find her brother Simon standing over her, furious with worry.

She didn't answer any of Simon's questions. She was trying to understand what had just happened to her, and as she thought, she became aware of an itching inside her mind. A fragment of the thing beyond the Spiral coiling within her own consciousness. The mere act of seeing it had allowed it to infect her, but only partly. She could feel its outrage at having failed to take her away completely and then cross over, and as she lay there on the damp stone she felt the tiny seed it had planted in her mind flicker and die.

But while that happened, her brother stepped over her to the pool, dipped his fingers into it, and tasted the liquid. She watched in horror as his eyes froze, he fell to the ground beside her and crossed over into the Real City.

She knew that her brother would find his way to the Spiral and go beyond the Real City. She knew that the thing waiting there would seize him and pass into him. She shook him, slapped him, but he didn't respond. He was gazing on another world.

She decided to follow her brother into the Real City and bring him back. But what if she passed through the Spiral and saw the thing beyond it again? The mere act of seeing it would allow it to possess her. She loved her young brother. She'd have done anything to save him. So she kneeled beside him, took one last look at her hands, and then drove her nails into her eye sockets, tearing out her own—

'Wait,' Danyl interrupted. 'You actually tore out your own eyes?'

'Oh, aye.' Cackle.

'Is that even possible? Wouldn't the agony make you lose consciousness first?'

'It were quite painful.'

But it worked. The Real City, Georgie explained, acted as a kind of airlock. One person could pass through to the Spiral, and then the thing beyond the Spiral could pass back, into our world. But if a second person entered the Real City, then the way from beyond the Spiral was blocked. When Georgie awoke in the City for a second time, this time with no eyes, she couldn't feel any pain, nor could she see the great plaza, nor the bridges, nor the Spiral. She could sense her brother, somehow, in the place beyond the Spiral and she could sense the impotent rage of the thing that dwelled there. Her presence in the Real City blocked its passage. It could not pass. Simon Ogilvy awoke, and so did Georgie.

They fled the chamber, but they took the wrong exit and spent days wandering in the darkness before they stumbled into the stormwater drains and a police search team found them. They were safe. But the seed that the thing had planted in Georgie's mind, which died, had taken root in Simon Ogilvy's mind, and thrived. He spent his whole life trying to return to the Real City and the thing beyond the Spiral.

'OK, stop.' Danyl was struggling to make sense of it all. He was also struggling to bear the load of Verity's weight. He lowered her to the steps and sat beside her, panting. Georgie stood and waited just out of the circle of his torchlight.

'Let me just understand this,' said Danyl. 'If someone passes through the Real City and beyond the Spiral, then the thing waiting there can enter into them. And that's bad, right?'

'Aye.'

'But it can't enter into them if there's someone in the Real

City? The City is a conduit, and if someone is inside it then the way is blocked?'

'Aye. But we don't have time to rest.' Georgie stepped towards him. The shadows ran from her aged, eyeless face as she approached the torchlight. Her eyes looked like mouths. She pointed at Verity; her head slumped on Danyl's shoulder. 'She doesn't have time. This'—she waved her hand, indicating the universe—'doesn't have time.'

Finally Danyl understood Georgie's plan. DoorWay. The Cartographers. The Real City. 'Because all those pilgrims were blocking the way!' he explained, proud of his comprehension. It all made sense! 'And now that they're awake, the thing beyond the Spiral . . .' his grin faded. 'It can pass through into Verity and enter our universe.'

'Aye.'

He stood again. His brain buzzed at him. He hoisted Verity onto his shoulder and started walking. 'And we're going to this underground pool because that's the source of the DoorWay compound. Your brother figured out how to create a synthetic version, but we contaminated the entire batch. So the only way through to the Real City is down here.'

Georgie did not answer. The stairs were levelling out. The roof of the cave curved up and out of sight. The walls widened. They'd arrived.

They were in a gigantic cavern. Water trickled down the walls and fell in columns from unseen outlets high above. The floor was submerged but the water was only ankle-deep. It was warmer than Danyl expected. A tepid bath.

Georgie led them towards the heart of the cavern. The humid air smelled of copper and rot. There was a faint washing sound, like a tide on a distant beach. It seemed to come from far below.

'Mind the vents.' Georgie pointed with her cane at a hole in the floor. Danyl detoured around it and peered down. The vent was a perfect circle, slightly wider than his hand span.

His torchlight lit up other circular holes, some as small as a fingertip, others too wide for him to jump across.

Georgie's voice rang out in the darkness. 'Over here.'

The pool was a smooth dip in the floor, like a shallow bowl. Its sides curved away out of sight. It looked like it was empty, but there were thin films of liquid dotting the basin at irregular intervals. They glistened blue in the torchlight.

Georgie tapped the floor beside the pool with her cane. 'Set your girl down here, dear. Mind her head. Don't touch the pool.'

Danyl obeyed. He stood and looked out at the emptiness, the glittering cascades of water dissolving into regions of mist, the rim of the pool extending out of the torchlight, and said, 'So this is the Chamber of the Great Sponge.'

'Aye.'

'And you're going to drink some of its milk.' He lit up a film of the blue liquid with his torch. 'And rescue Verity from the thing beyond the Spiral.'

'Aye.'

'Why do you call it the Chamber of the Great Sponge? Where is this Great Sponge?'

'Where is it?' Georgie cackled again. 'You're inside the Great Sponge, dear. You have been since you left my basement.'

60

Reasonable discussions and moderate violence

Danyl knelt in the warm water. He was exhausted. His brain buzzed and sang. He was inside a sponge.

Little flashes of light were appearing in his vision. A voice in his mind said, *You're not here. There is no sponge. You've gone insane. Totally insane.* But another voice told him that it was all true. *The sponge is real, and you should run from it. Flee back to the surface, back to the light.*

Which of the voices was Medicated Danyl? Which was the sickness? Which was the real, true Danyl? Or was Real Danyl gone, replaced by the babble of madness? Had Danyl ever existed? Danyl didn't know. He didn't know which Danyl to listen to or what to do. He was still struggling with this problem when he heard the sound: a loud splash and then a voice, out there somewhere, in the darkness.

Georgie heard it too. She was crouched beside Verity, tucking a shawl under her head. She stiffened. Her hands flew to the recorder which hung from a string around her neck.

They listened. There it was. More splashing. Footsteps. Someone was inside the Great Sponge with them.

Georgie said, 'It's the Adversary. They serve the thing beyond the Spiral. So long as there's someone inside the City, the thing out there can whisper to certain minds in our world and get them to open the way.'

'Why would anyone betray their own universe?'

'Oh, they don't know what they're doin'. The thing past the Spiral is subtle. Clever, like. That's why I had the Cartographers bringin' across so many pilgrims. The more from our side lookin' at the City, the harder it is for the thing to send a signal back.' She raised her voice and called into the darkness. 'Come on, Adversary. Show yourself.'

They waited in silence while the footsteps approached. Finally, a shape appeared at the edge of the light. It walked with a wounded, limping gait and clutched a club in one hand. Clothes hung from the figure in tatters. It was Ann.

Ann stepped towards Georgie. Danyl moved to intercept her. She pointed her golf club at him. 'Out of my way.'

Danyl did not move. Ann had blood on her torn jeans and blood on her golf club. Her face was scratched. Her hair was matted. But her expression was calm. She looked like a reasonable, intelligent person, except for the bloodstained club. Was she? Or was she an unwitting tool of the evil sentient mathematical universe?

Danyl said, 'We need to talk.'

'No, we don't. Move or die.'

'Ann, stop. There's so much you don't understand. Georgie's been telling me about the Real City. Did you know she discovered it when she was a kid?'

'I did know that.'

'She says it is a conduit for something beyond the Spiral but it doesn't work the way we thought it did. Instead of betraying our universe, she's saving it. And now she has to save Verity.'

'She's not going to save Verity, idiot. She's in league with the enemy universe. She's kidnapped hundreds of people. Drugged them and sent them to the Real City to open the way.'

Georgie started to speak, but Danyl held up his hand. 'Let me handle this.' He said to Ann, 'Georgie explained all of that. Sending pilgrims to the City blocks the way. It means the thing beyond the Spiral can't pass through, or manipulate the thoughts of people in our reality. See?' Danyl gave Ann his most winning smile. 'She thinks you're being secretly manipulated by the thing beyond the Spiral, and that if you kill her and stop her from rescuing Verity, then you're the one who'll destroy our universe.'

'Well, isn't that convenient? Have you considered that she might be lying? Or being manipulated herself? Or'—Ann's eyes narrowed—'maybe you're the one who's being manipulated. Maybe if I listen to you, the evil sentient mathematical universe wins.'

'Um, excuse me, but I think I would know if I was being subtly manipulated by another universe,' Danyl replied. But then he wondered: would he really? Where did his thoughts come from? His brilliant, intricate plans that sprang from nowhere, the brain zaps that punished him whenever he questioned them—was it possible they were some form of control? Something from an outside source?

He held up his hands, palms out in supplication. 'You're right,' he said to Ann. 'I could be under control. So could Georgie. So could you. None of us know if our thoughts are our own.'

Ann lowered her golf club a fraction. 'You're right,' she admitted. 'The mathematical universe could be manipulating any of us. Or all of us. Or none of us. We all want to save the universe.' She cast a dark glance at Georgie, who was watching them both wordlessly, her lips pursed. 'Or pretend to want to, but in trying to save it, we might destroy it. How do we know what to do?'

'I don't know.' Danyl waggled his finger at Ann. 'But you do.'

'Do I?'

'You're a mathematical genius. You understand logic. Right? Isn't this a logical dilemma? How do we think about saving the universe when our own thoughts might trick us into destroying it?'

'It is an interesting problem.' The gold club sank again. 'Non-trivial. It's more meta-mathematical than mathematical.'

'But you can solve it?' Danyl was filled with hope. Ann wasn't going to kill them. Instead, she would use her vast intellect for good. She'd lay down her weapon, figure out how to save the universe, and whatever the answer was, they'd do it, together. Everything was going to be OK.

Ann nodded to herself as she thought, untangling the complex meta-logic of their problem in real time. Her lips moved. Finally, a light went on in her eyes. She set her jaw.

Danyl said, 'Do you have the answer?'

'I do.'

'And?'

'I am my own thoughts,' Ann replied. 'I can't stand outside them and examine them. And I can't rely on anyone else to examine them, since that someone might be controlled by the evil sentient mathematical universe. Since I can never be sure of my thoughts, or your thoughts, it's logical to believe the thing that seems most likely and advantageous to me. And that is that I am not controlled by an evil universe. Therefore, I do control my own actions and I must make choices that seem logical, sane and just.' She raised her bloody golf club. 'That's why I'm now going to beat that old woman to death, and you too if you try to stop me.'

'Stop.' Danyl raised his hand. Ann stayed her blow and raised an eyebrow. Danyl asked, 'Is this about us?'

'Us?'

'You and me. Your strong tender feelings. The kiss? Because if you're putting the universe at risk because of your emotional instability—'

Ann raised the golf club once more. 'Time for you to die, Danyl.'

Danyl tensed. He closed his eyes.

Then Georgie, who had been silent and motionless, croaked, 'There's a way.'

Ann shook her head. 'No more tricks.'

'No tricks. Aye, you're right. There's no way to know who is tricking whom, or who controls whom. But there's a way to act without knowing. There is a way to seal the way.'

Danyl asked, 'What is it?'

'A sacrifice,' Georgie replied. 'A terrible sacrifice. It's hard, but it's the only choice.' She turned to face Danyl.

'My lad. This burden will fall on you. You must reach within yourself. You must find strength. You must—' She stopped. Her mouth opened and closed. She raised her hands and clawed at the air, then sank to her knees and toppled into the warm water, face down. Steve stood behind her, holding his taser. He tossed it in the air, flipping it, then he caught it and grinned at them.

61

The third dimension

'Dammit, Steve. Gorgon was just about to tell us how to save the universe.' Danyl pinched the bridge of his nose. 'Your timing couldn't have been worse.'

Steve stood over Gorgon's twitching, shrunken form. He looked confused. 'Save the universe? I thought she was trying to destroy it.'

Ann snapped, 'She is.'

'We don't know that. We don't know anything.' Danyl looked at Steve. His right arm was in a sling and his sleeve was soaked in blood. 'What happened to you?'

'Dog got me. What about you?' Steve pointed at the cut on Danyl's forehead.

'Orgy.'

'Ouch.' Steve rolled his head to unkink his neck, then looked around, taking in the sponge pool, Verity, Gorgon—lying beside each other, both unconscious—and Ann, who had her golf club raised, still poised to attack. 'So what happens next?'

'Let's turn Gorgon over,' Danyl replied. 'The least we can do is save her from drowning.'

'Agreed.'

They knelt beside the old woman and rolled her onto her back, positioning her next to Verity. Steve said, 'You know she was Matthias Ogilvy's daughter? And Simon Ogilvy's older sister?'

'She told me. How did you find out?'

'I found a secret archive of Te Aro Council papers hidden in Ann's office.'

'Hey, I found my book in there too.'

'Awesome, buddy!'

'Ann took it when she killed Simon Ogilvy.' Danyl looked at her. Ann was thinking again. Blinking. Lips moving without sound. 'When she saw that I'd seen the book, she tried to kill me.'

'Really? I thought she had a thing for you.'

'She does. She tried to kiss me earlier but I wasn't into it.'

'She seems like your type.'

'I guess. Things are just kind of confusing right now.' Danyl gestured at the sponge pool and the comatose bodies beside it.

'She is cute, though.'

'Oh, sure. On the other hand, she smashed Simon Ogilvy's head in while he was asleep. So.'

'Why did she do that?'

Ann spoke up. 'I was protecting our reality. I was sealing the way.'

'That's what she says,' said Danyl to Steve. 'But Gorgon thinks Ann is the Adversary. That she's being manipulated by the evil universe into letting it into our world, but she doesn't know it.'

'Wow.'

Ann said, 'A sacrifice.' She nodded at Gorgon. 'That's what Gorgon said before you stunned her. She talked about a terrible sacrifice.' She pointed at Verity, who lay peaceful and still in the warm water. 'Her. She's the sacrifice. Kill her now, and we seal the way. That was Gorgon's plan. So long as she's in the Real City, the universe has a conduit to our world. It can influence our thoughts. It can use her as a vector, travel into our reality and destroy it. But if she dies, no one from our side is observing the Real City, and the way is sealed. Then we close these tunnels. Collapse them. Destroy the laboratories. Block the way forever.'

Steve looked at Danyl. He said, 'That's a good plan.'

'Yeah, except for the murdering Verity part. We can't just kill her.'

'We're brainstorming, Danyl,' Steve told him. 'No blocking. No judgements.'

'It's her or everyone and everything else,' Ann said. 'We have to kill her.'

Danyl protested, 'Maybe we shouldn't do what we think we have to? Maybe we should worry about the morality of our actions? Murdering someone while they're asleep is wrong.'

'That sounds a lot like evil sentient mathematical universe talk,' said Ann.

'I won't let it happen.' Danyl positioned himself between Ann and Verity's unconscious form. 'To get to her, you'll have to go through me.'

Danyl did not think Ann would hit him. Something would stop her. Even as she raised the club, he hoped that she'd have an epiphany, see the truth in his words. Or Steve would tackle her from the side. Or Gorgon would rise up and shoot her with a dart. Someone else would materialise out of the darkness. Maybe, it occurred to him as the club swung towards him, the Great Sponge itself would intervene? But none of these things happened. Instead Ann hit Danyl in the side of the head with her golf club.

He didn't lose consciousness or go into shock, which was a shame because the pain was incredible. It felt like someone was holding a blowtorch right up to his skull just above his ear and pressing the blue flame into his skin. He dropped to his knees and held his hand to the side of his head. Warmth. Blood. Lots and lots of blood.

Ann raised her club again. Maybe something would stop her? Danyl was less optimistic this time. The sponge might save him, but it seemed more likely now that Ann would hit him again and kill him. He flung up his blood-drenched hand to ward off the blow, and the force of the motion splattered Ann's grim, determined face with arcs of ultra-red arterial blood. Her face contorted with disgust. She made a revolted choking sound in her throat and stepped backwards and disappeared.

~

Silence returned to the Chamber of the Great Sponge. It was broken by Steve, who said to Danyl, 'Are you OK, buddy?'

Danyl was on his knees, blood streaming down the side of his head. He did not dignify Steve's question with an answer. Instead he stood and staggered over to the spot where Ann had vanished. The surface of the water was troubled. Waves were spreading in concentric circles. They settled as he approached, revealing a vent in the cave floor wider than his arm span. At the edge, he stopped. A perfect circle of darkness—then something floated up out of it, gleaming as it spun to the surface. Ann's golf club.

Danyl said, 'She fell.'

'Why did she sink? Why didn't she float back up?'

'We're inside a sponge,' Danyl replied. 'I don't know how things work here.'

They backed away from the vent. Danyl tried to think through the pain. Why was he here? What was he doing before someone hit him? Then he remembered. Verity. He'd been rescuing Verity. He splashed over to her. 'I have to go back to the Real City,' he explained to Steve. 'That's how I save Verity. That's what Gorgon did. She gouged out her eyes then she went back in and saved her brother.'

'Why did she gouge out her eyes?'

'So she couldn't see the thing beyond the Spiral. It couldn't plant its seed in her. Look, I don't remember exactly, Steve, I'm in a lot of pain, but it made sense at the time.'

'Does that mean you're going to gouge out your eyes?'

'I don't know,' Danyl admitted.

'Buddy.' Steve knelt beside Danyl and touched his hand. 'It sounds like you haven't thought this through.'

Danyl felt weak. Dizzy. It was hard to think. He was running out of time. He was going to pass out soon. Then no one would save anyone or gouge out anything. Everything would be lost. He said, 'What should I do?'

'You have five choices,' Steve said. He ticked them off on his fingers. 'One. Do nothing. Maybe both Gorgon and Ann are wrong. Maybe there is no evil sentient mathematical universe. Maybe Verity will just wake up. Or maybe what's beyond the Spiral is heaven, and Verity has reached it.'

'But if Gorgon or Ann are right—'

'If they're right, then the evil universe uses Verity as a conduit into our own universe, which might be totally destroyed. So that's the downside there. Option two. Ann was right. The evil universe exists. The Real City is the conduit. We need to kill Verity before she wakes up. The downside there is that we kill Verity, which you oppose on moral grounds, but we need to keep it in the mix.'

Danyl rested his head in his hands. It was buzzing so badly he could hardly hear Steve speak.

'Option three. Gorgon was right about the Real City but wrong about the eye gouging. You cross the Real City to the Spiral, somehow, then touch it and that rescues Verity. Option four. Gorgon was right about everything. You gouge your eyes out and take the compound.'

'You said five options. What's the fifth?'

'Ah. This might be the most cunning approach. You don't take the compound, but you do gouge your eyes out.'

Danyl thought about this. He asked, 'Why would I do that?'

'If the evil universe is real, they'll be anticipating your choices. They may even have manipulated all of us into this position right here and now. Maybe the only way to beat them is to do the one thing they can't predict you'll do. Claw out your own eyes for no reason. Then we win.'

'Thanks, Steve. Good meeting. Good advice. Better than usual.'

'No problem.'

Danyl considered the five options. Thoughts and emotions sloshed around inside his mind, flooding his consciousness then subsiding. Feelings of anger; hopelessness. Love. He thought about his own brain: a small jelly inside his skull, brilliant with billions of electrical patterns, complex chemical gradients. A tiny fistful of organic matter containing infinities. But there was something wrong with it. Chaos in the patterns. He dug his nails into his skull and tried to think through the fog.

'Big issues to weigh,' Steve said, his voice low. 'Life. Death. Murder. Love. Existence. I think . . .' He hesitated, weighing a decision in his mind, then he decided. 'I think you need a hug.'

'I don't need a hug. I'm trying to—Steve, no. I don't consent to this.' But Steve was putting his arms around Danyl. Holding him close. Danyl was too tired to fight. He slumped against Steve and surrendered in exhaustion. He stopped thinking. It was nice to be close to someone, even if that someone was Steve.

And then the hug was over and Danyl's mind was clear. He knew what to do. In theory he could pick any of his five options but there was really only one path. The others were fakes: stage doors painted on the surface of reality. They led nowhere; they didn't even open. He wasn't going to abandon Verity to the Real City. His feelings for her were too strong. And he wasn't going to gouge out his eyes. He wanted to see what lay beyond the Spiral. To solve the final mystery. Also, they were his eyes. He'd grown fond of them.

He knelt before the pool, dipped his fingers into the bright blue film, and touched it to his tongue.

62

The end

He woke in the Real City.

It was a relief to be there. Calm. Dry. Safe. No one was screaming or being electrocuted. No orgies or dogs. No one smashing his head in. No pain. No Medicated Danyl or Unmedicated Danyl. Just the plaza, the bridges, the endless void above and beyond.

The Spiral.

It hung in the distance. A labyrinthine network of curves and shadows. A corruption at the heart of things. A new path led from the entry plaza directly to it.

So that was the secret of the Real City. Observing it did change it. The number of observers reduced the number of pathways. It didn't matter how far you travelled, the Spiral could be reached from the entry plaza only if you were the only person in the City.

Why? What did the pathways have to do with the fine structure constant? Who had built the Real City? Why had they designed it that way? Was it even designed? Or were its properties—like Danyl's own unlikely existence—just a cosmic accident?

If there was an answer to these questions, it lay beyond the Spiral. Ever since Danyl had returned to the Aro Valley he'd been beset by mysteries and riddles, and the only answer to any of them was another question. Now the ultimate solution lay within reach.

If Eleanor was right, then the Spiral offered illumination. Anyone who touched the Spiral would learn the answers to all the mysteries and attain peace beyond all understanding. Bliss.

But if Gorgon was right, it offered horror. Madness.

Annihilation. The mystery was just a lure. A phosphorescent light dangling before the open maw of a great fish in a drowned cave. Who was Gorgon, though? A crazy old lady who'd torn out her own eyes, that's who.

He stepped onto the bridge and walked towards the Spiral. He expected to feel something. Radiation. Power. Menace.

But he felt nothing. Up close, the Spiral looked no different from how it looked at a distance. It resembled some terrible energy frozen at the instant of release. The plaza that surrounded it was a featureless space with no other exits. When Danyl finished circling it, he found that his own path leading back to the main plaza was gone. He had come to a place without even the illusion of choice.

He reached out and touched the Spiral.

Epilogue

Verity woke in the back seat of a bus.

She must have drifted off for a second. The bus was crawling along Aro Street in heavy traffic. It was late at night. Heavy rain outside. The heater in the bus was broken and she was very cold, but she didn't mind. It felt good to feel things again. Even cold.

The streets outside were crowded. The bars and cafés were open. There were many house parties. People huddled in open doorways and garages or simply danced in the street in the rain. Verity's exhausted, half-awake, half-dreaming mind was beset with memories, prompted by the places the bus passed. There was her old art gallery. There was Eleanor's café, where she'd tested out the DoorWay compound after Simon had successfully resynthesised it, drugging her unsuspecting customers. Next they passed Devon Street, where Danyl and Verity had lived together; where Verity was happy, briefly, before Danyl had his breakdown and both their lives fell apart.

The bus stopped to take on more passengers at Aro Park. Verity pressed her forehead against the cool window and looked out at the stone table and chairs beneath the oak trees, now drowned in rain and shadow. She remembered sitting beneath those trees amidst shafts of blinding midday sun with Simon and Eleanor. Simon had held up a tiny capsule containing a glowing blue liquid. DoorWay.

'We're prisoners,' he told them, in a speech they'd heard many times before. 'We are the most hopeless, the most doomed type of prisoner: the captive who does not see his own cage. We feel alive. We feel as if we have choices. But we're like characters in a story. We feel alive only when we are observed. Our future is already written: we have no real choices, and if our story is not told, we cease to exist.' He flourished the capsule. 'This is our way out of the unseen prison. It is how we will tell our own stories instead of being trapped inside them.'

But three months later, when Simon lay cradled in Verity's arms with the side of his head caved in, Gorgon appeared and told Verity that what lay beyond the Spiral was not revelation or freedom, but, rather, unthinkable malignant horror. The thing beyond the Spiral had poisoned Simon's mind when he was a child, she explained, and to prevent it from crossing back into our world they would have to drug as many people as possible and trap them in the Real City.

Eleanor still believed that the Spiral led to freedom. She pretended to go along with Gorgon because she thought that bringing more people across might open a way through the City. But Verity didn't know what to think. She was numbed by the shock of the brutal attack on Simon and by the horror of Gorgon's revelations. She meekly obeyed Gorgon and Eleanor.

For the next three weeks, they spent their nights luring and kidnapping and drugging a few dozen of the braver and dumber residents of Te Aro. They were assisted by the creepy but obedient staff who worked at the second-hand bookshop Gorgon owned: they called themselves the Cartographers. They carried the drugged prisoners through the network of tunnels to Threshold, and when they'd used up all of the DoorWay compound they brewed up another batch under Eleanor's supervision.

'More,' Eleanor told them every night, as she sent them out to lure more victims into the bookshop. 'We need more pilgrims. We're close.'

And then Simon died. They buried him in a shallow grave on a high, lonely promontory at the edge of Threshold. More like a pit of mud, Verity thought, as a Cartographer shovelled on the last clots and smoothed the earth with his spade.

'Perhaps it's for the best,' Gorgon said as they struggled down the windswept slope, after the brief wordless ceremony was over. 'Now it's all done. The way will be closed. We can let the pilgrims wake.'

Verity agreed. 'We can.'

Eleanor gave them both a knowing look. She dropped back to whisper with one of the Cartographers, a repulsive goat-faced man who worked part-time at the bookshop and part-time at Te Aro Council as an archivist.

They did not wake the pilgrims that night. The next day, Eleanor sent the Cartographers into the valley to distribute more maps in blue envelopes, to lure more Te Aro residents into the bookshop. She stationed guards at the foot of the steps leading to Gorgon's house. 'To keep her safe,' Eleanor explained, before hurrying off to supervise the manufacture of another batch of DoorWay.

Verity took the compound herself. It was her first journey to the Real City since the attack on Simon, and she could see it had changed. The number of paths was different. Some were dead ends. Vast regions of the City, where she'd once wandered in those carefree days with Eleanor and Simon, were now inaccessible.

'We're making incredible progress,' said Sophus, the mathematician whom Eleanor had recruited from somewhere to help them reach the Spiral. 'We just need more data.'

'More pilgrims,' Eleanor told her Cartographers. 'More DoorWay.'

Where would it end, Verity wondered? How many more captives? How many lives stolen? Who were Simon and Gorgon, really? What had happened to them? Where did DoorWay come from? How many more drugged bodies would Verity have to carry through the catacombs beneath the valley? How many more adult nappies swollen with urine would she have to change? There had to be a better way.

Anyone challenging Eleanor was quickly drugged with DoorWay and dumped on a mattress in a Threshold townhouse. Verity knew not to make that mistake. Instead, she created a distraction. She wrote a note to Eleanor, pretending to be the mysterious Adversary that Gorgon had warned them about, and offered to meet her at Te Aro Archive, knowing that Eleanor would bring all of the Cartographers with her. Next, Verity sent several other interested parties—a giant, a band of idiots—to the same location. While they were all distracted, Verity left an apologetic voicemail for Eleanor, then she stole into Gorgon's house. She slipped past the old woman dozing in a rocking chair. She went down the steps to her basement.

She found the fissure in the wall and followed the tunnel as it spiralled down to the Chamber of the Great Sponge. She came to the pool with its thin film of bright blue liquid, the same colour as DoorWay. She dipped her fingers into the substance, and she woke in the Real City.

Whatever the substance in the pool was, it was different from DoorWay. The Real City seemed more real, somehow. Verity couldn't switch focus and glimpse the real world while she was trapped in the City. Reality was gone.

So she wandered the paths and plazas, waiting for the substance to wear off, waiting for the moment when she would wake, stiff and disorientated, back in the darkness of the Cavern of the Great Sponge. But the moment never came. She walked on and on, until she lost all hope of waking up. The substance in the pool had doomed her to roam the Real City forever. Eventually her corporeal body would die, and perhaps then she would be free of the City. Or perhaps not?

But then the City began to change. Rapidly. New paths proliferated, opening new routes, new vistas. Eventually she arrived back at the entry plaza, which now had 147 paths, the last of which vanished into the horizon, leading directly to the Spiral.

'That was us,' Steve explained to Verity during a secret late-night debriefing at the Te Aro Council offices. 'The number of paths in the Real City were reduced as a function of the number of people observing it. The more pilgrims seeking the Spiral, the more paths, and the more futile the search. When we drugged the last batch of DoorWay and sent everyone into an'—Steve hesitated, searching for words—'excited state.' He nodded to himself. 'All the pilgrims woke from the City, and you were the last one left inside it. The final pathway appeared.'

Steve sat on the handsome leather chair behind the Councillor's desk. He wore leather cowboy boots and a handsome cowboy hat that he'd discovered while rummaging through the closet of his new office, and a tartan bathrobe he'd found in Gorgon's house once he'd stumbled, exhausted and bloody but triumphant, back to the surface of the world.

Once dressed, he'd stood at the front door of Gorgon's house and looked out over Threshold as the dawn cleaned away the shadows and mist. The wasteland was dotted with wretched figures stumbling about, alone and in groups, naked, emaciated, with broken fingernails and bruised genitals; the people of Te Aro stood blinking and bewildered in the pale winter sunlight.

Steve took charge. He cared for them. He found them clothes. He ordered the Sufi Soup Emporium to construct a makeshift Sufi Soup kitchen so he could feed and hydrate them. He looted the lab and distributed antiseptic cream and bandages for their scratches and aloe lotion for their genitals. He found crutches to help them stand and walk. He deputised the Cartographers and ordered them to help. When everyone could walk, Steve used Lightbringer to smash open the large wooden gate at the base of the hill and he led the wounded procession slowly through it, down Raroa Road and onto Aro Street. The procession stopped at Aro Park and Steve stood on the stone table there and addressed the crowd through a megaphone, the rising sun at his back and the wind whipping open his dressing gown to reveal he was naked beneath it.

Steve told the people of Te Aro that he was their new

Councillor. He promised to be a wise and just leader. They had been victims of a mass kidnapping, he explained, and he had instructed his deputies to track down those responsible and bring them to justice. The crowd cheered. The deputised Cartographers applauded.

As for their hallucinations and last night's mass orgy, these were caused by a toxic mould growing in the tunnels beneath the valley, Steve explained. His first act as Councillor would be protect Te Aro from the mould by sealing the tunnels with tonnes of concrete, forever.

That's when things turned ugly. The Cartographers applauded, but the crowd did not.

The residents protested, demanding that this mould be cultivated and made commercially available to them. Steve refused. The crowd jeered and jostled closer. Someone demanded new elections. A new Councillor. Steve signalled to his secretary and his Deputy Councillor, Kim, who were waiting in the shadows at the edges of the park, and they turned on the firehoses and drenched the residents, driving them back, while Steve informed them over the screams that'd he'd cancelled future elections in perpetuity. And so, government and order was restored to the Aro Valley.

Verity sat in Steve's office, telling her story while Steve sat back in his chair with his cowboy boots on the Councillor's desk. The secretary sat off to the side; a shadowy presence taking notes of everything Verity said.

'I remember approaching the Spiral.' She pressed her fingertips to her eyes, concentrating. 'I couldn't believe I'd made it. I thought something would snatch it away at the last minute. But then I reached out and touched it. I felt the Real City melt away. A blinding light inside my mind spilled open, flooding me. And then I woke up.'

Steve asked, 'When you went beyond the Spiral, did you

see anything . . . noteworthy? Another universe, say?'

'No.'

'Any malevolent sentient beings? Mathematical or otherwise?'

'No.'

'Did you encounter any evil entity that seized control of your brain, of any kind?'

'Not to my knowledge.'

Steve tried to lean back further, but his ergonomic chair wouldn't allow it. Instead he steepled his fingers and said, 'And your friend. Your co-conspirator. Eleanor. Where is she?'

'I don't know. Have you tried her café?'

'Of course. My deputies have searched the entire valley for her. She's vanished.'

'Maybe she's left the valley?'

'That would be best for everyone,' Steve said. 'And the same goes for you, Verity. Oh, we could put you on trial. Imprison you in a café in the park. Set up a Truth and Reconciliation Committee and expose the horror of what you did to this valley, then pelt you with rotten beetroot.'

'You have no legal—'

Steve raised his voice, sharply. 'But we're not going to do that. We need to bury what happened here. For the good of the valley. I'm going to seal those tunnels. Destroy that laboratory. Impound that bookshop and turn it into a microbrewery. The mysteries of DoorWay and the Real City will be forgotten. The way will be sealed. Forever.' He turned to the secretary. 'Did you get her story?'

'Yes.'

'Yes, what?'

'Yes, Sheriff.'

'Stamp it "Sheriff's eyes only" and file it in my private archive. Then forget everything you heard here tonight.'

'Yes, Sheriff.'

Steve turned back to Verity. 'There's a bus leaving Te Aro

in one hour,' he said. 'My deputies will escort you to your home and help you pack. They'll make sure you're on it. And Verity? Once you've left this valley—don't come back.'

Verity stared out the bus window and thought about Steve's plan. Was the way sealed? She didn't think so. Simon Ogilvy believed that whatever lay beyond the Spiral was like water, and that our universe was a desert. Simon thought that anything vital or alive in our universe came from ideas that leaked through from another. All our ideas, our choices, all our free will derived from it. The Real City was one conduit into our universe, but there were others. Ideas broke through. People dreamed. They created. The world changed.

The bus turned. Verity shifted sideways. Danyl grunted as she bumped into him. She leaned her head on his shoulder.

Danyl. When she'd woken in the Chamber of the Great Sponge he was lying beside her, bleeding from a cut in his head. He woke a few minutes later, disoriented. Confused. Trying to speak. Making no sense. He couldn't walk, so Steve and Verity helped him up the tunnel to Gorgon's basement. When they reached it, Verity washed Danyl's wound and bandaged it. Steve inspected his eyes. 'His right pupil is larger than the left,' he said. 'That's a good sign.'

Verity stripped Danyl, dried him, and put him to bed. She laid cold compresses against his wound, and when his bleeding stopped and his breathing calmed and his eyes returned to normal, she climbed into bed next to him, and they lay sleeping together for twelve hours, until the leering archivist shook them awake and demanded Verity's presence in the Councillor's Chamber.

Danyl hadn't spoken much since then, but when Verity told him she was leaving the valley and returning to the seaside town where she grew up, he'd said simply, 'I'll come too.' And now here they were. Together. She took his hand

and squeezed it. She felt content. Safe.

The bus turned again. They left the Aro Valley.

They drove through the Capital. Steel and glass buildings towered above them: vertical planes repeating to the sky, mirroring the perfect, impossible architecture of the Real City. Verity gazed at it and wondered, how much of our world came from there? Was it trying to replicate itself? Was the Real City another reality or the future of ours?

Danyl saw it too. He squeezed her hand and said, 'Try not to think about it.' So she didn't.

Neither of them had much luggage. Verity had a sports bag full of clothes. She'd stowed it in the locker overhead. Danyl had a box on his lap. Inside was his book. The pages were torn and stained with mud and blood.

Verity nodded at the box. 'What will you do with that?'

Danyl smiled. It was a warm, confident smile, totally unlike the Danyl she'd once known. He seemed like a different person. A real person. He flipped through the pages. The words blurred, forming patterns. Images flicked by, half-registering in his mind, then they were gone. Eventually he reached the end and said, 'I have some ideas.'

Thanks to:

Steve Hickey who allowed himself to be both a character in this novel and provided valuable early feedback on it, in which he insisted I expand the role of Steve.

Elizabeth Knox who read what was supposed to be a final draft then met me for coffee and flipped through the manuscript, pausing at each of the most painstakingly crafted parts of the book and said, 'Cut all of this. This too. Lose this. And this,' and was right every time.

Fergus Barrowman, Ashleigh Young and everyone else at VUP.

My wife Maggie who is always my first reader.